P9-DDY-163

A Woman Called Moses

A Novel Based on the
Life of Harriet Tubman

Marcy Heidish

HOUGHTON MIFFLIN COMPANY BOSTON 1976

This Book Is The Property
of
CUYAHOGA COUNTY
PUBLIC LIBRARY

A portion of this book has
appeared in *Redbook*.

Copyright © 1976 by Marcy Heidish

All rights reserved. No part of this work may be reproduced or transmitted in any form by any means, electronic or mechanical, including photocopying and recording, or by any information storage or retrieval system, without permission in writing from the publisher.

Library of Congress Cataloging in Publication Data
Heidish, Marcy. A woman called Moses.
1. Tubman, Harriet Ross, 1815?–1913—Fiction. I. Title.
PZ4.H4593Wo [PS3558.E4514] 813'.5'4 75-40240
ISBN 0-395-21535-8

Printed in the United States of America

V 10 9 8 7 6 5 4 3 2

Parma Snow Public Library

For Jim

"The difference between us is very marked. Most that I have done and suffered in the service of our cause has been in public, and I have received much encouragement at every step of the way. You, on the other hand, have labored in a private way. I have wrought in the day — you in the night. I have had the applause of the crowd and the satisfaction that comes of being approved by the multitude, while the most that you have done has been witnessed by a few trembling, scarred, and foot-sore bondmen and women, whom you have led out of the house of bondage, and whose heartfelt *'God bless you'* has been your only reward. The midnight sky and the silent stars have been the witness of your devotion to freedom . . ."

Letter from Frederick Douglass to Harriet Tubman
Rochester, New York

August 28, 1868

Who's that yonder dressed in red?
I heard the angels singing.
Looks like the children that Moses led.
I heard the angels singing.

AFRO-AMERICAN FOLKSONG

cy76 76143

Contents

Journey

◆ ◆ ◆

"WELL, if it ain't Moses, hey you!"

I begin to come back to myself and where I am. Noise and people and a smell of coal, whooshes of steam outside, someone calling to me as I used to be called, faraway voice other side of the depot, the crowd. Must have dozed off, only dreamed that, waiting, eyes shut. *Washington-to-Philadelphia-express-Philly-Philly-step-along.* Home, waiting to go home, it's over, they're all free, should go, it's time, but even so.

"Moses!"

Now who on earth? Closer now, that voice, know it from somewheres, can't think, still swimming up from sleep. *Last-call-Last-call-Philly-Philly-change-for-points-north.* Confused, the clamor, too much. Someone's shaking me.

"Woman, you deaf?"

My eyes snap open. Shadrack. Shadrack standing there above me with a uniform and that evil smirk of his and only one leg. He leans on his crutch and laughs. A mean laugh, bitter.

"What call you got to be here?" My voice comes out tired, not sharp like I meant it to sound. I find myself staring at that bobbed limb.

"Guess I got a right to go home like everybody else. Well shit, no need to gawk, hate that, specially from you."

Can't help it. Don't like him, Lord knows I never have, but would you just look at that stump, the trouser leg pinned up around it.

"What you got there?" He seems to wink. "Special army pass say you can ride for free? Missy Moses she got her privileges, ain't that the truth?"

He leans forward, scoops the papers off my lap, grins. Sweet Heaven, my letters.

I reach up. He holds the sheaf away from me, teasing, making like he's going to read aloud.

"Go on, skylark then." I sit back. "You know you ain't able to read."

"Uh-huh, didn't you say once you got us free we'd all learn how? Wager *you* the one still ain't able — much good them letters do you. I learned, that's right, don't believe me? Lessee, say here, 'The bearer, Harriet Tubman, needs not any recommendation . . . noble spirit, high esteem . . .' Good Lord, who set this down? 'Using the skills she acquired on the Underground Railroad she made many a raid behind enemy lines as a scout and spy . . .' That so? Or you get someone to forge this here?"

"Damn you, nigger, give over."

" 'Nursed our soldiers during the late war . . . planned and conducted notable Combahee Raid, South Carolina, assisted by our brave Colonel Montgomery . . . such a servant should be paid by her country . . .' Shit, you mighty vain to carry this here about, now who penned it all? The *Honorable* Gerrit Smith, well kiss my ass, or did you kiss his? . . . and this one a Brigadier General *if* you please. Just got to glorify youself, don't you, well what'd you pay for this?"

I reach for the papers, I grab for them. No. I lunge.

Shadrack veers off balance, nearly falls, and as I settle back on the bench with the letters I'm dimly aware of someone turning around to stare. The crutch thuds closer. He plants it like a stake on the floor by my boots and leans over.

"Fine way to do what was one of your passengers. Course it don't matter now, you hear bout the resta them folks on that one escape you led us on, no? They all dead, see, oh pity you didn't hear. Killed, the mens was, that's a fact, was in camp with em. The womenfolks, they nursed in colored hospitals, cashed in with the dysentery, that's right, don't know bout the children. All that tribulation for nothin, only one lefta the group's me, and I ain't able to walk. Bout wipes out that one journey Moses led, don't it."

"Why didn't you all stay fixed North?" I burst out.

"Why didn't you?"

I look away.

"Ever wonder if all that work was worth your while, *Mo-ses?* Other folks you freed musta been killed, lost a couple arms, couple legs, maybe *all* them folks you saved been killed in this war that freed the rest, ever think on that? Anyways, all that counts for nothin now after what Mr. Lincoln done."

"You evil Shadrack, always been, now shove off."

"Ever think on this?" He brings his face closer to mine till his hair scratches my cheek. "Maybe you shoulda stayed set with your old mama and your old daddy, maybe you even shoulda stayed set with your man. Did all them voices and visions forget to tell you bout Mr. Lincoln? Didn't the Lord's angels speak on that to you . . . Goddamn, woman, you leave go of me!"

I have him by the collar of his coat, wishing I could stuff his devilish tongue down into his guts, but all of a sudden I loosen my grip, and Shadrack hitches away on his crutch, one shoulder heaving higher than the other.

For a long while I sit there, fingering the letters, seeing nothing but a blur around me. Them dead? This far along deaths shouldn't stun me. Should know how to mourn, to accept by now, instead of struggling for a way not to believe. Should be able to reason out how Shadrack's got to be wrong about everything else too, but my mind's a wall, the letters are wet.

New-York-New-York-change-at-New-York-City-Albany-Albany-Syracuse-Auburn-Albany-all-aboooard. All done, the war, the work that went before, done, that's my train. The conductor summoning the people, we've changed places, I'm the passenger now, pushed forward in a crush of travelers toward the sweating locomotive, up the high steps. I take the first seat I come upon, don't even look around. Home to Auburn, try to sleep, sleep it all away.

"Hey auntie, don't you hear me?"

Now who? Weary white face above a brass-buttoned uniform. The conductor sighs and jostles my shoulder.

"Said you in the wrong car, auntie. This one's whites-only."

"My ticket." I shove it at him. "Paid for."

"Lookit, no trouble huh, get a move on now."

He raises me to my feet. The ticket wafts to the floor like snow as he shoves me up the aisle. First Shadrack, now this; it all rises up within me, and I try to shake him loose, struggling harder as two other white men appear out of nowheres, their hands all over me, grappling, pulling. I bash one of them in the mouth quick and sudden, flail out with elbows and knees, drag my nails through a pale cheek.

"Awright nigger, you done it now, into the baggage car."

I thrash all the way up the aisle, but at last I'm pitched headlong into a dark place and a door clangs shut behind me.

Pain. My side, my shoulder. Sprawled amidst a vague clutter of bags and cases, I study on lunging at the door, but all strength is spent. I just lie here where I landed on the rumbling floor, feeling my side, feeling the old hatred rise up in me again as strong as when it was new.

Lord, the smell in here. A heavy smell, rotten. Seems to come from this trunk. A dripping sound, cold water spreading on the floor. Ice melting someplace. I reach out. Touch the trunk. It's crated up. My fingers snap back. I know what's in that long box now, traveling home like me.

Looking at it one way I can almost laugh, seeing myself as I am now, their Moses, like this, oh yes. There used to be trains all the time, mine, but here on a real one, here at the vocation's end, I feel like I'm back at my beginnings somehow. This day, this train, that meeting with Shadrack, especially this stink; they all carry me past the Moses-time to the early years which flash up clear in this darkness, as if the rest never happened.

◀ ▶

Midnight

◆ ◆ ◆

OLD CALLIE said Death was white, bleached out like bones, tall-built he was, and thin, with red coals burning in his eye sockets. He was no dark angel that one, she said, she'd seen him more than once, but Callie likewise believed she'd seen ha'nts and demons, and she wouldn't pass the boneyard alone.

Years later, I realized that Callie had fashioned her image of Death after my first master, Edward Brodas. The white folks used to whisper he was an albino; our folks muttered he was a freak of nature, and so he seemed with his pale hair the same color as his waxy skin, his pinkish, lashless eyes, and gaunt frame. The summer sun would send him into agonies which I secretly enjoyed watching, and it was doubtful I was the only one. During the lean times when I was small, when the price of wheat and corn was dropping, and the tobacco plantings were commencing to ruin large stretches of soil in Maryland, it appeared Marse Ed meant to get himself through by breeding and selling off slaves instead of crops. He'd come for us all, Callie would say, then bless herself.

To me Death was a stench, and at the same time it was Tilly, the loss of her. It was the stench hanging over the boneyard when I first attended a burying there, the same day my sister was taken. I must have been about seven years old then.

Mostly children never got to see coffle-gangs, but I'd been running through the woods looking for my sister, came out at the rolling-road, and nearly stumbled into one. I remember my first feeling was gladness that I'd found her, for I didn't comprehend what I'd chanced upon rightoff, I didn't even know the name for it. Chained slaves and auction blocks weren't common everyday sights to us, not there on the Eastern Shore, as the nearest big market was across the bay in Annapolis, and not then, when a flush time was only just passing away. For a moment I couldn't figure what she was doing crouched down in the shimmering July heat, lined up with all those people.

I recollect hissing at her, *tilly psst tilly hoo there s'me,* hissing a ways off from the roadside brush, for something made me know to keep back. She didn't hear me that time. An older Negro down the line had a fiddle clamped under his chin, and he kept bowing one high, tight note over and over till someone hollered for him to play a decent tune. A white voice hollering. Two white men, unshaven, in cowhide boots, rumpled trousers, sweat-yellowed open-neck shirts. *Drovers.* The word sprang into my head, I'd heard it before. I drew closer and saw that Tilly was roped around the waist to the other children, the grown slaves behind in a double row, braceleted and linked together with metal that gave off a dull, kind of beautiful sheen. And then I comprehended. But it couldn't be real.

"Tilly!"

She saw me and began to cry, but Tilly almost never cried. One time when we'd been playing in the woods she'd gashed her hand on a rock, and though she'd winced she didn't weep like I'd have done. It had amazed me. But here she was, bawling so hard she couldn't get words out, and all of a sudden she puked down the front of her shift, her new one made from a burlap sack scented with cloves. She was still retching and weeping as I bolted off into the trees.

I hid in the woods all the rest of that day and it wasn't till evening that Aunt Juba found me face down by the crik.

"O Aunt-Juba-Juba-Tilly."

I still remember how tall she appeared, looming up between me and an early-rising moon, but the next moment she'd squatted down to hold me. The smells of her tobacco chaw and dye from her bandana were close, comforting. She knew.

"Feel real tore up over it too, honey," she said. "You know she was like to my own same as you."

"Seen it. She puked."

"All right now. Easy. Go on, sob it out."

She didn't ask me how I'd seen it. Maybe she knew that too somehow. People said Aunt Juba had the gift of Far Sight, she was wise, and more than just a granny-midwife. She could cure ailing folks like no white doctor or nigger conjure man was able, but not from magic, child, she'd say, from the good herbs and years of doing with the Lord's help; don't have no truck with witchery. We'd often walked this crik together while she gathered in healing plants, and I felt we were deep friends, but for all my love and trust in her she couldn't even begin to make me comprehend why it had happened. I was barely able to believe my sister was truly gone.

Tilly and I had been near in age, the youngest of Mama Rit's brood, and long after our brothers had been set to work we'd run together through the woods, hunting birds' nests, catching crawldads in the streams, swapping cornhusk dolls and marbles. Even when she'd got big enough for choring I'd tagged along, helping her tote water to the field hands, and on Sundays we'd be scrambling through the woods again, calling out the words to our secret game:

Bring me my dress!
Yes'm I will.
Lace my stays!
Yes'm I will.
Whew that's tight now hold up the glass.
Yes'm I will.
Won't I be the finest lady at the c'tillion?
Tilly, I get to be ma'am now you been ma'am all morning.
All right but only for a little while, I'm older . . .

Aunt Juba was speaking, her voice steady above the whimpering I couldn't choke off.

"Honey, honey, recollect back on what I told you before. The Lord hold children specially close to Him, always done. He be sure to watch over Tilly wherever she gone. It don't mean she pass from His sight just cause she pass from ours."

I kept on crying.

"Child, you best learn here and now how to mourn proper,

there bound to be other times when you lose someone. There be times when you burn your grief away with anger, that's right, burn it out that way, and there be times when you got to run with your grief till it heal. But times come when you can't do nothin else but mourn, and you learn to cry till you commence to laugh and you cry out till you ride above them tears. That's why I mean for you to be at the funeral now, you big enough. Old David slept hisself away last night, you heard that, surely. Come to fetch you myself, everybody else give up they find you."

I didn't understand much of what she said, excepting about the funeral. I'd known it would be this evening, but I didn't want to go. I shook my head, stooping over fresh tears.

"Harriet!" Aunt Juba shook me gently. "Straighten up, child. Mind me. We best go direct, they likely started."

She bathed my face in the crik, shot a thin stream of tobacco juice into the bushes, and led me off through the dark without another word.

Our buryings were held at night. It had always been like that, and at the time I never thought to wonder why. I suppose now that our masters wouldn't have lost a workday off us that way, and a body wouldn't keep till Sundays, but maybe we chose the nights ourselves so that we'd have some peace without the whites prying into our own doings. Aunt Juba had told me of troubled times long before when prayer meetings and funerals needed to be kept secret. Back then, she said, a lookout was always posted, the path through the woods was marked with branches bent in a certain fashion, and the trees of the praise-grove were hung with drenched quilts to muffle sound. No fuss was made over us gathering when I was small though, excepting sometimes when the patrols were about, and that night I heard the end of a hymn sung out plain as Aunt Juba led me toward the ring of cedars where our funerals commenced.

All of it does not come back clear.

Most of the Quarter was there, but the faces smeared together in the wavering glow of the torchlight. Sweat-soaked backs and brows were clouded with mosquitoes, and a constant *slap-slap* at the whining pests came like a faint drumbeat under the singing. The preacher alone stood out. Tall and powerfully built, he seemed to anchor the circle of mourners as he rose up in their midst and strode to the open coffin. Amos was a shouting preacher, they said, one of the best when the Spirit took him, but for all that it was only scraps of his words that reached in between my thoughts.

"Dead. Brother David's dead. We raise up our voices and mourn our brother, we mightily grieve. But don't nobody forget. We all bound to follow him one day."

A flicker of heat lightning. Could Tilly see that from where she was and would it be raining there?

"You can't go nowheres my brothers and sisters, but Death will find you. You can't dig a hole so deep and bury youself that Godamighty's farsighted eye can't pick you out. All your friends may forget you but . . ."

I won't forget. Even when everyone else does no I will not ever.

". . . the Lord's good, the Lord's mighty to save, the Lord know all our names. Jesus who died and rose before us got His hands stretched out to our brother here, that's right, poor folks closest to the Lord's heart."

And children. Aunt Juba said about the children.

"Wasn't the Lord poor? Yes He was. Didn't He pass His time on earth with poor folks like us, like David, not with the high-and-mighty? Yes He done. And so I ask you to praise the Lord with me, praise . . ."

Old David's woman Lutie wasn't the only one answering the preacher through her tears. The Spirit was moving through this sober time, but I wished Amos would say something for Tilly's sake.

"David gone to live in Jesus our Brother, ain't that the truth?"

"Amen yes he is, tell it out."

"David gone to rise up into that almighty Grace with Jesus, our Jesus who stooped down and wore a man's life, died a man's death on our account."

"So true, oh yes, praise Jesus."

But Tilly, she didn't go to Jesus, she just went away, and what would happen, what else was it Aunt Juba said? That He'd watch over her, she'd said that.

She was nudging me up as folks moved into the solemn Spiritual Shuffle, clasping hands and telling each other's names out till every one had been called.

My sister Lutie bound to go, hope to meet you in Heaven . . .

My brother July bound to go hope to meet . . .

My sister Harriet hope . . .

When it was over six men shouldered the coffin and we followed behind, heading toward our own burying ground on the far side of a ruined tobacco field. The air was thick and moist as we moved along, and there was no breeze to carry off the stench from the nearby swamplands, a stench that seemed to grow as we reached the boneyard.

In the sputtering glare from the torches, the worm-eaten pine head-slabs appeared to be moving, pushing up against the milkweed and goldenrod that choked the place, and I could feel the dead lying all around us, shut up in their boxes, wrapped in lengths of rotting cloth. Briars reached out from the graves, bramble bushes tried to climb the fence, and mingling with the reek from the swamp was a heavy smell of decaying wood. I didn't wonder why most of us tried to avoid passing this way. The white people never came hereabouts either, saying the place was foul on warm days, but maybe it made them fidgety, maybe it gave them the same sense of slithery dread it did me.

I was trembling as they turned David's coffin so he'd face the sunrise, and while they commenced to sing him home I silently said the one name they'd left out of the Spiritual Shuffle. *Hark from the tomb a doleful sound* my sister Tilly bound to go *My ears hear a tender cry* my sister Tilly bound. *A livin man come through the ground* my sister Tilly bound and gone, hope to meet you. For me it was my sister in that box they lowered, and only the crushing pressure of Aunt Juba's hand on mine kept me standing. I wept till they'd filled in the grave, till folks were lighting up their pipes on the way back to the Quarter, and the preacher had turned back into what he was most of the time, only Amos the blacksmith.

I wept other nights later on, especially from watching my folks. For some time my mama's eyes were mostly wet, even while she fixed supper, sand-scrubbed her skillets, or did her piecing and quilting. On the odd evenings when she couldn't find enough work to do in her garden patch, she'd sit in the chimney corner fiercely puffing on her pipe, and as she watched Daddy break up the railing around Tilly's empty corn-shuck pallet, she bit clear through the pipe's clay stem. Her long days in the fields couldn't seem to numb her grievings then, and with my daddy it was the same. He'd come in from the timber yard with wood shavings on his clothes, eat little, and pace about in the firelight, working his jaw muscles as he flung his tall shadow across the walls. He still went out fishing or trapping some evenings, but there was none of the usual carryings-on when he came back with a muskrat from the marshes. Children from the other shacks still crowded around when they smelled roasting meat, but they'd fall silent and slink away just from looking at Daddy Ben's face. Even my brothers were quiet for a spell, and the unnatural hush frightened me.

In my earliest memories, our cabin had been a warm place for living in. Half the Quarter used to gather there at night, jawing and smoking by the hearth, while all of us children sat up on our pallets, listening to the talk. Daddy mostly told us the Fang-Tooth Catman would come get us if we didn't go to sleep, and we'd lie back down, only playing like we were asleep, overhearing everything anyways: all about runaways and thefts, crops and quarrels and courtings, all about the woman that got her ass branded for hitting the overseer who'd hit her boychild, and about the nigger who was so mean, when he was sold the traders sent him on home again.

Time and time again we used to hear Mama Rit set folks laughing with her stories, one in especial that she seemed to favor. It was about a slave who told his master all the hogs on the place had died from a sickness called Malletitis, and Old Master, believing the meat would be tainted, gave the dead hogs to his darkies for eating. "And you *know,*" Mama would say, "that nigger *give* them swine Malletitis, cause when he tapped Mister Hog between the eyes with a mallet, it sure set in mighty quick."

After everyone had left, we used to peek out and watch Daddy hanging up the blankets around his and Mama's rag bed in the corner. Late at night we'd hear them back there, laughing and shushing each other, whispering, making things creak and rustle, as we finally dozed off.

But there was none of this anymore. There was only that hush.

I'd lie awake long after everyone else was snoring and let my eyes wander over my brothers, sprawled all around the dirt floor on their pallets. Would William Henry be sold next? Or Benjie? Jamie? Robert? Would it be Mama and Daddy? Or would it be me? I was seized with the notion that whoever I stared at the hardest would be taken, and after a while I'd just turn my face to the wall. Daddy had knocked the clay daubing out from between the logs so we'd get more air in summertime, and I could gaze out through the gap next to my head. The slice of darkness I'd see there always appeared mysterious and smooth, flowing like black water, carrying me past the cabin . . . and then would come the voices again, crooning sometimes *with you with you* or booming, beckoning *come follow.*

Most nights I'd go outside to obey but there was never anyone there, only the dim, leaning cabins and the vague bulk of the hill which hid the Quarter from the Big House. Even so, I believed in this bodiless friend, and after the warm mellow night had lapped around me for a few minutes I'd crawl back to bed, drowsing at last, dreaming the old dream.

I'd be flying over cottonfields and cornfields and the corn was ripe, the tassels waving golden-brown in the wind. I'd fly over a town and a river, and the water would gleam under me like a mirror in the sun. I'd come to a hill and fly over that. I'd come to a fence and fly over that too. But I'd always get to a barrier, mostly a stone wall, and I couldn't fly over it. It would appear like I didn't have the strength, but just as I was sinking down, there'd be ladies over there, and they'd put out their hands and pull me across.

In the first few moments of waking from that dream, just before it had shredded away, I'd feel peaceful. Then the horn would call, my folks would hurry out. And I'd remember.

The sense of loss would strike me in the gut, and I'd sit there alone, scuffing at the floor with my feet, seeing her again as she'd looked that day, while the death-stench rose in my nostrils.

From that time on, Death was a stench, it was the loss of Tilly. But maybe Old Callie was right after all. Death was also white.

◆ ◆ ◆

SULLEN.

Willful.

Insolent.

I was often called such when I was small, and I don't suppose that's so wide of the mark either. Looking back now, it seems only natural that my childhood ended in a pigpen, and it makes me smile to think of myself as I was in those early years. I kept getting into trouble one way or another, mostly in my efforts to get away from certain people, certain places.

Old Callie's nursery for one.

She looked after us children who were too young for work, while our folks were out in the fields all day. In bad weather she'd have us in her cabin, and when it was fine she'd keep an eye peeled to us as we played out front of the Quarter. There was a suckling woman too, for the babies that lay in baskets hung from the lower branches of a tree.

Tilly and I had always hated the nursery. Mostly we'd sneak off to run around on our own, but now and then Callie would pull us along by the ear before we could go anywheres, and make us stand with the other children while she tried to teach us something Marse Ed wanted us to learn. Callie called it a "Catechiz."

Who give you a master and a mistress?
God give them to us.
Who say you got to obey them?
God say we got to.

What make niggers so lazy?
Our sinful hearts . . .

She'd never been able to keep us still long enough to get through the whole thing. As I hung around the edge of the nursery after Tilly was taken away, I could see Callie wasn't doing any better.

"What do God say bout work!" she'd be hollering, while all around her an open game of Driver-in-the-Field broke out wild and noisy. A boychild named Shadrack was playing Boss Nigger like always, beating the others with a hickory branch, even though he was older than me and didn't belong there. One time he saw me watching the goings-on and sidled over, thwacking his switch against his thigh.

"You too high-and-mighty for we-all now?" he yipped.

"Ain't so."

"You figure you too high-and-mighty just cause your daddy go up the Big House all the time? I know what he do up there, he suck Marse Ed's asshole."

I threw myself on top of Shadrack. He was little and wiry, easy enough to beat up, and I kept pummeling him till Old Callie's cane cracked down across my back. Before she could whop me again I was running off, babbling over my shoulder.

"My daddy do not suck ass no he don't my daddy proud he boss the crew that split the wood that make everythin in the world my daddy real valuable to master he foretell the weather for him yes he do and you ain't even got no daddy *Shadrack.*"

It was better playing by myself.

Even after I'd heard the other children had turned against their bully, and even though my games were lonesome without Tilly, I got a good feeling from running about in the woods. It was a sense of freedom, my earliest taste of it too, and it stayed with me. I'd belly like a snake through the tall grasses, barefoot, half-naked in my skimpy feedbag of a shift, and sometimes I'd climb up into a certain chokecherry tree where I'd pretend to be a bird. Straddling a high branch, I'd wave my arms, and then slowly, slowly make the tree swing this way, that way, liking the freshness of the salty, tidewater breeze against my face. Amidst the dapplings of sun and leaves I found a place for myself, and I'd spy around, hiding, exploring the plantation from end to end. I'd hear some whistling from the barn, carriage wheels on the Big House drive, squealings from the sow's pen on the far side of the pastureland, scythes whisking through wheat in the fields, and now and then a long, loud *Oooo-eeee watchit nigger!* carrying from my daddy's timber lot.

Other times I was nabbed to do small tasks before I could escape into my ramblings. Mostly I had to gather up kindling for the cookshed's fire, and I never did like it when they roped me in to help get dinner on. The cookshed was always one big hustling commotion, with pans banging, cutlery tinkling to the floor, lids slamming down, and hands snatching every whichway at crockery from the shelves and dried herbs hanging from the ceiling. It was too warm in there, cramped and stuffy, the air spattered with grease, rich with the smells of forbidden food. I'd catch a fierce scolding if I got underfoot, and I'd always fear Marse Ed would storm across the path from the Big House to see what the ruction was about.

That was likely when I concluded never to be a house servant, even though that's what Old Callie said good children came up to be, the lucky ones, they got to be real quality folks. I didn't care. I just wanted to be outside where I felt that nameless arm-flapping ease, working in the open with my own folks, and far away from that evil man who'd sold my sister. That was what I concluded, what I expected too.

But all of a sudden I was wrested out of my free wanderings. They stuffed me into a coarse cotton dress that felt like needles all over my skin, they were going to stuff me into a cart bound for Bucktown, they were going to stuff me into a house after all.

It was all right, my parents said it was all right. I wasn't being sold, I was only being loaned out in a kind of exchange to a weaver-lady and her husband. They'd have the use of me for housework while I learned weaving, and then I'd come back with a skill that would be handy to Master, handy to me as well; skilled craftsfolk had it better. In the meanwhiles,

Bucktown was close enough so Mama could come see me Sundays, and it wouldn't be for such a very long time, just a couple of years in James Cook's house.

Two years. That seemed a very long time to me indeed, especially in a house.

The Cooks' place wasn't all that different from our cabin down to the Quarter, excepting it had two rooms instead of one, and a loft where the white folks slept. The small room held only a creaky spinning wheel and the loom, and the larger one was fitted out real plain — just some stools, a wobbly table, a chest. That whole house was far dirtier than any shack I'd ever seen, littered like it was with broken bottles and chipped crockery. Chickens strutted in and out across the dirt floor, pecking at the food-crusted skillets by the hearth, and unwashed chamber pots were piled on the chest, next to a motheaten cloak. Although I was only a child I knew rightoff what kind of people lived there. They were trash. White trash. Daddy must not have been told.

Keep clear of trash, we'd all been taught that early. They were not only considered to be the laziest people alive, they stole from us, tried to get us drunk, and were mostly meaner toward us than the planters. These poor whites were also the patrollers hired to keep order in the district, catch runaway slaves, and check the Quarters once a month, but they often did more than that. They'd ride through, trampling our gardens, busting up our parties or prayer meetings if they felt like it, and some were known to torment whatever bondfolk they might find on the roads without a written pass from Master.

It seemed like that hadn't troubled Marse Ed when he'd decided to loan me out, but I decided straightaway that I wouldn't learn how to weave, and if I couldn't learn maybe he'd let me come home and then send me into the fields. The sooner the better, too. I missed my folks, and it was hard having to stay inside all the time, especially in that weaving room with fat Mrs. Cook.

I carded her wool all wrong, got in the way, played dumb, and the woman would slap me, cussing me out with a variety of names. Shit-brained nigger was the mildest of them, as I remember, but I can recall little else about Mrs. Cook excepting her shelf-like bosom and her onion breath. She soon gave up on me and sent me out to help her husband, who set me to hoeing his bean patch, cleaning the privy, tending the chickens and the goat. He'd cuff me after each chore was done, and then he'd stand pissing on the hearth, scratching his head with his free hand while he thought up more. It must have been a great thing for them to have a darky around, even a small one, and before long I was doing all the housework as well. I figured I had to get myself home somehow, and took the only means of escape I could think up at the time.

That time arrived on a drizzly November day when I was just coming down with the measles. My spots weren't out yet and I didn't really know what ailed me, but I ached everywheres and felt hot enough for it to be July. Nonetheless I kept silent and followed Mr. Cook when he bade me walk his traplines with him. It was a mighty effort to stay on my feet all that day, but in the midst of a drenching downpour I managed to turn the measles into pneumonia. Fever burned in me like triumph, I puked into a passle of muskrats, keeled over, and was carried home.

It was past Christmas when Aunt Juba had got me well again, and I heard that the Cooks had told Master I was too stupid to ever learn weaving. This bit of news delighted me far more than it did my folks, and it seemed a sure thing that I'd be sent to help out in the fields, but no. Marse Ed had concluded to make me a nursemaid, and oh what a lucky child you are, said Old Callie, you go thank the good Lord Jesus this minute. I'd be quality, I'd never be a common field hand, and I threw a tantrum on account of that, till Daddy Ben said if I didn't behave he'd wear me out himself. When I look back now, I see that he was afraid for me. He knew I wasn't stupid, likely knew something had gone on at the Cooks', and didn't want me to get so deep in trouble I might be sold off as a nuisance. But just then his anger was all I saw, and a temper on him that was frightening. In the end I did go up the hill to the Big House.

When I recollected Master's home later, I realized it wasn't really so grand as we all thought, nor so very big either, just a sturdy brick house painted white. Four large rooms surrounded the hall downstairs, with smaller, dormered ones under the gambrel roof, and a verandah running across the front, making the dwelling appear wider than it really was. There was no library or music room like I'd heard some other planters had, and I never saw more than three or four books in the place, as Marse Ed didn't set much store by such things. Even so, when I was a child it seemed a spacious mansion to me, floored with pinewood, curtained, and battened tight in the walls. In summer it was cooled by hilltop breezes and a cluster of shading plane trees; in winter fireplaces warmed nearly every room.

A different kind of living up there, to be sure. There were fewer drafts, fewer flies. No need to trouble over bad weather, no smoke-choked rooms, no thick cook-smells at all. Instead of itchy nigger-cloth, we had smooth castoff white folks' clothing to wear, rich leavings from the kitchen to eat, and the chores were easier, true enough. Also true: No end to those chores even after dark, no time to sit down for meals, and nowheres to stretch out for sleep, as I was quartered in a cupboard room which had once held linen. But that wasn't what made me conclude that I had to get out of there.

It was having to be indoors everlastingly, once more. It was the shrill, puling baby I didn't know how to manage, an infant that had been born only a few months before to Master's second wife, Miss Susan. And it was especially Marse Ed's presence. He never really hurt me, I have to say that much for him, and he only hit me once across the wrist when I permitted the fire tongs to fall smartly across his instep. He cussed at me continually though, and I never ceased to despise him; he'd sold my sister after all, and I hadn't forgotten that. But Mammy Portia was really much more dangerous. She carried the keys, ran a strict household, and appeared to think real high of herself as she bossed the rest of us, even Franklin, the aging butler and head manservant who was her senior. Portia wouldn't hesitate to box my ears if she thought I was looking insolent or if she caught me bungling, and she bashed me in the mouth the day I just happened to spill the baby's bath water in the hall where Miss Susan was likely to slip — and did.

Surprisingly, Miss Susan was the worst of all. I can still recollect the first time I was whipped with the rawhide after a series of blunders in the nursery. The whipping was carried out by Mistress herself, and I was just as unprepared for this new, skirted, straw-haired enemy as I was for the shock of the lash.

It caught me sudden, bit my neck and burned deep, stunning me so my eyes blurred and I careened from that single blow into a wall, where I sank down gulping, trying not to cry. The searing hurt would not let go, and wetness trickled from the ripped skin till it reached down between my shoulder blades. *You get up now, you heah,* she kept saying, as the baby commenced to wail and Portia's heavy tread sounded beyond the door. I just cowered there, rocking under the hot pain.

Miss Susan hadn't been married much over a year, and it was soon plain that my rawboned, long-jawed, toothy mistress was mighty unhappy. It was likewise plain that I was going to suffer for that, even though I left off purposeful bunglings after that first licking. I overheard Miss Susan telling Portia about her home in the Virginia hunt country, about the balls, the company breakfasts, the hunts themselves, and especially, endlessly, about her adoring daddy. I realize now she was barely more than a girl then, a girl who whimpered that she was still lonely and homesick in this Maryland backwater where she'd found no new friends, and Edward didn't understand her; why, when she'd asked him for a nursemaid she'd naturally expected an experienced mammy, not some stupid, sullen child. The darkies here weren't at all like her daddy's colored people save for Portia, she said, and her baby, her single consolation, was a heavy cross to bear as the doctor had said his lungs were weak.

She saved the infant's fuzzy hair cuttings in keepsakes on her vanity along with gilt-edged miniatures of her entire family, and many nights I'd hear her weeping as she clicked through the collection. It was after her worst crying fits that I had the most to fear. Oftentimes I'd be up late with the ailing, bleating baby and she'd appear suddenly in the nursery, swollen-eyed and rumpled, with the rawhide in her hand.

It got so I was terrified of the nights, even the peaceful ones. I'd lie awake in my cupboard room with the door open, listening for mother and child, bolting upright at the snap of a curtain against an open window, the chink of a chamberpot, the creak of a bed slat. In the days I was edgy too, jumping at the *thunk-thunk* someone made beating a rug out back or a tray clattering in the warming pantry below or even the slosh of a scrub brush on the stairs. The rare evenings that tinkled with music and laughter brought me no peace, though no one ever bothered me when there were parties, excepting when I had to lug the baby down to show him off for company.

As time passed tiredness and fear made me clumsy about the other chores I did. I mostly spilled oil when I was filling lamps, I'd track ashes across freshly mopped floors after kindling the hearthfires, and then Franklin would say I'd surely catch it. He never told on me, but I was always alert for the scents of rosewater, starch, or tobacco which signaled Mistress, Mammy, or Master. It seemed one of them was always after me. The only question was who it would be.

I hated them. I hated the house. I hated watching a new autumn and then another spring rustling beyond my reach, glazed over by the windowpanes. My attempts at acting dumb and insolent had got me nothing more than a scabby neck. It appeared like I'd been better off with the Cooks despite them being trash, and though I heard later there were plenty of good masters and mistresses, it seemed I wasn't going to run into any. I wanted to break the glass windows, break something or someone's head, and one morning at breakfast I guess I couldn't put up with the Big House anymore.

As I was standing at table behind Miss Susan she and Master commenced a great quarrel. All the while she railed at him Marse Ed kept reaching into the sugar bowl at my elbow, crunching the sweet lumps between his teeth like they were knucklebones. He left off doing that to pace about the room when Miss Susan rose to glare out the window, and I didn't even try to keep my eyes lowered like I was supposed to, in the pretense that darkies didn't notice white folks' ructions. I stared over at the sugar bowl, suddenly taken with a notion that it would feel good to grab a lump, something white and hard that belonged to them, and crush it up. Master started yelling, and the notion possessed me. He turned his back. Miss Susan was still facing the window. I put my hand in the sweets, but just at that moment they both swung around, and next thing, Miss Susan had the rawhide down off the mantel.

One big jump got me out the door. They were coming after me.

I scooted out onto the verandah, down the steps, and kept right on going. The footfalls and shouts faded away as I ran, but I didn't stop even so. Everything flashed by me in streaks till I didn't know where I was; I only knew my side pained and my legs were still pumping. When it felt like I couldn't gasp in one more breath I'd reached the sow's pen at the far end of the pasture, and I clambered over its fence, tumbled in, and fell flat on the ground by the sow.

I hid in that pigpen two days and two nights.

Just what I thought I was about is hard to say, but a swell of victorious pride filled me as soon as my wind came back. That was the biggest thing I'd ever done, that would show them, that was some kind of escaping, yes it was too . . . and so my thoughts rattled on for a while. Some kind of escaping indeed; it sets me to laughing whenever I recollect it.

There I was, feeling ever so daring and bold, staring bravely into an immense pink snout that poked me and snorted in my face. There I was, the heroine, sitting amongst six or seven squealing piglets, enthroned on their droppings, the sow's larger turds, assorted potato peelings, melon rinds, apple cores, corncobs, curdling gravy, mud, and sour milk. Finicky I was too, that first day, not about to eat any of those scraps. I'd steal out for food at night was what I'd do, and in the meanwhiles I scrunched down low whenever more slops were poured down the trough. It didn't occur to me to run off for good; I wouldn't have known where to go, and had no idea what lay past Bucktown. In the way of most children, I didn't think past the coming night.

But when that night did come I dropped into a deep exhausted slumber, and by the end of the next day I was so hungry I was fighting those little pigs for every potato peel. I'd also grown afraid of the sow. She didn't like to see her children's food stolen, and her beady eyes squinted at me as she'd heave up off her side, snuffling and grunting, to shove me away. The sun appeared extra close, extra hot, parching my mouth and throat, and the dense, dirty air gagged me. I'd tried to ignore it before, that pigpen's reek, telling myself it wasn't much worse than the privy, but it got to be overpowering, it was all over me, I'd become a part of it. Even so. I'd hold out. They wouldn't catch me, they wouldn't get to whip me again, hold out I would. I didn't reckon out how long.

The second night I heard my folks searching for me. My daddy's voice was hard and sharp-edged, he was swearing too, and he'd surely give me a licking if for some reason Marse Ed did not. *If* I came out. Then I heard Mama Rit and Aunt Juba, calling, calling, *Harrrr-iet . . . mercy now honey come . . . where's that child . . .* They moved off, faded away. And then there was just silence. Just me. I listened for those other voices that sometimes came in the nights, but heard nothing.

By noon the following day I'd had enough. I was choked with thirst, weak from hunger and sickened by that Godamighty smell. My family was all unsettled, and at that point a licking didn't seem so awful. It couldn't be worse than staying in the pen, so I'd just walk out straight and proud, direct up to the Big House, showing them I could at least choose the time of punishment.

When I appeared in the doorway of Master's dining room the family was just finishing the midday meal, and everyone jumped at the sight of me. My eyes peered out through the pig slops that still ran down my face, potato peels clung to my legs, I was plastered with mud and turds and likely some of last night's supper; Lord knows how I must have stunk. No single face appeared to me clear, and I only heard the crash of a plate some servant must have dropped, looking out at me from the warming pantry. The room began to spin slowly, a hand sent the rawhide zinging around my neck in one blinding stroke, and I was down on all fours with Marse Ed's voice above me. *Jeez-Christ, Jeez-Christ,* it spat, then ordered me to get my insolent black ass the hell out of his house for good, if I liked dirt so much I could just have my fill of it in the fields, that was where I was going, now march.

And that was where I was headed as soon as I was able, strutting out with the other hands at the sound of the driver's horn, finding myself side by side with Shadrack.

"Your daddy suck Marse Ed's ass to get you in the Big House," he hissed, "but no amounta suckass never get you back there now."

I gave him a murderous look and moved away, on account of what he said about Daddy Ben, but not on account of my changed fortune. Let him jibe about that all he wanted. Let Old Callie mutter I'd taken a long fall from quality. Let Master call me insolent, let my daddy holler at me for borrowing trouble, let anyone else consider me lacking in common sense. They just didn't comprehend.

This was what I'd wanted. This time, I believed, I'd truly won.

◆ ◆ ◆

FUNNY HOW just a few sounds or the look of a soft twilight can still put me in mind of quitting time in those fields; an easy mellow time walking back toward the Quarter together, time to let go, settle down, loosen up.

Through the dusk I'd see the outlines of a woman with a rake on her shoulder, a man pausing to take a leak, another wadding tobacco into his jaw. Amidst the faint calls of starlings there'd be the slow tramp of our boots, the clang of stashed tools, weary laughter and talk.

"Sure beat out tonight else I'd pick me off a duck out the Buckwater. They all bout landed in this week."

"Easier to grab a hen out the coop right here."

"Yeah, but Marse Ed he got tar smeared all over them fences now, figures that'd put a stop on thievery."

"Thievery? He say? Well, shit. The Man own us and them hens and the corn they feed on, that the truth? Then there ain't no reason why we can't eat his chickens same's them chickens eat his corn. Ain't thievery atall, property just shift around a bit."

"Aw*right!*"

Moving on home with the field hands, I'd sense a comradeship with those folks, folks who did real labor too, not like lighting lamps or washing baby-turds out of linen. I was amongst most of my family as well, right alongside Mama and my older brothers, grown men who'd moved out of our cabin. It felt fine being with them, it felt fine working out there at the start, it felt like God's gift to be a field hand, *uh-huh, oh yes, mighty mighty . . .* I can just hear myself babbling that at anyone who'd listen, never noticing the thin, pitying smiles I'd get for answers. But I was also mighty young when I started, not big enough to do much besides sowing seeds and picking worms off the plantings. Then, because I was husky and eager, I helped string up tobacco leaves, haul in pumpkins, pluck apples, and pitch hay for the stock. By next seed time I was more than helping.

The sharp-sweet smell of manure and wet earth got to be familiar, likewise the plow's screech as it grazed a rock, and the creak of the mule team's harness. A frenzy built around us as we hurried to set the tobacco seedlings in time, working straight through the Sabbath or a fine drizzle, and then the fields would calm some. Amidst the rustlings of young corn I'd catch a thread of my mother's singing, *come day go day God send Sunday.* A scent of stewing beans and pine kindling might waft over from the fire where Aunt Juba cooked our noon meal, and Shank, the strapping black driver, was always hollering from the fore row, "Hey nigger! You boy! I say what for you ain't to work, nigger, that mean you!"

From the beginning I never feared Shank like I'd done Mammy Portia, though he was massive, bulging with muscles, nearer to seven foot tall than six, and he carried a lead-handled whip platted with wire. Folks could recollect some other drivers before him, drivers who'd been mean with that whip, but not Shank. He was tough, he barked and prodded us to keep pace, but he worked alongside us and said he was no white man's nigger. Shank saw to it the work got done, that's what mattered, and if he had call to dole out a beating, he'd threaten a while, then snap the lash just above his victim's hide, never touching it. The field hand he'd spared always carried on something terrible for the sake of the overseer who sat his horse a ways off in the shade.

We didn't really need that overseer. There wasn't enough of us, just about twenty-five hands in the fields, though that varied. Sometimes there'd be less if the cropping wasn't good, and Marse Ed would hire folks out to other masters in a loaning system where the hired hand would pay Marse Ed a dollar a week out of earnings made elsewhere. In a good year we might be joined by hired hands from other plantations till there was maybe forty of us. Even so, we still didn't need that overseer, and they said McCracken was brought in when Miss Susan came, just to impress her. He didn't appear like he'd be much trouble at first, him but a young drifter with a nasal northern accent, new, green, and what most folks figured for a coward; a rare thing indeed. He tried to talk rough and menacing, but he'd never dared to whip a one of us, and was easy enough for the driver to twist this way and that. Sometimes we'd hide our smiles while we listened to Shank put him on.

"Real bad thing happen to this one overseer I worked for, real bad. This one nigger, was a big mother too, he fought back one time the bossman made for to whip him. Lord, he ripped that 'seer's pecker clean off, that's the truth, that's what he done, but don't you trouble youself none, Boss. You got nothin to fear on accounta me here to look out for you."

Whenever such skylarking went on my mama would suddenly find something very important on the ground between her feet, and as she'd lean down I'd see her shoulders shaking.

"Mercy, baby," she'd whisper to me, "that nigger sure know how to do a white man."

Quick to laugh, to cry, to forget bad times, my flighty child-woman of a mother had often seemed playful to all of us she'd raised. She appeared so to me firstoff as we worked side by side in the fields, even when she was showing me how to sucker tobacco or tend corn shoots. Big Harriet, or Big Rit, Old Rit, as she was called, had girlish ways and a giggly voice that almost made me forget her strong frame, muscle-corded legs, and the thick neck setting off her pretty, delicate face. Old Rit favored singing like she did storytelling, and her sorrow songs held a joyous note that rose above her labor, labor she taught me to do and do right.

I was glad of her teachings. When I'd become a hand I'd burned to show I wasn't stupid like they'd called me up at the Big House, and I yearned to work like I was grown before I truly was. But when I did get big enough to do all the important-seeming chores, I didn't care about them anymore. We worked hard, but it wasn't the toil that turned me around.

It was two people that changed things for me in the span of one year, my second in the fields.

A big man named Gideon worked out there with us, a man who stood pine-straight, near as tall as Shank. Gideon was known to have a temper and what with him being so strong too, everyone knew not to mess with him; even the driver let him alone. There wasn't any reason to push him, and more often than not he helped set the pace, even if he was getting on past his prime. You could tell how long he'd been in the fields from looking at his hands. They were so layered with callouses the palms seemed to have an extra inch of thickness, and callouses grew up over the horny fingernails as well. His skin was leathery, his eyes webbed in with a network of squint lines from a lifetime in the sun, and over the years Gideon had learned more about making things grow than anyone. Strange enough, there was a kind of motherly tenderness in this hulking man for the things he grew.

The crops had just commenced to poke through that second spring when Gideon called me over to a corn patch where he'd been putting in extra hours. He was crouched over some sprouts that had come up about eight fingers high, and he motioned me to kneel beside him as he took the shoots in his pawlike hands, touching them like he was stroking a child's hair.

"See that, Hat? I worked this patch four, five seed times now and this the first I ever got them things to grow right. Tobacco ruinated this soil before I took it over. Look at this here, she come up real strong at last. Go on, you can touch, but easy now."

Behind us I could hear Shank hollering, but he never hollered at Gideon so we paid him no mind.

"Feel that stalk," Gideon went on. "You able to feel the whole life in that plant right there under your hand. I worked this earth all winter, fed it, y'understand?"

Shank hollered again. There was a faint sound of a bridle and stirrups jingling nearby, but Gideon was too absorbed for looking up, and I in turn was tranced by the surprising gentleness of this towering field hand.

"Course it ain't like my own, what I got in my garden patch up to the Quarter, but still. Five years and now somethin to show. This here ain't bound to make no pig-shit ears neither, bound to bear beauties. Careful now, got to touch soft."

One last yell from the driver, and a whip handle cracked down on Gideon's back, the blow glancing off. We both leaped up and there was McCracken, off his horse and into the row, his boot crushing two of Gideon's plantings.

Before the overseer could even open his mouth, Gideon had jumped him and grabbed his whip so fast I didn't really see it happen. And then he just stood there, looming above McCracken, fingering the lash and looking murder.

"Keep away from me, you trash." Gideon spat. "Don't you never try that again, don't you never even come near me no more. You hear, boy?"

He took one step toward McCracken, threw the whip down like for a dare, but the overseer just snatched it up, backed off, and we didn't see him for the rest of the day.

That evening at quitting time Gideon went off by himself to close the pasture fence like always, but as he reached the gate he was surrounded by four white men who beat him with ax-handles and a bullwhip till he fell against the gatepost, dead.

Most of us saw it from a distance, turning at the sound of a ruction as we were heading out of the rows, and some said they'd glimpsed McCracken standing off a ways, watching from behind the fence. If he had indeed set it up we never knew for sure. Nor did Marse Ed, who only cursed out the nameless white trash that had come around and killed off one of his best hands.

The fields were nearly silent for a long while after.

"Why ain't they singing?" McCracken asked Shank, chewing his pale lips like maybe he feared we'd all turn on him at once. "Means something when they ain't singing, Jesus, I been here long enough to know that. Don't want no trouble, tellem to sing for God's sake, liven it up out there."

Still, there wasn't much noise through the summer, and surely no more put-ons from Shank that might scare McCracken again. As the steaming days drew on, there was mostly just the chopping of hoes and a steady drone of insects;

then in August came the singing of the grapevine telegraph, which McCracken couldn't hear.

The grapevine was made up of house servants who heard what was said at table, grooms who listened at the hitching posts in town, and hired hands who brought tidings from their own plantations. Our grapevine usually carried news of traders, auctions, or maybe a camp meeting in Cambridge. It had never sent such a message as it did then, a message that put me in mind of Gideon's rebellion all over again, but on a shocking, sweeping scale.

A slave-preacher called Nat Turner had raised an army of bondmen just over to Virginia, and slaughtered maybe a hundred whites in one night's time. Most of Nat's followers had been caught or killed, but planters up and down the Tidewater were seized with terror, a terror we could hear pounding up the drive and whirring through the Big House.

The evening the news came, nearly the whole Quarter jammed into Amos's cabin to whisper about the man we called the Black Prophet. Older folks could recollect rumors of other slave revolts and the hell that always broke loose on us afterwards, but most of the talk was awed, admiring. Nat still hadn't been captured, people said, they'd never catch that one, maybe he'd raise a whole new army, maybe . . . *Patrol!* screamed a child on lookout.

We scattered.

Mama started to chop up greens for supper as if to show everything was orderly and commonplace, just as the patrollers came down on us. They came through fast, riding across our gardens alongside the cabins, yipping like a horde of mounted demons, shooting wild. *Where you keep your coon preacher,* they hollered, and then we heard Amos crying out as they flogged him in his yard patch.

One by one the shacks were ransacked for guns, powder, and shot, none of which anybody possessed, otherwise there'd have been murder like elsewhere. Our place was turned inside out, crockery smashed, stools hurled into the fire, bedding torn apart. The air was flying with cornshucks and splinters. I was flat against the wall. Daddy's hunting knife was ripped from his belt as he tried to stand his ground before the hearth. They knocked him down. Mama's cleaver was snatched from her hand so fast it left a long, deep slit in her palm.

The patrollers roamed the Quarter that night and many nights thereafter with rifles over their arms, our curfew was the quitting horn, and Marse Ed got some rabble to guard the Big House.

All our gatherings were forbidden unless a white man was present.

All drumming, jubilee-beating, or rousing noise was forbidden.

All our passes to town or other plantations were stopped.

All books, tracts, and Bibles were banned from us.

Anyone teaching a slave to read would be jailed.

Any pair of slaves congregating would be lashed.

The door was wrenched off the privy.

The fields were watched.

The roads were watched.

We were watched, wherever we were, whatever we did.

We were getting ready for fall Hog-Killing time when we heard they'd caught Nat Turner, and we were in the midst of it when we heard they'd hanged him, boiling his hide down for grease afterwards.

Hog-Killing was mostly a good time for us, a time for partying after the men had made a big show, swaggering into the pens to grapple the swine while the rest of us watched. But that year it was different. There was no swaggering. There was no partying. There was no noise. It appeared like it was only axes and knives and blood, blood that left a sour stench in my nostrils, and then there was the stink of boiling hides as the dead hogs were thrown into caldrons of sizzling water. At last the scalded victims, scraped and hairless, were hanging from beams to cool, just like always. But not like always. Not that autumn.

As soon as the hogs had been cut up, the knives and cleavers were taken off us again, and that watchful silence went on. My dreams were filled with bloody vengeance for weeks, but then they sank away into empty sweat-drenched sleeps. The glory of the Black Prophet's rising seemed useless after all, all for nothing, excepting for the worse.

That next year was unsettled, and the one after it too, though not so bad. But even after things had calmed down and the patrollers had ceased haunting the Quarter more than once a month like before, a part of me felt changed, out of joint, out of place.

I guess that was the first time I'd truly comprehended what we were.

More and more often, I began to seek refuge in the praise-grove. Our prayer meetings seemed to take on greater meaning for me then, even though I'd attended them since I was small. In the grove or Amos's cabin, we'd join together till we were more than just ourselves, we were one in the Spirit, we were one in the Lord, we were one with each other, and that unity was able to lift me above tribulation when I was there. Amos would tell Gospel from memory, from his heart, the way his daddy had passed it along to him, preaching salvation through faith and suffering and love, and we'd glorify the Word, testifying, offering up our voices for a gift to Jesus. The Spirit would move through our hymns and holy dances, and I'd get to feeling raised up out of my body for a while.

But only for a while.

House servant, field hand, it appeared to make no difference which one I was after all. I brooded on that revelation during three more seed times, my body moving over the work, my mind spinning off on its own. I came up into early womanhood troubled, restless, but aimlessly so. Those secret voices which had whispered to me since childhood spoke louder, but I didn't comprehend them yet, believing they were only the praise-grove's echoings in my soul. It wasn't until Barrett's Jim came to spark me that my broodings blazed into open rebellion.

◆◆ ◆◆ ◆◆

I WAS LEFT FOR DEAD with my head busted, a ways off the plantation in the crossroads store. It was the summer I must have been about sixteen.

For a while afterwards all I could recollect of my whole life was McCracken grabbing the heavy iron weight off the counter scales, his arm snapping back, and a flash of white light as the pain exploded in my skull. Then there was darkness, a kind of breathing death that seemed forever, till the world began coming back, but only in pieces.

Cornshucks crunching under me. Warm stickiness running into one eye. Stabbing agonies in my temple. Something soft wound around there. Dry mouth. Flies crawling down a sweaty arm. Dense smell of food, bodies, smoke. Blurred firelight breaking into two fires. Then three. Then darkness again. Voices leaking through, urgent, closeby. And other voices, different, distant, only echoed rememberings.

"That mafucker McCracken, I swear I . . . Girlbaby? Girlbaby, don't you know your daddy, Harriet! . . . Lord, Rit, gimme a rag. Don't care what she done, this all on accounta that white trash sonabitch and that nigger from Barrett's."

"Hey y'all, put up them hoes just a minute, we got a new hand here called Jim. You figure you be able to keep pace, boy? We was supposed to get a strapper, not some little nigger made from wires. That make you mad, boy? Meant to. Best you comprehend to mind straightaway, you got me for driver now even if you does belong to Barrett. Just cause you hired out and able to save extries don't need to make you up-

pity. Someone show this nigger around. You there, Harriet! Hand him a hoe, I set him to work alongside you. Move it, gal!"

"Ben Ben, hurry! Run up the Big House, ask em to send for the white doctor, he bring her around, oh my Lord please."

"Mercy woman, don't move your hand off her head, that rag ain't stopped the blood, press down harder. I mean to fetch Aunt Juba direct, she better than any white doctor, and they wouldn't send one down here anyways, not after what they say happen. Be back."

"Heard on you Jim, leastways on your brother. Wasn't he hired out like you, didn't he buy his freedom with what he saved all the while? . . . Figured so. Concluded to try that myself if I get the chance on it."

"Shit, Hat, that way it take too long. I don't aim to stay around here and save till I got one foot in the boneyard, Lord no."

"Hat? Honey? You know your mama, don't you? Aunt Juba she on her way, you be to rights, be to rights, be to . . . ain't nothin, just a little blood is all, ain't nothin, nothin, oh sweet Heaven, can't you hear? Lord God, why do we birth these children, for what?"

"I figured what you got your mind all prepared for."

"Yeah, gal? What's that?"

"You mean to run off, ain't that right? Jim? Well, ain't it?"

"Hush, don't you say nothin bout it, hear?"

"She get to a place like this and that jumpy jackrabbity Jim he get away clean and clear, it ain't right. Hat honey, speak to your mama, oh baby, please."

"When you figure to run?"

"Soon's it look good. You cover for me when the time come, won't you, Hat?"

"Here she come now, thank Heaven, how bad she take it, Juba, say quick."

"Dear God . . . McCracken done this? If I wasn't a Christian I'd . . . No, easy, easy, she make it through. With the

Lord's help I just plain won't leave her go, but she be bad off a long while, may never be like before neither."

"But she come through, you hear that, Ben, oh bless God bless . . ."

"All right now. Know how you feel, Rit, but hand me that kettle. And Ben, you run fetch down all them herbs I got hung in my place. I surely ain't no doctor, but we do what we able. The kettle, Rit. And clean rags, many's you got. This here's bled through."

"Don't touch my neck, Jim. Don't! Them scars so ugly, ugly as that bitch what give em me. Well, ain't you mad over nothin? You the one set to run off."

"My own good sense make me want to run. Got that sense when they sold my daddy years past. Hey, come here. Don't have much more time outside tonight, your mama got her eye peeled to us. Look. Caught you a firefly."

"She let him mess with her, that's how it begun, Juba. I just know, shoulda told Ben. If he seen em over to the meadow nights he'd done that sorry nigger so's he never stand up straight again, let alone put fool notions in her head."

"Easy sugar, easy oh yes, almost now darlin almost oh yes now."

"Mercy oh Jim."

"Hurt you, sugar?"

"Uh-uh, not hardly."

"First time for you?"

"Course not! Course it ain't!"

"You figure she meant to run away with that boy and didn't say? Don't even comprehend why she was in the store, well, what you think, Juba? You and her always over by the crik together, didn't she say nothin?"

"White folks? You sure?"

"Told you, them Quaker ones don't hold with slavery . . . Now what you up to? Ain't no time to skylark, we got to get back in. Hat! Hand back my trousers, Lord sake."

"Not till you tell me more on them tunnels and that underground train."

"Don't believe Jim put much more in her head that wasn't

all ready there, to speak plain, Rit. Maybe he just raised up what was on her mind so's she was able to see it clear . . . No, can't say for sure . . . Now what's kept your old man with them herbs?"

"Waited on this a long time. Too long."

"Me too, I spect."

"Huh? Hold on, you concluded to come along? Ain't safe, not two at a time. Besides, you said you'd cover for me."

"Still can't comprehend it. Why on earth didn't she duck when she seen the Man rear back to throw that thing? Shadrack seen the whole bad business, was over to the store in the back room all the while. He say she just stood there and laughed at McCracken — Good Lord, laughed — just when he raised his arm. Now what you find to smile on in that?"

"Figure to grab some vittles from the crossroads store firstoff and then I be gone, Hat, clean off."

"Best you make certain ain't nobody in there."

"Well now, Rit, maybe McCracken meant to hit Jim, not her, just missed is all. Then again. Never mind. Got more rags?"

"You mean to run at night then? Jim? Ain't that so?"

"Raise up a little, honey. Try and drink this. That's it. You know this old face, know Aunt Juba?"

"What night?"

"Won't know till it come along, Hat."

"Hat honey, I got to give you another dose. Lift your head just a mite, there."

"What night?"

"All right, raise up again, you able to get this down? I know how bad it pains, somethin in this for the hurt, and boneset plant to make you mend."

"Tell me when, Jim."

"Certain you want to hear, honey, appears like Jim made it. We just past Christmas now and he ain't been caught. The reward bills even blowed down, first snow. Believe you meant to go with him, was sure all the while, so you drink this, get well, then you can try again. Always seen you headed for other things, child, if not now, another time. Drink."

Bitter, evil-tasting stuff running down my throat, my chin,

and the long-fingered pain reaching into my head as I lift up, but then I am drifting away on a purple fog of numbness, back into the whispering dark. I drift further off till that dark is lit by twisted, oil-soaked rags; it is the shadowed darkness of the barn, it is reaping time, the last one.

"Jim! What night?"

We're working late into the night cleaning up wheat, stuffing it into sacks, and there's a frenzy about the task; so much wheat, so many sacks to fill, and that grain must go to market at sunup. Everyone's weary, but McCracken keeps coming around to prod us, keeping himself on his feet with whiskey. We go on at a dragging pace, heads nod, hands appear to be moving on their own, but I am wide awake because across the barn I see that Jim is wide awake, edgy, jerky, and I comprehend it will be tonight.

Three hours to dawn and we still work, some folks dozing, grain spilling from loose-wristed hands, but beyond the slack faces Jim's head is cocked, the veins in his neck stand out, an eyebrow twitches. He looks over his shoulder, looks at no one, fills another sack. McCracken hasn't been by for some time now, maybe he's stumbled off to bed. Everything is still outside the barn, calm as a Christmas morning.

Two hours to dawn. A rooster makes an early crowing from somewheres. Jim's mouth tightens as he knots a full gunnysack with one sharp wrench. He glances at me, moves into the shadows toward another heap of bags, picks up an empty one, and steals out the barn door, that one sack strangled in his hand.

I wait some moments. Feel each one pass. Feel my blood bumping all through me. If I'm going to follow him it must be now, I have only instants to catch up, and I move past that same shadowed heap of bags, out the door into the star-sprayed night, and bolt off down the road. There's only the sound of my ragged breathing as I leave the plantation behind, there's only my boots thudding in the stillness and my heart drumming loud enough to wake the world. And then I'm rods away from the crossroads store where I stop, bend, try to catch my wind. I listen. Think I hear someone panting a ways off behind me, heavy uneven footfalls too, and, panicked, I plunge into the lamplit store. My eyes grab around, the counter, the shelves, the barrels, *there.* Jim, bending over an apple barrel in the back, turning just as McCracken bounds in on my heels; oh Lord, he wasn't abed, he must have seen me streaking past, and I have made this store Jim's trap.

The overseer takes it all in quick, me where I shouldn't be, Jim poised against the wall with an apple in one hand, a stuffed sack in the other, and sweat coming through his shirt. McCracken hurtles forward, clumsy from drink, and Jim sidesteps as the overseer crashes into the back shelves. Before he can right himself Jim is out the door.

McCracken bellows with a thickened tongue for me to chase that damn nigger. He is careening across the store heavy and slow, the fat rippling under his shirt, his face flushed with whiskey and what looks to be fright, but as he stumbles into the counter I turn to face him.

I reach behind me, slam the door shut and stand before it, spreading my arms till I am gripping each side of its frame. Jim might still get away if I can just *stand within the grace of light,* he'll make it if I can only *be not afraid,* and a deep feeling of power rises from my planted feet, it whirls up through my limbs to my head, my chin lifts, I hear myself laughing out loud at the overseer as I stand fierce and proud in front of the door, even as McCracken hurls his threat, even as he snatches the iron weight off the counter scales and takes aim.

"Do it again too, yes I will, stand up another time do it again."

A shriek, mine. It fills the cabin till I hear a chair overturn and Aunt Juba's face hangs above me. A hand. A ladle. A wormy, dirty-tasting brew in my mouth. I spit. She forces it down, holding my mouth open while she sits astride me.

"Hush honey, you got to hush. Marse Ed he on the way."

Through a dulled, whitish haze I see his pallid face and lashless eyes. There's another man with him, and the cabin is dead quiet.

"Well, here she is, name your price."

"Why, she's not worth a sixpence, you must be plumb crazy, Edward. She's so weak and scrawny I wouldn't think of buying her."

He comes again.

He comes every day, he comes with men who poke and jab and count my teeth, then go away till the next morning, when Marse Ed kicks the door open again and shows me to another could-be buyer. The crack of that door hitting the wall sends me off into the darkness once more, a darkness where there are torches in a ring, the stink of rotting wood mingles with the swampland's reek, and Tilly lies in a box facing the sunrise. I pass over into a deeper, blood-soaked darkness, I am rising from my stained pallet with a knife, I am slitting Master's throat and Miss Susan's, their blood runs out thin, white, and it freezes. The Lord will show me how to kill, I will rise from the dead with Nat Turner, I will slice open their bellies till their pale, frosty guts drop like stones around my feet, and I scream out for murder.

"Here she is, name your price. She'll make a good breeder once she's well, feel that, nothing wrong with this nigger's pussy."

Kill you, wish you killed, get off me, you bastard.

"Your price, sir? She was one of the strongest wenches I had before this unfortunate mishap, and will be again."

Spite you, smite you dead, I'll pray for it. Lord, take that man out of the way, don't even bother to convert his heart, kill that man, Lord, kill what is evil in Your sight, my sight, strike him down, for the arm of the Lord is strong, and you can't go nowheres my brothers and sisters but Godamighty's farsighted eye will pick you out, all your friends may forget you but Death will never forget you, and Old Callie, she said Death was white.

Another face looms up, this time a deep-black face, dwindling, then growing vast as night, a flat-nosed nigger face, and below it a skinny neck hung with a glinting coin and a rabbit's foot. Largo, the conjure man.

"Made a charm. Sprinkled red pepper out front the cabin, that draw off all the evil and pain, honey. Largo take it away."

"Don't draw pain, send it," I scream. "Put badmouth on Master, get him out the way, dry up his blood."

Aunt Juba shoves Largo out the door, sends someone for Amos, pours another brew down my throat, and then I scream only inside my head, kill him, kill him, kill that man dead.

And then I hear them say it: the words cut across the stuffy air to my pallet, *Marse Ed gone.* He'd died at table halfway through dinner, choked by a chicken bone caught in his throat, dead in two minutes flat. A Dr. Anthony Thompson was taking the place over, since he was Young Sir's guardian and Young Sir was but seven years old. No one would be sold off, thank the Lord.

Lord? Lord, I did it, I wished it on him. Wicked though he was, I'd no right to take a life, and I did, willed one away, oh have mercy on me, Lord. Cleanse me of my sin, for I have done what is evil in Your sight, cleanse me and I'll never have to do with killing, never, I swear. Cleanse me of blood-guilt, wash me with snow, turn Your face away from all my sins, and blot out all my guilt. I will rave my regrets in this fever forever, I'll offer myself up to You as fever itself, a burnt offering, fever me, forgive me.

The fever left off.

I was able to sit up.

Speak.

Feed myself.

Gray light ribboned across the floor from the wall chinks, the shutters were down, and it was so cold my pallet was drawn close to the hearth. Master had been dead a month, but I still felt tainted from that bitter, violent hatred, that murderous wishing, and for a time I believed I was unworthy of prayer. Even after I had confessed to Aunt Juba, even after she had said sharply that Jesus didn't work like that, nor did He listen to fool conjure men, I felt I was yet an abomination to the Lord. It was Aunt Juba alone who stayed my mind from craziness. She sat by me all that winter while my folks were out working, and kept me centered by talking to me, telling scraps of tales, or reciting Scripture when I asked her to.

" 'Then the Lord said unto Moses, *Now shalt thou see what I will do to Pharaoh, for with a strong hand shall he let them go, and with a strong hand shall he drive them out of his land.* And God spake unto Moses and said unto him, *I am the Lord.*' "

I heard her speak many passages from the Good Book that winter. She had a sharp mind on her, and recalled a great deal from a long-dead, pious mistress who'd taught her one Bible verse a day for ten years. That lady hadn't taught reading, only recitation, but she'd passed along rebellious texts by chance, not just the one we heard in the white church on Mission Sundays: *servants, be obedient to your masters with fear and trembling.* Aunt Juba never quoted that one to me.

Other times she'd recite what she taught herself, the names of her healing plants and what they did. I liked the way the words sounded.

"Grape root, dandelion root, sarsaparilla. Juniper berries and stinging nettle. Catnip, tansy, elderberry blooms. Enough? No? Sumach and yarrow for fever, squawvine for childbirth, skullcap for sleep."

Listening to those words, I could just see Aunt Juba striding the crik as she gathered in the plants, a tobacco wad bulging in her jaw, her straight-spined, six-foot frame etched out against a full moon. In her prime she'd been one of the best field hands on the place and would have made driver if she'd been a man, everyone said that. Her height and stance almost made me forget that age had commenced to thin her down, sagging and seaming her flesh, but high cheekbones still jutted up proud against webbed skin, the eyes were keen under heavy brows, and though her teeth had long been stained, they were all there. Mystical, practical, this farseeing, firmspoken wisewoman was the strongest soul I'd ever found to hold onto. But there were some miracles even Aunt Juba could not work.

In the end, she could not undo all the damage caused by McCracken's blow. For a time she wasn't able to shake my conviction that I'd brought a curse down on my head by willing death, and the first day I was able to move around the cabin without weaving, that notion of mine seemed oddly borne out. That was the day we ceased talking on how I'd run away again. That was the day I walked across the floor into a sleeping fit, and awakened to find Aunt Juba clapping her hands in my face while she yelled loud enough to stir the boneyard.

"Don't you comprehend what you done, child? You just gone off to sleep on your feet like a horse, been leaned against that wall I don't know how long. Lie down right here, that's it, easy."

She looked at my tongue, lifted my lids, probed the dented scar on my head, and went over the rest of me while a cold sweat commenced on the back of my neck. Then she rose.

"Nothin bad, Harriet, truly. Wasn't a shakin fit, thank the Lord, I seen that rightoff. Ain't nothin bad, you hear!" She spoke fierce, like to cover a ripple of anguish in her voice. "Maybe you go off like that again, maybe not. We just got to wait and see."

The next fit took me while I was on my way to the well for the first time, and Marse Doc Thompson himself found me slumped there with the buckets still yoked over my shoulders. He was calling to me when my eyes opened on his narrow, freckled face, and I cringed away, but he only pulled me to my feet and moved off, muttering sadly to himself.

I still thought the spells would pass as my full strength slowly returned, but they came on again and again, leaving me stooped over a rake handle in the barn or sprawled against the sow's pen with a pail of slops in my hand. One evening I couldn't play like they were just nothing anymore.

My brother Benjie and I had gone down to the stream to get washing water for Old Rit, and the last thing I knew I was bent over the bank, filling a bucket. Next thing, I was lying face down in the grass, soaking wet, puking up water and my supper while someone pushed on my ribs.

"Near drownded herself, just keeled over into the stream. If I wasn't here she'd drownded for sure." My brother's eyes hung above me round and scared. "What she got Aunt Juba, snakebite?"

"That broke piece of skull pressed in too long, I believe is all. I just bless God you was with her, you done right to go and run for me, Benjie. No more questions now. Help me get her home."

They both reached for me at once, but I flung them off and stood up. Nothing pained. Nothing felt wrong with me. But something was. Something always would be.

"Feel just fine, now leave me be," I snapped. "Don't you stare at me that way, neither of you, I can get myself home."

And I stomped off, but to the crik instead.

A while later Aunt Juba came down, and sat silent a ways off from me as we both glared at the water and slapped at sheep flies. After a long time her voice came through the dark.

"Lord knows I feel bad, I left you down, child. Wasn't able to get you mended just right."

"What you mean, left me down, saved my life's what you done." I threw a stone into the crik. "McCracken's to blame. But this still don't make me sorry for how I stood up in the store, never will."

"Good. You stay angry, Harriet, angry as you able. And there's one comfort in all this tribulation, even if it appears like there ain't no road out for you just now. Didn't nobody tell you yet, but Marse Doc was bout ready to try and sell you soon — well now he ain't. I just been up the Big House, spoke to him. He's came round to see he won't find a buyer for you, said your price never be above two hundred dollars anyways, and Lordamercy, he's took you for a half-wit! Got his mind set to put you in the timber yard where your daddy can look out for you, believes you be able to pick up chips, rake, and suchlike out there. Course I feel certain you can do far more if you don't take a notion to favor youself, why, you most as strong now as you was a year back. Leastways, honey, you be safe, not chucked off on some strangers."

But everyone appeared like strangers to me for a long while after that. It seemed I no longer fit in with other folks, excepting Aunt Juba, not since McCracken's blow.

I felt set apart by my sleeping fits, freakish and ashamed when I'd drop off in front of folks, branded by the deep scar in my temple. And at first I feared that one time or another I'd never awaken from a spell at all.

Shadrack added to my tribulation. He'd been partly faulted

for Jim's escape, just on account of him being in the crossroads store when it happened, and McCracken had put him on short rations for a year, watching him close all the while. Shadrack laid his miseries to me and didn't let me forget I'd got him in trouble. He rumored it about that I was crazed, and bullied the other young bucks into hooting at me, jumping in my path to ape my fits, drooling and falling down. Benjie or William Henry or any of my brothers tried to stop such doings whenever they could, but it didn't matter. I took to keeping clear of everybody, never bothering to seek company or consolation where I might have found it, save by the crik.

On Sundays I'd stand on the Quarter's edge like an outsider, watching. A group of folks would follow Amos to the praise-grove without me. A knot of men might be gambling with wood chips. Old Callie was mostly chasing chickens or children down the path. Mama's humming would reach me as she weeded her garden and William Henry twanged his jew's-harp in the doorway behind her. I'd watch folks jawing and gathering and strolling around, but I'd always turn away from the merriment when a young couple jumped the broom into marriage. No one would ever jump the broom with me, I thought, and my mind would turn to Jim.

No use in that. He wasn't coming back to fetch me, that was a sure thing. No use in studying on the Bucktown Quakers he'd talked of either. I'd never be able to run away, not with my sleeping spells laying me flat when least expected. Nor could I buy my freedom like Jim's brother had done, since nobody but hired hands got that chance. So I'd be what I'd always been; a small-time troublemaker, only an afflicted one, that was the only difference.

I still wasn't regretful over what I'd done, but I hated what I'd become. Aunt Juba got an earful of my miseries till I saw my talk pained her, and then I brooded alone over my damaged head, my blightedness, my stopped life. I'd pace the Quarter nights, gazing at the glimmering row of swaybacked cabins, lit by their many hearthfires. Sometimes I'd steal up close to an open shutter, and stare at what would appear like a framed dream: A woman with a pipe in her teeth, one eye shut against the rising wisp of smoke as she squatted over a basket she was mending. A man's large, knob-knuckled hand reaching to hang blankets around a rag bed in the corner. A girl-child sitting up in her straw pallet by the hearth, her eyes wide and white, as a deep voice said if she didn't lay back down the Catman would get her. Nothing, no one, had changed, excepting me.

One such evening Aunt Juba appeared by my side, and we paced the Quarter together without speaking, while she chewed tobacco and I smoked it, gnawing on my own clay pipe now. She paused, tried to speak, then hugged me to her of a sudden, and all at once I was weeping deep and heavy against her shoulder, holding my pipe away from us till it went out on its own. There had been no sobs like that from me since my sister had been sold long before, and I didn't weep again for many years thereafter. An emptiness came to replace the anguish, and my soul grew so barren it could not even bleed.

◆◆◆

THERE ISN'T MUCH I can recollect about my years in Daddy Ben's timber yard, that lost wasteland-time in my life when I wanted nothing, raged at nothing, cared for almost nothing.

Only fragments come back.

The timber yard: a sheltered clearing gathered in by watchful trees, a sun-striped place keen with the scents of split pine and fresh sweat, quickened by the *crack-crunch* of broadaxes, urgent with birdcalls and shouts from the crew. Me, crouched on its edge firstoff, a stocky, scarred, dull-eyed wench in a burlap shift belted with twine, booted and bandanaed in drab browns, fingering an ax-blade, terrified. Terrified of moving, of getting in the way, of getting pinned beneath a felled trunk. Behaving like the half-wit Marse Doc and Shadrack had called me. Favoring myself. Blank in the face. Listening to my voices crying out in that wilderness, voices only I could hear, voices that made no sense, for still they called *come, follow,* but where, how? And *ask, knock, it shall be* what? Ask for what?

The wilderness itself: trees crowding closer in the green heat, or standing back, stripped and stony in the cold, while the lumber crew echoed through them. Circles of changes in the woods, wondrous at first, then commonplace, just a way of telling time. Time that was passing, time measured out another way, by the comings and goings of northern geese. Time passing around me and over my head.

Later. Another image of myself, after Aunt Juba had goaded me into working: a short, square-built woman spreading thickened legs and raising a broadax aloft, swinging down hard and accurate, cording the same stint of wood as the men on the crew. A muscled woman, strengthened by the labor, dragging loads down the rolling-road with the team, hacking branches off felled trunks, sweating, unsmiling. The body moves, the face does not, aside from a glimmer of pain about the eyes. That amazing increase of bodily power tormented me, since it could be used for nothing but splitting timber so long as the sleeping fits lingered. And they did linger. They came less often, they passed more quickly, they weren't enough to hinder my labor — but they were enough to hinder me from anything beyond that.

Another fragment, a clearer one. An image of the only soul besides Aunt Juba I did fit with during those years: my daddy, to my surprise. He'd been the tall terror of my childhood, a man I'd never really known before, but out in the timber yard he began to take great pride in me for the first time. For once I wasn't in some kind of trouble, and I was the one child he had who plied his trade and plied it well. He didn't speak his love and pride outright but it showed in his face, in his voice, in the times he made for us after hours. That was when he'd lead me to private things he cared about; the secret paths to his traplines, an elm he'd saved from blight, a burrow of muskrats he liked to watch from the riverbank.

Daddy was an axman, bossman of the lumber gang, the best with a cleaver at Hog-Killing time, and a coffin-crafter too, but he had a hidden tenderness for growing things, and was schooled in woodlore. He began teaching me what he knew, a lifetime of learning, how to scent game or people, how to corner a raccoon or catch a fish with my hands, how to tell directions from the sun, the stars, or from simple things like moss growing down one side of the trees.

There was an excitement about Daddy Ben's teachings, for he was passing along the one thing he owned to leave a child, and after a time he shared his most valued possession of all, giving it away in bits and pieces when no one was near: his ability to foretell the weather from the thickness of a possum's coat, the feel of some bark, and especially from the patterns of the skies.

I'd stand watching him as he taught me, awed, and proud in my turn, of him.

Here was this great hill of a man, beginning to age but still straight, mule-broad across the chest, and above the trunklike neck his whitening beard and hair were thick as brushweed, tufting around a face the color of rich earth. When he'd plant his boots in the ground, raise a square, split-nailed hand heavenward and tell me what was going to happen next day, he seemed like a prophet about to speak in tongues.

A ripply cloudbank, did I see that? Yes? And did I feel the wind shifting around too? Well then, it would rain tomorrow.

And it would indeed rain. All hands idle.

That cluster of gold and pink clouds, pretty-looking ones, did I see them there at sunset? Well then, no rain romorrow.

And the weather would hold fine. As if he'd made it that way.

After a while I was learning, and that appeared to delight Daddy no end. His teachings had given my mind something to tinker with, and more than that, he'd given me a deep part of himself. I took what he offered mostly because it pleasured him and because I felt his love at last, but the woodlore was only a game to me then. And it wasn't enough. Not enough to ease my spirit or turn me around, and apart from moments with him or Aunt Juba I was still deadened, lost. For myself I cared nothing at all.

I didn't care that I was shambling with the broken-down gait of an aged woman, nor did I care that I'd taken to bootlicking Marse Doc whenever I saw him. Bootlicking made things easier, safer. A bull-bodied axman named Tibbit *yassuhed* and *yessummed* and rolled his eyes as much as Old Callie did, though he was the toughest buck in the wood lot. I didn't see why I shouldn't do the same. No one bothered Tibbit or Old Callie, never had. I didn't see why I shouldn't look forward to small events, the lay-by jubilees, Easter week, and especially Christmas when presents, whiskey, and several idle days were bestowed upon us. Such things were all I looked toward then, never looking past them, and one Yuletide I got puking-drunk, finding it very much worthwhile. Enough spirits from the darky-bowl, and I was able to cluster around the candlelit tree in the Big House parlor with the others, forgetting how much I'd hated that place, seeing it all through a kind of ripply blueness, something like the watered silk of Miss Susan's gown. Feeling becalmed and beautified by the whiskey, I bobbed my *thankee-sir* at Marse Doc for a red kerchief and a gold piece, then tumbled down the back steps, wondering why the Big House had ever appeared so terrible to me. If these holiday doings were created only to keep us content till the next one, I'd take that little contentment even if it made me sick afterwards. I didn't care.

I barely noticed how I badmouthed others and swore and took the Lord's name in vain, although I'd made a secret promise in the praise-grove never to do so. My talk amused the lumber crew when my father wasn't around, and made me feel like I belonged in the lot.

"Now May Ella," Tibbit said once, "that's a gal with tits."

"Old Melons Ella ain't got tits, she got cotton up her dress," I told him. "And shit, she'd lift her skirt for one tobacco wad."

"She say she got teethmarks in her neck from Marse Doc hisself, and he give her extries for the sugar."

"She say. Well, she put the marks in with a fork she stole, and each time they wear off she dig em right back in again. That ain't a fuck, not with a fork."

The crew doubled over with laughter.

"You get meaner every day, Hat," another axman told me, with some approval. "Just you watch your daddy don't hear that mouth on you. Anyways, we all able to agree May Ella surely won't make no angel when she cash in. Not with them tits and all and what she do, even if it ain't with Marse Doc."

"Angels got no tits," I said.

"You hear the preacher say so?" Tibbit again, chuckling.

"Just figures. Jesus, how they be able to fly through Heaven with tits to drag around, would weight em down."

More laughter.

"Ain't no nigger angels in Heaven atall, white preacher say." A snort from Tibbit at that teaching, contempt for it, and a challenge for me.

"White preacher don't know nothin," I snapped. "When

Isaiah come before the Throne on high, he seen angels all set to wait on the Heavenly King. Who else be bound to wait and serve up there ceptin nigger angels?"

Such evil talk didn't trouble me then as it does now, when I recollect it, but I did keep my blasphemous jokes to the wood lot. The rest of the time I scuffed around silent, not even caring how I'd come to look.

I seldom washed, ignoring the general fussing and scrubbing on Saturday nights. Dust exploded from my skirts, my bandana was a filthy rag, and I was crawling with fleas and lice. Ash from my pipe snowed over me as I moved about, great rents gaped under each arm, but nothing got mended unless Mama or Aunt Juba threatened with their needles.

It was a long time before I comprehended what I was turning into. It wasn't until one steamy August morning when I headed for the wood lot, ax in hand, and stopped first at the privy.

Shadrack was waiting outside the door, tearing at his fingernails with his teeth, almost like he was trying to hurt himself. He'd been doing that way since his crowd of young bucks had turned on him, and while he gnawed his hands he was mostly brewing up some trouble. I didn't feel like scrapping with him, so I flung the privy door open without glancing at Shadrack again.

Old Callie sat there over the middle hole, and in the dim, stewing light of the crapshack it seemed that I saw my own image reflected in her. Her greasy head rag hung partways down over her eyes, her torn skirts stirred, sending off a haze of dust-motes, and she growled, spilling pipe ash down her chest.

I slammed the door shut on that apparition, only to hear her cackling behind it, as Shadrack sidled over to me.

"What you scareda some old pussy like that for?" He snickered. "Figured you wasn't scareda nothin, Hat, or that just time past? Lookit you, you surely appear like to Old Callie, know that? Broke down, Lord, makes me laugh. Recollect when you thought real high on youself, you was too high-and-mighty to be a house nigger one time, ain't that the truth?

Recollect you was too high-and-mighty for this place altogether, figured to run off, but you couldn't make it, ain't that the truth? Figured you could stand up to the Man and get away with it too, that's right, folks said you was one fierce-born gal aimed for bigger things, well crack a eye at youself now. Shit, dasn't you?"

The privy door opened. Old Callie hobbled out, trailed by flies and a ripe, rotting stench. She blew her nose in her fingers as she gazed on me, cackling once more.

"Mercy, don't you waste your time on her, Shadrack," she said, from the side of her mouth. "This gal just a old dumb-wit, she don't comprehend what you say. Had her pegged for a dumb-wit way before she got bopped, couldn't even learn that child's catechiz I give her. She reckoned to come out better'n me and all us, well now she worse off, way worse off'n Old Callie. Never bound to amount to nothin more'n me, that's right, Lord, lookit her."

She commenced howling and chuckling, and I fled, forgetting the pressure in my gut, my hands slipping on the ax-handle as I ran.

Out in the timber yard I raised that ax and struck at a rock-hard maple, driving a blow deeper than I'd ever done before. That's for you, Old Callie. I reared back for another swing. For you, Shadrack. Another splintery crack. And one for you too, McCracken. This for you. And this. The tree crashed down just as the crew came out, cheering, and I was butchering that maple when my daddy dashed in sometime later, breathing hard.

He pulled me off aways where no one could hear him.

"Was just up the Big House, Marse Doc needed them reports on the timber I specked, well I figured that was all, and then he up and say he got a notion to hire you out."

Ben sighed. I looked up at him, stunned. Hiring my time. A dollar a week to Master, sick or well, rain or shine.

"Course there wasn't no way in the world we could hide how strong you got to be, Marse Doc always remark on that to me whenever he come poke around here. But maybe we can fix it so's you don't have to leave home, honey."

A dollar a week to Marse Doc and anything above that, mine to keep. Mine to save.

"Just sham a fit for em when they come to look you over. Sure hate to see you go, don't guess you want to neither."

Hiring my time like Jim's brother had done, Jim's brother who'd bought his way out.

"Hired-out ain't no holiday life. Lean spells come along, steady labor dry up, and then you got to scrounge for any old piss-work you able to find. Don't like to see my girl headed for hard times, besides . . . still so much I meant to show you out here."

I could save, I could work nights and Sundays. I could do it, Lord willing I would do it, no matter how long it took.

"Just play dead, Hat. Leave em take you for a half-wit again, won't nobody hire on some afflicted nigger."

"I ain't afflicted. Not like I was, nary atall. Ain't no half-wit, never been," I snapped, then gentled my voice. "Be all right, Daddy, no need to worry on me now. And I want to go. Got to."

Lord forgive me, forgive my faithlessness, all of it. A way was open after all, a way out still. And I hadn't even prayed. I hadn't even asked.

◆◆ ◆◆ ◆◆

HIRING MY TIME kept me on the move the next two years, working all over Dorchester County from Airey to Church Creek to Castle Haven to Windyhill a ways up the Choptank River, and across that river into Talbot County, though it wasn't common for hired hands to pass over county lines. Nonetheless I went wherever Marse Doc had a friend who needed an extra darky for a while, and I thrived on the movement and the work. It was getting me closer to freedom. It had given me a purpose again. And little by little I was beginning to collect a small stash of saved coins in an old flour sack, which I hung around my neck with string and kept strapped inside my clothes.

I commenced talking wages with other hired hands.

"How much you able to save?"

"Nothin to speak of. I got seven small ones back on the old place, my wages give em extries."

"Hey brother, how much you able to save?"

"Sugar, I don't save, I sprees, what else I got to pleasure myself with this side the Gates?"

"Know any hands able to buy freedom?"

"Know some as had a good chance on it."

"What you call a good chance?"

"Master that let us hire our time reasonable and price us reasonable. Best way to make high money's swamp work, but I wouldn't sign on for that, gal. Gang go out in February when things dry out some and you stay down there till seed time, don't do nothin but cut shingles and live in huts a possum wouldn't piss on. High money, but no ma'am, not for me."

I got myself hired on for the lower Dorchester marshes direct, with Marse Doc's say-so, since the winter months were slow and that way money kept coming in to him through me. Half of what we made down there went to Master, more went for our board, but a fair sum was left to us even so. The next winter I signed on with a swamp gang again, but during the greater part of the year my savings scarcely grew at all. Daddy had been right about hard times, and I began to comprehend why hired hands were paid wages at all. When we were with our own masters we got food rations, clothing rations, we got our keep. As hirelings we had to pay for all that out of our earnings till those earnings were nearly gone. I was feeling trapped and tricked and furious by the time Master sent me to John Stewart's place.

It was a place I knew well, right next to Doc Thompson's. Our folks oftentimes held prayer meetings and dances with Stewart's folks, so it was almost like being home again. The slaves there were a touch high-and-mighty about being Marse John's people though, and never ceased to tell you how their Man was one of those famous good masters. He tolerated no abuse to his darkies, tried to keep the patrols out of his Quarter, and had kicked more than one nigger-breaking overseer off his place. He was free with passes to town, gifts, and extras, and loved to dress up like Santa Claus for all the children come Christmas. The only thing some folks held against him was his passion for showing slaves off, making them perform feats of strength or skill to impress his guests.

For my part he could have been the Devil himself and I couldn't have cared. John Stewart gave me the chance I was looking for. He gave me my keep, since that was a practice he had with all his hired hands.

Hopes of buying my freedom goaded me to work harder than any overseer or driver could. I helped to set plantings and bring them in, and even lent a hand with house chores, but mostly I felled trees and split timber in the wood lot. Stewart did a sizable amount of business as a lumber supplier, and whenever he needed a load of beams carted someplace I hauled it for him, either on the road to Cambridge with the team, or along the path by the Buckwater River with the mule hitched up to a barge.

During the off-times I planted a yard garden out front of my cabin, raising beans, greens, and a·little tobacco to sell in town. The laws forbidding us to peddle had never stuck, so I hawked my crops on Market Sundays in Cambridge, and took in washing from a Quaker lady in nearby Bucktown.

In one year I was able to save more than I'd reckoned on, by working like a madwoman and keeping clear of any Saturday night or Sunday big times. Stewart's folks must have taken me for standoffish, but I didn't have much chance to worry on that, and when I did get to feeling lonesome I'd count my coins. The flour sack was getting heavier, but there still wasn't near enough money to offer Marse Doc in exchange for myself. This would take forever it appeared, but then Stewart made me an offer of his own.

He'd long owned an old, ruined, burnt-out piece of land that had once been a wood lot, and now he wished to turn it to use and profit. Try your hand at it, he said. Nothing to lose if the plot didn't flourish, a good deal to gain if it did, and a wench would be the easiest one spared for such a gamble. Ah, but an uncommonly diligent wench, he added, and went on for some time about a newfangled idea he had: *Incentive.* The Yankees, he believed, knew nothing of incentive. All one had to do was look at their mills and foundries, why the Yankees were simply unable to get the best from their own working class. Stewart's beloved but misguided Yankee brother-in-law himself owned a mill, yet he didn't understand that the institution of slavery was every bit as efficient as northern industry, more so, more so, *he shall see, he shall see it with his own eyes!* Stewart paced about as he spoke, and his clever, pointy face shone. Like to a raccoon he looked, with his bright eyes sunk in dark flesh-pouches, and his hands making little pawing motions at the air as he told me his theories. This would be an experiment, *our* little experiment, that plot of land. He would use incentive like so: if I could make the soil prosper, he'd give me a cut of the crops' market price, he'd even let me use one of his oxen, and that Yankee brother-in-law, *he shall see! He shall see it at last!*

Theories and brother-in-laws and Yankees didn't exactly fire me up. But what did stir me to the bone was the thought of the freedom-money I had a chance to earn from this little experiment. So help me, I would make that lot fertile, I'd make it into one big freedom-garden was what I'd do. Yas*suh*.

From early morning till long past late I was out there with the ox, pulling up stumps and rocks, filling in craters, and then plowing the field under once. The plowshare broke maybe six times before I was able to grade the land, lime it with clam shells, spread manure — and plow it all under again.

Stifling August, with its bloodless skies and droves of pest-flies couldn't put me off my labor. Broken plowshares didn't matter, they could be mended. Sudden, steamy drizzles didn't stop me, and they slaked the land besides. Up to my ass in weeds, dirt, and gnats, awash in my own sweat, stinking to Heaven, I smiled, thinking on the crops I'd set come spring. And when spring did come I planted feverishly, a little of everything, almost more than I'd be able to reap. No matter, I'd get the harvest in someways or other, and get a bigger share of the profit too, from whatall I had in the ground. This, the toughest toil I'd ever done, felt like it was for my own sake, not for Stewart's or any master's. Even the land felt like my own, and as I worked it I eternally blessed the Lord for this gift of earth, this way that would one day lead out. For a small thank-offering I gave up cussing and tobacco too; it was all I had to give.

On Sundays I'd tramp through the Sabbathtide stillness to Marse Doc's, hand over my dollar to him, and then join Aunt Juba by her crik. She was the only one who knew of my plans, and she was pleased by them, pleased too that I'd come back into my soul, as she said. Daddy was proud over what he'd heard on me from Marse Doc, but Old Rit sighed, missing me and her sons, for six of the boys were hired far off just then.

"One way or other I lose my children," she said, then added, "Least you don't appear like to Old Callie now."

Which reminded me.

One such Sunday I went to stand before Callie's cabin, wishing she'd come out. Come out and crack an eye at this gal now, old witch, I proved you wrong. I'm going to buy my freedom, and you can bet your lost teeth I'm nowheres like you, nor ever will be. Take a look now while you can, Old Callie, else next time you do, you might not see a slave.

◆ ◆ ◆

HE WATCHED me and I couldn't abide that.

He watched me as I peddled in town or delivered washing, but mostly he just slouched against a tree, grinning, sometimes whistling to himself as I worked through my third seed time on Stewart's plot of land.

Well, maybe I was flattered at first. Maybe I was even hoping he'd speak to me; I knew about him, even though he hadn't been around much the last year or two. Then I began to get irritated. Uppity of him to grin at a slave's labor, since he wasn't a slave. Uppity of him to lounge around, appearing so all-fired amused, staring at me like I was pushing the plow stark naked. Or was that some imagining of mine? Foolishness, that's what it was, this was no time to get notional. There was planting to do and plenty of it, for I needed another good harvest. That year, my fifth as a hired hand, I might have enough money to buy myself out, but only if the cropping went right. Distraction was just what I didn't need, and that cocky man was distracting if he was anything.

I tried to pay him no mind, but found myself studying him from the tail of my eye. He wasn't so very tall or strapping, but he had a sure easy way of holding himself, swiveling his hips as he shifted against the tree. Sinewy-firm through the body, he was too. His clothes were made from smooth goods, not what you'd call real flashy, just a bit fine for a Negro to sport every day. There was a reddish cast to the hair tufting out from under a raked cap, and faint freckles across his light-skinned face; a bad-boy face, changeable, tilting up at the chin. The eyes were quick, provoking, nearer to gray than brown. And that grin on him could light up a bat's nest. Somehow I felt plain before him, clumsy too, under his teasing gaze.

One day he stepped into the furrow I was planting, and stayed the ox with his hand.

"Appears like you labor like hell out here all alone, gal."

"Ain't so rough."

"Watch you off and on."

"Yeah?"

"Heard you got a good deal on with Stewart."

"That right?"

"Out to make youself a sweet handful or two, huh?"

"My sweet handfuls is my business, or whatall you call em."

"Somehow that don't sound respectable what you just said. My grandmama would called that sin-talk. Hey. What you mean to do with all them wages, heard you don't never spree or party even."

"You maybe got your nose where it don't belong, man."

"Easy gal, you awful touchy. Didn't mean nothin, just figured to come out and speak after all this time."

"I got this stretch to plow if it's all the same to you."

"What's the trouble? Your head give you a misery of a sudden?"

"No, just your slippery tongue."

And then I must have taken a short sleeping fit. When I opened my eyes he was holding me and hollering, his face puzzled, almost concerned. A smell of tobacco and new-laundered shirt cloth was close about me.

I righted myself, pulled away, and stared down at the furrow between my feet, shamed. It was foolish to feel so. I'd no reason to care that this fast-mouthed, twinkling-eyed man had seen my affliction, or that he'd got a close look at the knotty scar on my temple either. This man didn't have one thing to do with me. Not one thing at all. He was still gazing.

"Lord, you all right? What come over you?"

"Nothin. Believe I just got bored."

I prodded the ox and moved on down the furrow, leaving

him to watch me for a time. Then he snorted and took himself off.

They said you had to hand it to that man. He'd never known bondage, freedom had been his birthright. His daddy had got manumitted in an old master's will, set himself up as a tailor, and made out pretty fair till he'd taken off for the North years before. His son made out just as well, and had all kinds of things going. Firstoff, he'd wangled himself a peddler's license, but he was above hawking common wares like home-brewed persimmon beer. What he sold he got at no cost to himself, either. Housemaids around the county would pass him castoff white folk's clothing, which he'd mend like new and peddle about, earning himself a heap. He'd learned how to do mending from his daddy, and if sewing didn't appear proper manly to some, the way he did the housemaids for thank-you made up for it — that's what folks said. He had other deals going too, things no one knew about for sure, but it was believed he wanted to set himself up in some kind of shop or maybe a farm. Everyone was certain he'd do it one day too. That man could put on white folks like nobody else, smart as a fox he was, been places, seen plenty — that was one *bad* nigger, they said.

I'd heard the talk since I'd been at Stewart's, but took it mostly for tall tales. Could be he was just a gambler or a floater, gone for long spans of time, maybe doing as a traveling barber more often than making fancy deals. It was hard to believe he could make out as well as they said, not here, not outside a big city, not as a peddler. Some free Negroes did fair enough as smiths or coopers or even as dirt farmers, I'd heard, but with the others it was different. The whites were plenty suspicious of free colored folks, especially the rootless ones. It wasn't easy for such to find work in the county, excepting when extra hands were hired for seed time and reaping on the plantations. There were some we all pitied; the skinny, tattered, lice-ridden beggars and drunks who couldn't find jobbing to do and were forever getting beat up. I'd seen a few such folks scrounging slops from the hog pens and sleeping in privies.

Of course I wouldn't be like that once freedom was mine. I figured those no-accounts had got their liberty too late, after they'd been broken from years in bondage. They looked worlds apart from that clever-sounding man who watched me, that was for sure. And to tell the truth, I did want to believe the big talk on him after all. He was proof that free Negroes could do more than all right for themselves. That was the reason I couldn't leave off thinking about him. The only reason. Anyways, I didn't have to fall all over his feet or honey-eye him just on account of him being used to it, and I'd certainly never tell him about my savings. Let him make his own money off those other gals he was supposed to know, let him get his sugar off them too. I had my own freedom to think about, I had my work, my secret schemings, my voices to guide and comfort me, and I didn't have need of anything else. Did I?

That night I sat before my cabin after the day's labor in the field and the evening's labor over the Quaker's washing, not thinking much. There was a private murmuring amongst the leaves as the trees bent toward each other in the rippling air, warm air. It smelled of blossoms, summer, turned-over earth; it touched up and down my arms. The moon slid back of some elms and the darkness throbbed with crickets, then a pair of cats groaned nearby. For some reason I was twitchy, not ready for sleep even after all that work. I just kept sitting in the rectangle of light from my doorway, and all at once I heard him laughing. I couldn't see where he was. Likely he'd leaned himself behind some tree nearby, and I tried not to glance about.

"Got the yearn?" came his voice, mellow, but mocking too.

I glared at the dark and rose to go in, feeling hot in the face.

"Got the yearn to talk is all." He laughed again.

"Don't you pay no mind to the curfew?" I snapped.

"No call to act so huffy. Most you know on me's but a few words we passed today."

"Heard on you, John Tubman, big-time freedman with wenches and deals and whatall, a freedman what mocks at a slave."

"And you," he shot back, "Thompson's Harriet, work-all-the-time nigger, real standoffish gal what don't take to nobody."

I went inside, slammed my door, banked my fire, and crawled into my pallet, feeling like a fool. The whole Quarter could have heard that, and now he might not be the only one who'd figured I was waiting for him. Well, he likely wouldn't be sniffing about again and there'd be no more distracting nonsense. Likely I wouldn't see him another time, excepting maybe in town. I didn't know why that made me feel just a small bit low.

Saturday next I was in town to buy seeds. Stewart had let us off around noon like usual, and I'd gone through the fuss of getting a pass and catching a ride to Cambridge. Like always on such afternoons the town was rolling with carts and thrashing with people, but I'd grown used to dodging carriage wheels, careening barrels, and sharp elbows as I moved up High Street. A few darkies were buying bits of ribbon and tobacco, but most blacks were in their customary place back of the feed store, jawing, scrapping, smoking, and throwing darts while they waited for their masters. The regular collection of white trash idled about on one corner, slinging their cunt-talk at passing skirts, and swapping goods. And above it all hung the common town smells of axle grease, new-cut timber, horses, fodder, paint, and fish fresh from the bay. Everything was the same, almost predictable, but after I'd got my seeds and darted through a crush of hagglers, I glimpsed something that wasn't everyday Saturday doings.

Down at the end of an alley, I saw a handful of Negroes gathered in front of a free colored woman's shack. I'd noticed the woman sitting on her steps once in a while when I'd been in Cambridge before, but this day they were carrying her out the door in a coffin. Drawing closer, fascinated more than grieved by the sight, I wondered if there'd been an accident, a beating, or some kind of harassment, for she'd looked too young to have passed natural. I'd got so possessed by my thinkings on free Negroes' lives that now I even wanted to know how they died, and I was just rounding the corner of the house when I saw John Tubman crouched there, staring at his knees. He looked up, wet-eyed, and we both jumped.

"Get the hell away," he rasped. "Ain't your business, you got no rights to spy around. Said haul out."

I took off, startled at the sight of him gone so soft, but then I figured he'd only lost one of his wenches.

A short while later I heard his sister was the one who'd died. John Tubman had vanished directly after the burial, and there was the usual talk of him doing some fancy dealings up to Airey, maybe Baltimore. All the same, I wondered. I wondered about him even as summer commenced, turning from my work now and again with the feeling that someone was watching me. No one ever was.

Anyways once it got on for August such fancies passed and I ceased to think on anything excepting my harvest. In my greed for big profit I'd planted too much, likely more than I could get in, so I pushed myself hard. Toiling from can to can't, bone-tired, and troubled over wasted crops, I barely straightened my back up at all.

Then one day I heard him chuckling.

He had a growth of stubble on his face, his clothes appeared slept-in, but he was grinning like when he'd been dressed fine. Down on his luck though, surely. I stopped the ox near to him and cocked a hand on my hip.

"Heard you was out to make youself one sweet handful, John Tubman. Hard times?"

"Now you the one with your nose where it don't belong."

"Easy man, you awful touchy."

"Appears like you got more crops here than you be able to bring in."

"Appears like it."

"Unless you mean to bust ass, acourse."

"You worried? Shoot, I can always ask Stewart to hire on another hand just for harvest."

"I ain't bond, you recollect? Got no need to do this kinda work."

"Didn't say nothin bout you."

"Then what'd you look at me like that for?"

"Like what?"

"Besides, Stewart pays piss."

"Don't really need help that bad anyways."

But I asked Stewart all the same, and when I got out to the field next day there was John, poking at the ox he'd rounded up ahead of me.

"Come on, pretty baby, you just pull for John, what you got behind you's the sweetest freedman this side the Chesapeake," he was saying, then changed tone when the ox didn't budge. "Now goddamn, move your flea-bit rump else I beat the shit outa you."

"Give me that." I grabbed the prod from him. "Need for the ox to stay right there so's I can load up the sled as I go along. Got the wheat to scythe down hereabouts, you'd best start on the corn."

"Bless my soul, this must be Boss Nigger. Yassuh, here I comes Boss, don't you beat this poor darky."

"The corn. If it ain't too much for you?"

"A wench driver's too much, but I believe I just gone tenderhearted. Done this only for a favor, you comprehend? Jesus, you planted enough corn so's the whole county be able to wipe ass with the husks."

Still, we worked well together, sweating, straining, and snapping at each other under the hellfire of an August sun. Toward the week's end John said he'd got me figured.

"Gal, you got some overseer in your blood, that's what cause you to be so mean."

"I come down from pure Ashanti African. Aunt Juba said she believed so when she told me bout the Middle Passage on the slavers, her grandmama recollected it."

"Ashanti, Ashanti . . . recollect that name from somewheres. Believe I heard they sold other niggers to the traders in Africa, yeah, that'd be right."

"That'd be flat wrong, John Tubman."

"My my, mistress-ma'am she riled at this poor darky, this poor miserable nigger workin from sunup to sundown, oh Lawdamercy, don't beat me, Missy, I tries."

I turned with dignity to lift a heavy sack onto the sled, stepped on my skirt, and sprawled flat-out on the ground.

John commenced to laugh, and all at once I was laughing with him — didn't know why — but I wasn't able to get up till he pulled me to my feet.

Well. I always did pleasure in a good scrap.

Jibing at him kept me from noticing too much about John, but for all my pains I noted enough: the good man-smell, the long-fingered hands, and once he had his shirt off, the nap of fuzz running down the center of his chest. It was bad enough my eyes strayed to him in the days. It was worse that I'd begun to see him in the nights as I sat in my cabin, swatting moths, counting my coins and losing count. My hands would pause over the money, and I'd imagine him standing before me, shedding his trousers and kneeling to spread my legs open with both hands. His fingers would rub along the soft inner flesh of my thighs up into the pelt, he'd take one tit in his mouth, and his joint would swell, enter me, and stroke back and forth, harder, faster, till I'd be filled with sweet jizzom.

Whenever such fancies took me I'd stand up sudden, spilling the coins from my lap and cussing at myself. This wasn't what my mind should fix on. Best imagine the day I'd tell Marse Doc goodbye, best imagine what I'd say to him. Best not dampen my drawers over some man who didn't cast a thought to me, a man just doing a stint in the fields. Nothing was more important than my freedom, and I couldn't let anyone take my thoughts from it, not for an instant. I'd put my mind to night chores, I'd wash, mend, split kindling, anything that would keep the coins coming in; anything that would make it easier to face John in the fields after those secret lustings.

One sweaty, mosquito-ridden morning I had to keep clear of his eyes for a long while, till he brought me up short with a question.

"Don't you know nothin but work, gal?"

"Sure. Acourse."

"What'd that be?"

"Well I, uh . . . Know how to read the weather, foretell it too."

"Aha! Stewart ain't heard he got a conjure woman out here."

"Go on with you, John Tubman. I learned from my daddy, it ain't so strange. No stranger than the fancy stitchery you learned from your daddy."

"Shit, I didn't learn nary a thing from him, only picked up tailor tricks cause I watched him, not cause he showed me. That man didn't have time to show me more'n how to pee straight, wasn't around long enough. He got hisself all worked up for glory-land, and that was the big old North, lit out for it direct after Mama died. No I didn't learn nothin offa my daddy."

"Didn't you never try to follow him?"

"No."

"Didn't he never send for you and your . . ."

"Woman, I believe your scythe's bound to rust over while you just stand there and mouth off. Give me a hand here, I ain't of a mind to do all the work. Thought you was so hot to get your reap in."

As Market Day drew closer I hottened to the work like I never had. This year was different, this year I'd likely have enough to buy my way out, this was my last harvest as a slave. I labored hard, spoke less, and blessedly didn't take a sleeping fit till the final afternoon, when the crops were nearly all laid by. John was holding me as I came out of the spell like he'd done once before, and the smell of him, the feel of him was so very near I didn't twitch away. Racked out on the warm earth, cradled on his knees and against his naked chest, a lush laziness stole over me and I felt too heavy, too comforted to get up or even feel shamed by my affliction.

"You all right?" John asked. "Heard you get spells, never heard how come."

I looked into his face. He appeared sober, not teasing, so I kept my cheek next to his skin and didn't stir.

"Overseer, long time ago . . ."

"How'd he do you, gal?"

I told him, and he whistled through his teeth.

"That's what got you so hard-drove to buy your freedom, ain't it?"

"How'd you know I mean to do that?"

"Folks talk. Some say all you do's count coins nights cause

that freedom-money got you fired up like no man's able to." John chuckled.

"Well, I got plenty to fire me up over freedom and freedom-money. Go on and hoot, you and who-all else, but I be able to buy myself clear tomorrow after market. Won't nobody mock me then."

I moved off stiffly and began stashing tools. If only he hadn't said that. If only he hadn't laughed.

We didn't speak much as we hoisted the last sacks from the ox sled onto a wagon, and then it was over, our time together in the field. As John went whistling away into the dark I was stung by lonesomeness for a moment, but then the nearness of my freedom came on so strong it overpowered all else. I stayed late, nerved-up and sleepless, checking the wagon's load over and over. A snatch of music came from up the hill where Stewart was partying with some Yankee house guests, but I heard that just dimly. Everything faded excepting what I was about to do.

Next morning when I went to market I barely noticed frantic, teeming Cambridge around me, and as I drove back the hazy rolling-road, crowded with carts and shimmering with heat, seemed but a conjuration. I finally had two hundred dollars altogether. Two hundred dollars; that seemed a mighty fortune. Two hundred dollars; my price. Marse Doc had always wanted to sell me low, and I still had the affliction that devalued me before. Surely he'd take my offer, he'd be shet of me in a few minutes, he'd do it, please God. I was just decking out in Sunday best to see him when Stewart ducked through the doorway of my cabin.

He said he had a special job for me, I was the one darky that could do it properly, straightaway too, and his pointy raccoon's face quivered as he went on, talking high and fast. Of course I'd still be in time for the lay-by jubilee he always threw for his colored family, why, that would last three days this year, and the task he had in mind was a short one. I was to pull the barge upriver just a quarter-mile to the next wharf. He had some goods to get there in a hurry, and he knew he could count on me.

Suddenly I thought of throwing the coins at him and laughing, but I had to play things right now, keeping clear of any trouble that could spoil my plans. Anyways, this would be the last time I'd ever goad that mule up the river road.

But when we reached the river road the mule wasn't there. Stewart mumbled something as he strapped me into the beast's harness, and hitched me up to the laden barge. Before I could find my tongue he'd scrambled up the bank to higher ground, where a row of chairs had been set out beneath shade trees. Sunbonneted ladies sat there, erect and centered in flounces of bright skirting, backed by a line of gentlemen standing up stiff inside their morning suits, as if they were all awaiting a portrait painter. But no. Their fixed gaze was on the river road. They were awaiting a spectacle, an entertainment, and I suddenly comprehended. That entertainment would be me.

I stood stock-still in the harness as Stewart called for me to start.

He had me. He had me good, though he didn't know just how good. If I made any revolt before his company, if I did what I burned like hell to do Marse Doc would hear of it, and I'd be whipped, not bought.

I put my head down, and damn me, I pulled.

I pulled till the road blurred and sunbursts bloomed before my eyes. I strained and grunted as my own sweat blinded me, the harness seemed to cleave my flesh, breathing came harsh, joints cracked. And slowly, slowly, that barge came dragging behind on the water. Only to the wharf, only fifty paces now, then to Marse Doc, oh Lord. I was steaming like the mule itself while Steward babbled up there, and scraps of words fell around me.

"Won my wager, brother . . . incentive, I tell you . . . began as an experiment . . . Yankee industry be damned, sir, *this* is industry . . . with care a Nigra can . . . this is the one I spoke of at dinner . . . of course they don't mind . . . proud to be shown off. . . ."

As soon as it was over, I was running for Marse Doc's place, gasping, stumbling, dirtying my dress and apron before I found him in his garden. I leaped into his path.

"My God," he said, staring at me. "What's happened to you, child?"

"Nothin, sir. Just some chorin for Marse Stewart's company."

"Ah, one of his darky pageants again," he muttered. "Is that it? You want me to talk to him about it? Well, speak up."

I took a breath. "Come to say I heard on a buyer around for me."

"And you're frightened?" He made a cozy wheezing sound. "No need. I wouldn't sell you now, you're too prime, and I doubt there's a soul could pay your price easy, eight hundred, maybe a thousand. Good God no, I wouldn't let you go even if I got an offer like that. I'm more in a mind for buying than selling, we're high on the hog this year. Harriet? Now where in creation are you running off to? Harriet!"

I fled, blurry-eyed and choking, till I found myself back at Stewart's, stomping through that picked-clean field I'd worked so hard. Heaving and ranting, I commenced to uproot the bare stalks around me, kicking dirt in the air, ripping up everything in my path like I was trying to destroy the entire lot. When at last I dropped down panting, I saw John Tubman watching me from the edge of the field, and I cussed him out for spying in language I'd forbidden myself.

He walked toward me anyways.

"Heard bout Stewart," he said.

"Don't care what you heard, get away. Don't want to see you or no free nigger never again," I screamed.

"Huh. So Thompson wouldn't bite neither." He made a low whistle.

"Leave me be!" I turned away, put my apron up over my face, and wept.

His boots kept crunching forward nonetheless till he was holding me, and though I squirmed at first he didn't let go. After a time I leaned to him, sobbed myself out, rested. And then a terrible shame crept through me. No one had ever seen me so bared excepting Aunt Juba, and that was different. I shrugged away, muttered something, then ran for my cabin just as a thunder shower commenced.

It was a steady downpour by evening and the roof leaked, dripping rain on my forehead as I lay on my straw pallet, but I didn't care enough to move. The wetness on my head felt like old blood. The numbness of my limbs, the swirling in my brain brought back the nights I'd lain half-dead from McCracken's blow. But I couldn't escape into a delirium this time. I was too old to will my master dead, and there was no overseer to blame here. At bottom the fault lay with me. I'd put my trust in Stewart's everlasting fatherly goodness. I'd put my faith in Marse Doc too, and in myself, steadfastly believing that I could be different, that I could buy myself out with a hired slave's wages. Shamed and sickened, I sank into a half-sleep, listening to the murmuration of the rain, listening for some comfort from my voices.

"My cabin's flooded clear through."

It murmured louder, that voice, repeated itself, and I woke, then sat bolt upright when I saw him. Well, what had I expected, one of the Lord's angels come to my shack just because I was feeling lowdown? It was only John who stood dripping before me with a lantern in his hand, a skillet on his head, and a roll of blankets sticking out from under his coat.

"Merciless out there, don't look to let up," he said. "Got water three fingers high on my floor. Shoulda patched the roof weeks past, that's for sure."

I stared at him.

"Real grateful for the invite." He grinned at me. "Reckon to just bed down over here by the hearth."

"Say *what?*" I started to rise, remembered I was naked, and sank back again, pulling the covers around my shoulders.

"No cause to raise the devil, you bound to wake the whole Quarter."

"Man, you listen, just hold on. You bust in here halfway to dawn, hand me that story, just commence to bed down, don't ask me even — now who on earth you figure to be?"

"Just figured you'd make a poor wet nigger welcome."

"And your sass atop it all."

But I still hadn't told him to leave. I only pulled the covers up over my head and turned my back, feeling shamed again. He pitied me, this freedman, that was why he'd come.

For a while I heard him fussing with his things, felt his gaze on me now and then, but I never moved. The noises softened, his blankets rustled on the other side of the cabin, and then all was still. The rain appeared to shift into a soothing rhythm, and my shack seemed tight and warm as I lay there wide-eyed and dry, the covers shielding me from the roof's drips.

I put my head out. He looked to be asleep, likely lulled by the rain, and I crept over to him, holding my blanket around me. He was curled up inside his bedding like a mouse wrapped in its tail, but after a moment he pushed the covers from his face and I saw his eyes were wide awake and glimmering. He smiled, reached out to ease the blanket off my shoulders, and drew me down against him.

◆◆ ◆◆ ◆◆

BELIEVE IT, I never did think John and me would jump the broom.

I really don't know what I was thinking during those first few weeks after Marse Doc turned me down. It appeared like I'd never be able to buy my freedom till I was old, and I still believed I'd have no safe chance at running away on account of my sleeping fits. So there I was, stuck again, angry, lost; but this time there was a difference. There was John.

Looking back now, it seems strange that the two of us took up together. Him, a freedman, easy, good-timey, not the sort to get pinned down. Me, a bondwoman, a workhorse, muscled and plain, hardly the kind of pretty yellow gal John was known to favor. And yet he courted me, honeyed me; no one had ever done me that way before. Nor had I really wanted it while I'd been caught up in my freedom plans, but just then I needed John's wooing and comfort. Everything else seemed to have fallen apart, I was down, he was there. At the time it didn't feel like a mistake.

I believe it started out mostly as a distraction for me. Partly it was bedding down with him nights, it was the way he bedded me too. Partly it was tramping through the woods with him come Sundays, fishing the streams, paddling in the Buckwater's mudhole. It was the small things he showed me — how to shoot the rifle he could own because he was free, how to sew, how to feel easy with folks, how to party. It began like that.

Little times, just us.

Big times, partying with the folks in the Quarter.

Two strands. They cross in my memory like bright threads zigzagging through plain cloth; hard to say which came when and on what day, and I don't recollect when it first formed clear in my mind that I'd got around to loving him.

"Hey Hat, no time to swim, we got to get ready for tonight. Hat! You don't mean to jump in there *naked?* Anyone could happen by."

"Well, you seen it all before and a dunk's one way to get cleaned up for a dance . . . whew! . . . ain't so cold, c'mon. Didn't the Lord make us like this and find us good?"

"You got to bring the Lord into everythin, even the swim-hole?"

"John, you bashful after all, else you ain't able to swim."

"Awright lookout! . . . Bleh-*chew*, Jesus, cold."

"Figured you wasn't bout to come back up. You able to swim or not?"

"Best be able, that's for sure. If I sink here, won't nobody be there to set the floor tonight."

You should have seen that man set the floor out there all by himself at the commencement of a dance, hands on hips, chin thrust out, tapping the dirt floor with his boots like he was patting it down firm. He'd get one sweet beat going and then the music would start up underneath, zinging off a fiddle and a washboard, shaken out of beef-rib clappers, drummed from a hollow stump with tanned hide stretched over it. The music would grow from a tick to a patter to a throbbing wild-sweet sound, steady though and even, till we were all stomping it out, clapping it out — you couldn't stay still. Other folks would rock into the dance with John, as many as there was room for, up, moving, singing as they stepped the floor. *Hold your partner where you at* slap-thunk-slap *dance pretty mama till the floor go flat,* faster, building, the beat taking me with it, stirring my feet, my hands. *If you work all the week and you work all the time* stomp-clappa-stomp *white man sure to bring the nigger out behind,* louder, faster still. And John would be out there keeping pace, dancing with a glass of water on his head while folks laid bets on how long he could go without spilling two drops. And, Come on, he'd call to me, show you how.

"All right, show you how to hold a rifle proper. Lord, woman, it ain't no broom. Now. See that bead there on the barrel? Line that up with this groove here on the back, that's it. Now line em both up with that stump yonder. Pull your breath in. Jam that butt into your shoulder good."

"Now?"

"Now. Squeeze the trigger easy."

"Mercy, would you look, I hit it! No, wait, give it back, I just begun to catch the knack."

"Powder and shot cost me, know that?"

"One more time. Watch this."

Stewart figured he had a right to come watch us if he sent a chicken down to the Quarter for our parties, but we didn't take to being watched. Like our prayer meetings, the dances were our own times apart from the whites, so we'd mostly trap game ourselves for the feasting, and fetch along jugs of home-brewed beer or cider. On fair nights we'd set tables out under the trees, and if it rained that didn't matter. We'd just crowd into one of the larger cabins.

I'd never joined in such doings while I was working so hard for my freedom, but John had often mingled with slaves when there were big times. He set me right at ease, and I knew most of the folks who came around anyways. They'd sneak over from Doc Thompson's and other nearby plantations, gathering with Stewart's people to forget the week's toil by dancing it off whenever there was a Saturday night we could meet. Everybody would be fresh scrubbed and decked out in party threads kept aside special, often dyed red; our jubilee color. We'd sport ribbons and buttons bought in town, trimmings borrowed from somewheres, and finery stitched up when we got the chance.

"Mean to get this quilt all pieced up before we gone, come on, Hat, you got to help."

"I got field nigger's hands. You the fancy stitcher."

"You ain't so bad with a needle."

"Yeah, just botched this here's what I done."

"Keep them stitches closer together, hon. Hurry now."

"Huh. Lack patience for this kinda work. How on earth'd you ever stand still long enough to learn from your daddy?"

"Said we wasn't to speak on my daddy, recollect?"

"Ow! Sheesh."

"Well give it here then. Still mean to get this done even if you sit there with your fingers in your mouth. One patch more."

"Best patch your shirt too, you be out there in the center tonight like always."

The two of us would be out there, hands on hips, slapping our feet down hard against the dirt floor while the music whirled up through my bones and everyone rapped time. John taught me Pick-Cherry and Two-Hook-Hands-Go-Round, showed me how to jab my elbows out sharp and quick when we did Cuttin-The-Pigeon-Wings. And all the while I'd be watching John, him moving so loose and fast and fine, I'd be thinking, that man is my man, that man will be loving me up an hour from now.

"Babe? Babe! Wake up all right now."

"Huh what . . . John? Sun up? Horn blow s'soon?"

"Still dark, easy easy."

"Some dream . . ."

"Musta been the mean kind, you hollered. Cussed a streak too."

"Was Marse Doc . . . Stewart there . . . can't catch it back."

"Baby, ain't no need to let Stewart and Doc T. into your sleeps now, that's all over, past."

"Cold. Hold me. John?"

"Mmm?"

"Nothin. Warmer. Stay?"

"Right here, babe, right here."

Amos came over from Thompson's one night and said with all due respect, John and me were carrying on sinful. He'd marry us if we wanted, if Marse Doc gave consent. I didn't say anything. The preacher left. John sat with his pipe in a haze of smoke, silent for a long while, but he stayed that night anyways. Next evening I went over to talk with Aunt Juba. She said it was best to get married right, but marrying a freedman was uncommon, maybe asking for troubles; of course she'd come if we did conclude to jump the broom, she wanted me to know that. She looked worried. I went back.

"You want me to keep away nights, Hat?"

"Uh-uh."

"Why'd you go see Aunt Juba for?"

"Just gone to talk is all. John, what you want with me anyways, me a slave . . ."

"What you think?"

"Dunno."

"What'd Aunt J. say bout me?"

"She say . . . nothin. Well, stay around if you got a mind to."

"Like this? Not hitched?"

"Oh I just dunno. Up to you."

A week later we jumped the broom.

Sometimes our masters married us on the verandahs of the Big Houses, but this was different, bond marrying free. Anyways, I just couldn't see myself standing up there before Marse Doc, and those Big House slave weddings were no more lawful than ours, they only had more trappings. There was a lot that had to be left out of the vows in those ceremonies too; we couldn't promise Master we'd love and cherish till death parted us, nor could it be said that what God had joined let no man put asunder.

So the wedding was in the Quarter where it belonged, with Amos to join us and our own folks clustering around — Stewart's people, Thompson's, free Negroes from Cambridge, and others we'd partied with, many of them bringing food or music-makings for afterwards. Tables had been set outside with cider jugs and loaf cakes, and the breeze brought the smell of roasting meat and brushfires. It was a hazy warm October day, and since it was autumn I had a garland of bright maple leaves on my hair instead of the dogwood blooms spring brides wore. My mama placed the wreath on my head just before I walked over to the preacher.

Amos said the ceremony, a short one which I don't recollect and likely didn't hear; I was gazing around from my family to Aunt Juba to John. He gave me a ring hammered into shape from a penny, and two of my brothers stepped forward with the broom. They held it maybe a foot above the ground, John and me joined hands, shut our eyes, and jumped over, clearing it easy. And Amos said:

"Now you married."

◆ ◆ ◆

IT WAS hard for me to comprehend why John didn't mind living with me in Stewart's Quarter. He said his shack had caught fire, maybe true, though I'd never seen it, and sometimes I doubted he really had a place of his own to stay in. He might have just boarded with other free Negroes in Cambridge after his sister died and her house was torn down; the white townspeople had put a stable up where it used to stand. Anyways, Stewart hadn't objected when I'd asked about John moving in. All the Man wanted was for John to pay him some a month for keep, so we lived there. John got to be the center of the Quarter just like he'd always been the center of the dances, and if anyone was riled or suspicious about him living on the place I didn't notice. Folks would come by nights to hear his stories, and soon most of the parties were held in our cabin.

Now you married, Amos had said, but in the beginning things didn't appear so very different from the way they'd been when we were courting.

"That bash sure broke up late tonight. Say babe, you looked real fine, stepped it out good."

"Oooh man, am I beat. Can't be long till sunup."

"Appears like you bout ready to fall asleep on my shoulder here."

"Might . . . Honey, why you got to go and tell everybody you made me tame?"

"Don't mean nothin by it, come to bed now."

"Help me off with this would you, watch out for them pins."

"Raise up your arms. Ow, shit! There. Mmm baby. You too beat to give me some sugar?"

"Well I was. With my threads still on. C'mere. You know you one sweet man even if you talk too big?"

We did get on pretty well that first year, or maybe it was longer than that. I was still saving money in the flour sack, freedom-money for someday, but I wasn't laboring as hard anymore. Stewart had taken me off that plot of land I'd made to flourish. It had grown too big and productive for only one wench to work, he said, it needed a pair of strapping bucks now. And, I thought, he had won his precious wager. Stewart sent me over to his timber lot again, and I got John hired on there also. We worked together for a time till he tired of that. He quit, I stayed. He trapped and hunted, we still held dances, but after a while they ceased to appear so grand to me. John got hired on in the fields for spring planting and reaping time, but then he was out in the woods with his rifle once more. I was still in the timber lot. Sometime afterwards he commenced to do as a traveling barber, going all around the Bucktown District, coming home nights smelling of pomade and lather. He tired of that too. And from thereon it was different with us. The party times grew fewer, dwindled, almost disappeared. And our own times together — there got to be less and less of those, they changed, and as they did everything else changed around them.

Two strands again, but not brightly colored, only criss-crossing, confused, a tangle of quarrels and discontent and absences.

The first time John went off on one of his journeys he left without telling me. I came in from the lot, got supper, waited, then asked around. Someone said John had talked just that morning about jobbing up-county for a spell. He was away the better part of a fortnight and I was mad with him all the while he was gone, but when he came back that man appeared so broken I couldn't say anything. It looked like maybe he'd got beat up or leastways hassled, and his cap was gone, so was his pipe. Lucky he still had his free-papers on him, lucky he hadn't taken the rifle. He didn't look at me, just sat down hard on a stool, and I stood next to him not knowing what to do. I tried to touch him once but he snarled, and then he suddenly put his face in my skirts. He wasn't crying, just holding on like this was the only safe place there was for him.

Next day he had to get himself registered at the courthouse like all free Negroes. Once a year, they had to pay to get their papers stamped. He had to register his rifle, had to get his peddler's license renewed, he even had to register some mangy flea-bit hound that followed him around sometimes, even though it wasn't really his. All that cost plenty. I gave him the money.

We pressed close together that night in bed, not loving it up, just holding. Neither of us said a word. I thought he'd stay around for sure, but the following morning he was packed up and ready to journey again.

"Man, where you off to now?"

"Just up to Airey. Business. Like before."

"Castoff white folks' clothes from house gals?"

"Maybe."

"You mean to bring em back here to mend up?"

"Likely."

"You mean to peddle the stuff hereabouts?"

"Doubt it."

"I could get you hired on at the lot again."

"Like a slave? Had enough of that. Been on your apron strings too long anyways."

"Well go on then."

"You be good in the meanwhiles, you hear?"

"Me? After what I heard on them housemaids who pass you the stuff, you dast say that?"

"Now don't you start no fusses, I got to get a move on."

"Got to get a move on myself. To the lot. Like a slave."

Winter. Timber cut, log-rolling done with, workload light. Whitewashing everything, the whitewash like glue; folks said you could tell it was February if it froze before you could smear one coat on. Whitewashing and mending the pasture fence and the field hands' privy and the Big House porch.

Frost-bit fingers and feet wrapped in gunnysacks, too cold to ramble about, nowheres to go nights but home. John away again, away for a long while; it had been like that for some time, him home a few days, then off for weeks, and I felt stuck. Stuck standing on the ration lines like usual to get my pint-a-salt, peck-a-meal, strip-a-fatback. At a standstill, white-washing.

Strange, I hardly missed John that much anymore. I'd got used to this, didn't feel lost or lonesome, just angry, restless. Being wedded to him somehow made me feel more like a slave than ever. Like I was a nigger and he wasn't, and I had to live with such a man, or halfway live with him. Maybe he did get roughed up by some patrollers that one time, but the other times he'd come back whistling, and it seemed that just being able to journey around was worth the risk. It killed me that I couldn't, he could. So long as he had his free-papers on him he could ramble around the county, maybe even out of it, while the farthest I could go was Cambridge, and then only with a pass, only with permission. It was coming clearer how things were, how things would always be with us. I think it was winter then.

"How long you figure to stay around this time, John Tubman?"

"Hard to say. Done real big, made out fine this round."

"Maybe one day we be able to scrape up enough money to buy me my freedom after all. You know I save every extra I make like I always done."

"You still on that, gal? Figured you'd gave up long ago."

"Figured how? You know I never truly give up on it, I talk bout it mostly."

"Well, everybody talk. Met this nigger up around the bay, he talked on and on bout some plantation he believes to own one day. Hey, things all right. I always been here and there, you always been here, but we got somethin steady now. Things all right."

"Yeah. For you. John, don't it never trouble you I'm bond? Or maybe you like to be the only one around here with free-papers?"

"I got to buy some tobacco, back in a while."

"Don't you hear me, man?"

"Later."

Nights John was gone I took in washing from that Bucktown Quaker lady, the one I'd been doing for ever since I'd commenced hiring my time. A horse-faced woman she was, long in the teeth and jaw, kindly in the eyes. She gave me mending to do, darning as well as the wash, and she paid well. Almost more than the wages, I was glad of the labor. It kept me from pacing, gave me something to do with my angry nights. One time I punched the needle through some cloth so hard it flew across the cabin and I lost it. I was still saving money in the flour sack. Not much hope in that, but it was all I had.

"What you say we throw a real big time in here tonight, babe?"

"Big time for what?"

"Me home again."

"Don't feel big-timey."

"Ain't you glad I'm to home? Shit, sulk and scold's all you do anymore, brings me down just to look on you."

"Told you what's got me troubled, John."

"Been like this I don't know how long. Why won't you leave me near you nights? Should be real sweet in bed after I been gone."

"Man, you can't whistle in here whenever you please and spect me to roll over on my back direct, just cause you concluded you had enough travels for a while. What'd you jump the broom for anyways, safe sugar in one place, cheap keep, a mammy to do for you, what?"

"Gal, I heard enough outa you. Wonder what else you got on your mind makes you so cold. Way you behave you likely carry on while I'm off, that it? That it? . . . Jesus Christ, don't you never do like that again, no one spits on me. All right, we get this straight now."

Daddy asked about my swelled-up eye. I told him I'd poked myself with a rake handle, told Stewart the same thing when he asked, and the Man seemed to believe me even if my daddy didn't. Ben was around the wood lot often just then; even at his age he was still the best timber inspector thereabouts, good for five dollars a week at Stewart's, Barrett's, as well as Thompson's. Sharp, my daddy, in many ways, and he kept after me: Had that free nigger bashed me, had he, well he'd answer for it, just wait . . . but I kept saying no, it was the rake handle, dark barn, clumsiness. There weren't many bondwomen I knew who'd snitch on their men in case it got to the whites, but I did tell Aunt Juba, her alone. She asked me if I was happy. I said I didn't know anymore, something kept me with him, there were some times when it was good. She asked me like what. I couldn't remember at the moment. She spat out her tobacco wad, and said there was nothing she could do for it, just leave it take its course. I played like she meant my eye. Lord, she looked old, frail. I went back without troubling her anymore.

"Said I was sorry."
"Heard you."
"Aunt Juba patch you up?"
"No."

One night when I was by myself Shadrack came over from Doc Thompson's. I opened the door, saw him, slammed it.

He shouted from the other side about some news I ought to know, but if I didn't care to listen, it didn't bother him none. Maybe I'd married freedom, he hooted, married it since I couldn't get my own, well that was no cause to act stuck-up, that didn't make me different, that wouldn't help me if the rumors were right. John Tubman couldn't rub off on me that good, John Tubman had other wenches anyways so I'd be a fool to . . .

I opened the door again and clouted Shadrack across the mouth with the flat of my hand. He slunk off, and I started out for Thompson's to see what he'd been taunting me about. I ran into three of my brothers on the shortcut path; Robert, William Henry, and Benjie, on their way to find me. They told me what had happened and what the rumors were. No danger to Mama and Daddy, they figured, nor to our older brothers hired up-county; the strong talk centered around us younger ones. We whispered on what to do, what if, tried to plan in case. But all the while we were huddled together I kept thinking, Not without John, even after our bad times, not without John. Benjie said nothing would happen till after the funeral if at all, we had a few more days to think on it, sleep on it. And the next morning my man came home.

"John, you got to listen. Marse Doc appears bout ready to sell some folks off. Old Marse Ed's son Young Master he just died — lung fever — Miss Susan she may go back to her daddy down to Middleburg and leave the place to Doc Thompson. Someone seen a trader around already. John! Don't you hear me?"

"I hear, no call to yank my arm out the socket, no call to carry on like this, where's your head at? Good Lord, one white boy croak up the Big House and the whole Quarter come down with rumor sickness. Won't nobody be sold, no reason for it. Doc T.'s always run the place since he been that boy's guardian, now he just get to own it outright is all. Anyways, the Man wouldn't sell you off, not your folks neither. He ain't bout to part with prime niggers, useful ones, you oughta be able to figure that youself."

"Still that chance, nothin's for sure, I don't mean to risk a sale, never let them do me that way. Besides I reasoned it out you and me we'd be best off up North. Studied on it all last night. Down here we always got this Godamighty difference between us, drives us apart more and more. That's why we ain't like we was, but up North it wouldn't need to be like that. The boys and me already talked it out, we all best go."

"You got it all planned out for me? You stand there and tell me what to do, don't even ask? Well listen here. If I wanted to go North I'd be gone longtime past. North, shit — cold as sin, with niggers crammed into mills, crammed into towns, nothin more from what I heard. Never made my mind up for that, ain't no fool."

"John, sweet Heaven, now's different. Can't you make your mind up for it on my account?"

"And how far you think we'd get, me and three slaves? Patrol be down on us in no time, and what with your affliction, they'd catch you first fit you took on the trail."

"Oh no they wouldn't, I worked years with that affliction and done fine once I got used to it. Fits don't need to hold me back, not now, I got that reasoned out too. Oh John, I want out so bad, won't you come?"

"How many times I got to tell you? Things all right."

"*Don't!* Don't you say it, nothin's all right, ain't been for years. You blind, you scared, Holy God! When you ever comprehend, John Tubman? You look at me, I said look. I'm bond. I could be sold. This time, next time, time after, well dammit man, can't you care? Can't you? You mean to drive me so's I run off alone, that what you want?"

"Oh Jesus, Hat . . ."

"You tell me, John. Tell me straight out, I don't hear you with your face up against the wall like that."

"Said no, don't want you gone, babe. Lookit, smooth down now, help you buy your freedom soonest. Got somethin big ready to come through, that's right, up to Airey. Yeah, and then we start to save that money all over again."

"All over again?"

"Yeah, scrape it together between us, fill it back up, be easy."

"Fill it back? John, what you done?"

"Made you a promise, that's what I done . . . Dammit, woman, why you got to drag that old sack out for? Didn't give me half a chance to tell you, course I meant to pay you back, was in a squeeze. Just borrowed, ain't all gone. Chrissake, don't you fly at me over nothin."

"You no-account yellow bastard, that was my freedom-money, stole, not borrowed, oh yes that's right. You want them coins so bad, well here's the rest — right in your teeth, man."

"Shit, stoppit! You gone crazy? Your freedom-money, your freedom, you blame your tribulations all on me, well Jesus, you don't even know how to lay blame right. You don't even know bout your mama, don't even know bout her first master or his will. Blame old man Green, not me. You mighta been free, nigger, and there'd be no ructions like this atall."

John stomped out. I just sat there on the cabin floor gazing at the spilled money, at his things, at the door swinging back and forth in the breeze. After a while I crawled around, scooping up the coins I'd thrown at him, put them in my apron pocket, sat down again. The dirt floor felt damp, that's all I noticed. John's last taunt was the only thought I had. It faded away, and no other thoughts came. There was a haze before my eyes. I couldn't move.

◆◆ ◆◆ ◆◆

LORD KNOWS how long I would have squatted there if Stewart hadn't sent word for me to drive a load of timber into Cambridge. The wagon was already packed and hitched up to the team; I had little more to do than steer it, a simple task I did almost blindly, trying to sort out the clutter in my head, scarcely noticing the sun-and-shower patterns of the morning around me.

By the time all the wood had been delivered, I'd seized on one notion in especial, and then I did something that could have got me whipped.

Instead of going back direct I went to the courthouse, took out the five dollars I had left, and paid a lawyer to look up the will of my mother's first master. The lawyer looked back sixty years and said it was time to give up. I said to go back further. He looked back sixty-five years and then he found the will.

It showed that the girl Ritty had been left to old Master Green's heir, a Mary Patterson, to serve her and her issue till she was forty-five years of age. But Mary Patterson had died unmarried soon after the bequest, and as she'd made no provisions for the slave she'd inherited, Ritty was legally free at that time.

Only no one had told my mother that. She'd been but a child, too young to question things, so she'd been sold straight back into bondage. And once a Negro was sold back, that Negro was a slave again, no undoing it.

I walked out of that courthouse near unable to feel my legs

and sat down hard on the wagon's seatboard like I'd been dropped there. I didn't notice the day had deepened into late afternoon, didn't even recollect unhitching the team, or driving back onto High Street till someone jumped out of my way, hollering that I'd best keep my thick nigger wits about me. Habit alone was guiding my movements while my mind remained stunned, frozen over the thing I'd just learned.

My mother should have been free all these years. Her children, by law and by rights, should have been born into freedom. Tilly would have escaped that coffle-gang. I'd have a hide clean of lash scars and a head clear of affliction. All of us would have had other lives, if only Mama Rit hadn't been tricked, if only she had known. John had known somehow, maybe from his daddy, but I guess he'd kept such hurtful tidings from me till our quarrel had brought them out; he'd known too that nothing could be done to change things.

It's still hard to say why I didn't turn that wagon around and ride right out of there, run away then while I had wheels under me. Maybe I was too dazed for reasoning anything out. Maybe I wanted to see my family one more time, to say goodbye or round up my brothers to come along. But deep down I believe it was John holding me back. At that moment I still wasn't certain if I could bring myself to leave him, even after all that had happened. And so I just sat there with the traces slack in my hands, numbed, letting the team take me back, while my head dinned with voices.

Come.

They'd catch you first fit you took on the trail.

Follow.

Don't want you gone babe.

Be not afraid.

One way or other I lose my children.

It is only I.

Don't like to see my girl headed for hard times.

With you always.

Don't want you gone babe they'd catch you don't head for hard times one way or other I lose my girl don't want you to don't.

Come only I with you follow not afraid come.
Always seen you headed for other things, child.

Aunt Juba's voice echoed in my head last of all, clearest of all, and of a sudden I whipped the horses into a faster pace. Had to get to Aunt Juba, needed her, she'd do or say something that would decide me, lend me strength. Had to get to her direct.

Back at Stewart's, I left the team still hitched to the cart, then scrambled off, short-cutting through the woods, stumbling into jagger bushes, tearing my clothes, plunging on. I didn't stop till I'd reached the edge of Marse Doc's Quarter, where I shrank back suddenly, panting.

The patrollers were roaring past it.

Through the dusk and the beginnings of a fine rain, I saw vague forms scuttling for shelter, one falling as the horsemen whooped by and lashed out with their riding crops. And then they were gone, hollering in the distance. The Quarter remained still, but I edged up closer. There was Daddy's cabin down toward the far end of the row and near to it, Aunt Juba's. I rushed toward her shack, calling her name.

She was there in her trampled garden, sprawled on her back where they'd knocked her down, with her tobacco chaw still wadded in her cheek. The horses must have ridden over her. There was blood. Her clothes were torn. Her eyes still gleamed from a battered face. All feeling quit my limbs as I sank down beside her and squeezed her hand, but it was limp, she was not even able to press my fingers. My teeth chattered though it wasn't cold, and my words came out in a rattle.

"My Lord oh Aunt Juba, say what to do, where's the pain, say quick, get you mended, how?"

She seemed to smile at me.

"Put you to rights, come out fine, just fine, please God, just say what to do."

"Get me inside?" A voice that wasn't hers, thin, small.

I picked Aunt Juba up in my arms, carried her into the cabin, and laid her on the rag bed in the corner. Kneeling by her, I dimly felt the warmth of the hearth at my back as firelight wavered over the walls and onto her face. A thin stream of dark juice trickled out at the corner of her mouth, drippings from her tobacco chaw, I thought at first, but the juice was red. Her eyes were still open like she could see, but when I spoke to her again, I knew she saw nothing more in that place.

I grabbed her fingers, jangled them, shook her by the arms. I screamed for her, clapping my hands in her face like she'd once done to bring me out of a sleeping fit, and then I dropped my head into her skirts. Sobs wrenched me like I was a child again and she was standing with me down by the crik, telling me it was time I learned how to mourn proper.

A hand pulled me off her. Summoned by my cries, folks from the nearer cabins had come on the run to cluster around the rag bed, and I was pushed back against a wall till I could hardly see Aunt Juba. She had shattered into the Quarter's many faces, and I shut my eyes, unable to watch her go from me.

After a time I thought I heard Daddy's voice mingling with the others in the shack. My eyes opened, searched about, could not sight him or Mama, and of a sudden my guts went runny. Daddy Ben and Rit not there, but they'd have heard the wailing if they lived, they'd be here by now, their cabin was only two doors down. Ben and Rit not there, and old themselves too, maybe they hadn't been able to scramble out of the patrollers' way either, oh my Lord. I bolted from the shack.

Daddy's place was empty, appearing like it had been left too soon, too sudden. Ashcake was on the coals, and shelled corn waited in a gourd by the hearth. I picked through their ravaged yard, then dashed up to the other end of the Quarter and into my brother's cabin, Robert's, the last one in the row.

Inside was warmth, cook-smells, and an orderliness that seemed unnatural to me just then. Robert was smoking, his wife Elvina had just pulled a long-handled skillet from the hearth, and Benjie was there with William Henry, both of them sitting around on a chest. They all started at the sight of me. My skirt was slivered, arms scratched, and I must have been wild-eyed.

"The old folks," I rasped. "Where?"

"Good Lord, them patrollers get you?" Robert rose sudden, snapping the pipe from his mouth.

"No, Heaven's sake! *Where they at!*"

"Only over to the cookhouse, went just before that trash ripped through here." Robert sat down again. "Nothin amiss, Marse Doc sent for extra help. They got maybe fifty callers up the Big House come to pay Young Sir last respects and stay for the funeral. Ain't able to handle it all. You all right? Appears like you ready to fly apart. Listen, bout that sale talk . . ."

"Don't matter. I already concluded to run off. Now." The words sounded simple as I spoke them out loud, though I didn't know just when they'd formed clear like that. "You still got your minds fixed to go like last night?"

"We stopped by Stewart's earlier on to tell you," Benjie said. "That sale talk bout whispered itself out, was just talk, bless God. Trader we seen, he just come by to pay a sorry call, nothin more, and Daddy say things sure to stay even. Anyways this ain't the night for a run, patrollers around, rain — best we wait. Thank the Lord ain't no one bound to be carted away after all."

"No one ceptin Aunt Juba. In a box. Patrol just stomped her to death. That's right, don't you hear nothin up this end?"

They stared at me, glanced at each other, half-rose. I went on.

"Well, I still mean to go. Tonight. My mind's set. Be off soon's I tell the old folks goodbye somehow and stop for my things. You conclude to come, meet me at Stewart's direct. I just got to get out now, straightaway."

I left them whispering amongst themselves.

It wouldn't be safe to tell my parents openly, not with them so near the Big House, but I had to let them know I was going, had to let them know myself. I crept over by the cookshed and hid in the shadows, feeling the ground under my feet turning to mud, watching the place. Daddy was just going in with a load of kindling in his arms, and I saw my mama's head passing back and forth behind the half-open window. Then Daddy's was framed there too.

Crouching down back of the woodpile, I thought for a moment. The white folks would think nothing of it if they heard some darky voice making a tune. Soft but plain I sang:

I'm bound to leave you
Bound for Jordan's other side. . .

Daddy's head came up, listening, knowing my voice; comprehending my meaning. He started to move, stopped himself, his cheeks wet. Oh Daddy, sorry, got to even so, waited too long. I sang again.

I'm sorry friends to leave you
Farewell oh farewell. . . .

Then I turned and made the short tramp back to Stewart's.

John wasn't there. The cabin was dim and damp, untouched by either of us that whole day. So much the better. I didn't want anyone standing in my way now, and it was an effort to hold back a little while on account of my brothers. They didn't come. It was time. It was past time. I commenced gathering up my things.

Even after all that had happened since morning, there was no tiredness in me. Just a flapping in my chest, a fuzziness in my head. I steered myself around the place with jumbled directions.

Dry clothes, put them on, well just drop the wet ones anywheres, don't matter, some ashcake, that smoked meat too, and yes the hunting knife surely, best take the quilt clean off the bed and bunch it up, might look like a peddler that way you never know, hope these boots will last, maybe that hat will keep the rain off, ticking bag, knife, quilt, well then girl, get moving, easy now, out the door straight to Bucktown, farewell oh farewell.

I left him his gun.

◆◆◆

THE HORSE-FACED Quaker lady opened her back door to my knock, and I stared at her shoes, wondering what to say. Nothing much, I figured, not till she looked to be trusted. I babbled apologies about the lateness of the hour, and how I'd been trying to peddle this quilt all the day, and might I just come in to dry off, that rain appeared like it wouldn't quit.

She was watching me close. Her eyes flicked over my bulging ticking bag, the knife at my belt, the quilt crumpled up just as it had come off the bed. She glanced up at the sky. The rain had quit indeed, though I never even noticed till that moment; my clothes were still dry, and a soft dripping sound came from the eaves of the Quaker's house.

"I should like to see thy quilt by lamplight," was all she said. "Come inside."

I followed her into the kitchen, saw that she bolted the door, but I took in little else about the place excepting that it was warm and plain. My boots made muddy blotches on the pine floor. My breathing sounded loud and sharp in the stillness. I knocked against a table, then jumped as a stick of wood shifted in the stove. The quilt dropped. She was still watching me.

"It is a fine piece of work indeed."

"Ma'am?"

"Thy quilt."

"Oh yes, the quilt, thank you ma'am."

She hadn't really looked at it. I hadn't really heard her.

"Thee looks weary. Did thee intend to peddle thy goods further north if thee didn't find me interested?"

"Could be, ma'am, could be," I muttered, shaking my head and staring down like I didn't comprehend her whole meaning. The poor thick-witted nigger wench was a safe enough guise for a time, it was what most white folks expected to see anyways.

"Will thee go on tonight?"

Her skirts skimmed the quilt on the floor, leaving it untouched, as she set new milk, bread, and cold ham on the table before me. I didn't move nor could I touch the food, though I hadn't eaten all day and my belly churned. The place was too warm, bright. This place was locked. This lady was waiting on me, which in itself was strange enough to seem alarming, and she appeared to have guessed my purpose. Maybe Barrett's Jim had been wrong about these folk. After all the woman was white as well as Quaker. She had no reason to help me, she could turn me in, she could collect a reward.

She repeated her question. I didn't answer.

"Best eat thy food," she said, and busied herself at the hearth.

I remember that I ate standing up. At that time it wouldn't have occurred to me to sit in the presence of a white person, and I tasted nothing of the meal. When she spoke again I spun around, startled, though her voice was low and her back was turned. She might have even been talking to herself.

"I wish it could be understood that we are different. Others have come. It is all right. Truly. I'm afraid I'm of little help. However. Does thee know the Choptank?"

An odd question. I'd seen it hundreds of times stretching beyond Cambridge. I'd worked up and down its banks. It had gleamed in my earliest dreams.

"Yes'm, I know the river."

"Perhaps thee did not know that it leads north to the Delaware border? Yes, and perhaps thee did not know that if one keeps north just a little way beyond its source one comes to the town of Dover. Dover, by way of the Choptank. There are Friends in that town, and free Negroes, but one must be careful where one knocks. If thine errand does take thee north, thee might find an Underground Railroad station at Dover, and a ticket to Philadelphia."

She turned, gathered up the quilt, and gave it back to me, then put out her hand. From long habit I flinched, and her eyes appeared saddened for an instant. She drew her hand back, and did not make to touch me again.

"If thee can reach the river before dawn, thee may be fortunate enough to find a boatman at Reedy Cove. He is often there, and though we do not know who he is we know he is a friend. A carpenter some say, or a fisherman, thee can trust him. Remember, thee are journeying from midnight through hope to God be praised." She repeated that last, as if it were a prayer. "Remember that."

She lifted the lamp high to show me out, and at the door we both paused for a moment, standing together within the circle of light rippling over us. It felt like we were bound together by what was unspoken, by the surrounding quiet, by that ringed brightness. For the first time I returned her gaze. This stranger, this queer-spoken woman, was giving me something with her eyes, and I saw a friend trapped in a white face.

She turned down the lamp's wick so that it was dark when she unbolted the door, and I gave her the quilt before I stepped out.

"Godspeed."

The door shut, swift and silent.

I moved through the dark, damp air till the lights of Bucktown had disappeared behind me. The night held still, stood back, let me pass. No one was about. My stride lengthened. Before daybreak I'd reached Reedy Cove.

A rowboat stayed there in the shallows.

I dropped flat on the ground, peered through the tall marsh grasses, and got a glimpse of the boatman.

He was hunched down in his skiff, a shadow within a shadow. I could just make him out in the dimness, and I crept closer, sensing it was safe. There seemed to be a gentleness about the man as he lifted his head, half-turned for an instant, then leaned over his oars as if he was waiting for something. I cast about in my mind for what the Quaker had said, found it, murmured it.

"Journey from midnight through hope to God. . . ."

His back was to me, but I saw he nodded, then pointed upriver. I waded the few feet out to the boat, climbed in over the bow, and lay flat against the bottom as the skiff swung into the Choptank. I saw nothing, heard only the creaking of wood, the murmurations of the river, and felt the current flowing beneath us.

The oarsman sliced the water clean without much splashing, and we slid along like a spirit ship under a spell or a blessing. When I dared look up, I could not tell if the rower was colored or white. All I was able to see was a back bent low inside a big, threadbare coat, hands in shabby old gloves pulling on the oars, and on his head, the tattered brim of an old hat, the inside of it gone. The night mists shrouded him as he carried me on, and the river moved under us like in the old dream; the air hung over us, peaceful, hushed. After a time the sky brightened. The skiff slipped into a shadowed cove, and the man put up his oars.

I waited an instant, but he neither turned nor spoke, so I whispered my thanks, climbed out, and dodged into the cattails along the shore. When I'd got myself hidden I looked back, but the boat and its captain had vanished.

Day was busting wide open, all birdsong and sun, flinging grasses, river, and shoreline before me in their ordinary, solid colors. I felt alone, exposed by the morning, and though I was upriver a ways, I wasn't so far from home either; the boatride couldn't have lasted more than two hours at the most. It would be dangerous to move any farther by day, and I knew I'd best hide there till dusk — but no, I could not, I would not think of holding still, not now, not at the very beginning.

Between the river and its bank lay a long stretch of marsh, thick with tall, guarding grasses. I took off my boots, tied them around my neck, and began slogging through the reeds. Water rose above my knees, the current shoved against me, but I pushed myself, trying to move quick. I couldn't. The grasses thrust themselves in my path, cutting my hands as I fought them off. The sun, flaring in my eyes, climbed higher till it was directly above.

Noon. Everything washed-out, bleached by that light, everything looked the same. Was I getting anywheres? A heron skimmed the river, passed me, vanished. Lord, this will to hurry, and yet this weariness like a weight to lug along. I remembered I hadn't slept at all the night before, and of a sudden I splashed down, shaking my head like a wet dog. Lapping a drink like one, I got a mouthful of brackish tidewater, spat it out, struggled up, stumbled on. I found I was pulling myself along by the weeds after a while. Everything kept blurring before me, and after I'd plunged down three more times, I knew I couldn't keep going without a rest. Panting, soaked, dazed, I clawed my way up the slippery bank, fell flat in the brush, and sank into a sleep right where I dropped.

I woke to see the afternoon sun staring down at me like it was pointing me out. Anyone might have spied me as I dozed. There were plantations just a bit inland at the heads of small, winding rivulets emptying into the Choptank. Besides, I'd lost time, valued time; even though this was Sunday they might have found me missing by now. The patrollers could be out with the nigger-dogs, and I feared those dogs, every slave did. Those hounds were trained to maul their prey, and we'd all heard of runaways who'd died from being bitten countless times; it was said one fugitive had a nose chewed clean off. A cold sweat came over me. My skin prickled as I jammed on my boots and dashed off, thrashing through the brush, tripping over roots, scrambling on all fours till I lost sight of the river. Unable to stop myself, I careened along till I thought to have covered a powerful distance, but all at once I was back by the Choptank again, not much farther along than when I'd begun that panicky flight.

I made myself hold still, breathed deep, and cussed my foolishness. It was crazy to move on land where the dogs could scent me, crazy to crash about like an ambushed deer, when after all I was my daddy's daughter. I listened. All I could hear was common critter-sounds, so I shoved some ashcake down my throat and took off my boots once more.

All that day I waded upstream against the current in the marsh by the riverbank, and as I walked my mind commenced to ramble on its own. It didn't turn backwards like I'd expected, to John, or my parents, or Aunt Juba, but centered solely on the work I was doing here and now.

This labor was not like any I'd done before. No master had ordered me to it, I had chosen it. Somehow this felt akin to birthing-labor, although I had never borne a child, never known the kind of pushing pain that comes with a lying-in. Even so, I felt I was in labor with myself just then, pushing to bring myself forth into new life, and I never did know of a birthing that came painless.

The evening drew down misty and damp by the Choptank, and the river became a dim, chill presence around me. A watery moon rose, swam higher, and as the night deepened, the air grew cold. After a time I couldn't even feel my feet or their broken skin. My head rattled on my neck, my body jerked out of control, piss ran down my leg. The darkness itself seemed to shake before my eyes. Fearing I'd pass out in the water and drown, I dragged myself up the bank once more.

Spring rains had made the earth so soft I kept sinking into mud as I climbed, grabbing at weeds to keep from slipping back. At the top, I sat hard in sucking mud again, and fumbled in my ticking bag till I got some food to my mouth. My whole being ached for rest, but the wind blew straight through me, my soaked shift was plastered to my skin, and I didn't see how I'd ever find a place warm enough for sleep. Snapping my head up, I forced myself to move into the woods, where rain-swelled buds heavied the branches.

There I found a pine grove, with dry ground and mounds of fallen needles beneath the trees. I gathered great heaps of them together like I was fixing a burial mound, and burrowed into the pile. My wet dress felt like a winding sheet, but the needles held in some of my body's warmth, and my eyes finally closed in a shallow sleep.

About three hours to dawn something seemed to warn me awake, and I started up, listening. There was no sound save the rumorings amongst the trees and the questionings from an owl, but sleep had quit me. I brushed the pine needles off and stared about. Nothing, no one, but I crept away even so, sighting the North Star off the bowl of the Big Dipper. This star was steady, though the Dipper had swung around, and it led me straight till I heard the river shushing along by my left ear. I was still on the proper path with star and water for guides, my strength had returned, and I figured to walk in the woods till my clothes dried out; no use courting fever so early on. But when the woods ended at daybreak, all cover ended with them, so I'd figured wrong after all.

The riverbank there was open, steeper. I could see no safe way of sliding down into the marsh grass below, as a few early boats were already plying the water. And ahead of me lay a different kind of danger. It was a field, an open space I'd have to cross one way or another, though the only cover was from last year's dead cornstalks that hadn't been plowed under yet. Some of the stalks were broken down, leaning over, others stood tall, and in some places they would come no higher than my knees. A farmhouse rose beyond the tawny expanse, and at any time someone might come out to enter the field; I could only hope that if someone did, it would be a trustworthy Negro, for I surely wouldn't be hard to spot against the pale crops. Here was a choice, then. I could risk hiding near the field till dark, or I could risk getting myself through it now.

A moment later I took a breath, dropped flat, and crawled directly into a row between the cornshocks. Then, for all my mock bravery, I cowered for an instant, unable to stir. Another breath, and I was forcing myself to move again, crabbing forward, pushing with feet and elbows and hands. As I tried to get a firm grip on the soil, my fingers plunged downwards till I was wrist-deep in mush. The rains had been here as well, and once again the whole front of me was plastered with mud; as I wallowed there, all I could think on was the sow's pen, so long before. It was agony going so slow, an inch at a time, shrinking into stillness after each movement, cringing as the sun hit my back, waiting for a boot to strike my shoulders. I barely breathed. Dirt clung to my chin; I tasted earth, spat it out, and burrowed along once more, stopping, starting, listening. After a while, gasping was what I heard, my own snuffling, and a *wisk-wisk* whenever I jostled the stalks. I can still recollect how panicked I felt once I'd got to the middle of the field, looking back, looking forward, surrounded, no fast way out.

But at last the cornshocks were dwindling away. The field ended. I stopped. Listened again. Rose into a crouch. And shot out of those crops on all fours into the brush beyond, where I lay panting like a hound in summer, scraping the mud off my chin, thanking God.

All was still. It didn't appear that any farmer had noticed my wormlike passage through his dead corn, and I couldn't see the house anymore. The Choptank glimmered off to my left. Its bank wasn't too steep there, so I slid down till I was in the concealing swamp grass again, where I bathed my face and took a long drink. The river was no longer brackish, nor as wide as before, and it looked to be shallower. I could wade across it if need be, but up ahead the river changed color in a certain spot by the bank. That would be one of those treacherous deep places amidst the shallows, and I'd have to be careful soon, for the footing on the swampy ground nearby might be faulty.

Weary from my struggle in the cornfield, stiff all over from tensing each muscle so long, I splashed carelessly through water and reeds till I'd almost reached that spot, and then everything was gone, the river, the grasses, the sun. Only my voices remained, booming a warning in my skull.

When I returned to myself from the sleeping fit, there were men talking close by, and a thwacking in the brush along the riverbank, just over my head. I dropped flat in the marsh grass, frozen, alert.

"Goddamn nigger," said a voice above me. "Tricky. Always say they may be niggers but they can still be tricky. Reckon you'd know her, Luke?"

"Hell yes, she got that scar on her head. Don't always get a mark like that to go on, a clear one, know what I mean? She be hereabouts if she got this far."

I was hid in the tall grasses, mostly covered by the water,

but those patrollers were so close I could smell horses, whiskey, tobacco, even sweat. And then I heard the dogs. There must have been a whole pack of them leashed together, yelping upwind of me — thank the Lord, at least they couldn't sniff me from there.

"Reward money's damn good just for some wench." The voice moved farther off. "Hey Luke! See anythin?"

"Nope. Leave the dogs loose, told you we shoulda done that straightaway."

By that time I'd eased myself out of the marsh and into the river's deep place. Up to my mouth in water, I took one quick quiet breath, and sank below the river's surface. My lungs shoved against my chest, and my whole being felt to bursting, but I didn't dare come up till my eyes began to darken.

I let air out slow. Held my head back. Raised my nose out. Breathed. Sank again. *Oh Lord.* Nose up. Breathe. *God please.* Down under. Up, breathe. Under again. *Sweet Jesus.* Up once more.

Tilting my head back, I lifted my face partways out of the water. My eyes rolled toward the near bank, where I couldn't spot dogs or men for the moment. Longingly, I swung my eyes over to the far bank across the Choptank, and saw a doe poised on the river's edge. An instant later she darted away with a flash of white tail, upsetting the brush as she went.

Next thing, the dogs had scrambled into the shallows upstream and commenced to paddle across. Those beasts were ready to chase any game, no matter the number of legs on it, and they'd be able to pick up the doe's scent once they'd reached the other side. I raised my ears out and heard them howling while the men shouted, hustling to mount. The slavecatchers had been watching this bank close, so it was doubtful they'd seen the deer, and they spurred their horses into the river, likely believing the dogs were on my trail. As they splashed off, I wished with all the strength left in me that the waters would rise and swallow them like the Red Sea had done Pharaoh's chariots.

After they'd disappeared into the woods beyond the Choptank, I pulled myself back up to the marsh grass. Bless God. I lay there for a short time, gulping air, but soon enough I was moving again.

Fright pumped a false sense of strength through me. I waded knee-deep in the river, then waist-deep, wishing all the while I could run on dry land. But I couldn't quit this water, I had to kill my scent on account of those hounds. Nor could I quit the screening grasses either, since the alarm for me had clearly gone out.

Now and then I glimpsed a house atop the bank, and heard a distant clank from the fields up there, the bark of a common farm dog, and once, the faint wail of a child. Madness it was to keep going by day, but still I went on; went on till I'd passed a broad creek draining off the Choptank, till I'd skirted two towns, and the river had become little more than a weed-filled, tree-lined stream. I'd no notion I'd passed into Caroline County, I'd no notion of anything by then, and even fright couldn't push me any longer. It had ceased to block out the deep soreness of each joint and sinew, and I felt suddenly old, wounded in a dozen places, shaky in the knees, dizzy and sick from hunger.

I sank down in the swamp grass as evening settled in with a flock of wild ducks, and all warmth drained from the air. There was nothing left in my soaked ticking bag to eat, and I just sat there in the fading light, staring blank-eyed at the water till a small fish came close, nibbling at the river's surface. That snapped me up, and I moved near, reached up under the fish and grabbed it fast. Flopping in my hands, its gills shuttered open and closed, but I was so starved I tore into that creature with my teeth all the same. Wounded, but not dead, the fish slid away from me, its gills working, one eye partways dislodged, and I spat up a mouthful of scales. I grabbed it again, drew the knife from my belt, and carved what I could out of that small, slimy carcass to feed on.

The night's chill fell over me as I crept to a drier spot in the marsh and covered myself with reeds. Curled up, knees to chest, shivering, I dozed on and off. Between my dreamed prayers strange images floated by, none of them reflections of the past, but shadows of things I'd never looked upon.

I saw a gentle face that had no lips, and a great spired city, and an aged white man who stood in a road like a signpost; then all I saw was the road itself, an endless one taking me back to cattails and swamps. I could make nothing of these dreams, but they kept rousing me, and before the night was done I'd commenced to journey once more.

When the sky lightened I was journeying still. The river had shrunk, dwindled, and soon it was just a strand of water caught amidst some stones. Bless God, I must have reached that place called Delaware. Shelter and safety couldn't be far, neither could Dover.

I followed alongside a road, figuring it would lead to the town, or close enough so I might begin seeking a friend. Joyed and grateful, I hurried on, then stopped short all at once. The dinning of hoofs reached my ears, and a moment later I was flat down in the brush. If that was slavecatchers, there was no river to hide me. And if they had dogs with them this time as well, they'd get me for certain. Curse them, damn them, rot them to hell, I was so far up I thought I'd done with that wicked trash.

They were slavecatchers indeed. I could tell as I peered through the bushes, but it was a different group. These men didn't have hounds, thank the Lord, and the horses trotted on without stopping. Nonetheless it was some time before I could leave off feeling trembly and runny in the gut, and although these nigger-hunters had passed me by, I knew I wouldn't be safe anywheres near the road. I'd have to leave that guiding pathway and loop around under cover, hoping to find Dover somehow.

Deep in the woods I felt for moss on the northside of trees, and all that day I moved from trunk to trunk, watching, listening, my heart jabbing against my breastbone. My limbs began to pain something fierce, as did my head; my skin felt hot to the touch and I couldn't seem to get my wind. But again, I was too scared to stop. Leastways Dover was within reach, surely I'd be able to last a while longer, and it would be easier finding my way at night, when I'd have the North Star to follow.

But late in the afternoon clouds moved in thick and fast,

masking the twilight, and there was no North Star that night, only a steady, drenching downpour. I pressed through it, wet to the bone, finding little shelter even from the big oaks. And then I began falling down. Over and over, I tore my knees on rocks, busted my palms open, and bit through my lip till I tasted blood. I couldn't comprehend what was going wrong with me, why I was weakening, losing a hold on myself.

The tree-moss appeared to be lying all of a sudden. It just didn't feel like I was moving north, and every time I got the trees lined up right, I'd feel drawn off to another direction. Was that east? South? I didn't know, and anyways the woods were spinning in the storm, spinning so fast they scooped me up and flung me into a gully where I must have passed out.

I awoke flailing my arms, fearing I was about to drown. Mud and water rose around me, and a rotten log floated by my side; the gully had partways filled with rain, and when I stood up the bilge ran over my fevered body like sweat. With a shock I saw that the storm had ended and dawn was beginning. I'd lain in that ditch most of the night, wasting the darkness, but that didn't seem to matter just then. What mattered was a dry mouth and an empty belly, so I lapped water from a stump-hole and gnawed the green sprouts poking up through the soil, only to retch them back up. Doubling over, I forced myself to rise.

Somehow I was still groping for tree-moss as the woods thinned, but by the time they ended I was on my hands and knees, hitching along, grunting like an animal. Confused with weariness and fever, I crawled right out of the trees into an open field.

I stood upright where anyone could see me, staggered farther into the field, wavered on my feet, and sprawled flat. I didn't try to move again, didn't care what happened to me anymore. All I wanted was rest, and my eyes closed. Just as they did, I felt hands grabbing my shoulders, pulling me up, and I stared into the face of a white man. I was too weak to struggle. He started to drag me away, and then I must have passed out again.

When I came to, I was lying on my back with something soft

and heavy covering me. I twitched my feet. No boots. Boots gone. There was a layer of cloth around me, cloth I was wearing, dry cloth. Not my dress. Wet dress gone.

My eyes opened on a tiny windowless room which circled slowly around me. Lamplight spattered over whitewashed walls, and holding the lamp was the man who had grabbed me; a sharp-featured rawboned man standing next to a fat, bosomy lady. The two of them blurred over, swung into clarity again, and as I opened my mouth to scream I realized they were alike in some way. Their clothing seemed to match. It was dove-colored, plain. That gray hue, that simple garb, a memory flashed. The woman's head, capped, a cap with two long streamers. Quaker. Bless God.

"Underground?" I croaked.

"Indeed. Under our woodpile. Thee are safe." The man said that.

"Dover?"

"Yes. Rest."

"Ticket to Philadelphia?"

"Rest now."

They smiled, smeared into the lamp's glow, and I drifted back to sleep, wondering if the Lord had guided me to this safety, or if it had been the moss on the north side of the trees after all.

I stayed buried under the Quakers' house for the better part of a week, fevered and half-delirious at first. The woman came often to bring broth, poultices, clean linen, or to empty the slop bucket. She'd squeeze her bulky figure through the small doorway in one wall, grimacing, but then she'd smile as she tended me, sometimes forcing ugly grunts through her delicate mouth. Whenever I tried to speak, her eyes would follow my lips, and I comprehended that she was deaf.

Once she made her queer noises, motioned with her hands, and raised her eyebrows in a question. The room was still hazy, she was still moving in and out of a blur, but I figured she was asking about my journey when she pointed to the scratches on my arms. I rasped out the story only to find I was nearly shouting toward the end, and her eyes were still blank.

She shook her head and quit the room. Moments later she returned with paper, ink, and quill. Her face shone as she handed the things to me. She'd found the answer.

I shook my own head then, but she still gazed on me, eyes eager. All I could do was ink the quill and make an *x* on the paper.

She nodded and took the things away.

Other times I tried to question her about the railroad and the network of northbound tunnels I'd heard about down to home, but she couldn't read my lips. Maybe there weren't any such things. Still I wondered why these white Quakers hid escaping slaves; there could be nothing in it for them excepting a lot of trouble if anyone caught them. When she came again, I asked her.

"You help me, why?" I repeated, motioning with my hands till she appeared to comprehend. After a few moments she pointed upstairs, but I didn't take her meaning.

"Who bid you do it? Who you work for?"

Her gaze remained fastened on my lips as I said the words several times. Then she stood, placed one foot over the other, spread her arms straight out from the shoulders, and let her head fall limp to one side as she shut her eyes. When she opened them again, I nodded.

That image stayed with me a long while after I'd recovered, departed from the Quakers, and continued my journey alone once more. The man had given me directions to another friend, the woman had given me a bundle of food along with my mended clothing, and though these white folk seemed almost too kindly for belief, they had somehow renewed my spirit.

And so I went on, tramping through woods or creeping past fields near the main road, but not too near, using it only for a guide like I used the sun and stars. I remember how whole I felt during the next two days and nights of hiding and traveling, even when weariness set in again, and my boots chafed fresh blisters raw. I also remember wondering where the train was, and the tunnels; maybe that underground road was so secret I'd never find it, but no matter. I was getting free anyways.

By the third morning I'd edged past one large town and reached another, called Odessa. I circled it in that shadowy hour before sunup, watching lights flickering here and there, narrow and wavery as candlewicks. If daybreak caught up with me, I was to head straight for the Quaker meeting house and hide. But I'd been told to search out a certain house and barn if I could, while it was still dark. They were on the town's outskirts, and it was nearly dawn when I found them.

A small frame dwelling, with white stones built into the chimney, ringing it. A barn beyond, with whitewashed doors. I hesitated, trying to sniff out a trap or find some sign that this was truly a safe place, and in the end I concluded not to approach the house itself. Instead I dodged into the barn and hid in a stall, thinking to wait there till I'd seen what sort of people lived on the farm.

It didn't take long. Almost as soon as I'd scrunched down I heard footsteps, glanced out, and saw a hefty colored man reaching a harness down off a peg. He was dressed neat but plain — patched shirt and trousers like the stablehands wore down on Marse Doc's place, shabby boots not so different from mine, and he was whistling a bit of a tune my mother used to sing in the fields. Sweet Jesus, that man had to be a slave, a slave going about his morning chores. So the people who owned this place must likewise own slaves, and Lord, I'd got myself into the wrong barn somehow. I waited a moment after the footsteps had clumped out again, began crawling toward the door, and had almost reached it when the big Negro loomed up in front of me, blocking the way.

"Ahhh," he said. "Always on the lookout for such as you. Best come along now, best be quiet bout it too."

I edged away, and for some reason the man broke into a grin.

"You figure me for a slave, that right? Uh-huh, and you figure my master he got me on the lookout for runaway niggers so's I can turn em in, collect a bonus?"

I was still backing off, trying to figure how I might get past him, and darted forward as he doubled over with laughter. He caught me by the arm.

"Hey, easy now. I'm free, sister, this here's my own place.

Always help runaways when I'm able is all, and you sure appear like one to me."

The shame I felt was terrible. My own kind, and I hadn't trusted him.

"All right, it don't matter," he said. "Come upon a runaway one time who was more'n edgy, was ornery too, bit me's what he done. Well, never mind now. You be to Wilmington soon, on wheels all the way. That's your last stop before Philadelphia."

"On the train?"

"Train ain't safe hereabouts and it don't run over Wilmington Bridge. We go in my cart, got to haul some timber in anyways. Here, put these on, the hat too, that's it. Bridge got guards, and handbills been posted for a wench with a scarred head. Less chance they notice you in them rags, besides which Market Day's tomorrow, bound to be a crush to get lost in. Hurry now. Be there by evenin."

We were. As we inched across the jammed bridge amidst a crowd of buggies and wagons, I was sitting right up on the seat next to the man, dressed something like him in a farmboy's clothes and a floppy straw hat. Up ahead I suddenly saw the guards, and my eyes stayed on them, riveted.

"Just behave like natural," my driver said from the side of his mouth. "You be safe enough this way. If I stashed you in the cart and they find you down under — girl, you finished. Ain't likely they'd look for you flat-out up top. Chew?"

He offered me a fresh wad of tobacco. I shook my head.

"Chew." He commanded. I chewed.

Lucky I didn't swallow the thing. Behave like natural, well what was natural? Surely not this. I never felt so bared in my life, perched there in plain view where anyone could point at me, take a shot at me even. Oh yes I chewed, right into the lining of my cheek.

The guards didn't seem to notice us on the swarming bridge. We crossed over at last, drove past some cows grazing on the town's outskirts, down several unpaved streets, and stopped in a shadowed, empty alley. The man bade me stay rigged out like I was; he said he'd fetch the clothes another time. Then he handed me my bunched-up dress and an armload of kindling, and told me how to find the house on Shipley Street where I was to deliver the wood.

"God bless, sister," he said as I clasped his hand in thanks. "Almost there."

Almost there, last stop before Philadelphia, twilight coming down fast to hide me; everything felt all right, and I found the house with little trouble, fitting it with what the farmer had said. Through the growing dusk I thought I saw two or three colored people hanging about one side of the dwelling, and felt their eyes on me as I rapped at the back door in the way I'd been directed.

I believe I expected to be welcomed by a Negro, but when the door opened there stood the tall, crease-faced white man of my sleeps, another Quaker smiling down on me from under a shock of frosty hair.

And so I met Thomas Garrett, my friend to this day. He has never let me forget that I introduced myself to him as Thompson's Harriet rather than Harriet Tubman; I recall he answered that by presenting himself as Garrett's Thomas. I recall, too, how uneasy I felt with him there at first, Quaker or not.

He took the kindling from me and laid it in a corner. Then he drew me into a curtained firelit room, down a hall, and through another door. We came out in a cobbler's shop, lined with racks of shoes. We paused there, and though his blue eyes crinkled at me, I could have sworn one of his ears twitched like a dog's does when it catches some sound. My palms were wet as he strode to the window.

He lifted an edge of the curtain, raised the sash a few inches, and hollered.

"Gentlemen, please! Won't thee go home now? I'm most grateful, but thy supper is waiting. *And* thy wives. All's well, assuredly." He shut the window, fixed the curtain, and begged my pardon. "Some of my friends are a bit oversolicitous since my arrest. Kind of them, but they sometimes stand guard till all hours. I've startled thee?"

"Arrest?" I ran my tongue around the inside of my mouth.

"Oh, that was last year." Thomas spoke offhandedly while

he tinkered at the edge of a tall shelf of shoes. "Another Friend and I were brought to trial for helping fugitives, it was in New Castle, not here. Thee can see we survived. I was fined of course, had to put everything I owned up for auction, but my friends bought up all my possessions, returned them to me, and I added an extra story to the house so I could hide more fugitives. Did thee notice it? No? Come."

I'd been so absorbed in what he was saying, and so amazed by the easy way he spoke of such things that I wasn't prepared for what happened next. A wall of shoes swung out, revealing a sloping passageway which ended at the threshold of a narrow door. Thomas went up ahead of me, matter-of-fact and whistling, turned the knob, and I caught a glimpse of a small chamber beyond. The other Quakers' hiding place had been only a partitioned bit of cellar with a hatch in the roof giving on the woodpile, so at the time Thomas's secret room seemed to appear almost by conjuration. Clearly, it had been built special, putting me in mind of Marse Doc's wall safe, and if such was needed there must be danger close about, all the time, had to be.

I cleared my throat as I gazed up. "They search your house a lot?"

"Never yet, thank heaven. But a hidden compartment can offset many . . . inconveniences, let us say. We Friends are forbidden violence and the telling of falsehoods, so we must resort to other means when the need arises. All the same, most manage quite well without such a luxury as this." He drew me into the secret room and continued. "I know of one Friend who was nearly invaded by bounty hunters soon after he'd welcomed some fugitives into his kitchen. However, these particular agents knew him, knew he'd never bear false witness either. Sometimes I think those people reckon up our piety according to whether or not we disdain buttons as worldly adornments — some of us do, some of us do not, he did — at any rate. The search party simply rode off when this Friend said he had no slaves on the premises. Of course he wasn't lying. To him, to all of us, no such entity as a slave exists. Hungry?"

Before I could answer Thomas had left me there, returning moments later with a kettle of stew, a jug of milk, bread, cutlery, and plates, all balanced perilously in a basket.

"I forgot to take supper myself," he said as he spread the things out on the floor between us, sat down, and bowed his head.

"We thank Thee, Lord, for this good meal, which as every meal is made in remembrance of Thee. We thank Thee for Thy Light which illuminates every soul, and for Thy Spirit ever with us, by which the holy men gave forth Scripture." He paused for an instant, flicked an eye at me. "And we thank Thee for that Scripture which teaches that the stranger who dwells with us shall be unto us as one born among us."

I thought of the deaf Quaker lady, added an amen, but felt startled even so at hearing a white man pray like that.

It was more than a little startling to be sharing a meal with a white man too, him and me cross-legged on the floor together, but there seemed nothing odd about it to Thomas. He just sat there with his plate on his knee, mopping gravy with a chunk of bread, asking after my journey, and soon enough he'd got me feeling easy. I found myself talking of the earlier part, the tougher part when I'd been all on my own, and of the woodlore I'd learned from my daddy.

"Thee knows a great deal," he said through a cheekful of stew. "Many fugitives perish for lack of such knowledge. I've often wondered if I'd be able to survive such an ordeal. Tell me, what kept thee going through the worst of it?"

I told him something I'd concluded during the long days of sloshing through the marsh grass. It had formed clearly in my mind, I believe, after that first brush with the slavecatchers.

"I'd reasoned it out that I'd got no rights atall," I said. "But then I reasoned I did have the right to die. And I had the right to try and go free. I'd have one or the other then, and the Lord would take care of me."

Thomas nodded. "I thought it might amuse thee to know how much thee are worth."

He took out a scrap of paper. It was printed with words and a small woodcut of a Negro carrying a sack-and-stick over his shoulder. I knew that was one of the handbills out for me even before Thomas read it aloud, and I was nowheres near amused.

"I didn't mean to distress thee, it's of no importance. I've been advertised myself. Yes, truly! In a Maryland newspaper, someone offered ten thousand dollars for my capture. Impudent of me, and highly immodest, but I wrote back saying I was worth at least twenty." A roar of laugh.

Impudent indeed. I liked that, and felt easy again.

"And," he went on, chewing, "when I offered to collect the reward in person some people had a few things to say about my impudence, only that's not what they called it. Well then. Thee shall stay here tomorrow while I tend shop, and at night thee shall take thy last . . . gracious, what's this?" Thomas flushed, finding a rip in his shirt I'd noticed earlier. "I shall have to mend it, my wife's away on a visit, that's always when I tear things. However, I believe women should vote, it follows therefore that men should learn to sew, though I'm certain thee has never seen one wielding a needle."

"John. My man, still down to home."

It just came out, I hadn't planned to say that. And then I was making a great clatter with the plates and cutlery, trying to cover this sudden wash of homesickness, unprepared for it. A picture of the old Quarter rose in my mind, bringing images of all the people I'd left, their faces clear and close and sunlit. My eyes were stinging. I could feel Thomas watching me.

"Why did thee choose to take that right thee mentioned, the right to try and go free?" he asked after a moment.

Yes. He was doing well to remind me. I told him of all the badness I could recollect, paused to think, and added something about the voices, how they'd always seemed to be leading me this way. Then I broke off, looked down. I'd said too much, he'd take that for darky superstition or madness, surely.

"I believe in such things," he said with a quietness, no trace of mockery in his tone. "Voices. It has been so with me. The first time when I was a young man, and bounty hunters kidnaped a free colored servant right out of my father's house. I made chase . . . it was during the ride. Some scoff at what they call my mysticism. With certain others it can be shared."

He looked thoughtful, held my gaze an instant. Then he collected the supper things and wished me a good night.

A surge of impatience chafed me all the next day as I paced about the secret room. That brief wave of homesickness was forgotten, and I willed the time to pass, unable to tell what time it was, in a sweat to start, to move, to cross over. Soon, it would happen soon, if nothing went wrong. Please God, let nothing go wrong. Not now, within reach of it all, the last stop, the last hours of waiting so long. Whenever Thomas came up with food I was right by the door, hoping he'd say we could leave.

Deep in the night he came to me again with a candle in one hand, a pair of new shoes dangling from the other, a gray cloak and a veiled bonnet over his arm.

"Thee must wear these. I'm often watched by some who are not friendly guardians," he said. "If anyone is about, perhaps they will just think me a discreet sinner, smuggling a woman out of my house in the dark."

My hands fumbled as I made ready, and then we went down together. Thomas rearranged my veil, snuffed the candle, led me straight out the front door, and as if I was a fine lady, he handed me up into his carriage.

I couldn't think as he drove me along, my mind was rushing ahead of us, streaking, blurring, and then the carriage halted well beyond Wilmington's outskirts. I laid the cloak and bonnet on the seat, and was just bending to the shoes when Thomas climbed inside with me.

"Keep them." His voice was low. "This is a safe road, it leads to the turnpike, thee can reach it by sunup. Thee will see a stone marker where the roads meet on the Pennsylvania border, and beyond it thee are no longer bond. Follow the pike to Philadelphia, but take care, bounty hunters hang about the city. My friend William Still at the Anti-Slavery Society can be of help should thee need any."

I climbed out after him onto the narrow road, and he held out his hands. I pressed them.

"Godspeed," said Thomas Garrett.

I was walking before the carriage had even clattered away, and barely heard it go, hardly saw the path. It seemed I couldn't move quick enough. I broke into a trot, yearned to run, forced myself back into a walk for fear of making noise. Each step felt important. I was walking into my freedom. It was coming closer, coming on with the dawn, oh Lord so near now, nothing could happen to stop me, nothing could go wrong, faster, had to reach it faster. In the end I was running after all.

The sky was peach-colored as I came to the turnpike, saw the marker. I walked forward. Touched it. Stepped past it. And stood stock-still on the other side for I don't know how long. At last I wiped the wetness from my face and looked at my hands to see if I was the same person now I was free.

The sun streaked through the trees, and there was such a glory over everything.

Through Hope

◆ ◆ ◆

THEY TELL ME to rest myself, everyone's been telling me that since the train carried me home here to Auburn. It's almost two years past Surrender, Year of Our Lord eighteen sixty-seven, work done, so rest yourself, they say, it's time. There's Old Rit and Daddy Ben to look after, they remind me, look after your own kin, look after yourself and rest, high time.

More than a few people seem to think of me as an old woman now, just because the sleeping fits come on more often, and a touch of rheumatism steals into my joints. Or maybe it's because I appear so burnt-out after all the years of labor, though I'm not quite fifty. And no, not yet burnt-out, not old.

I'm restless fixed here in one place, and some believe that's on account of my argument with Uncle Sam. I've yet to see a cent of pay for my war work, but I don't know if that's due to me being female or colored, or both. My friends do what they can about it. Gerrit Smith and Mr. Seward and others petition Congress and write more letters, knowing I need the money. But all that's not what causes me to feel restless.

When there's not another thing to mend around my house, and there's not another weed left to pull from the garden, and no more crops to peddle in town, when there's nothing further I can do for the Zion Church, and I've told my daddy the same war story for the nineteenth time, I still can't stay set.

Sometimes I walk over to the Auburn depot and board the first train that's bound southeast. I might journey to Boston or New York City and visit old friends, I might go speak at a Women's Suffrage meeting, and then again I might not. Often enough I just ride the cars; what happened on the way home doesn't stop me. The feel of movement once again, the stations, conductors, passengers, freight — they remind me. Even though my train was far different and only those words are the same, they remind me, and the rocking motion soothes me for a while.

Still, I don't like to be gone too long. People come to my door almost every week now, the ailing or aged or penniless colored folks uprooted by the war, with no place else to go. I take every one of them in. The house is always full, what with the pilgrims who sleep upstairs and most of the Zion congregation centering down here in the evenings. That should calm my spirits, but I lie awake, pace about, and then some crippled young man in an old Union coat knocks at the door. There are many like that who come, and such men always put me in mind of Shadrack, his final questions. And again I wonder how much I've truly done for my people. Anything, a little, enough? Those years on the Underground Railroad, how do they apply now, how do they signify? I doubt them. Another knock at the back door, and I put my doubtings aside for a bit, wishing these folks would come around to the front instead.

Day before yesterday a young woman came by, a woman roundabouts thirty, the same age as me when I first reached Philadelphia. She'd just got to Auburn, planned to settle here, would have to find work. Might she just take a load off for a few minutes, she wondered. It was dinnertime, so I asked her to stay, and told her about a shop in town where she might get hired on. That's all I was able to do, but she thanked me, thanked me so much I couldn't comprehend why or what for. I'd done nothing much at all.

But how fine it was, she said, feeling to home in a strange place all of a sudden, how fine to get a steer in some direction. Her eyes were brimming.

And then I comprehended why, I remembered. My own first welcome, that early joy, how it had been with me then.

◀▶

◆◆ ◆◆ ◆◆

THERE IS A NEGRO CHURCH on Lombard Street in Philadelphia which I found my first night there. It was open, empty, so I went in, climbed up past the choir loft, and out into the belfry where I twirled around, trying to keep from pulling the rope, raising my hands till they met and clasped over my head. *Oh my Lord here I am.* People moving in the street below didn't hear me, didn't see me. It didn't matter. The city leaped up, welcoming, winkling with a thousand flames from gas lamps and trash fires and bright windows and I was above it all, *I did it I'm here up here O Jesus praise You free.* A breeze stirred the bell's clapper just enough to make a small ching of sound, a tongue echoing mine, announcing me to myself and God and everyone, and I stretched forward, arms out, eyes blinded again, *Crazy this is Here I am Girl you watchit you don't fall off now Here is Harriet Tubman.*

I didn't sleep that night.

For most of my life, hatred and struggles had kept me going, but there in the newness of freedom the hatred had vapored away, leaving me light, buoyant. It seemed I wouldn't need the old ways to get me through anymore.

That whole day I'd walked all over Philadelphia, unable to get enough of it, and everything appeared so fine and big and baffling. Streets: crossing, winding, hilly streets, or broad flat ones mostly paved with flagstones, many with wells at the corners. Streets with names like Chestnut and Spruce, others shaded with double rows of plane trees, buttonwoods, willows, streets scrubbed and sparkling, near flooded in the morning by the Fairmount Waterworks. Streets lined with grand black and red brick houses, houses shuttered with bright green, fronted with flower beds and steep flights of steps. Streets racing with hansom cabs, hackney coaches, mail carriages, fire-wagons, shaking and grumbling where the railroad tracks ran straight through past Dock and Broad. Streets from Front to Eighth at Market filled with open-air sheds, hawkers, wares, buyers, flies, and the inky smell of fresh-dyed cloth, *For pennies! For pennies!* Above, beyond, masses of pale young leaves in Lemon Hill Park, and over down another way, mills, smokestacks, taverns; tenements swarming with whites in Kensington, and blacks in Moyamensing; lumberyards, coal yards, alleys, archways, printshops, pawnshops, and rows upon rows of stores. And not one auction block. Not one nigger pen. Not anywheres. And so all of it looked good.

It wasn't the city itself that stirred me so much as other things. Almost everywhere I'd gone I'd seen colored people moving about, and not a one of those colored people was a slave. I had to keep reminding myself: There are no slaves in this place. That nigger there is not bond. That nigger is free. And that one. And me. I had to keep reminding myself of that too, even as I settled into Philadelphia.

I asked directions of other Negroes and they talked to me, asked me to come in and sit awhile, come in and eat.

Where you just new from? They'd ask, and I'd tell them.

You been here long? I'd ask, and they'd tell me.

Sam and me we come up from Delaware years ago, pass her the biscuits. You got a place to stay yet? . . . This here's Lizbeth and Cal Williams from two doors down. Lizbeth's daddy come up from Virginia when he was only small, and Cal's own granddaddy he fought in the Independence War near to here . . . how you called? Harriet, well you sit tight now, going to put a fresh pot on . . . need more chairs in here, you found work yet, Harriet? I do for a white lady over to Chestnut, day-labor . . . try the mills, the shops, hand your mug up. Sam, you tell her . . . Hell no, jobs ain't all that hard to find. Me? Just unloaded a ship from England, man upstreet works the lumber yards. More greens? Lizbeth here's a seamstress, you able to sew? . . . What *I* do? Take the dead under's what I do, been a family business since way back . . . Come by the church tonight Harriet, Mother Bethel on Lombard, meet the preacher . . . pass your plate over, just taste this pie, then we show you around.

They showed me the Colored Benevolent Societies, the Shelter for Colored Orphans on Callowhill, and their school on St. Mary's; they showed me all through the Negro section. Like the Quarter down to home, this community appeared to be one sprawling family. Keeping close around their own churches and streets, these folks dealt with their no-accounts themselves, watched and fed each other's children, looked out for each other. And even if many of the dwellings weren't all that much better than the shacks in the old Quarter, even though there were rats in the alleys beyond the finer houses with gardens and wells, the people here were different. They were free.

Inside of one day, my second in Philadelphia, they'd found me lodgings and a place to work. I moved upstairs into the Juniper Street home of a colored caterer who took in boarders on the side, and I started cooking and cleaning for a Quaker family in Spring Garden. That sort of labor never did agree with me, but I was beginning to grasp what this freedom truly meant, what I was suddenly able to do with it, and nothing could shake my joy right then.

True, I couldn't go on the streetcars on account of being colored. I couldn't get hired on part-time in a lumber yard when I tried, on account of being a wench. I wasn't safe around the Irish who lived in Kensington and rioted against us several times that summer; they were new arrivals themselves, many of them, and feared we'd crowd them out or steal their jobs.

But that was all right. It was all right because I was free, and there were so many more important things that came with that word.

I was a wage earner and every single cent I made was mine to keep, mine to spend as I wished, mine to save. I could change jobs if I wanted and no one could stop me. I could walk from one end of town to another, or even move to a different city altogether, and I wouldn't need permission or a pass. I could learn to read if I chose, I could own a Bible, I could one day own a house. There were no more ration lines to stand in, I had full say over what I ate and wore. I could belong to a church run by my own people, and I wouldn't have to sit up in the balcony there. And above and beyond everything else, I didn't have to fear being priced and marketed and sold along with horses and hayrakes and harnesses. Not there. Never again.

Most people don't count such things as rarities or rights, or even think about them, but to a newly freed slave such things were more than rights. They were privileges. Gifts. Blessings. And yet my jubilation changed somehow, almost as soon as I'd fully comprehended just how much I'd gained.

One evening at the end of the first week I went off to buy myself some goods for a dress, just something that would feel new like everything else did, and the clerk threw in for extra a bit of old stained lace. I stood before the glass in my room that night, pinning and stitching the cloth around me, holding the lace here, then there, trying to pleasure myself with this small finery. Laughter reached me from the family below, snatches of talk, and a woman's voice humming, then breaking off to tell a story.

My hand paused as I held the lace up to my throat, and the eyes in the mirror looked sad, not pleasured. My mother had owned something she'd called lace, a scrap of webbed cloth, and she'd fastened it to her dress with a store-bought button whenever she'd decked out for a Saturday night big time. For some reason I recollected that just then. Even how the button looked. Carved. Pretty. A red one. My mother.

Amidst my own giddy joy I'd forgotten. Mama, Daddy, my brothers, nearly everyone I cared about most were just what they'd always been. My world had been transfigured, but only mine. And after that flash of recollection things were different with me.

Another night soon after, I woke up for no reason in the

deep hushed hours, and found I'd got the quilt bunched up next to me, my arm flung over it. For a moment I didn't know where I was, or why I was sunk in this feather bed, or where John was off to this time. Then a fire-wagon banged through the darkness outside, I saw the outlines of the pine bureau, the straight-backed chair, the vague puddle on the floor which was a braided rag rug. Boardinghouse. Philadelphia. Free. All right now all right turn over. I went back to sleep, but it was the on-and-off kind. Tossing about, I was suddenly troubled over my brothers, wondering if they tried to follow when I ran off, gave up on finding me, and turned back.

As cloudy light commenced filtering through the window, I was pacing around the border of the rug. By evening I'd recollected what Thomas Garrett had said about the Anti-Slavery Society and his friend there, William Still. During the short time I'd been in Philadelphia I hadn't met anyone who'd known Mr. Still to talk to, but many had mentioned the Society with pride. It kept an eye on nigger-hunters, put out tracts, arranged boycotts of southern-made goods, and helped fugitives to get settled. There were a good number of white folks in the Society, all-right folks with connections reaching far down as Richmond, maybe farther than that, no one knew for sure. Much of the Society's business was secret, and was conducted at night. Maybe William Still would be at the Anti-Slavery Office this night.

As soon as I'd got off work after supper I was searching for the place, asking directions of a man I saw standing just outside in the dim street.

Time and time again I'd been warned against speaking to strange white folks in case they turned out to be slavecatchers, and this man might have been white. Then again, he could have been high-yaller. It was dark, I wasn't sure; anyways he didn't look suspicious. Slavecatchers skulked around alleys wearing slouched caps and cheap flashy goods, but this man was dressed plain, poor. A shabby big coat hung from his stooped shoulders, a tattered hat-brim encircled his head, and he had a gentle weary manner. Somehow I knew it was all right to approach him, and without a word or question he led me to 107 North Fifth Street, where he pointed upwards at the curtained lamplit window of a large dwelling.

That was it then, just a room above someone's house, nothing remarkable about it. I don't know what I'd expected, but it was surely more than this, and I turned around to my guide. He'd already gone, so I knocked at the door beneath the bright window. The curtain stirred. After a moment a voice called for me to go around back through the alley where I found another door and knocked again.

Footsteps sounded like they were thudding down some stairs within, and then the same voice asked who was there. I gave my name, mentioned Thomas Garrett's, and a man let me in. I could barely see him as the hall was unlit, but I fumbled my way up after him, and entered the chamber above.

The place was musty, cluttered, plain. Crammed bookshelves lined the walls, and more books were stacked on the bare floor. In the center of the room, a pair of benches flanked a potbellied stove, straw pallets lay heaped in a corner beyond, and a lamp stood on a crate near the window. Another lamp wavered on a rolltop desk against the far wall. A young colored man sat back there, his face thin, eyes keen, hair close-cropped. The other man, the one who'd let me in, was Quaker by his dress, fair-skinned, and bearded. I addressed him as Mr. Still, but the Quaker shook his head, said his name was McKim, and introduced me to the Negro.

William Still and I have laughed about that confusion since. In fact my first meetings with two of my deepest friends were thrown askew by the habits I'd learned from slavery.

Looking back now I realize my apprenticeship began with that clumsy introduction, though I didn't know it then. The year that followed is just one fast streak in my memory. It was a year of learning, of misering my wages, a year pointing in one clear direction.

As soon as I'd been told no one could be sent to steal my kinfolk off of Doc Thompson's place, I resolved to go down and rescue them myself. And so I passed most of my evenings at the Anti-Slavery office, poring over maps with William, discovering what the Underground Railroad was truly about, listening to the Society's members talk, listening especially to William Still.

He wasn't president of the Society as I'd first thought, and wasn't secretary till three years later when the Vigilance Committee formed, but he took a big share of running the place. William lived downstairs and had runaways coming to his door at all hours. He'd helped steer many escapes toward that office with the letters he wrote, and I heard about several of those runs. Some were dazzlers, like the flight of William and Ellen Craft the year before. They'd come up from Georgia riding openly on trains, staying in the best hotels all the way, with Ellen passing for white and William passing as her manservant. But most escapes were ordinary ones like mine had been, scrambling and hiding all the way up, and it was those escapes I wanted to hear about. I wanted to know of every detail, every step, every dangerous town, every route north from Maryland. It was then that I discovered my inability to read had caused my memory to stretch, to clamp down on things, and hold them.

While I was learning, I was helping out around the place too. I ran errands and aided the runaways who'd been directed to that office first thing. When packages of food came from other Anti-Slavery groups I took a hand in distributing them; when our own colored Dorcas Societies supplied clothing I helped deal the goods out. I tried to find jobs and lodgings for the new arrivals. I talked with them. I watched them.

There'd be a commotion on the stairs before a group crushed in, tattered and muddy, filling the room till it appeared small. Old people leaned on sticks, young men and women leaned on each other, children ran around, babies squalled. All of them would be hugging, weeping, laughing, thanking God, and their jubilation made them beautiful. Sometimes I'd leave such a group bedded down there late at night, and once I'd reached my lodgings I'd feel too stirred up for sleep myself. And I'd think, if only I could see Daddy smiling in that place, and Mama, my brothers, if only soon.

I always asked if anyone had heard news from Dorchester County, and sat by William Still as he read the slave advertisements in southern newspapers, among them the *Baltimore Sun.* There was never any hint of trouble about my folks, but William found out about some other bondmen who'd been cried for sale, and escaped to Baltimore where they needed to be rescued. I was allowed to go down with another agent by boat to help guide them north.

After my return I felt ready to go back alone. Soon it was summer, and I was ready indeed. I'd got enough money saved to set the old folks up right and help my brothers get started. I'd gained enough knowhow to bring them north safely, Lord willing, and I'd even got my hands on a rifle, knew how to use it too; it was like John's. The only matter I hadn't reasoned out had to do with John himself. I was still partways angry with him, and yet I seemed to miss him even so. Maybe I'd try to find out where he was, but maybe it was best to let things be . . . I put such thoughts aside. The big thing just then was getting back down, and I'd conclude what to do once I got there.

When I told William I was finally going, he leaned both elbows on his thick record book, and frowned. It was dangerous, he warned again. Once I entered a slave state I'd be considered bond, I could be sold back into slavery, I could be caught, killed.

I nodded. He'd told me that before.

He didn't have the right to tell me what to do, he went on, no one did, no one was sending me. But had I given no thought to my personal safety? Had the idea of capture never entered my mind? Was I really willing to risk this freedom I'd struggled so hard to gain?

I nodded again.

And then he laughed out loud, delighted, he said, that he hadn't been able to shake me from my purpose. I believe he was writing my name into his records as I walked out the door.

Never to this day have I forgotten how I felt as I reached the stone marker on the Pennsylvania border, the one I'd touched and wept over when I passed it coming the other way. No tears the second time. I strode across that line defiantly, with a clear head and a cool sense of what I was doing. I wasn't scrambling or hightailing it out of any place, I was deliberately arrowing back down, and no matter what the whites considered me below that border, I would always think of myself as a free woman.

For some reason I wasn't afraid.

◆ ◆ ◆

THE OLD NIGGER boneyard on Doc Thompson's place rose up before me, making a ragged outline against the dark. After a moment I slid under its fence, crept in, and squatted behind the tallest headslab with my rifle in one hand.

I hadn't recollected the place as being that small and overgrown. Many of the grave markers were tilted over, partly hidden amidst weeds and blackberry bushes, so the burying ground appeared more like an untended garden. The death-stench of my earliest memories was gone, and a cool breeze carried the scent of magnolia through the star-seeded April night. There was nothing here to frighten me anymore; in fact it was the safest spot to wait, with no one around excepting the harmless sleepers. My old dread of this boneyard seemed to have quit me at last.

All at once I veered off balance. My knees had gone watery against my will, the rifle trembled in my hands, but it wasn't a childhood terror that caused me to shake. A larger fear had grabbed onto me, abrupt and unexpected. It was the fear of what I was about to begin, and there was one moment when I wanted to run from that graveyard, the plantation, the county, and most especially from this thing I'd been given to do. Kneeling in the weeds, I felt hollowed out and empty of the glorious power that had poured through me earlier that night. All I could do was wait for the Lord to fill me up again as I kept vigil for the first passengers who would follow me north on the Underground Railroad. If only they wouldn't be too afraid to come and come soon, before the time was lost, before this mission could shred away into the dark like the vision that had brought it to me. And if only I could still my lingering grief that these awaited passengers were none of them the kin I had hoped to fetch.

The old folks would not be coming.

I'd met Daddy Ben behind his cabin some hours before, signaling to him with a song, and he stumbled out, groping for me. Lord, how thin and brittle-boned he felt in my arms as he kissed me and touched my face, asking over and over if I was all right. For one chilled instant I feared he'd gone blind, because he had a rag tied around his eyes, but in a whisper he explained. They'd questioned him about me, they'd likely question him again, and, straightspoken as he was, he'd always been a poor liar. This way he could tell the white folks direct and clear he hadn't *seen* me, so they wouldn't be able to sniff a falsehood, suspect something, and call the patrollers out. It wasn't just an old man's foolishness, he insisted, but I think he was also afraid he'd break down weeping at the sight of my face, and such a show of weakness would have been unthinkable to Daddy Ben.

As for going north with me, he wouldn't hear of it, turning stubborn and snappish the harder I pressed him. He and Mama were too old to travel. They'd slow me down, get us all caught. The journey would likely kill them besides. No way. No contradicting. No. He wasn't of a mind to quit his home yet, he said. It was different with me, I was young. At his age he'd only feel to rights in a place he knew, he was too rooted here to be pulled up now, and no, he would not call Mama out, she'd carry on, alarm more than two counties was what she'd do.

It was plain that Daddy was terribly afraid for me. He rattled off that speech quick and breathless like he'd practiced it for such a time as this, all the while tugging at my sleeve, trying to hustle me away from the Quarter. He ended by begging me to get myself north direct where he prayed I'd have the sense to stay put. Then he cleared his throat, held me to him once more, and turned to fumble his way back to the cabin, shaking me off when I tried to help him. Before I could even ask after the rest of the family, he was gone. I knew I couldn't drag him out against his will for other reasons besides his pride, so I just crouched behind his shack for what seemed a long while, my eyes blurred and moist. A half-moon was rising as I slunk off in search of my brothers.

Not a one of them was left on the place. Their cabins were filled with lights and children and folks I didn't know real well. Sick with fear that the boys had been sold off, I hunted up Amos, the old preacher. He told me they'd been hired out for a year at least; Benjie, Robert, and William Henry had been sent down to Fishing Creek only a few days before, and the others were scattered all over the Shore as far south as Bishop's Head, as far east as Sharptown. They were out of my reach just then. The preacher gave me a hasty blessing and a quick shove, urging me to get back out while I could, and with the Lord's help make it safe across the line again. Amos had always been a man of great faith, but from the pressure of his hands on mine and the look in his eyes, I knew he never thought to see me alive another time.

And I was indeed acting reckless. For some moments after he'd gone I stayed behind the Quarter, hunched over, fists in pockets, head bowed, feeling too wilted and dispirited to move. But then I rubbed my hand over my face, stole off the plantation, and before I fully realized what I was about, I was heading by way of the woods for Stewart's place. Heading for John.

Twice on the way I stopped, once I very nearly turned back. This hadn't been a definite part of my plan, and I still hadn't reasoned out for sure if I'd go looking for him even after I'd reached Daddy's cabin. If my folks had joined me I might not have gone to Stewart's at all, though it's hard to say. Even then I wasn't certain how I felt toward John or what I wanted with him, and the Lord only knew how he'd be feeling toward me after a year, but just then it seemed I was driven to find out. No, tempted. Tempted to see him another time, maybe to ask him to go north with me — then again, maybe not. I didn't even know that much for sure as I neared our old home. It was lit and shuttered, though John had likely moved on, and whoever lived there might be able to tell me where he'd gone. Thinking only to whisper a question, I kept to the shadows while I rapped on the door.

The man who opened it a crack was John. Why he was still living in Stewart's Quarter I neither comprehended nor cared about at first, for there was a sudden squeezing in my chest as I gazed on him again. His open shirt showed that nap of hair climbing toward his throat, and the smell of him was close, that smell I'd lain with. But his eyes were glassy, blank; he hadn't recognized me. Firelight had dulled his sight to the darkness, and I was still in the shadows with a broad-brimmed hat pulled low over my face. Moreover I was clad in an oversized man's coat, which concealed both my form and the rifle slung down my back. The coat was covered with burs, likely reeking of the swamps and barns I'd slept in on the way down, and he must have taken me for some tramp as he stood squinting in that sliver of light, making an impatient noise in his throat.

It was really only instants that we stood there so, though it seemed longer, and before I could gather myself to speak the cabin door opened wider behind John. A gal appeared in the amber rectangle with him, a tall, fine-boned gal, tiny about the waist, with hair near as straight as a white woman's, hanging long and loose down her back. She was pulling her dress up over her bare shoulders, and I caught the flash of a marriage band on her finger as the cloth moved up to hide the smooth scoops of her breasts. Her eyes wandered toward me, gentle and questioning.

I spun around and walked off quick. Somewheres behind me boots crunched on the path, then stopped as John's voice asked who was there, but I only quickened my pace, making for the woods. Dimly I heard a door shut but I didn't turn at the sound. I just kept moving, eyes stinging, as I scraped burs from my sleeve, and flung them out against the dark, angered at myself as much as hurt. What had I expected, him waiting there with the quilt turned down for me? And after all my struggles against men who'd owned me, what was I? Just a wench who needed a good bedding to put her to rights? A freed slave who couldn't let go of old times? The prodigal wife wanting her welcome? No, surely not. And him? Well, I should have known better, John Tubman was not a one to let himself starve for long. Besides, I'd done with him long before, else I'd never have left him the first time. I should have known that too.

Black-bodied trees fell away from me as I stepped along the trail through the woods, somewhat stiff-limbed like I'd had a spill, but dry-eyed, lighter in the feet after a while too. I didn't stop till I was back on Doc Thompson's place again, sitting on the bank of Aunt Juba's crik.

For the life of me I couldn't figure out what I was doing there, or why I couldn't seem to quit this plantation I'd fought so hard to escape. The crik's wisewoman was gone; I wasn't able to bring her north any more than I could carry the family I'd come to fetch. Maybe it was just confusion over my blighted plans that had made me seek this water where I'd always found peace, where I could rest for a little time and regain my strength before going back. Suddenly weary, I stretched out on the damp ground, but all at once my head snapped up again. Someone else was near. I didn't know why I hadn't seen him before.

A man sat on the bank a ways downstream from me with a net in his hands, looking to be seining the crik for crabs. Shadowed as he was by the thicket of swamp willow at his back I couldn't see him clear, but took him to be colored, since some folks did come down there, and it wasn't all that late. It appeared like he hadn't noticed me, but even so I decided to stay crouched down till he'd gone off. Feeling oddly loose and easy, I watched him pulling in his catch.

In his net were fish, silver-bodied and gleaming in the moonlight, multitudes of them, flopping wet and living and beautiful as he drew them in. He turned slightly, bending toward the crik. Moonlight caught the tattered, empty hat-brim crowning his head, the stooped shoulders inside the simple coat. And there was that gentle air about him. I remembered then, knew who he was. I'd met him twice before. The peacefulness of his presence lapped around me, and I called out softly. He did not speak though it seemed he smiled, a smile I sensed rather than saw. Then he rose, stood over the radiant water, and gathered in the net till the shining fish were brimming from his arms. I called to him again. Just a whisper of sound came forth, but he must have heard. He nodded to me, and again I sensed his smile before he was gone, treading softly away.

The smell of damp earth was in my nostrils as I lay with one cheek pressed against the bank. Before me the crik ran on under the moon, empty. For a moment my mind was vacant, and I remembered nothing more than a child does upon awakening from a dreamless, safe sleep. I straightened up, expecting to feel chilled clear through to the bone, but my body was warm as new-baked bread, and blood coursed through my veins like heated wine. Then something began coming back. Seen darkly at first. A shred, a strand. An outline. The crik, a clue. All the while the warmth was growing within me, racing, rushing me to my feet, and I rose, spreading arms and legs wide to let the rich feeling of power run to the ends of my flesh.

I understood.

For a moment I knelt at the water, bathing my face. Then I turned and stole back to the Quarter.

Sneaking through the darkness behind the row of cabins, I whispered at a window, crouched through a sagging doorway, and squatted in a shadowed corner beyond the hearthfire's light. I hadn't really thought much about the danger, not then, not yet, not with the flush of the vision still upon me. I spoke with a man who'd just got over the worst beating of his life, I talked with a woman who was being cried for sale, and all the while I held my rifle in plain view like a silent promise of protection. There wasn't time to visit more than two shacks, but that was enough; the word would be passed to anyone else wanting to run. The power and sureness bursting within me must have radiated outwards, for folks sat easy, seemingly unafraid to have a posted fugitive under their roofs.

They comprehended the need for haste without being told, and plans were made fast. They were to bring nothing save what food they could tie up in kerchiefs, and as much clothing as they could put on their backs. They were to come singly, allowing me enough time to get to the meeting place and check it first. They were to go roundabouts, by way of the praise-grove; if there was danger I'd leave a signal, branches turned back in the manner we'd always used when there was the threat of a patrol. Then they would head for the one place white folks were most likely to keep clear of, the one place where slaves would have a decent excuse to be gathering if they got caught: the burying ground.

And so I'd come to stand there, waiting. They'd had more than enough time, nothing had gone amiss, I'd left no warning signals. Maybe they'd changed their minds, maybe they'd run into some trouble I hadn't foreseen, maybe they weren't coming. Maybe I half-wished they wouldn't.

Inwardly empty again, burnt-out where the power had blazed through, I pondered what I was doing. If any of these people got caught or killed it would be on my head. Running off alone had been different; that had been my own risk, my own hide. Now I was risking others, reaching into lives beyond my own, and perhaps it was vain pride, not vision, that had made me think I was worthy or able or knowing enough to save them.

A shadow flickered over the fence, then another. They came one by one like I'd bade them, and they must have passed the word indeed, for there were more than I'd expected; a baby too, bundled so hugely in pale blankets its dark, sleep-creased face seemed small as a raisin. Seven slaves clustered around me so close we were nearly standing on each other's feet, and I could feel a tremor rippling from body to body like wind crossing a lake. As we waited for any more who might be coming, my mind raced through all I'd ever learned about the Underground Railroad. The runaways glanced uneasily from the graves to the rustling dimness beyond the fence, then jolted suddenly, freezing into themselves as some animal thwacked through the brush. Moments passed. A bulky form rose up before us, and I tensed till I saw it was a man I'd spoken with earlier, leading a child. Seconds later another man followed, and a feverish whispering swarmed from the group, the kind of hushed fast chatter folks make in sickrooms. I couldn't afford to hold back much longer; they'd lose nerve and I might too, but then one last shape detached itself from the night, clarifying into the spare outlines of an old woman. The whispering had swelled near out of control, but I stopped it with a sharp hiss. All eyes returned to me, eleven pairs of fear-bright eyes fastened on my face and the rifle resting in the crook of my elbow. I gripped it by the forestock in my left hand, nodded to them, and pressed their cold fingers while I formed the runaways into a line, with the biggest man on the end. Then I moved up to take my place at the front.

"No talk hereon," I said over my shoulder.

I raised the rifle's muzzle high enough for all to see, and gestured with it toward the field beyond the boneyard's northern edge.

We crept off through the dark, and I could feel each one of them at my back, their closeness, their presence rushing forward to enfold me. Warmth poured through my body again, strong and sweet and searing, as I comprehended what I hadn't grasped before, even down by the crik. It was right that this strength should come from the twelve who followed behind me, after all, and I saw it clear. These passengers, who were no part of me by blood or marriage, were kin even so.

These were my people.

It was plain at last. The stirrings I had felt in Philadelphia, the happenings of this night, the vision . . . all those strands came together at once, forming a pattern which suddenly made sense. I had come down for one set of kin only to find another set in those that walked with me now. And if they were kin, then there were others who were the same, waiting unseen to be led out of bondage, and beyond those others there were more. It wasn't a single journey that had commenced in that boneyard; it was as many as the Lord chose to send me on, though how many journeys or how many years of work there would be, I could not know. Nor was it for me to number them.

This, then, was what I had been molded to do, for this had I been given life. All the waiting, the rebellings, the restlessness, the strengthening labor, even the trials and defeats had been preparing me for this time and the times to come. Everything I'd learned from slavery and escaping, from Aunt Juba and my father, from bondfolk and masters and abolitionists alike had been readying me. The mission was clear, it was accepted, and from then on I never worried on the dangers it would bring. Wherever the Lord sends a servant the way is prepared and the paths made straight until the serving is done, and the servant no longer needed. My end was never in my own hands anyways.

For just an instant I thought on John standing in a sliver of light, a half-open door. I wouldn't forget, but I was free of it now. That was finished.

I looked behind me at the figures wading through the dark, knee-high in mist, my passengers, my people.

This was truly begun.

◀▶ ◀▶ ◀▶

I WAS TEN YEARS on the Underground Railroad. Those years stand apart from the rest, like a life within a life, and all my other days seem to cluster around that time of ripeness and mission.

It's still hard for me to speak openly about the Underground, as secrecy became a deep habit with us on the Road, and it was our best means of protection. Big tales and legends were allowed to grow up thick around the real work, and I wouldn't be surprised if the Railroad people started a few of them, hoping to confuse slaveowners and bounty hunters. There's even a legend about how the Railroad got its name, and this is the way I heard it told.

A master was running after an escaped slave, following him close for a good distance and keeping him in sight most of the time. Then the fugitive crossed a narrow stream, vanished all of a sudden, and couldn't be found anywheres on the other side. His baffled owner cussed a streak, and finally burst out, "That nigger must have gone off on an underground road someplace." Still shaking his head, Old Master took himself home, repeating the tale afterwards till it stuck.

Maybe there's some truth to the story, but if it really happened, the runaway must have just dodged into a house where someone hid him pretty quick. And so, Old Master was partly right after all. That slave had indeed gone off on an underground road, and his owner had likely stared straight at it. The sheltering house held a stretch of that road, which zigzagged north through many other dwellings.

I marvel now at my own confusion about the Underground Railroad while I was escaping, looking for tunnels and trains on the way. The only tunnels I've ever seen ran between certain homes and barns, so fugitives could be hustled from one to the other if a search party stormed in. Of course there wasn't any train either, much to my surprise at first. Railroad-talk was a way of speaking in code; it was safer to mention tickets, passengers, conductors, and stations, rather than forged passes, and the names of runaways, friends, hiding places. In fact the real locomotives, what we called the surface lines, were used sparingly and with the greatest caution.

In the beginning, I'd supposed the Underground was run only by white folks, but our people always did a large share of the Railroad's work. I had free Negroes for contacts in Maryland, saw slaves help other slaves off again and again, and up North, in Anti-Slavery Societies and Underground stations I met the great black abolitionists: men like William Still, Robert Purvis, David Ruggles, Stephen Myers, Jarm Loguen, Lewis Hayden, and that giant of them all, Frederick Douglass.

I worked with them. I worked with soft-spoken Quakers and bold-tongued Boston abolitionists and German farmers whose speech I could barely understand at all. I worked with tradespeople, market women, preachers, peddlers, roving barbers and rich benefactors, and I used them. I used everyone who could be trusted to help my passengers with whatever might be given: shelter or supper, money, medicines, blankets, or buggy rides, a pair of spare boots or a piece of information. With the Railroad's people I worked, but it was my own people I was working for, and all the while I felt the Lord working through me, gently using me as an instrument of His will.

I had no real home then, nor did I feel the need for one. All my time was spent in preparing for the raids, working in Cape May's kitchens till I had enough money, and then in the raids themselves. The years were no longer divided up for me according to the seasons, they were ordered by the rhythms of the work; when I would raid, and when I would ready myself for the next one, when I would rest, and when I would recommence once more.

"In such a short time you have transformed forty slaves into men and women," William Still told me, but added, "We are afraid for you. Please. Be more careful."

The reward for me had jumped to five thousand dollars.

I went down again. Forty wasn't enough, nowheres near, that was nothing.

"Dorchester County is being plucked of slaves like a chicken of feathers," said Still the next time I saw him, then frowned at me. "But you seem to have an utter disregard for consequences."

The reward had hit ten thousand dollars.

I went back. There was so much more to be done.

"She is becoming the greatest heroine of our age but she will be burned alive whenever she is caught, which she probably will be, first or last." William passed that opinion along to me from an abolitionist clergyman in Boston, and frowned again.

The reward had gone up to twenty thousand dollars.

I headed south. So many more waited, asking me to come for them the next time.

And I had no intentions of getting myself caught, let alone burned alive. I don't mind saying that I never did have any taste for becoming a martyr, and bother the reward money anyways; there'd always been handbills out for fugitives. I only went where the Lord sent me, though some have smiled to themselves when I said that, and anyways, I was careful. I spent days planning routes and scouting around the plantations I aimed to hit before I ever set foot on them, striking mostly on Saturday nights or holidays. Printers' shops were closed then, reward posters couldn't go up direct, and the patrollers would be away, hunting, wenching, or drunk. And I moved in secret, in disguise, in the dark.

Indeed, my movements were only seen plain by the slaves who waited for me, by William Still who noted my raids in his logbook whenever I came his way, and by the stationkeepers who helped me and sent each other scribbled messages about the fugitives they passed. I always asked to hear these letters read aloud, so that I could fix the words in my memory in case something went wrong. Afterwards, those coded jottings came to stand in my mind as markers for each journey, each length of the Railroad's track I'd traveled, and each step taken deeper into the mission.

Dear Sir:
By tomorrow evening's mail you will receive several volumes of the "Irrepressible Conflict" bound in black. After perusal please forward and oblige.

And it was up past Hurlock, Bethlehem, or Preston, Denton, Bridgetown, going north by east. Templeville past Suddersville, Millington to Warwick, almost to the border, skirting round the towns. Crossing made at Elkton over into Delaware, Marshallton to Brandywine, Wilmington ahead. Moving north in market carts packed beneath potatoes, reeds or greens or onions, sometimes loads of coal. Moving north in buggies, hid in box-bed wagons, wagons with false bottoms, trapdoors, and strong locks. Riding north in coaches, carriages with curtains, sometimes in a trading ship sailing up the bay.

But north mostly by foot.

Below Wilmington, especially. The slave states naturally held the greatest danger, the fewest friends, and the least chance of finding a safe set of wheels. Zigzagging so as to throw off any pursuers, I'd push my passengers on till their freshness and zeal for freedom had drained from them, and even the youngest ones were leaning on sticks, their feet plastered to shoe leather with masses of busted blisters. All the same, we'd have to make a run for cover if patrollers got close, and I'd drug folks' babies with laudanum till the danger passed and we could go on again.

To speak general, we moved by night. Of course that was safer, but it made the traveling hard for the runaways who didn't know the trails as I did, and sometimes during the worst, wearying tramps through dim swamps and blinding woods, one or two would beg me to leave them behind where they'd dropped flat. There were moments, I knew, when the

North seemed unreachable to them, freedom had become just a faded notion, and the only thing that felt real to my passengers was how bad they were hurting. I'd help them along, I'd carry their children, I'd let them rest awhile, but no one got left behind, not ever. Too many secrets could be tortured out of them if they got caught or crept back. But more than that, I wouldn't even think on abandoning a one of them with the freedom I'd promised them still out of reach. Sometimes, when coaxing failed, I prodded folks along with my gun and made one simple threat: "Dead niggers don't tell tales." The fallen passengers always found they were able to get up.

Bless God things hardly ever reached that point. My people had been strengthened by slavery, by their labor, and rough living, and the field hands who made up most of my parties helped the softer house servants.

To be truthful, a few passengers sorely tried my patience — one in especial I recollect well. Others didn't once complain, several seemed to pray their way north, some skylarked with the grumblers. Every escape group — excepting one, the one that went wrong — quickly got the feel of a close-knit family, a family going through hard times together. And because I loved these folks I was often silently wrathful that it had to be such a long walk for them, that I couldn't do my passengers the way Levi Coffin did the slaves he passed through his Cincinnati station.

Levi Coffin is a Quaker, called by some the president of the Underground Railroad. The Lord only knows how many souls went through his hands to freedom, and from what I've heard Mr. Coffin had a way of finding conveyances for his freight like no one else. One worker on his route had a special built three-seated wagon, curtained all around, which could hold ten people, and they say that wagon made runs straight through from Kentucky to Canada. Levi Coffin himself was daring as well as canny. I've been told he once got some twenty-odd fugitives through Cincinnati in daylight one step ahead of the patrollers, by renting a hearse, forming a solemn cortege behind, and cramming the black-plumed carriages full of slaves.

What I wouldn't have given for that special-built wagon

sometimes, or even a hearse to take us out of Maryland, but more often than not we had to tramp out through the swamps and riverbeds, through stifling airless heat that made everything appear to waver and tremble; or out through the trees in the dark, through woods blurred and rustling with rain that turned the ground soggy and soaked clothes against skin.

Things did get somewhat easier, if only for a little while, once we'd made it to Thomas Garrett. I always thanked the Lord for that friend. He was the best connected, boldest stationkeeper I ever met, and I ran about eighty-five fugitives through his stop. Thomas knew that any white could grab Negroes on the roads without free-papers, and he had a number of ways to send us on safely, many of them with wheels attached. Sometimes his friend Hannah Marsh carried us through Chester County in a wagon filled with beans and spinach; Thomas's own carriage or a rented one might make a run for me up to the Mendenhalls' station ten miles away; or he'd get hold of some brick-hauler who'd pack us beneath a load and cart us over the Pennsylvania line to the station kept by the Darlingtons. Even when we went out of Wilmington on foot, at least we went with new shoes from Thomas's shop, and we were often dressed up like working folks, carrying rakes or shovels over our shoulders.

> *My Friend:*
> *Business is arranged for Saturday night. Be on the lookout and if practicable let a carriage come and meet the caravan. I send thee nine bales of black wool bound for the British Lion this time.*

And it was up from Wilmington, Wilmington past Claymont, on through Chester County, Philly, and New Hope; Ohlerstown past Frenchtown, Freemansburg past Easton, Nazareth, and Milford, stop at Sparrow's Bush. Or it was up to Camden, cross the Camden River, find the house in Burlington known as Station A. Station B was Bordentown, leading to New Brunswick, leading to the Raritan, Rahway if it's clear, then to Jersey City, cross the bay by ferry, over to New York. Moving north in hiding, hiding out in belfries, attics, or a coal bank, corncribs or a barn; dodging into privies, woodbins, or a smokehouse, staircase rooms or stables, cupboards, closets, coops.

But hiding mostly out in the open.

Clever sliding panels giving on secret rooms weren't always around when we most needed them, nor were they all that commonplace. Snug, bright-windowed, welcoming houses didn't crop up by magic, one after the other, along the route. Indeed, there were many cozy-looking dwellings that had to be given a wide berth, even in Pennsylvania or Jersey. Kindly stationkeepers, beckoning with lamp in hand, could not be conjured to appear in the middle of a marsh.

Of course I recollect with gratitude the many stations that did shelter my passengers, the warmth, the safe, solid feel of walls around us. But more often I remember groups of folks trying to grab some sleep in scorching summer noontides, with nothing around them but muggy sour air, and swarms of sheep flies rising from a swamp. And other, chillier memories come back clear: runaways clustered on a blue comforter someone had spread on the frozen ground, that cloth appearing like a raft floating on the dark hilly earth, backed by bone-white sycamores; the thin look of a wintry river with dead branches drifting there, and a flash of red, a cardinal watching us from a tree, watching me go off to pilfer food from a barn.

I always signaled when I returned to an escape group after I'd left to hunt or scout or steal, and folks knew not to show themselves unless they heard a certain whistle, or a whippoorwill cry I'd make near water, where such birds never call. Secret signals did play their part on the Railroad, and there were many of them. Certain hymns, such as "Steal Away to Jesus," summoned slaves off plantations. In one northern town the password "William Penn" summoned stationkeepers to their doors, and a hoot owl cry, known as the "river signal," alerted others. But what has always stuck to my soul far more than these signs was the calls and murmurings that passed between me and my passengers as we'd crouch down to rest on the trail.

The runaways might be hunkered down in a dry ditch, covered with pine boughs. Now and then one of them would serve as a lookout, but more often than not I chose to keep watch myself, huddled up with my gun at hand, trying to stay awake. Sometimes they would commence the talk, sometimes it would be me.

"Cold?"

"Uh-*huh.*"

"Crowd together more then."

"Mercy, you know how cold it is?"

"Say how."

"Cold enough to make me conclude it ain't safe to take a shit even. I'd freeze more'n my ass off."

Soft laughter.

"Sweet Heaven, then hold it in, Clem. Wouldn't risk them jewels you got if I was you."

More laughter, fading into silence. Then the wispy voice of a child wavering toward me.

"We safe?"

"For sure."

"You put the baby's nose in the stink-rag again?"

"Baby's asleep natural now. The laudanum's just for bad times."

"This ain't a bad time?"

"No, honey. This a good time."

"Safe?"

"Sleep now."

"Cold."

Or sometimes after a panicky run through some woods, splashing across a stream, flopped down on the other side, they'd start it.

"Them nigger-catchers seen us, know they done."

"Didn't see nothin. Hush. Keep down."

"Lord God, we treed for sure. They musta heard us."

"Couldn't hear nothin but their own horses. Rode by too fast."

"Them dogs trained to chew us to pieces, that's a fact."

"They didn't have no dogs, now hush."

"This child's peed his pants. Scared out his head."

"Scare him more if you don't hush."

"It over?"

"Bless God yes. They way up ahead now."

"We got nowheres to go then."

"We backtrack is all. Just a short while."

"Then north again?"

"Soon. We all to rights, praise Jesus for that."

"Appears like He still got His eye peeled to us."

"Always. No more danger for now."

But the danger never did let up, even as we moved farther and farther north.

Dear Sir:
Uncle Tom says if the roads are not too bad you can look for those fleeces of wool by tomorrow. Send them on . . . no back charges.

And it was up the Hudson River, stowed aboard a vessel, otherwise the land route, slower, safer still. Up from Tarrytown, Ossining, and Peekskill, on past Kingston, Albany, and west. Schenectady past Amsterdam, Utica, Oneida, on through Syracuse, Auburn, almost there. Stop with Frederick Douglass, Rochester his station, shoving off for Shelby, onward toward the Falls.

Niagara Falls was the last door, the last stop.

Soon after I'd started to work the Railroad, Congress and President Fillmore had sold their souls to the Devil by passing and signing the Fugitive Slave Act, which said that runaways found in the North were still their master's property, and could be seized and returned, all neat and legal. Slavecatchers looking to win a bounty began sneaking around all over the free states thicker than ever, spying on colored folks, grabbing at some who'd lived there from birth. Vigilance Committees sprouted from the Anti-Slavery Societies, and abolitionist mobs stormed jails where recaptured fugitives were held.

Two bold rescues were made, a third one failed and a frightened boy named Thomas Sims was sent back from Boston to Georgia where, I heard, he was badly beaten before a cheering crowd. He was only the first to be taken. Free Negroes choked the roads with cartloads of belongings; in some places whole communities picked up and moved, heading for the surer safety of Canada.

I tried to ignore this new law for as long as I was able.

There'd been bounty hunters in the North before this, kidnapped colored folk too, and besides I just hadn't wanted to believe that our country would do this to us. But after a time of obstinacy, rage, and finally bitterness, I'd comprehended that Uncle Sam couldn't be trusted with my people. This blow didn't stop my work, however. I never even thought about giving up the mission which had only just commenced. Nothing had changed, excepting that the Promised Land was farther away, colder, and British-ruled.

Dear Sir:
I understand you are a friend to the poor and are willing to obey the heavenly mandate, "Hide the outcasts, betray him not that wandereth." I understand also that you are in shipping. I would be glad to know what are the prospects if any of exporting a perishable cargo of poor goods.

And it was down through Buffalo, Fredonia, and Westfield, down the Allegheny, moving south once more. East from Pittsburgh, Harrisburg to Reading, down through Philadelphia, Wilmington, below. South through Delaware, south through Maryland, back along the Choptank and the Eastern Shore.

Often by foot.

Often out in the open.

Always seeking to free more of my people.

◆◆ ◆◆ ◆◆

NINETEEN TIMES I went South for my people. By the grace of God I was able to deliver roundabouts three hundred souls in all, and somewheres along the way I came to be called Moses.

Tales spread about this Moses in the Quarters and the Big Houses of Maryland, tales that grew and built so big I was barely able to recognize myself within them. It was said that this Moses could part waters, lick five patrollers barehanded, and bound through impassable woods like a deer. Moses had sight sharper than a hunting owl's, scented out nigger-dogs or slavecatchers two counties away, and spoke with the Lord's angels while in a mysterious trance. According to the legend, this tall strapping raider stalked the Eastern Shore as invisible as the night itself, and was thought to be a man at first, had to be; no woman could steal slaves right out from under their owners, no wench could lead bands of grown men. It was even thought for a time that Moses might be two or three people going under the same name, each of them armed with hatchets, swords, and rifles.

I'm still not sure how all this got started.

Maybe the stories grew because the planters at first refused to believe that an ordinary Negro was making off with their slaves, and it was even harder for them to understand why they couldn't seem to do anything about it. Maybe the folks in the Quarters wanted to have a legend to tell their children about, and tales spun by hearthfires can always do with a little embroidering. Or maybe the stories centered on me because other so-called abductors were scarce. Even the abolitionists didn't like to mess around with those sort of doings, which could be considered kidnapping, or the violation of states' rights. Agents might come down to help fugitives along the way, but I was a conductor who struck directly at plantations. There were a few others like myself that I'd heard about, a colored man who hung about the Virginia Tidewater for a while, a white man who worked Levi Coffin's route for some years, and a Negro in Ohio who got caught and was hurt bad. But these men, brave and beloved of the Lord as they were, did not appear to the bondfolk of Maryland, who had likely never heard of them. The slaves on the Eastern Shore had only heard of me, and for those who didn't want to risk running off alone, I was the one they could find in the way of a guide.

Some of the legend's roots are clear enough though, for all its extra trimmings. I surely never bounded anywheres like a deer, let alone amidst thick trees. Scrambled, yes. Feeling my way was often more like it. But I did get through deep woods with the guidance of the stars, the sun and shadows, and a pocket compass I began to carry later on. If my sight or hearing seemed keener than other folks' it was because all of my senses were forever tuned to danger signals, and of course those mysterious trances were only my sleeping fits; they were a help as well as a hazard, for sometimes during those spells I heard most clearly the voices that had been sent me from childhood. I never took on five patrollers barehanded, nor would I have tried to, though I did smash one overseer's jaw with the butt on my rifle when he got in my way at the commencement of a raid. Over the years I had to do a few patrollers the same way when they got too close; the sound of a shot would have only brought down more trouble, and I'm afraid that's what kept me from killing them, rather than the Lord's commandment. As for being invisible, I took great pains over remaining so, and as for those tales of parting waters, I just knew where the shallows were in rivers we had to cross.

There was nothing miraculous about what I did, but still, the Moses legend served me well in many ways. In the earliest years of the mission it protected me somewhat, for then the slaveowners lacked a clear description to put on their reward posters, and the slavecatchers didn't know for sure just who they were hunting. Not knowing has a way of scaring people, too. The planters might have believed this raider would steal into their bedchambers and slice their throats, and I relished their fear, which begot confusion. Frederick Douglass felt as I did, although he was never a conductor himself. He said that each master should be left to imagine himself surrounded by myriads of invisible tormentors; let him feel his way in the dark, and let him fear that with every step he took in pursuit of flying bondmen he ran the frightful risk of having his brains dashed out by some invisible agency.

Too bad things couldn't stay like that.

But even after the planters had managed to tie Moses with Doc Thompson's runaway Harriet, I still got use out of the legend. It spread through the Shore's grapevine telegraph, alerting bondfolk to my arrivals and drawing them near, which helped me round up escape parties quicker. Speaking of Moses was fairly safe too, if it was done in a reverent manner; masters were used to their slaves' Scripture talk, and those slaves could make it hard for a white man to figure out if they were discussing the Prophet or the raider. But most of all, my code name gave me one of the best ways I knew to contact my people without endangering either them or myself. I used a certain signal-song to warn folks that I was closeby again, blending my voice with theirs as they sang over their work or lulled sleepless children. Sometimes I'd commence the melody out back of the Quarters, or while I was crouched behind a stand of trees edging a wood lot, or as I hunched down in the brush that fringed a field. And always the warning song was the same:

Who's that yonder dressed in red?
I heard the angels singing.

A cabin might grow hushed of a sudden. A footstep might pause on the path.

Looks like the children that Moses led.
I heard the angels singing.

A head might lift over a hoe, a broadax might hang in midair for an instant.

And then in the nights as I scouted about, taking in the lay of a plantation, I might overhear a few words, a murmur, a stirring in the Quarters that would let me know the signal had got through, and those who wanted to travel were making ready.

The slaves mostly knew who I was, despite the yarn-spinning. Few appeared troubled that it wasn't a strapping man who waited on them in boneyards, marshes, or fodder houses, just the short ox-built woman I was, with no resemblance to a prophet of any kind, for sure. They joined up, followed, and trusted simply because it was known that I'd never run my train off the track or lost a passenger. Still, I believe the legend did rub off a little, and it helped folks to keep faith in me, especially strangers from other counties who might have expected a more awesome conductor. Just as well it rubbed off. There were many moments when blind faith was needed.

Orders had to be given on those escape journeys, strict ones, with no time for explaining much and, excepting for one raid, these orders were followed with very little quibbling. There could be only one leader on those ventures through enemy territory, and even the men who towered over me seemed to accept my leadership. It was when I took a sleeping fit that they showed the full measure of their trust, gathering around my splayed body in a protecting circle until I got up again. Only one runaway ever moved toward the weapon in my hand.

It was my passengers' trust that turned each raid into an escape. If I was Moses, it was my people who made me so: my people who had reasoned their minds out for freedom and had cast aside everything they'd been taught to believe about themselves.

The planters often said niggers were naturally stupid, God made them that way was all.

A white Mississippi man named Cartwright, calling himself a doctor and hailed as a scientist, worked up a theory that blacks ran away on account of a certain mental disease called drapetomania, common to Negroes and to cats. Cartwright also believed he'd discovered some proof that the Negro brain froze in cold climates, causing insanity, and he therefore insisted that out of kindness to darkies, they should be kept in the South.

Most whites didn't go quite that far, but created their own notions about darky dumbness. I don't know how many times I've heard it said that niggers are so slow-witted they can't stay awake as long as whites, that niggers are too lazy to be smart, that it takes two niggers to help one to do nothing. And of course our owners tried to keep us as ignorant as they wished us to be. Some planters taught their slaves to read, but not all that many. Several masters taught their bondfolk other things however, like that old catechism of my childhood, and some very strange facts about the North, where horned abolitionists were supposed to feed upon black flesh, which they considered a delicacy. A number of slaves were also told that Canada was across an ocean, Pennsylvania was a barren land beyond an impassable river, and one freedman told me he never did know if Boston was a city or a state till he got there.

But despite this mind-twisting and the lack of book-learning, despite that image of niggerness many whites held up for us, thousands of my people ran away, and they were smart about it too. I saw that in the three hundred folks I rescued, and heard about others.

A slave named Henry Brown boxed himself up in a crate, had it addressed for Philadelphia by a friend who could write, and arranged to be shipped from Richmond to freedom by the Adams Express; William Still had been there when the package was opened in the Anti-Slavery Office. Ellen and William Craft certainly used wits just as keen when they made their famed flight from Georgia, and I met other runaways who were very canny about their escapes too, though they were lesser known.

Some of my passengers traveled the roads or crossed counties to reach me, and several came in such well-done disguises I didn't know what to make of those folks rightoff. There was a man who wore a loose shift over his own clothes and a wig he'd created out of a horse's mane; there was a woman who arrived in a suit of men's clothing, with a false beard covering most of her face. Others came with stolen town passes in their pockets and hoes over their shoulders, pretending to be hired hands on their way to jobs. One couple had thrown the nigger-dogs off their track by burrowing into graves deep enough to kill their scent. Some came with passes they'd forged themselves; those were the ones who had learned to read and write on the sly, while apprenticed to craftspeople in towns. I carried passengers who were as well schooled in the healing arts as Aunt Juba had been, and several who were as wise about woodlore as my daddy. But a great number came without any arts at all, without disguises, learning, or skills, and it is to them that I give the greatest accounting for brains. Those folks, who'd never read a book, never seen a map, or gained any new ideas from the free Negroes of the cities, had still concluded to get themselves out.

And yet the planters said niggers were naturally stupid.

The planters often said, too, niggers were naturally docile, God made them that way was all.

Most masters believed their darkies were content in bondage, and needed to be taken care of; slaves were considered a burden and a duty to their white fathers and mothers. And the masters had proof of this, they thought. After all, slaves were always singing, meaning they were content. Slaves hardly ever killed themselves, also meaning they were content, and they meekly hemmed-and-hawed when they had to address white folks, always staring at Master's boots.

The planters didn't labor, we did, so maybe they didn't know that all kinds of folks seem to sing while they work, to pass the time or keep the pace. Frederick Douglass believes that slaves sang to ease their minds. I believe my mother trilled in the fields to distract herself from the dullness of her toil. And our parties were hardly celebrations of slavery; those dances simply helped us to forget we were bondfolk for a while.

Maybe we didn't kill ourselves out of respect for the life given us by the Lord, and I figure it to be a sign of strength that we chose to live through the rough times. And as for that notion we needed the whites' care? We all helped take care of one another so much, I believe that's another reason why we didn't blow ourselves out; we needed each other. Docile? The planters always did fall for that act when we put it on. Bootlicking was indeed one way to get by, and often enough when I'd mumbled at Master's boots, I was either scared with plain good reason to be, or I was hiding a mighty rage.

My passengers carried plenty of rage with them too, not natural meekness. More than one had set fire to a barn or storehouse before they'd concluded to haul out for good. Some crept to me out of the woods where they'd hidden out and lived by their wits for months, even years, in a kind of halfway escape, and when they surfaced to join my parties, they were matted with leaves and burs, as wild-eyed as John the Baptist. I've heard of a slave who tied himself to the underside of a night train, and by that bold act got himself free in a hurry. One runaway got loose by ripping a wooden gate off its post, and used it to float himself down a rapid-moving river. I've been told about a whole group of bondfolk that escaped during a hard winter by tucking themselves into a stolen sleigh, which they later tore up to make a bridge over a stream. There was also the fugitive who was stopped by a patroller, and cut that white man down with a scythe; many others ran off armed with cleavers, meat hooks, hunting knives, or pitchforks. But again, it was the passengers who came to me unarmed, trembling, bearing only rabbit-foot charms for protection, that I counted the bravest. For they too had concluded to take what was maybe the biggest risk of their lives.

And yet the planters still said niggers were naturally docile and stupid, God made them that way.

The same was said of me after I began speaking at abolitionist meetings in Boston, between raids. I was told how the proslavery men felt about my lecturing, one writer named Robinson in especial.

Those who listened to me were traitors, he stated, traitors who were shouting about a poor, weak-minded Negro woman. The South had lost over fifty thousand dollars' worth of property to that deluded Negress, and he demanded why large congregations of whites and well-educated people would endorse such an imposition on the constitutional rights of the slave states.

Such congregations of well-educated whites in Boston would have laughed Cartwright and Robinson out of their halls. Those blazing-tongued, nasal-toned New Englanders held that slavery violated God's Higher Law, and they'd been fighting for my people's freedom while I was still a little nursemaid in my old master's Big House. They stood up for us, they supported my work, and backing them were the black abolitionists who helped hire halls for rallies, gave money to William Lloyd Garrison for his radical sheet called *The Liberator,* and, it is said, held up Garrison's right arm. And so, whenever I had the chance, I addressed these friends, many of whom I'd met on the Underground Railroad. I spoke on behalf of my brethren still bound in the South, and I also began speaking out for my sisters everywhere, for Women's Suffrage. Sometimes I just sat back and listened to my tall, bespectacled, fine-spoken friend Sojourner Truth, the earliest black female lecturer in the country, who talked up straight and stirring for both causes far better than I ever could.

I remember the first time I sat on the speakers' platform in Melodeon Hall. It was like a camp meeting in there, all manner of carrying on and commotion, speakers standing up, stopping in midsentence till some hecklers in the back left off booing, people shouting others down. The air was flying with tomatoes, rotten eggs, and spitballs fired from other hecklers who'd climbed into the windows, yelling catcalls and profanity.

Faces swam before me, William Lloyd Garrison, Frederick Douglass, dandily dressed Wendell Phillips, all those well-known men other people have written or told about. I remember trying to tie what I knew with some of those faces. Thomas Wentworth Higginson, that muscular youngish man, was a Unitarian minister who'd preached himself right out of his pulpit for the cause; I'd heard that somewheres. That balding man beside him was another preacher, Theodore Parker, said to be brilliant, dedicated; I might have met him at the Alcotts', or maybe it was the Emersons' home. And there was Gerrit Smith, rich as Solomon and more than generous to the movement; I'd sheltered fugitives in his Peterboro station. But before I could nod to him, someone had stood up in front of Smith's chair and the crowd shuffled together. Only Garrison seemed to stand out plain, appearing to enjoy himself thoroughly. He'd been in this a long time, had fought proslavery mobs in the streets, and had been jailed at least once for his own safety. His eyes glimmered up at me from behind his specs, and around him was a group of colored folks who'd come to watch and listen. I found myself focusing on them, as someone nudged me to my feet.

"I came up like a neglected weed," I began, "ignorant of liberty, with no notion it was meant for me. I wasn't happy or contented, and every time I saw a white man I feared I'd be carried away. And don't you believe me to be the only one who's felt so. I never seen one escaped slave who wanted to go back and be a slave again, not one amongst hundreds."

Someone threw a tomato at me, a freckle-faced, coppery-haired heckler who was perched in a windowsill. I picked up the mush, sprayed it back in the general direction it came from, and the hall rocked with cheers.

"I think slavery's the next thing to hell. There's folks say it's real easy on us, safe, there's folks always will say so, but you know different, you my friends. Mrs. Stowe's book just been read to me, and I tell you, even her pen can't begin to paint what slavery's truly like. Now I hear they made *Uncle Tom's Cabin* into a play. Well I don't want to go see my people's tribulations acted out on some stage, not after I lived through real bondage, not after what I see each time I go back south. Best we work against the live evil, not watch it play-acted, best we work till one day the slaveowners got to give up. My people must go free, the Lord ordained it."

Cheers again, stomping feet, then a commotion on the floor.

"What's fair compensation for a slaveholder?" someone called.

"The state prison!" Another man, on his feet, overturning a chair.

"Sir, you must address this question seriously. I favor abolition myself, but just compensation is due . . ."

He was booed down.

"Send the niggers back to Africa for gold!" The window-percher again, screaming, red in the face, near out of control. He fired a volley of spitballs at me.

I fired one of them back, hard.

"Too late for that," I shouted over the noise, and at last the hall quieted some. "My people must go free. Here's where they must. The white folks carted us here to do their drudgery and now some say to send us back, even got a place picked out called Liberia. Well they can't do it, we rooted here and we can't be pulled up, we rooted deep as anyone else who came over the seas to Uncle Sam, and that'd be everybody in this land, North and South. And who mostly built that South? Us. Was mostly our hands that pushed back the trees and made things to grow and raised up fine mansions. Our hands. Negro hands, that's right. My people belong to this land, gave to this land, and in this land my people must go free."

And I sat down. Amidst the applause another speaker stepped to the rostrum, the Reverend Higginson, I think it was. He was saying how much I'd done for my people, how many I'd liberated, again calling me the greatest heroine of the age . . . I stopped listening and turned inward.

There I was, the woman they called Moses, at the height of my powers, with more bondfolk waiting on me, others already saved, and this white man numbering my raids and rescues. But whatever else I'd done these past five years I still hadn't been able to free four people I dearly loved.

◆◆ ◆◆ ◆◆

BY THE MID-FIFTIES I'd brought off all my own family excepting for my parents and two of my brothers. I longed to see the old folks living out the rest of their time in freedom, I missed them, but all the same they weren't a great cause for worry. At their age it was most unlikely they'd be sold since they wouldn't be worth enough on the market. Besides which Daddy was stubborn; I'd seen him on and off since my first raid, and he'd always refused to come away. It pained me to leave him and Mama there, but at least I felt certain they were safe.

I couldn't say the same for that last pair of brothers remaining in bondage. Benjie and Robert weren't so young anymore, but they were still prime, and they still could be sold. They were a great worry indeed, especially because I couldn't seem to find them. Whenever I went down I asked after the boys, tried to hunt them up, and always it was the same. They'd been hired out. Maybe down to Cedar Creek. Maybe over to the Somerset County line. Maybe Benjie was one place, Robert somewheres else, those two were always moving around. No one knew for certain. Robert's wife Elvina has passed in childbed, Benjie didn't have a steady woman who waited on him. Even Daddy wasn't clear on where they were half the time.

Finally I concluded to make a special Christmas journey for them. Hired hands mostly got the better part of holiday week off so they could visit distant kinfolk, and my brothers would likely come home to Doc Thompson's then. I planned to wait for them near Daddy's cabin, only I'd have to get word to my brothers somehow, making sure they'd pay that Yuletide visit, warning them to keep low, to wait, not to show themselves. It would have to be done with care so as not to put the old folks in danger; it would take planning, and in the midst of that planning a message came to me from William Still. Benjie and Robert were being advertised, they'd be cried at auction soon after New Year's.

It was the night before Thanksgiving when the note came, I remember that. Boston reeked of turkey and baking, the streets were slick, a flutter of snow was in the air, and the Anti-Slavery Office was almost empty. I was there with the colored man who often read me correspondence or penned my replies, and I'm afraid I kept him up half the night helping me work out a letter we sent down to Maryland. Anything in writing was risky; the note had to be coded and it couldn't carry my name, even though it was going to Jacob Jackson. He of all people would know what to make of that odd-sounding message, purposefully odd because he surely wouldn't be the first to see it.

Jacob was a free Negro who plied his cooper's trade a little ways from Bucktown. He did well enough for himself by underselling the white cooper in Cambridge and by lettering signboards now and then, since he could read and write. He'd moved in near my old home around the same time that I'd commenced running slaves, and I used say the Lord must have put him there for me. Jacob was one of my best contacts, canny, shrewd, a good friend too, and when I arrived outside his cabin late that Christmas Eve it seemed he was ready.

He'd hung some washing out on his porch, and by the glow from his hearth within I could see a red kerchief tied off to one side, already stiffening with frost. All right then, no danger about, that was Jacob's ordinary signal. I whistled to let him know I was back, then went to a clearing in the woods beyond —an old cutting-lot littered with stumps and piles of rubble where two figures could blend in easy enough. Stamping my feet against the cold, I poked about there in the dark, waiting on Jacob. He never came out direct, leaving some time between the signal and the meeting, to make sure he wasn't followed; in the meanwhiles I was safe enough in the lot despite the skull-like full moon carved into the hard wintry sky. It was unlikely anyone would pass that way, but if so I might have been taken for a short-statured man gathering up kindling, clothed like I was in trousers, a big coat, and a wide-brimmed hat. There was no cumbersome rifle to stick out anywheres; I'd switched to a Colt revolver, which was strapped in my waistband, and my hand only moved toward the pistol from habit when I heard footsteps. I knew Jacob's stride, and a moment later I spotted him, along with a boy he'd brought to stand lookout.

They paused nearby, and as Jacob spoke to the child I could see his breath hanging on the air. Amidst the whispering I caught the word *Moses*, and the boy cast a white-eyed glance in my direction. He edged toward me, reached out one finger, touched my coat quick like it might burn him, and bounded back to the lot's edge where he stood shivering.

Jacob's boots crunched toward me over the brittle ground, and as the steely moonlight caught him I saw he was grinning.

"Boy's scared shitless," he said. "Guess he got to touch you all the same just to say he done it, what with all the stories he heard on Moses. Never mind, he sure to stay fixed there. I told him you was able to cast spells on patrollers so's to freeze em stock-still, and boychildren best not run from you, else they freeze up too."

"Sweet Heaven, Jacob, spells! Well? The letter, you get it safe? Able to make it out?"

"Comprehended rightoff it was from you and what you was after, who else'd write me so oddlike? All's fixed, got word to the boys easy enough. Said for em to wait in that old toolshed on Thompson's place, figured that was safest to stash em in, it ain't used for much but storage now. Be here before first light tomorrow mornin if they walk lively tonight."

"Bless you. Figure you wasn't the only one to read that letter."

"Uh-uh. Post clerk and some others gone over it fine by the time they called me in. Wanted me to tell em what it meant, huh, turned out I wasn't much help somehow."

"They make you trouble?"

"Shit, no."

Jacob rocked back on his heels, spat, smiled, and crouched down on his haunches. He was small-built, wiry, and carried a few scars from his youth, when he was known to have been a real scrapper. A shiny stretch of bare skin split his whitening beard down the center, but there were no new markings on him, he was all right. In fact he appeared very much pleased with himself as he commenced to tell what had happened.

"Always pleasured me how I could put on the whites so good, well I never done a better job on em than in that post office. They was all hot in the pants, likely they believed they was on to some scent — folks been pretty nerved up and notional since you run off that last big bunch. Well, they paced up and down, farted around, huffed and puffed while I read that letter, and I took my time over it, moved my lips real slow, even though I got what you meant first thing. You shoulda heard em, all jumpy, killed em they couldn't make that letter out, oh they did go on. 'What this here mean, boy? What it mean *give my love to the old folks*, you got old folks, boy?' 'Nawsuh,' I says. Comprehended you wanted me to tell Ben from that, so I just played dumb while they got ruffled over the next part. 'What you think this here mean, boy, *tell my brothers to be always watching unto prayer so that when the good old ship Zion comes along they're ready to step on board*, well what that mean?' Course it couldnta been plainer, but I just scratched the old wool, you know the action, said I couldn't figure it, the letter couldn't be for me, never heard on a W. H. Jackson what signed the letter. They don't know I got a son in the North what can't spell even, but you and me just talked on him last time you was here. In the end they looked real busted cause they wasn't able to find nothin out, scrunched up together near the stove, broke out a bottle. Appeared like they forgot I was still there, so I ambled out slow as you please, and Lord, they even forgot to take the letter offa me. I burned it first thing."

"Owe you, Jacob, owe you plenty."

"Don't owe me nothin, what else I got to liven up my old age with? Spect you want me to rip down the reward posters soon's they go up, like before?"

"Yeah, and burn em too. And Jacob . . ." I took a breath. "You ain't said how the old folks been, they all right?"

"Appear just fine. Now that Thompson's got em partways retired they able to take it easier. Course Ben was real unsettled when he heard that sale talk, kept it from Old Rit, but once I said you was on the way he smoothed right down again. Meant to ask, how'd you know to come fetch the boys this time outa times?"

"Friend in Philly. He read the bids in the papers, told me. Sorry, no witchery to it atall."

"Well, that surely will leave the children down, they come to hear me tell stories sometimes. Guess I just have to spin one up." Jacob allowed his voice to rise just a bit. " 'Yes, children, I seen Moses and Moses come on accounta she seen a vision. Angels fluttered down all over Moses' bed in the night and they show her folks in chains, and then a big lightnin bolt come and hit the bed, burned up the mattress, and Moses know what she got to do.' "

"Get out the bed pretty quick, I'd say. Go on with you, man, look what you done."

The trembly boychild had edged up closer just in time to hear that last part, and a trickling sound had commenced of a sudden. He'd peed down one leg, then jumped back from the puddle, likely believing he was in the presence of some power-struck conjure woman.

Jacob laughed, collected the child, and turned to me once more.

"You welcome to get warm first at my place . . ."

"Kindly, Jacob, but it ain't safe. Got to get a move on anyways," I said. We went through this every time.

"Ain't you able to hold still one minute now you comprehend all's to rights?"

"Not till I see the boys in that toolshed . . . God bless . . . take care now . . ."

Before dawn my brothers were there as Jacob had promised. They were crammed in with five others, amidst heaps of old sacks and coiled rope, broken plow-handles, and an old pair of chaise wheels. At first I saw all this only dimly, at first it was just Benjie and Robert who loomed up clear, close, in my arms, shouting in whispers, Benjie and Robert and me together again.

"How many years it been, lose count. Hat, I do believe you got shorter. Bless you, somehow Robert and me we took a notion you'd come."

"Looked up and down for you both time upon time . . . Mercy, you still able to pick me up like I was only small."

"We meant to run off anyways, but didn't know just how to go. Likely you been up and down so much you able to sleepwalk it, well that's what they say."

"Not hardly. Put me down, let me look on you. Robert, you commenced to go gray there, and there, and . . ."

"Baby sister got herself a pistol!"

"Oh Benjie, man, good to . . . look at me, almost got the weeps."

"These all my friends from where I was hired, yeah, they caught the freedom-feel when they heard."

"Always glad to carry more passengers, but we best hush up now."

"Hat, you certain nobody won't sniff us out here?"

"Nobody but Daddy, Jacob told him where we'd be hid. Place ain't been touched for a good while, you can tell just from the look to it. Doubt a soul come near today, what with Christmas and all. Get some rest now. I can keep watch."

They were all sleeping as a chill, reddish dawn filtered through the cracks in the shed's wall. Before the plantation commenced to stir Daddy was there, bringing ashcake and salted meat, wearing his blindfold again.

"They all right?" He whispered after I'd pressed him to me and guided his fingers over his sons' faces.

"Just wore out, they had to walk a long ways. Bless God they didn't hit snow. You figure the weather's bound to hold?"

"Long enough. When you set to move?"

"Tonight. Where's Mama?"

"Still asleep. Didn't tell her nothin, and don't you make no sign to her neither. She'd carry on, give it away. You be safe here today, I got my eye on the shed, but almost no need. Overseer's away, he got kin to visit, and besides you know the

Christmas Day fuss. Marse Doc be busy with his house guests, and we got two hogs down here for our jubilee. No need to wake the boys yet, the whole Quarter do that soon."

Before long I knew we'd be hearing folks scrambling for the privy, then hustling to get scrubbed and decked out. There'd be a hush while everyone was up the Big House for prayers and presents, and then the partying would commence, up the hill and down in the Quarter. It would go late into the night.

". . . mean to come back and see you off, speak to em then," Daddy was saying as he rose, started to go.

His hand floated blindly on the air, searching out Benjie's sleeping face once more, and of a sudden I grabbed his fingers.

"Lord's sake, Daddy, listen to me now, you and Mama come too. I maybe could get you a mule to ride on, a horse, could even put you on the steam-cars. Leastways take that rag off your face."

"Hush, you bound to wake em all."

Ben felt his way out of the shed and whispered to me through a wall chink.

"Honey, we been over and over this. They come around each time Moses hit the county, they ask questions and I always been able to say I ain't seen you, able to look em straight and say it, they believe me."

"Told you, don't know how often now, if you'd come away you wouldn't need to do like that, there'd be no more questions. Why on earth can't you reason it out to leave? When the boys gone off tonight what's left to hold you and Mama?"

"Child, child, my home's here, don't you comprehend yet? Whole Quarter's like to kin, always been. That cabin there, built it myself one log-rollin time before your mama and me ever even made Robert. Recollect one night the chimney caught fire, Rit and me got up, moved it away from the shack, saved it. That cabin's my place, so's the woods, the woods is home too. Maybe I don't own it legal, but this all feels to be mine, ours. I lasted out five, six masters, and I got no intents to die in some strange place." He turned, put his hands out, and felt his way back.

All that day I watched him. Ben still held himself straight

and appeared fit enough, but he moved slow as he gathered in kindling or toted water. Daddy seemed a smaller man all of a sudden, his flesh sunk down closer to the bones, muscles slack. I don't know why this surprised me, or why I'd never expected him to age. Maybe you never do with your folks. Maybe I'd just never had a chance to study him that long for a good while. He must have been into his seventies then.

It was hard watching my father, knowing we couldn't venture out to speak with him; it was even harder watching my mother since we couldn't even let her know we were there. Old Rit was looking out for the boys. She kept coming out of the cabin to stand on the frost-stiffened path, gazing southward, shielding her eyes with her hand from the spikes of wintry sunlight. There was a smell of roasting goose on the air; she'd likely fattened it all year for this time, for her sons, and she was wearing her best clothes. I hadn't seen Mama since I'd escaped, and in the meanwhiles I'd remembered her like she'd been out in the fields when I was a child, a younger mother, giggly, pretty. This wasn't the same woman. Rit appeared to have dwindled, the body stringy, the clothes hanging loose, chest flat, face oddly hard, almost bitter. No one had told her that the boys wouldn't be making their visit, but I think somehow she knew.

That was one of the longest days I'd ever passed on the Railroad, and I blessed the darkness when it came down around us at last. There was music and jubilee-beating in the Quarter, music up the hill as well. The plantation had faded into vaguer outlines, Old Rit had gone inside. It was time to go.

Daddy walked a short ways off the place with us. He'd still insisted on that blindfold of his, so I had him by one arm and Robert had him by the other. When we stopped to say goodbye Daddy Ben gathered us to him all at once. He'd wait till he lost sound of us, he said, then he'd go home without the rag over his eyes . . . no, he did not mean to trip over nothin, go on now, God bless, well go on.

We left him standing on the edge of a field with that piece of cloth over his face, pressing his palms together, his feet spread apart and firmly planted, stubborn and proud as ever in his bondage, in his old age.

I remembered him often as he looked there, even after I'd got Benjie and Robert and the others safely to Canada, settling the boys in St. Catharines where I'd taken the rest of my brothers. I saw my parents in the faces of aged fugitives I carried on following raids, saw them in crowds, in bare air, and thought of them at abolitionist meetings when I spoke on the others I'd rescued.

It seemed there'd be no peace for me until I'd got the old folks out. My nights thrashed with vivid dreams, leaving me limp afterwards, scalded with drenching sweats. There was something wrong; these were more than common nightmares, more than ordinary worry. Some warning loomed up in those restless sleeps. No voices. Just blazing images, urgent ones, and I trusted the sign unquestioningly though I didn't fully comprehend it. Aunt Juba might have been able to explain the premonition to me; Thomas Garrett later understood, for he believes such things are the workings of the Holy Spirit.

Whatever. I didn't care just then who'd understand and who wouldn't. Somehow I knew I must hurry. There wasn't time to trouble over disguises or keeping my cover, so I appeared openly in depots and steam-cars. There wasn't time to work till I'd raised the money I needed either, and I rushed into the New York City Anti-Slavery Society with a single clear intention: to beg. Ordinarily I'd have been shamed by doing suchlike, but again there wasn't time for shame, or for arguments with a pale, young arrogant clerk who flat-out told me to leave. I couldn't just walk in and demand twenty dollars, he said, who did I think I was? He must have been new; I'd never seen him before, and the main men of that Society were off lecturing. I just planted myself in the doorway like workmen I'd seen out on strike, and announced I'd sit there without taking food or drink till I got the funds I'd come for.

After a while the clerk let me alone, likely believing I was some poor half-cracked darky with no place else to go. People began trailing in and out of the office. I made sure they noticed me, and by midafternoon I'd gathered enough contributions to get me going again; a wild-eyed Methodist missionizer had even thrust some kind of holy tract into my hand along with a coin. I dashed for the Forty-second Street station.

All the while I was hastening south, I tried to figure some means of carrying a pair of old people who'd never be able to walk a full mile or last out days in the open. Once I'd got them on a locomotive they'd be all right, but they'd have to be hustled off a good distance from Thompson's place before I'd dare let them surface. Certainly nowheres closer than the Greenwood Depot just over the Delaware line would do, but Greenwood was a full night's ride, and that was pushing it. A horse would have to be stolen along with my parents, a good strong one, and I'd need to throw together some kind of a buggy . . . those chaise wheels I'd seen in the toolshed when I'd run off my brothers . . . still on the axle . . . rope and boards and nails in there too . . . likely long gone by now, all of it . . . have to wait and see . . . in the meanwhiles all I could do was to keep on moving south.

Fidgeting like a six-year-old in church, I sat in a dim, empty car on the night train bound for Wilmington out of Philadelphia, unable to close my eyes. The car swayed and heaved, and beneath my feet the floor bounded, then shimmied as the wheels ran over a bad stretch of track. For all its hissing and rumbling and clanking, the locomotive didn't seem to be going fast enough. I'd have felt better outside running, instead of sitting there helpless in the swinging, yellowish light cast about from the kerosene lamps in the ceiling. I looked out for some sign we were nearing Wilmington, but the train must have been between towns. The clear June night was glassed in and steamed over behind the jammed-shut windows, and the only thing to watch was the sparks sprayed backwards from the engine winking out like dying stars. Or fireflies. Used to catch them when I was small, catch them in my hands and watch my fingers go all ghostly. Tilly had cut a firefly open one time to find out what made it do that way, and Daddy had said . . . what was it he'd said? He'd said something, couldn't remember what, wanted to, Daddy, oh my Lord. The image was there again, Daddy in some kind of trouble, in danger, only I couldn't see what it was; he was standing there waiting behind a pane of glass, fogged over, fading from me, don't go not yet I'm coming wait, but there were men coming too, like in the vision, white men, white men asking something, voices now, no more images, voices I could barely hear. *Don't know, you tell me. You the nigger expert, read through what we got here, Roy.*

My head snapped up and out of the sleeping fit.

They were standing in the aisle up ahead of me, glancing over their shoulders in the swaying sallow light, trying to keep their footing as the floor jolted. A smell of whiskey, tobacco, and leather lingered at my shoulder. They must have only just passed by. After an instant they sat down on the edge of a seat, more like they'd been thrown there by the train's motion than by choice, seemingly unaware that this wasn't the whites-only car. After one fast sideward glance, I turned my face to the window again. I'd seen their types before, slouching in the alleys and slums of most big cities; they all looked alike to me, with their quick eyes slithering in weaselly white-trash faces, rough manners and speech, and twin bulges at their hips, the one from a whiskey flask, the other from a pistol.

Papers rustled, and they commenced talking together, sounding somewhat slow-witted or maybe a touch drunk, their voices carrying farther than they intended. They were mouthing what was on the latest advertisements. The worst thing I could have done just then was dash for the next car; that would have brought them down on me for sure, so I kept my seat and tuned my ear to their talk.

"This here's for one name of Jericho, that'd be a man I'd spect, lessee now. Hiram, Luther, ain't we got a wench here somewheres, ah there, well don't hush me, it don't matter. 'Tall slender woman, mulatto, could pass,' wrong one. Ain't much of a reward for Missy Mulatto anyways, well maybe we still get lucky."

More rustlings.

" 'Short woman, muscular build, deep color, pure Afri-cain. Late property of Doctor Anthony Thompson, Bucktown District, Maryland.' "

I moved my right hand under my coat till I'd got the pistol

from my belt. Keeping it hidden within the folds of my skirt, I reached in my ticking bag for that missionizer's gift. With the tract tented over the gun I was able to raise it a bit higher, but still well below the back of the seat ahead of me. My eyes stayed on the window as I listened sharp.

" 'Scarred head, scarred neck and shoulders,' hang on Roy, here come the good part."

Lowering the pistol, I held the tract before my face like I was reading it. My hat and collar was likely covering all scars, but I had to make certain.

"Jee-zuz, we maybe just hit paydirt, worth twenty thousand dollars. *Twenty thousand dollars!* Some kind of ree-ward for a nigger that can't even read or write, say so here."

I could feel them looking back at me, and I just prayed I'd got that tract right side up, what with all the lettering on the front of it.

"Aw shit Roy, this one can read sure enough."

Right side up it was, whatever it was, whatever good that would do me.

"Even so we may as well, she be worth somethin even if it ain't . . ."

I coughed to cover the sound made as I cocked the pistol, but there was no need. The train's whistle covered the sound instead, and from somewheres behind me the conductor was caroling *Will-mington-next-stop-Will-ming-ton.* The locomotive began slowing down, but the town ahead was yet invisible. If these men wanted me they still had time to move, but they commenced to quarrel amongst themselves and I only caught the last part of what they said.

". . . and maybe worth nary but piss. Anyways if we take her we got to guard her all night, can't make no deals this hour. Up to you. You want to stick to that nigger, do it, but I got a mind for Maureen's place, and I surely ain't about to bring her in there."

A snort came from the one called Roy. "Oh no you don't, you ain't stickin me in that sorta fix, shit no, well never mind. Tomorrow . . . likely some good prospectin over to the river . . . yeah, they run em in there sometimes." The train jerked, sighed, and stopped. "Sweet Mo-reen, les go."

Believe me, I didn't wait for them to get up, and I kept the pistol cocked just in case as I took myself off that train. Lord knows I would have shot them if I'd had to.

After a brief stop with Thomas Garrett to pick up forged passes, and to tell him what was coming day after next, I was southbound again on another steam-car. Thomas would have protested if he'd known what had just nearly happened, but the surface lines were still the fastest way to go, and had to be risked. Well worth it too, for nothing else went wrong, and by the following evening I'd reached the old folks' cabin. I sneaked around the back and peered through the half-open shutters.

Daddy wasn't there.

Nor was he outside, or in sight at all, but through the twilight I saw my mother going into the privy. I went after her, wrenched the door open, and caught her standing frozen before the six-hole seater, just dropping her skirts. I fastened the door behind me, locking us in with the dense dark stink of the place, and saw her face, striped with the fading light that leaked through the wall cracks. Her eyes snapped at me, shocked, relieved, angry.

"Mama! What happened, where's Daddy?" I rapped out.

"Up the Big House again, don't you touch me."

For an instant I wondered if she was in her right mind, but cast the thought aside and kept on.

"Trouble?"

"They ask him the same things over and over. Maybe he helped some niggers off."

Oh Lord. "Not the boys?"

"After that." Her eyes narrowed at me.

"Spill it, Mama, they done somethin to him?"

"Ain't harmed him. But folks say it bound to come up for trial first or last." Her voice was flat. "And then he be good as dead, for sure."

"He won't be, I mean to fetch you both out tonight. Just move his trial to a Higher Court is all."

"I said don't touch me. And don't you try to make it a light thing. You got your ways, likely you seen this was to come somehow, but sweet Heaven, do it need to take this kinda tribulation before you come to fetch your mama and daddy?"

"He'd never come before. Now Mama, there ain't time to fuss."

"Fuss! You-all behave like I was a child, that's right. Ben say later you and the boys was right here that time and nobody told me, concluded I'd carry on, spoil the run. Well it ain't so, I wouldnta done, ain't no baby, ain't no fool. Why didn't you leave me see the boys? Why didn't you never say one word to me all these years? Don't you hush me. If you'd ever asked what I'd got reasoned out in my mind we wouldn't be in this tribulation now. Wanted to go North from the first when I heard what you was about on the Shore, but Ben he just laugh, and you never come and ask me, only speak with your daddy." Her voice softened then. "Can you still save him even so? Still get us off someways?"

Feeling shamed, I nodded, then put out my hand to her, and that time she let me touch her.

"Sorry, Mama, truly, ask you now. When they send Daddy back — they leave him come home nights? — all right, when they leave him go, tell him I'm behind the cabin, get him out there to speak. Tell him you and me got everythin planned too."

I explained it all to her, about having to go get a horse, and what I wanted them to do and bring when I returned. The signal was fixed, everything was set to go. Everything excepting for my father.

I waited behind the cabin, and in a short time Daddy did come out back. But he kept his hand over his eyes, and was just as stubborn as ever.

"Don't mean to ask this time," I told him. "You leave with me tonight is all. They through with you for now?"

He nodded.

"All right, I told Mama what to do, and you just act like ordinary till I come back. Sun's only just down, we got time. Daddy! Don't you hear?"

"All bound to blow over," he whispered. "What can they do to a old man anyways?"

"Will you look at me? God's sake! You won't need to tell the Man you ain't seen me, you won't be here."

"Won't risk you on my account," he said, fierce. "They got their eyes peeled to me. If you make to run us off they be sure to catch you, Lord, string you up. Won't have it."

I shook him like I was trying to jar his eyes open.

"You mean to be so Godamighty proud you won't let nobody try and help you, even your own? All right. You be a stubborn old man. You march back in there and you study on how bad off Mama's sure to be once they cart you away. And after you study on that a while, you look out for me again, right here." I brought my mouth up to his ear, and hissed into it. "And you get outa that cabin, you and Mama. You get around back real quick, and you get youselves North with me direct."

I let him go, and moved off. When I looked back over my shoulder he was pacing there, arms behind his back, head bent.

About two hours later I was behind the shack again, making a low whistle.

Nothing happened.

Smoke was chugging from the chimney, the place glowed at the windows, and I heard sounds within. They had to be there. But alone? Maybe something had gone wrong, someone had come, more questions.

I whistled again.

A quilt tumbled out of the window facing the back of the Quarter. Mama clambered after it carrying two small cloth bags. And at last Daddy stepped out over the sill slow and careful, till he was standing before me, meeting my eyes.

They knew without being told to keep silent, and I led them off to the old praise-grove, our way lit by a skyful of stars and a three-quarter moon. When we entered the circle I heard them pull in their breath.

It was still there, the contraption I'd rigged up, looking strange and funny and dangerous, caught by a shaft of moonlight. The only thing that appeared natural about it was the mare I'd borrowed, a strong, piebald workhorse, chomping grass like nothing odd was hooked up behind her at all. I'd fitted the mare out as best I could with a straw collar that had been hanging in the toolshed, and hitched her up to what was little more than that pair of chaise wheels. There was a board nailed firm to the axle for the old folks to sit on, and another board swung with ropes where they could rest their feet. I roped the quilt down on the seat, hoping it would cushion them some; without springs, and with the pace I intended to set, it was going to be one jarring, bone-shaking ride. Mama and Daddy climbed on, and I swung more ropes around, one over their laps, a double length stretched behind to keep them from falling over backwards and one more in front for them to hold onto.

I tried all the knots twice, untied the mare, and led her out of the grove at a walk till we reached a partly overgrown wagon trace where I mounted the horse, then brought a stick down on her flank.

And so my parents commenced their first and final journey.

It was a wild one; I'm sure none of us could live through anything like it again. I drove that beast as if a legion of demons were at our backs, zigzagging, jolting over chuckholes, cutting across fields, and tearing down back roads while the horse steamed and bled, spewing foam into my eyes as I lay flat on her neck. Low branches lashed me across the face as I swung right, then left, trying to miss craters or fallen logs I could barely see in the faint, silvery light; behind me the old folks gasped as they grabbed for the ropes and each other. The earth quaked, the clear sky shook above us, and the moon bounced up ahead.

Each time I stopped to breathe the horse, I was half-surprised to see Mama and Daddy were still hanging on, their eyes big, fists clenched, chests heaving. Then we'd start up again, while all inside my head were spinning thoughts. Would the axle crack, a spoke, a wheel? Would the horse give out, would the old folks keel over, fall off, let go? Could I run down anyone who might try to bar the way without wrecking the buggy, and what was that stickiness on my palms, blood or only sweat?

More than halfway through the night, the mare jumped a boulder which caught the left wheel, and the buggy flew into the air, nearly overturning. I pulled up short to find my parents hanging half off the rig, and I held them till they ceased trembling; till I ceased trembling as well.

"You all right? Mama?"

A nod.

"Daddy, you?"

Another nod.

The breath had been near knocked out of them, but after I'd tied them down again and found the wheel was only scraped, my daddy's voice wavered on the air, telling me to get on with it.

The sharp stars hurtled across the blackness as we galloped, trotted, rested, dashed off again, and then the stars were fading. Dusky, formless trunks rose up alongside us, sank away, and rose again in plainer shapes as the dark drained out of the sky. We were racing the dawn.

I beat the horse harder, kicked her sides like I was trying to stave in her ribs, and hollered loud as I dared. More light, faint and thin, lifted the treetops out of the dimness. The road blurred beneath the slamming hoofs, and that rig creaked and screamed like it was about to fly apart. The sky went lemony and the east glowed like from a hidden, white-hot fire. Behind me, the buggy swayed, the heaving horse faltered and slackened her pace. And just then the sun flashed like sparked gunpowder through the trees, low and piercing. We were just outside of Greenwood.

I walked the mare into some woods not far from the small whistle stop of a depot, tethered her to a tree, and helped my folks down.

They blinked at the brilliant morning, took some shaky steps, and then we just leaned against each other, stiff and sore and winded. And safe. Smiling. Our eyes and mouths were rimmed with dust, but after a gulp and a wash at a stream, the old folks seemed to rights again. I beat out their clothes, straightening them here and there; they had to look collected for that train.

We stopped just within a fringe of trees near to the tracks, and I gave them the passes and tickets. Then I took a breath. This would be hard.

"You got to go on your own now for a little time. I can't get on this train with you, not hereabouts. Someone could pick my face out easy from the posters, don't want you nabbed on my account." I didn't mention what had happened on the way down, so as not to frighten them. Two old people like that, dressed poor but neat, with passes and tickets; worthless to bounty hunters, they'd be safe.

Their faces were blank, but their eyes showed hurt.

"No danger if you go alone, no one here's never seen you, and you likely ain't even been missed yet. It's all right, don't you see?"

No answer.

"It's all right, now listen. Wilmington's where you get off, Wilmington, remember that, they call it out just before the station. There's a Quaker, my friend, all set to meet you, and I be there to catch you up tomorrow." I described Garrett, told them when to give their tickets, what to say and what not to, and how long the ride would be.

But still those blank faces, those sad eyes on them.

"Ready now? Should be almost time. Remember to wave the train down when you hear it whistle, else it won't stop. Well. Best say goodbye here, I got to stay back in the trees. Don't want nobody to see me put you on."

I reached for them, but they didn't move. They just kept staring at me, the small yellow tickets lying in their open, upturned palms.

"Can't you come on this one time?" To my surprise it was my daddy quavering so. "Course it don't really matter, just figured to ask. Can't you?"

I shook my head, trying to fight down the urge to go along with them anyways, and then I commenced a light quick babble, repeating everything I'd just told them. My voice reached that false, foolish pitch people use for coaxing children to bed. "Why, you sure to do real fine, and won't the boys be clean amazed when they hear? Just act real easy, sit back like you done this every-day-and-Sunday, and don't you carry on, Mama, mind me now, behave like you real bigtime . . ."

"No call to talk like your daddy and me's babies." Old Rit closed her fingers over her ticket.

Ah, I'd hurt her pride again, well thank Heaven for it.

"You sure can act ignorant sometimes, Hat," she said. "We knows how to behave."

From behind a maple I watched them wave the train down and board it, holding themselves stiff and dignified, Daddy Ben leaning down to hand my mother up like he'd seen gentlemen do ladies all his life.

In the moments before the three-car train started up again, I caught a glimpse of them, Daddy seated closer to a window, his head like to a silhouette behind the glass, with the lighter tones of Old Rit's face outlining his as she perched by his side. Both of them sat up straight, staring directly ahead, motionless, and, I thought, proud as well as scared. They didn't turn their heads and look for me, protecting my cover, and so they rode off without a glance when the train lumbered away.

From Wilmington all the way to St. Catharines we'd be together again, and in the meanwhiles they'd be all right. I knew it, sensed it, as I stood amongst the trees, a breeze snapping my skirts and the sun dappling over me. The air flowed cool and smooth across my skin, making me feel washed clean, and that day is still as shining fresh in my mind as the morning when I first crossed the line myself.

◆◆◆

ST. CATHARINES lies just over the Canadian border between two Great Lakes, only a few miles past Niagara Falls. I remember it for the black freedfolks' settlement it sheltered, and as a terminus of the Underground Railroad in the fifties, with fugitives coming in by rail, by foot, or by boat across Lake Erie. Songs of praise have been made about the new country and its queen. The ground has been kissed numberless times. I've seen runaways throw themselves down there, weeping and thanking God, sometimes to the embarrassment of white seamen who ran the slaves through. Maybe the pilots didn't comprehend that St. Catharines was the Promised Land and the New World for many of my people, just as surely as the port of New York City was for white immigrants who'd crossed an ocean.

In the early days, however, St. Catharines was a cold, cheerless Promised Land indeed. I can recollect the first time I ran slaves straight through to that place, straight into the depths of a bitter winter. Those fugitives had been bruised, frost-bitten, and starved when they crossed the line, but they blessed the Lord for their deliverance even so, touching their mouths to the soil, only to burn their lips on the ice. They had to earn their bread by splitting timber in snow-steeped forests, hewing out clearings and building houses, and as I helped those pioneers start all over from nothing, I saw the question in their eyes. This, the reward? This, the land of milk and honey? No use in being free if you freeze to death, they muttered. Even a man such as Frederick Douglass says that when he arrived in Canada he stood there ragged, lonely, and forlorn, feeling it was a cold wilderness for a fugitive to face after the trials of escaping.

But things had changed fast. Those runaways I'd carried on my first journey to St. Catharines realized that anyone who'd been a slave could stand plenty. Older settlers helped the newer ones through the Januaries and Februaries, through the strangeness, and the shock of standing alone after a lifetime of being bossed and numbed by the sameness of plantation routine. Log cabins sprouted everywhere, fields were cleared, and the work went on without any fear of the whites nearby; the Canadians never made any trouble I heard about, and I found them welcoming and good-willed. In Queen Victoria's Dominions we had the right to own land and vote in county elections, while Uncle Sam slapped our rights down with the Dred Scott decision.

By the late fifties, the freedfolks' settlement in St. Catharines numbered roundabouts six thousand souls. A school had gone up, and more than one church, a cemetery had been hallowed, and a small jail built for the usual no-accounts that plague every community, colored or white. There was a railroad junction by that time too, even a telegraph, and the log cabins were giving way to finer houses of frame and brick.

It was to this place that I finally brought my folks in that summer of 1857.

It seemed strange to them, I could tell, even though they were too polite to say so. The Canadian summer must have felt chilly set against Maryland's lush, steamy Julys, but surely they'd be used to the climate and settled in before the first snow fell. I knew they felt somewhat lost, but that was bound to wear off; three sons and a daughter surrounded them, children they'd never thought to see again, and their reunion with William Henry was especially joyful. I'd brought him and his bride there years before, and they had babies to show off. The other boys had gone farther north for work, but they came down to visit soon after the old folks arrived.

I didn't want to leave the Railroad and root in Canada myself, but I thought it best not to tell Mama and Daddy. Not yet. Not till some of the strangeness had worn off. And anyways I'd reasoned it out to stay until I'd got them set up proper in their new home.

That home was a well-built, snug, two-room cabin, left empty by a young family who'd outgrown it, and the place was already floored and battened when my folks moved in. I promised I'd get them a real house someday, a fine one, and in the meanwhiles Daddy and I whitewashed the cabin together, while my mama scrubbed it down and swept it out. One day I came back from town with glass panes for the windows, another day I carried in yard goods for bedding, and helped them find cook things, build furniture, and set the glass. I lived there too, sleeping on a cornshuck pallet like I'd done as a child, till Daddy built me a bedstead; why that made me uneasy I knew, but didn't care to think upon just then.

Other things were making me uneasy as well.

The cloth bag, for instance. One night I'd dropped off early, curled up in the chimney corner, and awakened sometime later to the sound of whispering. Ben and Rit were crouching over the hearth, untying the bag. They were so absorbed neither of them noticed my eyes opening on the sack, and on the things they lifted out of it, one by one, to hold up in the firelight: A green ribbon, frayed and split. Half a set of beef-rib clappers. A Christmas gold piece. An ax-blade gone to rust. A wooden wall-peg. An ear of hardened, red corn. A wooden spoon with a face carved on the bowl, tattered cloth wrapping the handle.

From that bag they could conjure up the Saturday night big times back on the old place, when they'd decked out in ribbons and danced to the jubilee beat of the clappers. Yuletide at the Big House could be conjured too, and likewise the woods, the cabin, and the cornshucking parties where the man who found a red ear got to kiss the prettiest wench. And they could also conjure back the owner of that crude doll, the girl-child who was left far behind somewheres in the invisible South.

For an instant I wanted to rise from the chimney corner and sweep every bit of that stuff into the fire. Those times were over, well rid of, not worth remembering. My folks would have done better to carry away the boot heel a patroller had once left in their trampled garden after a rampage, or some lead platting from a whip, or a bill of sale to remind them of how things had really been. But then again I knew how hard it was to leave home, no matter what kind it was; I myself would soon have to part with this Canadian home where I'd settled for such a short while. That leavetaking wouldn't be easy. I closed my eyes again.

As the summer wore on my uneasiness grew though there seemed no real reason for it. My folks were in good health, and the cloth bag's trinkets were fondled less often in the nights, as far as I could tell. I also discovered that Daddy had an old sock stuffed with coins, saved from years of hiring his time as a timber inspector. He and Mama were able to buy things, so there wasn't any cause to trouble over money. The work on the cabin was progressing, we'd almost got all the windows glassed in, and much of the furniture had been built. Next week I'd go, next week I'd rejoin my other life, my vocation, in a fortnight I'd go, in a month, sometime soon. And yet I lingered. Just a little while longer, I told myself, just till the cabin's done, just till they feel to home in it.

In late August Benjie and Robert left St. Catharines, moving to other settlements where there were great stretches of land to claim. Mama and Daddy were downcast for some weeks afterwards, though my brothers would be able to come back for visits; they'd left with that promise. It was a comfort to the old folks that William Henry's family was still closeby, and I was yet under their roof, keeping house for them like a proper daughter. They stuck closer to me than ever after the others had gone, following every movement I made with their eyes.

They stuck to me and to their hearth as summer snapped into the chill, brittle blue autumn that seemed to come up so quick in Canada, and my mother commenced to complain about the cold. I worried. She fretted. I repeated every speech I'd ever made to new freedfolk about the winter in St. Catharines. She said it didn't chill your bones like this down to home till Christmas. This was only September. Well. I'd just see them through the first snow was all; by that time the cabin would be done and they'd be settled in.

It came early, the first snow, in mid-October. I rushed through the light flurries into town where I tried to hunt up some presents for my folks, something to ease the time of parting. Tools for Daddy, though he had more than enough as it was; a new clay pipe and some yarn for Mama, though she had plenty of both. It was evening when I returned with my gifts to find my mother wrapped up and shivering on the path, waiting on me. She was shivering with cold, I thought at first, but then I saw it was excitement. She took the packages from my hands, bade me close my eyes, and led me inside.

The whole place had been swept and scrubbed again from top to bottom. Firelight gleamed on the polished kettle, and the cook things were neatly laid out on a table Daddy had made of fresh-hewn wood. He must have just put it together too, for that morning it had only been in pieces. My folks opened the door to the smaller room, and I saw there was a new quilt on my bed, racing with red and blue patterns. Then Mama spun me around to see the windows. Curtains frilled there, white ones, just hung, still stiff. Old Rit must have been sewing and piecing late into the nights, hiding things, keeping secrets, and the both of them must have worked all that day to surprise me. The cabin was finished, settled into, shining and lit and alive with color, and my parents' eyes glimmered as they watched my face.

"*Curtains!*" was all Mama said, but she didn't need to say more. I knew what she meant. Slaves and trash had shutters. Fine folks had curtains.

Ben walked around, looking at the curtains, the cook table, and the quilt on my bed. He nodded.

"Feel to home here, first time," he told me. "And acourse we done this for you too, honey. Only natural you settle down with us now."

Of course. Only natural. What I'd felt growing around me had finally been spoken out loud, and I couldn't bring myself to tell them no. Not then. Not the next day either. Nor the next.

Through the rest of that month I kept finding tasks that seemed to need doing. I built a fence around the cabin, limed the privy, corded enough wood to last a winter and a half. Tried to speak at mealtimes, smiled brightly. Couldn't sleep. Grew thin. Rambled the woods, the town, and returned to mend the gatepost, patch the roof. Then the gatepost again.

And when at last there was no more work left to do I just paced, outside, inside, round and round the cabin, while my folks watched, saying nothing. Leaving them by the fire, I'd retire early and pace all through the nights, thinking on folks squatting by other hearths. What of them? What of the ones I'd promised to come back for next time, those who should be settled in St. Catharines too? Maybe they thought I'd forgotten. I'd never been away from the mission this long. It was the first of November.

One night I stood by the window in my room, neither pacing nor sleeping, just gazing out the window. The stars wheeled around, looking dulled and very far away behind the glass panes, and for a moment my lids drooped. I was back in Philadelphia circling the border of a rag rug, and then the old dream unraveled before my eyes, the dream of flying over rivers and fields . . . my head snapped up. That was a childhood dream. It was long past the time it should come again.

The door scraped open behind me, footsteps padded near, and Daddy's hand appeared next to mine on the sill. It was a while before he spoke.

"You want to go back down." He told me, rather than asking.

I nodded.

He stood there for a time, neither telling me to go or bidding me stay. Then he cleared his throat.

"Your mama figure John Tubman's still in your head. She got it reasoned out you hope to find him one time you go back, him turned up amidst some runaways."

I looked away from him and said nothing. Let him think so then. That would make it easier. That was something he and Mama could understand, something anyone could see as natural, me leaving to seek a lost husband. It was enough for me that I knew different, though I had no words to make plain this vocation's pull on me, even when I should be feeling settled, content. Yes, let them both think that, it would lessen the hurt.

After a moment Daddy sighed.

"I be sure to tell Rit tomorrow," was all he said as he left the room.

In the morning I was packed up, dressed warm, and standing before them, fumbling for words.

"William Henry's real closeby acourse, next nearest neighbor almost. He be sure to have you for Christmas dinner, surely will, and what with all them grandbabies there and the other boys come home, you won't have time to miss me. This ain't goodbye anyways, be back before you can turn around twice. And meanwhiles you still got kin to look out for you."

My mother clung to me, but over her head I saw my father nod, like he truly comprehended.

"Best get a move on," he said, "Get south before the weather snaps cold down there. Well, go on now, best make time."

But his lips trembled and his eyes filled as I held him to me, then walked out the door.

◆◆◆

THERE WAS A SENSE of urgency upon me as I returned to the Railroad in the early days of that November, moving south below the snow, going backwards through the seasons till I was passing into what was only late autumn in Maryland, and a mild one too.

I'd been gone too long. I was fretting to begin again, and had one plantation clearly in mind for this strike, but yet I was dragging, continually weary to the bone, and sleep did not refresh me. It was a kind of drained, dead-limbed weariness I hadn't known since slavery, and for some reason that scarred place in my head, quiet for so many years, was jolting with pain.

One morning while it was still dark I paused to rest in some woods till nightfall, safely concealed in a cavelike place formed by the overhanging bank of a shrunken stream. Suddenly my legs gave way, throwing me to my knees, as dust motes glowed and darted before my eyes. Hungry, I was just hungry; that was all it could be. I crouched there, fumbling for the food in my ticking bag, then unfurled the bedroll I'd carried with me, slung over one shoulder. Wrapped in the blankets, I hunched up against an oak, knees to chest, head sunk down, just dozing really. All the while I was aware of the small sounds in the woods, the early birdcalls, the branches creaking; also keenly aware of this new bodily weakness, troubled over that and the misery in my temple. Maybe I'd only gone soft in Canada with the old folks, maybe it was only taking me a while to get used to the Road again. Maybe I was falling ill.

Too tired even for sleep, I stayed hunched over, leaving my mind to ramble off on its own, rambling backwards to John Tubman. I'd had no man since him, and only desired one now and then. In certain tired, idle moments I'd sometimes have fancies of a man touching me, thrusting into me, a lover who was always black, often faceless, but mostly he was John. I seldom missed John excepting after those unbidden dreams, and even then I didn't miss our home, or our courting, or our having been wed. What I appeared to miss was his body around mine, the feeling of being caressed and nibbled at and entered, though I'd never thought of seeking John again, or messing with anyone else. I didn't need a steady man; this life I'd chosen left no time or space for one. Any carrying-on might distract me, derail me, make too many demands, like it had happened before. But even so, there were those times. And yet just then I felt too drained even for small, lustful fancies. I only wanted someone to hold me and touch me and rock me like a child.

I lifted my head and watched some massed, brown leaves floating in the narrow stream, as a colorless dawn gave way to clouded, stony daylight. Mostly I found comfort gazing at the woods, but this time none, and I pressed my face back against my bunched knees. I'd have to own it, there was no point in making up more excuses about what was wrong with me. It wasn't that I'd gone soft up in Canada, I hadn't been there long enough for that, and I wasn't sick. It was only that I was starting to burn out at last.

I'd been on the Railroad going on eight years almost without a stop, and those stops had been filled with work to settle folks up North, or low toil in kitchens to raise funds. Pride had kept me from thinking these labors could ever wear me down, and I'd ignored small signs which warned it might happen. But I could put them from me no longer, they weren't small enough anymore. I could only huddle against that oak, wondering if I was still fit to lead. A numbness came over me. The air grew warmer. My bones ached. I slept.

My eyes opened later on the beginnings of a ruddy sunset which turned the stream into a trickle of wine, and light blushed over the ground onto my skirts. It had been like that all the way down, red skies either starting or finishing the nights, marking off each step I'd taken back to my people; red, the color of the Lord's people, the people Moses led, the people who were bound. I took this for a sign, and prayed for the Lord to fill me where I was used up, to make me more than what I was, to sustain me in spirit if my strength must wane. Lord, I asked, walk with me now, help me. Light my soul with Your grace so I can still do Your work, power me on, Lord. Let me see You in the faces of my people like always, lead me, lead them, please, my kind Jesus.

As I stooped to wash in a still part of the stream, the horizon's glow caught my face for a moment and caused it to be reflected before me in the water. Beneath my bandana the eyes were hollowed but bright. The image showed a woman who appeared closer to fifty than forty, but the broad features were set firm again. A driven look was just starting to form on my face, and I knew it would be so thereon in, for this recognition of bodily weakening would make me push myself harder against the day when I might give out entirely. Suddenly I grinned at my mirrored self for looking so stern and sober and desperate. The sky's redness lingered for an instant before the darkness folded down, and then I walked off into the final lap of that particular journey.

Last time I'd raided a certain plantation in Talbot County, I'd promised a bondwoman named Mary that I'd come back for her and her man; he'd gashed his leg in the wood lot and they hadn't been able to travel back then. They'd both of them been all prepared for going next time I came, and they'd likely kept watch for me, maybe wondering why I'd made them wait so many months.

Their Quarter appeared calm as I approached it through a clear autumn night that was snapping with starlight, and the row of buckling shacks seemed to line up firm and clean-edged against the sky. A stealthy glance into the overseer's cabin showed me the Man was abed with a bottle and a bruised face, but even if there hadn't been that measure of safety I still would have crept directly out of hiding, for as I crouched behind Mary's place, I heard the sound of soft moaning from within.

The shack was dim and close inside, choked with fire-ash, and five or six women were clustered around a figure on the floor. Mary was half-squatting, half-sprawled there, near naked, and what was left of her shredded clothing was meshed in the lash stripes on her back. There were deep welts on her face too, even on the heavy tits which hung above a child-swollen belly.

I leaned to her, tried to take her hands, but she didn't seem to know me, and flung herself out of my reach. Her head snapped back, mouth open, teeth bared like an animal's, and she let go with a low tight sound that seemed to go on and on. Sapped and tormented by her burning wounds, she was also going through birth pains, and judging by her belly's size, it was a birthing that had come far too early.

Someone spoke up behind me, an old woman. Her voice shook with sorrow, with anger too. She might have been Mary's mother.

"Her man got hired out yesterday, Moses, far side the county, just a while since we got the word you was on the way. Mary she like to went crazy, jumped Mr. Jay — overseer — hit him, spat his eye, called him a lowdown trash bastid. Was the first white she run into after she heard Sam gone, well you see how the Man beat her. Master over to Easton, else he never let it happen no matter what she done." She turned toward Mary. "Can't keep her abed, can't do nothin with her. The granny-midwife's took sick, but we done all we able. Just ain't no way in the world to hold her still so's she be able to rest, maybe heal after all, please God."

She hadn't even let them grease her. A pot of lard was smashed in a corner, rags and poultices were thrown every whichway. Mary commenced to thrash once more, then grabbed on to the edge of a table with both hands. Her body jerked, arching over into a crouch, and a pulpy mass began squeezing out from between her legs. It was the baby that hadn't finished forming. Layers of purplish mush came with it and after it; knotty blood-ropes, dark clots, and wetness spread around her. She wasn't yelling, just panting, eyes wandering; odd that she didn't cry out. We held her, called to her, grabbed for rags, a blanket, water. It seemed only a short while before she went slack and heavy against me.

I walked out into the fresh spangled dark, and stood there for a moment, eyes brimming. *Damn. Damn.* All at once I smashed my fist against the cabin, then again, feeling neither bruised knuckles nor torn skin. *Folks say it's easy on us, always will, safe.*

Later that night I struck Mary's plantation hard, picking it as clean of bondfolk as I knew how. I'd remember her. Let her owners remember this.

Almost as soon as I'd got that group safe in Canada I fell ill at my parents' place for a month, left in spite of their protests as soon as I was better, and went to work in Jersey to raise money for the next raid. It wasn't until March that I was able to get back into Maryland.

If my own bodily troubles were making me desperate, Mary's loss made me more so, and what I encountered upon my return to Dorchester County nearly turned my desperation into a murderous despair. It took me a while getting down, for that spring was troubled, almost as bad as '55, when rumors of a slave revolt had crackled round the county, and the patrollers had been all over the place. Once again the roads, bridges, and towns were filled with patrols, and as I passed just below Cambridge I spied a piece of their work.

It was a black man swinging from a gibbet by the side of a wagon trace. From the distance and through the brush, he appeared more like a dark scarecrow flapping there, set off against a steely blue sky and the field beyond. I couldn't see him plain till I drew closer, what with the flies clouding his head and a gathering of turkey buzzards. I stepped forward, shooed the buzzards off, and they looped slowly above me as I gazed on the hanged man.

He couldn't have been up long; the birds hadn't got a

chance to pick him over too bad yet. His eyes bulged, his tongue thrust out. There was a sign strung around his neck. I couldn't read it. I didn't need to. The man was Jacob Jackson.

He blurred in my sight. For a moment he was Nat Turner, he was Denmark Vesey, he was Gideon from the old days on Marse Ed's place, he was every Negro who'd rebelled, been martyred, and made into an example. But when my eyes cleared, he was Jacob again. My friend.

I am totally certain that if any white man had come upon me then, I would have shot him without a word or question. But I was left alone at that gibbet, and although it was most unwise to do so, I took my knife and slashed through the rope around Jacob's neck. I buried him in the nearby fallow field, and that night I ran off the largest escape party I'd ever carried, signaling them with the one song it was forbidden us to sing, "Go Down Moses."

But Moses hadn't been there for Jacob Jackson, Moses hadn't been there for Mary. True, I had been there for hundreds of others, yet it wasn't enough; there were so many who must be delivered out of that land. Somehow I'd have to go down more often. Run more off. Move faster. Push myself harder. Take still more. Run greater risks. Beg money. Make extra journeys. Carry more still.

I began to dream continually on numbers. The numbers of souls I'd freed, by the Lord's grace. That set against the number still bound. The number of fugitives Thomas Garrett has passed through his station, almost two thousand by then. That too, set against the number in bondage. The numbers of freedfolk in St. Catharines, the thousands who had fled during the fifties on their own, with the Railroad's help. And that again, set against the numbers of my people enslaved in the South. Three million, the abolitionists said there were; that figure loomed large in my brain, nearly blotting the others out. I was unable to picture what a million or two or three million looked like, so I dreamed instead of fingers, counting them, fingers spread, pointing, webbing together, locking at the knuckles, breaking apart, stretching.

These dreams, in which I lusted for my people's lives and souls, were far stronger than my earlier dreams of fleshly lusts, and they were sometimes followed by another, which came often during that month after Jacob Jackson's death.

I'd see myself in some wilderness sort of place where there were rocks and trees under a bluish light, and I'd feel someone or something staring at my back. I'd leave off whatever it was I was doing there, turn, and catch sight of a serpent coiled on a rock, a beautiful proud creature, big around as my waist. It meant me no harm, I could sense that, and I was drawn to it rather than afraid. As I'd watch a man's face would slowly take shape on the serpent's head, an aged white man's face, bearded, with gray eyes that would keep gazing on me ever so wishful-like. Then, flanking this serpent would appear two others, smaller ones, also with white faces, though these were boyish and beardless. That wondrous trinity would look at me longingly for a time. All at once, a great crowd of people would thicken around them, people I never saw plain. I could not stop them as they struck down the great bearded head and the younger ones, till all of them lay there, smote dead.

Try as I might, I could not comprehend the meaning of this dream, though I pondered its message each time it came, reaching into my mind for old Scripture lessons to aid me. Taken one way, it could be a warning of some kind, for the Lord God said to the serpent *thou art cursed and dust shalt thou eat.* But a warning against what? Some temptation in my path? *And the woman said, the serpent beguiled me.* Perhaps the dream was pointing out some source of added power I could not see, though I prayed for it daily, a hidden wellspring of strength or support to help me go on with my work. For when the Lord told Moses to cast his rod upon the ground, he did so, and it became a serpent, and the Lord God said to Moses, *put forth thine hand and take it.* And when Moses took it up it became a rod in his hand, an instrument of power, a sign.

One way I saw the dream, then the other, and at last I gave up trying to read it, for if the Lord meant me to comprehend the message He would reveal it in His time. Anyways, that apparition didn't trouble my rest too often while I was leading that big escape party out of Dorchester. My energy was always entirely taken up by a journey, especially just then, when that energy seemed to be draining away.

It was when I'd finally got those fugitives free and I was back in Canada for a while that I'd sleep every night with the man-headed snake on my pillow.

◆ ◆ ◆

OLD BROWN.

Captain John.

Osawatomie Brown.

He came to me in St. Catharines while I was still between journeys. He came to find me in the woods where I was splitting timber, and he must have been watching me for some time before I noticed him. When I turned around he was sitting patiently on a rock, peeling an apple with his jackknife.

Although it has been said that John Brown was crazed, I saw no madness in him. What I did see was a spare, strong-built man, hard and taut through the body, dressed in farmer's homespun and cowhide boots. He was beardless then, but appeared older than he was since his springy brown hair was starting to go white, his face was seamed, and though his mouth was firm and his nose was stark, there were pouches under his eyes and sagging lids above. Those eyes were deep-socketed and gray, reflecting light as water does, and they looked at me with an odd wistfulness, like I was a sign to him, an answer, a key.

I tried to help him out and thought I had. He died anyways, and I still wonder if that wasn't partly my fault. But there was no hint of future bloodshed there at the first, no sign that anything could go wrong, no mention of Harpers Ferry in that bluish wooded twilight when Old Brown came to me for aid.

"Fred'k" had sent him, he said, meaning Douglass, and I had no reason to doubt this. I knew the two had been friends for years, and I'd also heard that a white man named Brown had lately got the backing of the Boston abolitionists for some undertaking or other. I'd naturally figured it had to do with Kansas; there'd been rumors of some ruction Brown had caused at a place called Osawatomie or Pottawatomie in that troubled state, a ruction between Free-Soilers and those that wanted slavery to spread west. No one seemed to know just what had happened, but there wasn't any question about what side John Brown was on. Anyways Douglass trusted him, so I asked him back to my parents' cabin. My folks were away visiting their sons, the place was quiet, and I stirred up the fire, offered him a chair. I kept a watchful silence as he finished off his apple, tossed the core on the flames, and leaned to the hearth till his face ripened in the warmth. He began to talk softly of "Fred'k," of the Canadian freedmen's settlements, of the chances of a mild spring and a rich harvest. When I think back on it now, it strikes me that he wasn't speaking of the ordinary sort of crops, but I didn't take his full meaning just then. I held to my silence, waiting for him to reveal what he'd truly come about.

When he said he had a plan to free the slaves, a plan he called the great work of his life, I felt suspicious, puzzled. There seemed no reason why this white man should be so fired up about my people's cause. I questioned him.

Brown answered me in a roundabouts way, but he answered me well, telling of the time he'd lived in North Elba, New York, with a community of Negroes. He laughed as he recollected it, laughed in that soundless way of his with only his shoulders quaking, and I comprehended he was laughing at himself. In the beginning of his days at North Elba, he said, he'd thought to teach the Negroes how to farm better; it seemed his neighbors had finished by teaching him.

Never before had I met a white man who'd chosen on purpose to dwell amongst colored people. That alone was enough to make him seem crazy to most folks, but John Brown had chosen such a life. As he talked of the shared living, the big times, the kinship he appeared to have found in that settlement, it struck me that he hadn't stayed in North Elba to shock folks, or to satisfy some curiosity. He'd liked it there, and I began to warm to him.

In his quiet, flat tones, he went on to speak of the violence over the slavery issue in Kansas, and he just barely touched on what he'd done to earn him the title of Osawatomie Brown. From the little he said, however, I was able to figure pretty close what had happened. John Brown, it seemed, had fought pro-slavery men in Kansas with his white sons at his side, and that image of him stunned and kindled me. This was the first white man I knew who'd taken up arms in my people's behalf; it wasn't until the war that I witnessed that again.

I trusted him by the time he'd got around to talking of his beloved Alleghenies where he'd once been a surveyor, the mountains which were the basis for what he called his great plan.

He believed that God had given the strength of the hills to freedom, as he put it, and had established the Alleghenies as a refuge for fugitive slaves. He intended to penetrate Virginia with some trusted friends. He would establish a permanent armed force in the heart of the South, holed up in what he termed the mountains' fastnesses. He'd place about twenty-five armed men in squads of five on a line of twenty-five miles, and send them down into the fields from time to time to get slaves to join him. And so his forces would grow till they could run off larger numbers of slaves, keeping the bravest ones with him in the armed mountain camp, while sending the rest to Canada on the Underground Railroad. He would spread the operation outwards to other localities as his numbers increased, for he believed that if slavery could be weakened in one county, it would weaken the system throughout the state, and after a time throughout the South. He mentioned past slave revolts. He talked of Nat Turner, saying that the Black Prophet had held Virginia in terror for weeks with only fifty men; surely the same number, once it was built up, could shake slavery out of the state this time. Only this time there would be no open rebellion, there would be no rash steps, he assured me. The plan had been forming in his mind for ten years, he went on. It was designed to destroy the money value of slave property by making such property insecure. He was convinced that the slaveowners would never give up until they felt a big stick around their heads. How long could we wait? He asked that again and again, of me, of the air, of himself it appeared.

His words were carefully chosen. The voice was calm, firm. But all the while he spoke his gaze never quit my face, like he was silently asking, almost begging me to join him. Once again I saw the yearning-eyed apparition of my dream.

I was already stirred and tempted by his plan, but I still had questions that needed answering. Brown did not shirk from my continued prodding. He narrowed his eyes and nodded to himself, as if my carefulness proved or confirmed something in his own mind, something I could not read, though I knew it had to do with me.

"Most bondmen don't know how to shoot a rifle, never got the chance to learn," I told him. "What'd you figure to arm the slaves with, firstoff?"

"Pikes first. Later, guns. Give a slave a pike and you make him a man. Deprive him of the means of resistance and you keep him down. Remember. Christ once armed Peter."

"Supplies could run out quick, specially food. What'd you plan to live off?"

"The land. And we'll also live off the enemy. Slavery is a state of war and must be treated as such."

"And money for arms?"

"So far my call has met with a hearty response, so I feel sure of tolerable success."

"Then you got the abolitionists behind you?"

"Yes, fully."

"You go under their orders?"

"What I have done in Kansas," he said quietly, "was by the authority of God Almighty and what I intend to do is by the same authority."

"And you feel easy in your mind the mountains make plenty protection?"

"Yes." His tone was firm as he added, "Jehovah will protect us. We will be His Gideons."

"What more do you need now?"

"Men."

He sought to recruit them from the freedmen's settlements in Canada, but believed the freedmen would harken more keenly to a call from their own leaders; the support of influential blacks would make him even more certain of success, he said. Then too, he needed an expert on southern terrain and northern routes, on the art of stealing slaves off plantations, on plotting strategy, on keeping military discipline amongst small bands of men. He needed me.

Our regard for each other deepened as we labored over his maps, and often we talked far into the night, though we were looking at the plan from somewhat different angles. For Brown it was a political tool which might turn Uncle Sam around if all went well, and he likewise termed it a holy crusade against the Great Whore of slavery. For me it was a means of widening the Underground Railroad, a way to reach thousands more of my bound sisters and brothers than I or the Railroad ever could. It was an assurance that my work would continue, an assurance which came just at the time when I was starting to feel myself wearing out. Our different outlooks didn't change the plan itself, however.

While we worked, I drew on all the knowledge I'd gained from the Underground Railroad. In truth, only someone who'd traveled the Road could have told Brown which trails were safe and which place was thick with patrols, where there were friends and where there were spring floods, what swamps to avoid, what woods were impassable, and most of all what areas had the most slaves. We were a week in our scheming together, and during that time I came to notice that we saw in one another parts of ourselves.

I saw this man as a Negro, and I was never able to shake the impression from my mind. Frederick Douglass observed that John Brown was as interested in our cause as though his own soul had been pierced with the iron of slavery, so maybe that was why I felt as I did. Maybe I'd linked him in my mind with Nat Turner, a resurrected Nat Turner clothed in pale skin. Yet that thought in itself was odd, for the old man was not planning slaughter like the Black Prophet; he'd told me so over and over. I recollected my dream, but did not speak of it. Its meaning still wasn't altogether clear to me, and at the time it seemed a sign of power, not a warning.

Just as I saw John Brown as a Negro, he in turn appeared to

see me as another man. Even before I'd heard that Brown's letters often referred to me as "he" rather than "she," it was clear. One night as we worked he tipped his chair back against the wall, gazed on me, and narrowed his eyes.

"You," he said, "are the most of a man that I've ever met with, a better officer than most I've seen. You could command an army as successfully as you've led your parties of fugitives."

To his mind, only a man could do such things, and I let the matter be. Maybe it was a deceiving snare, us seeing each other as we really were not, but even so, in that way we were able to feel a deep bond. I think we came to stand as signs to one another, joined by that plan we believed in. With the Lord's help it would all come to be, and soon.

But shortly after John Brown left me, saying he'd send word when all was ready, it appeared like this plan would not come into being soon. There were rumors that a traitorous follower had spilled everything to a Massachusetts senator. Brown had vanished back into Kansas, and no further word came. The recruits I'd gathered fell away, having their own work to do, forges to mind, fields to harrow, shops to tend, and the abolitionists seemed to have lost all contact with their man.

For some reason I didn't feel badly disappointed or impatient during that time. I sensed it wasn't over yet, and though it wasn't clear to me just how, I knew that John Brown would be back. I must wait on him too, since he'd placed such great trust in me.

And yet I could not wait.

I'd been idle too long and the Railroad was pulling me back into itself, back toward my own mission. I could not sit still while my people waited on me. They were where they'd always been no matter what might be changing elsewhere, and they couldn't be asked to stay even a little while longer on account of a plan, a promise, a vision.

I was heading south even before I'd fully comprehended what I was doing. It felt right to be back on the Railroad, it was where I belonged, but all the same I wondered if I was being disloyal to Brown. If his troubles passed over quickly and he was able to recommence his grand design, he wouldn't be able to find me rightoff; if he needed more colored recruits, I wouldn't be there to raise them. Yet, if I stayed put, waiting faithfully on him, I would betray my own people and my own vocation, one that had been given me long before old Osawatomie Brown had come out of the wilderness.

I told myself that somehow he'd find me when his moment came around again. Meanwhiles I journeyed, worked to earn more funds, and journeyed again, through a summer, a winter, the beginnings of another spring. And still John Brown had not come back.

It was March when I arrived in Boston, partly to raise more Railroad funding, partly to seek a loan from friends for my new home in Auburn, New York. Another friend, Senator William Seward, had mortgaged it to me on easy terms, and I'd settled my parents there in a staunch abolitionist town, in the fine house I'd promised them before, near a sizable Negro community. But I believe I'd also gone to Boston to seek some news, some sign of Brown.

As I walked the brick-paved streets near to the Common it felt like someone was watching me; but no, it was only a pair of lovers on the Courting Walk. I stepped along a bit hastily since slavecatchers slouched about the city, and I shouldn't have even been in that part of town. Again that sensation of eyes upon me. But it was only the old apple woman scrunched up in a shawl, her tempting, rounded red fruit arranged in baskets at her feet. Even so, I passed along faster through the early morning haze, approaching the Negro section near Faneuil Hall at a trot, and ducked back into my boardinghouse doorway sooner than I'd meant to.

A white man ducked in directly after me, drew near, and spoke my name.

I lowered my head and kept silent. From the tail of my eye I could see he was tall, young, slender, and almost too pretty for someone of his sex. I knew him, I thought. Seen him somewheres. At an Anti-Slavery meeting? At someone's home here in Boston?

He spoke to me again with a wrinkle of irritation in his

voice, like he wasn't used to folks not answering him, but still I kept my face turned away till he murmured that a friend from Kansas wished to see me. The friend was closeby in the American House, and the youth, who said his own name was Franklin Sanborn, offered to take me there.

I reached into my ticking bag for three daguerrotypes I always carried with me, images of William Lloyd Garrison, Gerrit Smith, Wendell Phillips. Even though I knew this girlish-built young man for certain now, I could never cease being careful, and would not speak till he'd named each picture right. Then I followed him out the door, through the streets, down an alley, and into the parlor of another boardinghouse where I sat in a musty-smelling, overstuffed chair, waiting. All at once he was there.

John Brown stood before me and for a moment I was stunned by his appearance. The gray eyes gleamed like flint above a long, startlingly white beard. His loose coat hung from him like a prophet's robe, and he held his strong, wiry body as taut and tall as a spruce tree. He was flanked by two younger men who bore him some likeness.

We talked and went over the maps again in his room. Brown said he feared his backers might have grown unnerved, maybe reluctant, after this long delay and the past year's treachery. Would I stand with him still?

I would.

And bring recruits with me when it was time to join him in the mountains?

I would indeed.

He was going to make his move soon, before any more betrayals could occur. He had already ordered a load of rifles, regrouped his forces, and proudly introduced his two sons Owen and Oliver as comrades-in-arms. When, he wondered precisely when, would be the optimum time to start?

I suggested the Fourth of July.

In the meantime I would return to Canada and raise recruits once more, so that all would be in readiness when he was. And yet, for the first time since I'd known John Brown, I felt uneasy. The dream image had held true, but if it was the warning it seemed then, I still believed we could outrun it together.

Back in St. Catharines I awaited his summons and fixed my sights on Independence Day.

◆ ◆ ◆

I WASN'T ABLE to wait quietly. Maybe John Brown had stirred me up more than I'd realized; maybe the tame task of raising recruits for him had made me itchy. Whatever the reasons, I got myself caught up in a big ruction only a month later, as I was passing through a New York town called Troy. For the first time in all my years of freedom work I came out in the open and snatched a black man from his captors, though I was not on the Underground Railroad, nor under the protection of darkness. I rescued the man flat-out, down-front, in the staring daylight of a city street.

His name was Charles Nalle, and though I barely remember what he looked like now, apart from the fact that he was tall and high-yaller, I remember his terror as I dragged him through a screaming mob. The mob had moved against Nalle's captors, since that poor man had just been arrested as a fugitive and was held in the Commissioner's office, pending his return to bondage in the South. I recollect the marshals who brought him down to the street, the mob's frenzied charge, and I was charging with them, at the forefront, till I had the prisoner around the waist with both my arms. The rest is a smeared image of thrashing limbs, snatching hands, flying rocks, fists, and chisels, while Nalle and me crashed to the pavement. All I could think on was that I would not leave go of him, even if the marshals got through that screeching, mauling crush to nab us both. This fugitive too had to be saved.

He wasn't sent back South, bless God, for in the end the

mob won out. Nalle's friends helped hustle him off to Canada, and I had to spend some time in hiding till things calmed down. To speak the truth, if it hadn't been for that piece of work, I don't know how I would have kept still, waiting for the Fourth of July.

I was at large by then. I was in Boston, I was ready, and so were my recruits. To distract myself I addressed an Anti-Slavery rally in Framingham, then hurried back. Nothing. No word. The white folks sent red flares against the sky, but no signals went up from the Alleghenies where I supposed John Brown to be. Independence Day passed, and there followed more silent days and nights. No one had received word excepting Sanborn, the month before, and this was an odd request for even more recruits. Some believed Brown had postponed his plans again, some said they'd heard he was in New York, others said Maryland. No one knew for sure.

John Brown had vanished just like he'd done the year before during a time of treachery and trouble. Maybe there was new trouble. Maybe that load of rifles hadn't arrived. Maybe there was good reason for some of the abolitionists to commence losing faith in their man and in his scheme. There had been delays, there had been one near-betrayal already, and there was other work to be done. There had also been many people beside Brown who'd had plans to aid my people; plans that had come to nothing, I was told.

Frederick Douglass seemed to think that Brown was still unable to arm and equip himself properly for the dangerous life he'd mapped out, and I figured that was what had caused the delay. The old man was likely holding off till he'd got all to rights, thereby cutting the chances of failure.

Douglass's words were of some comfort. Leastways, I figured, Brown wasn't going to make some poorly thought out strike all of a sudden, but would bide his time, building his strength. In some corner of my brain I'd always feared he'd jump in too quick and get caught like the Black Prophet he so admired, but now I felt reassured. Reassured but restless even so.

If I'd known right then where he was I might have tried to

find him, though that could have been a foolhardy action, a giveaway of him if I was followed. At any rate I'd no notion of where to commence searching, save for scouring the entire Allegheny range in Virginia. The hide-out he'd chosen was to remain a secret till the last; a wise thing too, for if his followers were questioned they couldn't tell what they didn't know. And if I myself didn't know, there was nothing I could do about it just then. It could be another month, another year, and I could not halt my Railroad work that long; as it was, spring had slid into summer without any sign from me to my people. I reasoned it out in my mind this way: Brown was not planning on only one move but several, and even if he did commence his mission while I was away I wouldn't be gone all that long. I could still catch up to him with my Canadian recruits after I got back, and surely he trusted me enough to know that I would come quick as I was able. In the meanwhiles I could make one escape journey with a fairly easy conscience, promising myself I'd check in Boston for word from him directly upon my return.

Soon after, I was prowling about my old home down to Dorchester County again, and once I was back on the Railroad all other things quit my mind excepting that drive to rescue more of my people. My own mission had drawn me back once again, and I believe the call within me had grown so strong over the years that it had the final say over my life, and nothing, no one could keep me from it.

I brought off another group of runaways, got them safely past Niagara Falls, but almost directly afterwards a raging illness struck me down. It took me even as I was pushing myself back into Massachusetts, seeking news of John Brown. A colored family in New Bedford sheltered me, and walled up in their house I lay fevered and delirious for some time while the earth spun in crazy wheels around me.

I didn't know that Brown had sent one of his sons North to find me, or that a bearded man calling himself Isaac Smith had rented a farm near the town of Harpers Ferry. Because I'd fallen ill in a place unknown to my friends, I didn't hear that this man had been asking for me in letters to his backers. Nor did I know that Frederick Douglass had been called to a secret meeting in Chambersburg, Pennsylvania, or that Douglass had been told to bring me there. I only heard of these happenings later, when it was almost too late.

When my delirium left off I didn't know how late it was, not rightoff, though I knew exactly what I was doing in New Bedford; my mind had frozen on the last clear thought I'd had that September day when I'd took sick. Only it was colder now. The sky had deepened in color. The leaves were coming down. It was October. My Lord.

Still weak, I dragged myself to Boston where I learned all that had happened. I also got the feeling something had changed, something had been said to Douglass that cast new light on the matter, but Frederick wasn't around then to tell me what it was. Anyways, I knew nothing big had commenced yet, so I did my best to get down to Harpers Ferry fast. John Brown mustn't think I'd let him down. I'd promised to be with him, and I would be.

Only I couldn't seem to move as quick as I wanted. There were delays connecting trains, there were long periods of waiting in depots that kept me pacing. There were times when I traveled partways on foot, but even then my steps seemed to drag like I was holding myself back for some reason. Well, maybe I was still a touch sick, but that was no excuse, it had never been, not on my own freedom train. I'd walked miles while weak, starved, or tortured by the pain from my old head wound, and I'd been able to go faster than this. All of a sudden it appeared like there were a thousand little towns in New England rising up before me like barriers, but at last I reached New York. I bought another steam-car ticket and sagged on a bench, deciding against a night train. Best to rest till the next day, best to arrive fit. An ailing woman was just what Brown didn't need right then; he was expecting a general. I'd get there soon enough, and send for my recruits once I'd reached him, but Lord, what was fretting me so about this delay? Be there soon, tomorrow, first thing.

But the next day I went nowheres and did little more than listen. I was listening to a man with a red face reading out words that crackled off the wires.

INSURRECTION HAS BROKEN OUT AT HARPERS FERRY

WHERE AN ARMED BAND OF ABOLITIONISTS HAVE FULL POSSESSION OF THE GOVERNMENT ARSENAL. Next day, that was what the telegraph told New York. EVERY LIGHT IN THE TOWN EXTINGUISHED. ALL ROADS LEADING THERE ARE BARRICADED AND GUARDED. TRAINS STOPPED AND FIRED INTO. BYSTANDERS CITIZENS SHOT DOWN BY REBELS. It couldn't be him. I wouldn't believe it. THE INSURRECTIONISTS SAY THEY HAVE COME TO FREE THE SLAVES AND INTEND TO DO IT AT ALL HAZARD. ADDING NEW FLAMES TO THE FIRES OF EXCITEMENT THE NAME OF THE LEADER IS OSAWATOMIE BROWN. Oh my Lord. IT HAS BEEN SUGGESTED THAT THE SECRETARY OF WAR BE NOTIFIED AT ONCE. But why the arsenal? A government arsenal at that? He never mentioned such a thing, well pray God he gets himself directly out of it and back to hiding without sending any more messages. Dear Lord, did he somehow figure this was the only way he could let us know he'd meant what he said? BAGGAGE MASTER OF MAIL TRAIN TAKEN PRISONER. THE LEADER REQUESTED ME TO SAY THAT THIS IS THE LAST TRAIN THAT SHALL PASS THE BRIDGE. IF IT IS ATTEMPTED IT WILL BE AT THE PERIL OF THE LIVES OF THOSE HAVING THEM IN CHARGE. Hostages then. Good. He could still barter his way out with them. THE TELEGRAPH WIRES ARE CUT AND THIS WAS THE FIRST STATION I COULD SEND A DISPATCH FROM. I could not get through to him then, all I could do was pray and keep vigil.

It was a torturous vigil that ended almost two months later on December 2, 1859, when I wore a black armband to a crowded prayer meeting in Boston's Tremont Temple. It was Martyr Day, a day when the bells never ceased tolling, a day for weeping, which I could not do; the hurt was too near the bone to bleed. Oh let us rend our garments and pour ashes on our heads, come, let us tear at our faces with sharp nails, for this day he is gone from us. It was the day they hanged John Brown.

Through my guilty grievings after his capture I'd tried to find a way of comprehending what had happened, what had changed Brown's mind. Perhaps he'd thought to rally the slaves with that single, stunning raid, perhaps he'd been planning it all the while in some secret nook of his brain. Then again, he might have concluded to try and ransom the sins of slavery by crucifying himself in one great and final act of martyrdom. But maybe he'd only grown desperate, believing his support to be drifting away, and then neither Frederick Douglass nor I had come to join him. His calls to me had gone unanswered; he might have taken my silence like a denial. And what if I had been there? Could I have saved our old plan or would I have gotten caught up in the new one, till I was fighting and killing side by side with Brown? Could I have saved his life and those of his two sons, or would I only have lost my own?

I didn't know. I hadn't been there. And now he was dead.

Time and time again in the past weeks I'd thought back on that vision which had first revealed John Brown to me. If the dream had been sent as an omen of danger, if the serpent had been tempting me toward bloodshed, then the Lord had preserved me from death. But if the dream had held a true promise, if the serpent had been the Lord's own rod and staff, then I was guilty. I had failed John Brown and my God.

I didn't know. The sign was a mystery. I mourned.

Yet one thing was clear where all else was murky. I hadn't been at Harpers Ferry, whether to save, take, or lose life, because of the Underground Railroad.

◆◆ ◆◆ ◆◆

IT WAS BACK to the Railroad that I turned once again.

If the Lord had indeed preserved me from death so that I might continue with my mission, then continuing was my task. My vocation had not been lost, my people still needed me, maybe more than they ever had, and there was work waiting to be done. Remorse could not follow me where I was going, rememberings would not hunt me down there either, for the danger-filled toil of an escape journey had always taken the whole of my mind and energies. Besides, I'd gotten one matter reasoned out before recommencing my raids.

I'd studied for a short while on reviving John Brown's plan as it had first stood and carrying it forward myself, but I'd soon cast that notion aside. The plot's secret details had been given away, an investigation in Washington was revealing more, and the times were troubled. The South had been taken with a mighty panic, far worse than the one after Nat Turner's revolt; once again slaves and free Negroes were dragged from their homes to be punished for an uprising they'd had nothing to do with. There was serious talk of war too, but that wasn't the main reason I'd concluded to leave things be. I'd come to believe that any scheme for freeing slaves in a big way would first or last spill my people's blood. In my lifetime alone it had happened like that twice, and we'd bled enough. The Lord only knows how much I wanted to see my people sprung from bondage, all of them, but I didn't want them to die doing it; the thought was unbearable. Why us? Why should we have to pour ourselves away against an evil we'd never created? John Brown had said the crimes of this guilty land would have to be purged with blood, and maybe he was right. Maybe I wasn't willing to move boldly enough. But I'd been too long in the vocation of helping people start life anew, of saving lives, of guarding them, to stomach such a purge. And unless war did break out there was still another way to free slaves. The old way, the slow way. My way.

Even so, my vocation appeared changed to me. Compared with John Brown's mighty plan, my work looked small, nothing sweeping, nothing near enough. A few souls rescued here, a paltry fistful saved there. Not quite three hundred people freed in almost a decade of labor. Little numbers. Meager clusterings of fugitives. If war didn't come, if I went on for another ten, even another twenty years, I'd still not be able to free a thousand, and it was for this that I'd abandoned kin, friends, an ally, a home. Maybe I'd done so for a mission that didn't really count for much in the larger framework of things. On the few escapes I led after Harpers Ferry, I no longer felt like I was a force to be reckoned with, a threat to the slaveowners and all they stood for.

It was in the Railroad that I searched for answers at last, even as I search there still, in my memories. After all, it was in my role as Moses that I had hoped to make some sense of my labor, my life, my own bondage, and my soul. It was as conductor, raider, outlaw, and slave-thief that I thought I'd known myself best. It was in my vocation that I believed I'd truly known my Lord, and had heeded the voices that from childhood had beckoned me to *come, follow.*

Surely this was the path marked out for me, and my small works counted for something. Surely, Lord, if I'd only freed a single slave it would have still amounted to Exodus again, Exodus for one, and surely each soul is precious in Your sight. Surely You intended me for the Railroad, and did not mean for me to set the mountains gleaming with guns, to purple the land with my people's blood.

Yet, in the wakeful nights that come to me now that it's all done with and can't be changed, I look for the Moses I was and can't find myself. I look for the fugitives I rescued and number millions missing. I look at the Underground Railroad and see only questions, questions which have been deepened by time and seared by a great war.

Be Praised

◆◆◆

Ever wonder if all that work was worth your while Moses? Maybe all them folks you saved been killed in this war that freed the rest . . . Anyways all that counts for nothin now after what Mr. Lincoln done . . .

You evil, Shadrack, always been, now shove off.

Heard bout the resta them folks on that one escape you led? They all dead, see . . .

Them dead, all?

Killed the mens was, in the war. The womenfolks nursed, cashed in with the dysentery. Don't know bout the children . . .

Why didn't you all stay fixed North? . . . I look away, won't believe.

Ever think on this? Maybe you shoulda stayed set with your mama, your daddy, even with your man . . . All that counts for nothin now, all that work . . . Did the Lord's angels forget to tell you bout Mr. Lincoln?

I have him by the collar of his coat wishing I could stuff his devilish tongue down into his guts, but of a sudden I loosen my grip. He hitches away.

New-York-New-York-change-for-Albany-Auburn-all-aboard-Auburn . . .

. . . I wake. The room comes back. Not the B. & O. depot, just home. Home in Auburn. I'm only clutching the quilt on my high old bed, not his collar. Shadrack's not here, nor ever likely to be, and I don't want to recollect him. Not him or that one escape journey, been able to stay my mind from it so far. Got to get up, move, walk around.

Rising, I pull a shawl off a peg and feel the chill floorboards pressing up against the soles of my feet. I light a candle, pause, wander down the hall. Maybe I'll just check on these folks I shelter here though I know they've been abed for hours. The candle flame trails before me, flickering. I shield it with my hand and pass into the next room.

This child here, she's sleeping sound enough. An orphan, maybe seven years old, maybe eight . . . *Martha?* She stirs, turns on her side, crams three fingers into her mouth. Not Martha, she's got her own name. It's just my mind playing tricks.

This young man, next room down. Tall, husky-built, he's too long for that bed. Must try and get hold of a bigger bed, must try and remember that. He doesn't move as the light from my candle wavers over him, and I see he's thrown the blankets off. I lean forward and reach them up over him again, covering the marks on his bare back. Yes. Before he was in the war he was bond.

Mama, Daddy, they rest together in another chamber, in this house I bought for them, for them alone really. But farther down the hall there's that old woman with the rheumatism who sleeps with her Bible, and that young gal who's staying till she can find work. They're all right, they don't need me haunting their bedsides.

Enough.

I go back to my own room. Glance at the rumpled bed. Conclude to leave it be. Still holding the candle, I pace about.

. . . that one journey Moses led . . . killed the mens was in the war, and the womenfolks . . . ever wonder? . . . Back and forth, crossing and recrossing the floor, I come to a stop at the window. The candle is reflected against the panes, and my face *. . . only one lefta that group's me . . .* I snuff the light, pinching the wick hard. In the dimness the curtains prickle like a border of holly, but no. Only starched muslin. Raising the sash, I lean out *. . . They all dead, see . . .*

Below, the porch shows up plain in the moonlight. An old man who sleeps downstairs scuffs across it and heads in the direction of the privy. With my elbows on the sill, I look around at nothing special *. . . all that tribulation for nothin . . .* the yard, the sheds,

the fence, the porch again . . . *ever think on this?* . . . I look away . . . *all that work for* . . . them, didn't I give them something even so? . . . *bout wipes out that one journey Moses led* . . . surely not? Is it?

. . . *that one journey* . . . that other porch. Hughlett's porch, where it commenced in the dark as I watched.

◀▶

◆ ◆ ◆

I HEARD THE DOOR spring open. Heels clapping on wood. He couldn't see me, there was no moon. Was that Hughlett himself or one of the guests? Hard to tell, hard to make him out either, just the outlines of a swallowtail coat against the bright house. He turned slightly. My eyes picked up a faint gleam from his studs and scarf pin, the vague creaminess of a waistcoat. The man strode to the edge of the verandah, pissed out over a frosty bush, went back. The door shut. I stayed. I kept on watching.

The last of the buggies had drawn up some time earlier, they'd all been taken to the carriage house by the grooms. Everyone was inside, everyone had come, a great crowd of them. The laughter and buzzing and babbling grew larger, spilling out through raised windows. Despite the chill night it must have grown too warm in there, what with the banks of candles, that huge, blazing log, that crush of bodies. I crept closer, well below the verandah but near enough to spy through an open casement, an amber square bordered with holly, set off by the dark. The danger of it, being so close, this excited me. Just till they got rolling, just till.

A hand lifted a wine glass into the square of light. A woman's hand, pinching the stem below a quivery red triangle. The glass tipped back beyond my sight, then returned, drained clear. A silver tray rose to take it. At eye level with the tray, a little colored boy got up in a powdered wig. A wig, Heaven's sake, and such saucy eyes beneath.

Children, white children. A streak of them running by the window, shrieking, sleepless, bright spots of color on pale cheeks. They ducked down under the sill, maybe under the tree; I could see only part of it, a mass of green done up with ribbons and berries and small candles. A long taper reached over, kindling the wicks one by one, the narrow flame threading upwards and away. Good. Almost ready.

The window emptied of all excepting that slice of evergreen. I heard a jumble of footsteps, a tinkling crash, a chair scraping out. They'd gathered in another corner of the hall.

And then at last, the music, the singing. I could tell by the loud raw-pitched voices that the wine tray had been passed several times before; there would have been a nog bowl somewheres too. Under the voices a spinet clinked into the first carol, the notes punching out over the still brittle air. The party was rolling indeed. I moved off.

GOD BLESS THE MASTER OF THIS HOUSE
AND ALL THAT ARE THEREIN
AND TO BEGIN THIS CHRISTMASTIDE
WITH MIRTH LET US SING . . .

Down past the carriage house, sticking to its far wall, its shadows. From within I heard the rattle of dice and weary laughter from the grooms. On past the stables, the smokeshed, the well, the cutting garden. Down the hill, keeping low, meeting no one. Turning once, I saw the Big House shining above me against the star-strewn sky. It had never appeared so grand in daylight, but just then it seemed to be all windows, light-streamers, and music.

THEN LET US ALL MOST MERRY BE
AND SING WITH CHEERFUL VOICE . . .

The Quarter. Bigger than Thompson's but likewise hidden from the Big House by a hill, its hearthfires glimmering. The caroling was a bit fainter down there, but still plain enough as I sneaked back of the cabins. I made a low whistle. It was arranged. They knew where to meet me. Here and there I peered through cracked shutters.

For we have GOOD *occasion now*
This time for to REJOICE . . .

A cloak snapped down off a wall peg.

A sleeping baby was muffled up warm, lifted against a shoulder.

A bony seamed hand reached out, the palm tawny and calloused. First the walking stick. Then the bundle.

I whistled again.

then sing with voices cheerfully
for Christ this night was born . . .

Heading toward the meeting place, I looked back over my shoulder. Dim figures were slipping past the spaces between the cabins, reappearing, vanishing. One sped across the front of the row, a shadow blinking against the flushed windows.

. . . *did from death deliver* . . .
when we . . . *forlorn* . . .

The fodder house. Small, cramped, the walls only wide-spaced slats. Soon they were there, five grown ones, a child, and an infant, scrunched down amidst the heaps of chopped stalks. They jumped at the sight of me. I reached out to touch them all, feeling again the rightness of it, the love. Then I took the pistol from my belt.

"No talk. Line up. Hold hands, stay close."

I took a fast look around outside, ducked back in.

"Now."

They followed me out of the fodder house, their breathing sharp and shallow. We crept alongside a fence till it ended, skirted a stretch of brush, a stand of trees.

. . . *upon this night* . . . *born* . . .

The music had faded away by the time we'd reached a field of dead cornshocks. I led them into it, and then the only sound was the rustling we made going through. Going fast. Going out. And like always, a ripe strength filled me as I felt a new escape party at my back. The stalks bent around us; here and there a dried cob crunched underfoot. I looked back, looked ahead, all the while sensing the runaways' excitement and fear.

Deeper into the field.

Chill damp air lay against my cheeks, but the weather wasn't bad for that time of year, not real bitter. Thank the Lord, no snow yet. So long as the weather held, my passengers would be warm enough, leastways while they were moving. Just thrashing amongst these crops likely kept their minds off the cold.

All at once I heard a rustle that didn't come from us. A hurried *shush-shush* a good ways behind, toward the place where we'd entered the field. A steady straight-on purposeful sound that an animal doesn't make. I stopped the group an instant. That other noise stopped with us. I started my passengers up again. That other rustling recommenced as we did. Once more I made them halt. Listened. Heard nothing. Went on. Heard it yet again. Someone surely was back there, unable to see where we were, tracking us by the sounds we made. And those sounds couldn't be helped.

No one stampeded, no one else seemed alarmed. The runaways must have been listening to their own noises, intent on each step, and their ears weren't tuned like mine. Just as well. I said nothing for fear of touching off a panic, and only moved them along faster, trying to get clear of the field. They kept pace, still holding to each other and to me.

At last the stalks sank away, leaving us on the fringe of some woods. I felt for my passengers, pushed them over to one side, and whispered a single direction.

"Down."

They dropped. The warning in my voice was enough to keep them there, silent. I crouched at the field's edge, waiting. The thrashing grew more frantic. Came closer. A figure emerged from the cornshocks. It wavered there for a moment, almost a shadow, hard to make out. I dived on it quick, locking my arm around a wiry neck as I jammed the pistol into his back. In the starlight I could just barely see the man was black, but I didn't loose my hold.

"Ow shit leave go don't mean no harm."

"Who you!"

"S'me, Thompson's Shadrack, you got no call to half-choke me."

"You best say quick why you followed us."

"Catch you up is all, figured to run."

"Yeah? Without the others? Didn't hear nothin bout you."

"Only just concluded to go last minute, heard you was around, heard you signal, seen you clear out. Was hired over to Hughlett's, see, and I . . ."

"Shut up. Get your ass over there."

Lord, this was one man I hadn't wanted to lay eyes on again. I recollected him, we went way back, and no, didn't want to carry him North; first time I'd ever felt so about a fugitive. But it was a point with me never to turn anyone away, and besides, this nigger would mouth off if I left him behind, he'd do it out of spite. Hating him, I yanked Shadrack over to the others. They appeared frozen, scared numb by what they'd just witnessed.

"Nothin gone wrong," I said. "Just one real late-timer runaway here. All right, everybody up. Shadrack, I said get up. No more trouble, hear me?"

We cut directly east toward the Nanticoke River, and reached it around three hours to sunup. Salty moist air rose up at me, welcoming, familiar. I'd followed this river on most of my past raids since it ran north like the Choptank, but wasn't so well-known as an escape route, and thereabouts the Nanticoke was smaller, with fewer towns to dodge along its banks.

My passengers stirred and whispered behind me. They could barely see that swatch of water blending with the dark land and trees, but I knew it was a kind of road marker for them. It meant they'd truly cleared the plantation, it was proof of the distance they'd come. Not such a great distance, but something, the first step away.

Even so, they were beat out from the night's walk. I could feel their weariness as they sagged against me and each other; dim, faceless, leaning figures. It was cold. A December wind sliced off the Nanticoke, damp and steady. The baby whimpered. The child whimpered. Someone sneezed. I motioned them on just a little farther.

There was an old shed some rods away, back in the woods, hidden by dense trees. A free Negro might have lived there once, but no one used it anymore. No one even seemed to know about it. I'd come upon the place on an earlier journey, and whenever I returned to the shed it was thick with dust and cobwebs, clearly untouched between times. All it sheltered was some boards piled up in a corner, coils of rotting rope, and the remains of a fishnet. Whatever. Within the windowless walls we'd be safe for a time, shielded from the wind, and maybe a bit warmer. Everyone crushed through the crooked doorway after me, blowing their breath out, slapping arms, stamping feet. I still couldn't see them plain, so I went around placing my hand on each head till I'd counted seven, reaching down lower to feel for the child.

"This safe, Moses?" A man's voice, not Shadrack's, one of the two I didn't know.

"For sure. Been here with others, nothin once gone wrong. Just talk down, stay in. Anybody got to piss, do in the corner. Dig into that food you slung along, but keep some for farther on."

A match scraped on a boot heel. It flickered out, leaving a smell of sulphur on the air, before I could see who'd lit it. There was a scrabbling noise where that pile of boards always lay.

"No fires." I spoke firm into the dark. "Sorry, but there's one thing ain't safe. Someone could spot that fast, the whole place could go up besides. Best everybody try and catch some sleep, we move again at dawn. Herd together and the chill won't feel so bad, rest easy. The white folks got that party to snore off and come day they bound to have thick heads. Then there be callers and church and holiday dinner and whatall — they won't miss you for a good while. I be just a ways off past the door to keep watch. Wake you when it come time."

They were settling down on the dirt floor, rustling and munching and making a soft murmuration. The baby's cries ceased as a sucking sound commenced. A deep yawn, then another. Peacefulness folding down.

"Bless you, Moses." That voice, fluty and calm, must have belonged to the old woman I'd glimpsed in the fodder house.

"And you. Rest now. Be back."

I went outside.

Everything was blessed quiet in the woods. Cold but not unbearable. The wind had quit. The trees stood stiff around me, their topmost branches webbing against the sharp stars. No sign of anyone else, no sign of pursuit; Christmas morning coming on, all to rights so far.

A sudden twinge of pain caught my temple, a harsh one, just for a moment. It didn't matter. The beginnings of another journey always got me to feeling so good I was able to cast that trouble aside. Wrapped in my blanket, I sat on a log and watched. A silence had falled over the shed. No doubt they'd all passed into a sleep. The stars swung around, softened, grew fainter. My head drooped forward. I dozed, woke, nodded off again, always listening, listening even so. No warning noises reached me. The night finished calm.

Just before dawn I roused my passengers.

◆◆◆

IN THE WAVERING MILKY LIGHT I got my first plain look at them. The night's voices had become faces and the faces had become people, and the people had names and airs and ways about them.

"Before we start, say quick what you called by. You?"

"Josiah Bailey. Joe." Big man towering over me, in his prime, huge bald head, scarred cheek. Mild voice, oddly gentle face above that massive frame.

"Bernette Wilson, that's me." She spoke right up. Young, pretty, smart-eyed. A lift to her chin. Willowy, man-pleasing figure of a gal, but tough, strong.

"And you there?"

"Tazwell Robinson . . . my woman, Addie . . . child's Martha . . . and the baby here, mean to baptize him up North so he begin right." Easy and open, this man, short-statured and lean, with a springy stride. Coppery skin, wide smiling mouth.

Addie didn't say anything, just cast her eyes down. Shy woman, dark, built squat and heavy. Smooth face on her, smooth hands trembling as she drew her children close. And Martha, roundabouts seven, was all spindly arms and legs, her cloak hanging from a narrow little body. Pointy chin, and frightened eyes staring from beneath rows of neatly platted braids.

"Rebecca's how I'm called. My Christian name's all I set a great store by." The fluty-voiced old woman, a good ways past sixty, puckered skin, not many teeth, but tall and solid. Must have been a field hand like the rest appeared, excepting for Addie. Serene and firm-spoken, this Rebecca, she'd do all right.

"Well, Shadrack. You and me surely ain't strangers." Lord no.

I lined them up again.

"Hereon keep it quiet, if you got to speak, speak down. There be some times for talk, specially when we rest. Mostly don't journey by daylight but we best get a good jump on em before Christmas pass, it's our grace-time. Let's go."

All that day we walked through the muddy eastern marshes, sometimes by the Nanticoke, then looping inland for a while, zigzagging, always screened in by the tall grasses. No boats could be seen, no people, and only once the slope of a gabled roof rose in the distance, looking small as a peaked cap. A weak winter sun slid up the sky, and a smattering of wild geese honked past, breaking the stillness for just a few moments. Ahead the grasses rippled on and on, drab, bleached, tiresome to watch, and the trees beyond stood gray, deadened. Even so, there was a smart step to my people at first, a sense of purpose and maybe triumph. It hadn't gotten hard yet, everything must have seemed within close reach.

"*. . . on my way anda won't turn back, yes Lord, on my . . .*"

That sounded like Tazwell, but he'd trailed off suddenly before I turned around. Likely he'd just caught himself, recollecting the danger, and I knew the thought of it would keep slipping in and out of everyone's minds. It was out there somewheres, only concealed for the time being. And for the time being, not such a mighty presence, not so near, not in the commonplace daylight and the newness of escaping.

"Good you come, Moses. Wonder how old Master bound to end his Christmas when he find us gone. Wager he go out and get hisself drunk all over again."

"Bernette, I just hope. Hope he ain't even able to sit a horse. Best we all move quick before he do find out anyways. Pick it up back there, Tazwell, Shadrack. Too early to drag."

"Lord, I ain't seen so much mud since we dug that new privy for . . ."

"Sshh. Keep it down now."

Up through the grasses, over to higher ground, small hillocks of earth, then slime again, slipping along, screened in . . . *Ooops shit . . . hush!* Cattails, reeds, we pushed them back, pushed ahead on into that Christmas morning.

"Daddy, when we get presents?"

"Not now, Martha-baby. Be real quiet."

"But we always get presents, Marse Will he always give em out."

"She just a child, Moses, she don't comprehend."

"Martha? Got some molasses candy and a sugar-tit for you. What you want first, baby? . . . The molasses?"

"Martha, you thank Moses now."

Everything the color of doeskin, there's a dull sameness to a marsh, and Christmas had always been brightly colored for them before. Would others besides Martha think back on the way it was down to home, and maybe lose drive, missing it? I knew this was the best time of year for bondfolk, and likely the hardest time of all for them to cut loose. But they'd come nonetheless, they were still coming on behind me. If they were making shiny memory pictures in their minds it didn't show as I hustled them along.

"Rebecca, you all right?"

"Can't complain. Bless God, He give me a strong constitutional. Was able to outrun a man when I was in my prime."

"Well that's fine. But stay to the front like you been so's I can keep you in sight."

"Don't mean to be no burden, Moses, not on you or nobody here. I lay my burden with Jesus, He help me make it through."

A thick spate of clouds, a chill over us for a time, silence as I walked them ankle-deep in water a ways. But field hands knew cold, they knew outdoor struggles, and hurts worse than cuts from sharp-edged grasses. These folks were wearing their summer and winter issue both, layered over them so thick as to make them almost shapeless; that would help if the weather worsened. The clouds shoved off toward the south, the sun came out again. A little warmer then, back onto drier land, and the pace quickened just a little too.

"You awful quiet Shadrack, what you so broody bout?"

"Just can't believe you turned up to be Moses for real. Heard on you acourse, but still . . . ever kill anyone with that pistol?"

"Thank the Lord, no. Hope I never need to."

"Say Taz, told you me and Hat Tubman come up same time. Recollect when she wasn't no Moses nohow, nary but a . . ."

"All right, enough talk now. Pick it up folks, we got to make time."

It didn't look like we were getting anyplace. The marsh grass never changed much, excepting that here it was eye-high, there it reached only to my chest. Sometimes a patch of open water shone in the distance, then sank away behind the reeds, and everything appeared the same as before. But we were indeed getting someplace, getting farther inland.

"Bout wore out, what you say we rest?"

"Too soon. You done good so far."

Further into the marsh, slowing down a bit.

"Drier hereabouts, good place to stop."

"Can't yet."

"Well, when?"

"Not yet. Hold on a while longer."

Zigzagging back toward the river once more. Slower still.

"Mama, can't go no more, tired . . ."

"Somebody carry this child. Joe, you got the shoulders for it, you want to hoist Martha up?"

"Wheeee . . ."

"Hush, honey. Addie, let me take the baby now, spell you some."

"I can manage . . . well . . . all right . . . careful, Moses."

Closer to the river, sticking to it, screened in. Glancing back I saw how dark we all appeared against the tawny grasses, especially at noon, sun high but dim. Rest-time. They ate what was left in the bundles they'd brought.

"Mercy, this ashcake's like to a rock. All we got left in here, Addie, maybe I can break it three ways."

"Don't you crack a tooth on that thing, Tazwell. Done that once myself and swallowed it right down, the tooth, was fit to choke."

"Huh, they don't mention suchlike in them big tales they tell bout you, Moses. Say, how far's Canada?"

"Not so far's it appears just now. What you troubled over, Addie?"

"Dunno . . . oh, I guess . . . well Canada appears bout as far off as . . . as Heaven to me is all."

"Then your master surely won't be able to meet us there, you figure? Here, believe the baby wants suck."

"Want a drink myself, shame us big folks can't have a tit each to our own come mealtimes."

"Bernette! Girl, you come out with the blamedest . . ."

"Yeah, well you know some milk'd do you good too, Taz, do everybody. Anyways there's this here."

"That water may still be a touch brackish . . ."

"Phooo-eeee! Sure is."

"Never mind, we be to good water soon. You all bout done? Up children, get a move on again."

Midafternoon. Our shadows were falling directly in front of us as we reached Marshyhope Creek. It branched off from the Nanticoke, narrower, reedy, but the water there was sweet. We drank, went on.

"What we keep walkin in and out the water for?"

"To kill our sweet scents."

The freshness from rest and food wore off, our shadows were lengthening, falling east of us. The footsteps behind me grew slow, uneven. Blisters don't take long to rise; I often forgot that, my own feet were so calloused by then. Dusk was getting ready to come down, and a shivery dampness was rising from the marsh, the creek.

"All right, we bed down here."

"*Here,* Moses? Flat-out in the middle of nowheres? Never be able to sleep with all this water around."

"Dry enough place. And this marsh got to be somewheres in creation, that's a fact. Supper first."

"Nothin left to eat. We finished off every scrap at noon."

"Never mind. Got some in this sack somewheres . . . there . . . hold this, will you . . . should be some cheese and . . ."

"Hat Tubman, what you done? Pilfered Hughlett's smokehouse?"

"Don't see it that way, Shadrack. Always figure it's rude to turn down what gifts the Lord send my way. He just happened to send these whilst I scouted Hughlett's place is all. Well, children. Christmas dinner."

"Ain't bad, ain't bad atall."

"Pass that here, appears like enough to . . ."

"Hold it. Where's Rebecca gone?"

"Behind you, Moses."

"Good. You want to say the blessing first?"

After we'd eaten I went off alone to look around, came back as the sky faded, and watched my people from a little distance. I saw a tight group pressed close together, encircled by the endless marsh and the unseeable danger and the faraway hope; a row of heads, a cluster of bodies, uneven, separate, yet one.

A breeze came through the cattails, whispery and thin. The water gurgled closeby. As the darkness came down a few hushed words reached me; folks making talk to hold back fear, to keep touch with their voices, letting each other know they were there, all right, near.

They answered my low, whistled signal, and I went to them. Together we cut great swatches of reeds till there was a pile to burrow under, a sharp slick shelter for sleeping. They all crawled in, the heap writhing as they settled themselves.

Through the whisking and muttering, Joe called over to tell me he'd stand lookout next turn.

I sat up keeping vigil as the night deepened, grew larger. It was cold. There was no fire. But there was a warmth.

◆◆◆

"WAKE UP! Come on, up now!"

"Whas happen . . . ?"

"Who . . . Moses?"

"They on us?" "S'wrong?"

"Time children, got to move before first light. Hush! Ain't nobody on us, get up."

I rustled out of the pile with them, looked around, and saw Joe's dark bulk nearby where I'd put him on lookout a while before. He'd brought a blanket along and had it tented over his head, but when I came toward him I saw he was wide awake and watchful. We whispered together. He'd seen nothing amiss, everyone had rested deep, there'd been no sound from anywheres; fact was, he'd just prowled about to make sure all was to rights.

It would be safe enough to move my passengers even though we'd be going inland, leaving the protecting water, journeying a few miles west of the Marshyhope.

"Keep ahold each other, remember. Don't nobody get lost now."

I put Joe at the end of the line, and went up front. The rest followed like sleepwalkers through the dark grasses, stumbling, stiff-limbed from resting on the damp ground, and I pushed them hard. Had to get there, Christmas was over, the night slipping away. She'd be waiting if nothing had gone wrong.

The sky had grown faintly bluish by the time we'd reached Hurlock, and I halted them within a fringe of trees bordering the village. They were shivering, still drowsy too, but as they peered out each one seemed to come awake with a snap.

"A *town?*"

Addie clutched her children and Tazwell moved his family back a pace. He was staring at me, they all were. Shadrack jerked my sleeve.

"You crazy? Ain't no way in the world we make it through there without somebody see, you bound to get us killed."

"Just hold on. Use your eyes, man, that town's asleep. Don't mean to march you down the main street neither. We skirt the place is all. Now, there's a . . ."

"Still don't smell right to me. Best we keep to the marsh."

"Hush your face this instant. Do just like I say and listen up. Everybody. There's a friend on the watch for us closeby. We move in pairs, safer like that, a group's too easy to spot. Joe and Bernette, one way. Rebecca, Shadrack, another. Taz and Addie a third, and I got to ask you to trust me with the children. We all headed for the same house, but once you get there, don't nobody go near the door. Creep on your bellies around back, hide in the haystacks direct, and stay put till I say different. No talk, no moves, you comprehend me correct?"

I outlined the three different routes, said how the house looked, and made them repeat it all back to me.

"Go on now. Quick. Got to get there before sunup."

As soon as Addie was out of sight I drugged the baby with laudanum, just enough to give it a short silent sleep, then crept past the town with the infant on my hip and the girlchild clinging to my hand. Martha was shaking from cold or fright or both, and when I looked down at her I saw her lips were fixing themselves for a wail. I whipped the sugar-tit out of my bag and plugged her mouth with it like I was corking a bottle.

Her eyes smiled up at me, surprised, and as we moved on again I realized that child hadn't smiled once till now.

We reached the house ahead of the others, crept around back, keeping low, and I buried Martha in a haystack while I knelt behind it, whispering to her.

"Mmm, don't that hay smell fine?"

"No. Want Mama."

"She be here direct, honey. Meanwhiles you just rock your brother, but don't make a sound, all right?"

Martha's face came through the hay, along with the hand that held the sticky sugar-tit. Her wide eyes glowed with tears, and her face was puckering for a howl again.

"You a great big gal, too big to cry."

"Mama she big and she cry."

I stuck the sugar-tit back in her mouth.

A moment passed. Another. Two shadows slipped through the field, disappearing into a haystack farther off. Only instants later two more figures slunk into hiding, but one pair was still missing. I crouched there, every muscle tensed. Judging by the size and shape of those figures I knew it was Tazwell and Addie who had not yet come. Maybe they'd gotten lost, maybe they'd wandered into the town, and that town would soon be waking. Martha quavered at me through the candy.

"Mama here yet?"

"Sure, honey."

She peered around, sniffing a lie, and tears streamed down her face as we waited.

At last, two more forms crept through the field and into another haystack.

"Mama!"

I had to hold the child back.

"You be with her soonest, Martha. Meantime stay put, just hold tight to the baby. No tears, keep hid, promise?"

A small nod. Promise.

I pulled the hay down over Martha's face and remained hunched behind her stack. Might be best to shift them all to the barn before it grew any lighter, but for some reason I delayed, peering out at the house.

It rested there, dark and still, but as I watched the back door opened quietly. Through the changing light I could see a white apron, Quaker headcap, pale face and hands. She kept standing on the small back porch like she was taking the air, maybe gazing around the field. I motioned to her, then crept forward.

As soon as I reached the porch she held a finger to her lips and gripped my arm hard. Her eyes flashed some warning as she jerked her head toward the barn, brows raised, questioning.

I nodded toward the haystacks which were catching the first flecks of new sun.

The Quaker let out her breath like she was relieved of a mighty trouble.

Above us, within the house, there was a sudden stirring; a clatter, a crash, a pair of rough voices. My friend vanished through the door at once.

I turned to scuttle back toward the hay just as an upstairs window scraped open and slops from a chamber pot splattered down next to my left shoulder. Directly overhead a man was leaning on the sill drawing in great breaths of morning air while he spoke to someone else in the room with him. The words weren't clear, but that was no Quaker talking.

Daring no movement toward the field, I shrank back against the clapboard wall. The voice withdrew, boots thudded off and out of my hearing for a moment, then came to a halt in the kitchen just behind me. More muttering, her voice, theirs. I'd only taken two swift steps when the footfalls neared the door.

I dodged back to the porch, reached under my coat to grasp the pistol in the waistband of my skirt, and tore the kerchief off my neck. Facing away from the door, I knelt on the porch stairs and was polishing the lowest step with my kerchief as two men came down past me, followed by the Quaker.

They stopped nearby to offer her gruff thanks for the night's lodging while I went on scrubbing like I intended to take the paint off the wood. From the tail of my eye I saw that the haystacks were deathly still. My hidden hand kept a firm grip on the pistol. I knew what those men were. Oddly enough what came into my mind was not a prayer, but something Jacob Jackson had once said to me: *Act like the way they spect niggers to act and they don't mostly notice you.*

The boots crunched toward the barn. A short time later horses clattered away, and my friend was beside me. She seemed to be panting.

"It is clear now, Moses. Do get up, I didn't think to trap thee out here. Scrubbing steps! Those Godless men usually lie abed late. I was invaded by the heathen last night — of all times, with thy passengers due. It may be sinful, but I simply cannot love all my enemies." She blew her nose hard.

There was nothing angelic about Leah Jenkins. A rail-thin, tall, sharp-featured woman, her long nose was always tipped with redness, as if from some continuous cold. The bluish veins standing out at her temples ran toward the creases in her forehead, her skin was chapped, her hands rough and red-knuckled. Past fifty by then, she and her man had worked hard to build up this farm; they'd also worked hard in other ways, for us.

I motioned toward the haystacks once more. "Small shipment for a change."

"Thee can move them now, I'll come after. Thank Heaven thee put them in the hay first, not in with those wicked men's horses." Leah Jenkins blew her nose again.

Moments later my passengers were in the barn.

The Jenkins's station was reached through a hatch in the floor, hidden just a few paces from the cow's stall. I scraped some straw away, lifted the trapdoor, and we climbed down a ladder into the room below. Mrs. J.'s voice floated above us.

"Are thee all in? Yes? Then I'll close it now and cover it . . . best light the lamp . . . I'll be down again the other way in a moment . . ."

The hatch shut down as I lit the oil lamp, and the room flickered up around us. It wasn't so very much bigger than a smokehouse. The walls were battened with pine to keep the dirt from sifting in, and the boarded ceiling was pierced with a row of small air-slits which opened directly on the barn itself. The place smelled of manure, feed, leather, and stock, but it was clean and bare. A pile of blankets lay in one corner, two slop buckets stood in another, and the lamp had been in its usual spot by the narrow door in the far wall.

My people appeared to be caught between wonderment at this secret room, and suspicion of the strange white woman. Tazwell and Addie gazed about just like I'd done the first time I'd been in such a hideaway, and Rebecca settled herself on the floor. The others pressed close to me, whispering questions. Joe sounded mightily alarmed.

"You sure this ain't a trap? How come she shelter slaves and slave traders alike? Seen that trash before, Cummings and Baker, blackbird-pushers at-your-service, seen em in Cambridge, that's a fact, that's who she had in there."

"Smooth down, they wasn't here to do business. Traders and other folks too, they come by sometimes just to stop the night, then go off again. Miz Jenkins can't turn some away and others not. She'd be a fool to rile a slave pusher, specially with a station under her barn, she best act easy so's they don't sniff around. Good people, her and her man both. Quaker. They hid me and passengers on four, five journeys now. All's to rights here, truly."

"Appears odd, even so. Why'd white folks want to help us?"

I told Bernette, told them all as plain as I was able, and then the door in the wall opened. We caught a glimpse of the tunnel running between the house and the hidden room before the Quaker came forward, carrying a basket and a candle. She kicked the door shut behind her and laid the things down.

"Folks, I want you to know Miz Leah Jenkins."

Everyone hung back.

"Thee are most welcome. My husband will be sorry to have missed thee, his sister was taken ill suddenly . . . I know . . . I always seem to take some getting used to. There should be enough food here for all, I hope, and I shall be back again later. Before it's time for thee to go, perhaps thee will accept some warm things for the rest of thy journey? Meanwhile take what comfort thee can."

She went off, clanging the bolt on the other side of the door, and the moment she'd gone everyone commenced talking at once as they passed the basket around.

"Bread's still warm can you beat that . . . she seem all right even if . . . Apples! Catch, Addie . . . speak odd, but shoot, guess she no different from them Bucktown Quakers . . . Martha, you too big to mush up potatoes and smear youself like a . . . yeah, they wasn't trash, never owned one nigger, they . . . snug in here anyways and . . . well get your big feet out my face . . . no one'd never catch on we was . . . chicken wing? Split it with you . . . Moses, you say you been here four times and nothin . . . ooops, watchit, milk in that jug . . . wonder how long . . . beat out, just hit me . . . Lord forgive us, we forgot to say the blessing . . ."

Shadrack surprised me, he was so good with the children. He managed to get Martha laughing aloud, tickling her and singing nonsense songs till she climbed into his lap, and he rocked the squalling, newly wakened baby too, once Addie had nursed it.

Tazwell, it turned out, was a storyteller.

"My daddy always used to spin tales bout a slave called Pompey. One time this Pompey he helped his master deck out fine before a duel. Then he just stand back and gaze at the Man.

'Well,' old Master say, 'Pompey, how do I look?' The slave say, 'O massa, mighty mighty.' 'Mighty what?' Master ask, and the slave tell him, 'Mighty noble.' Master got a question, 'What do you mean by noble, Pompey?' and Pompey say, 'Why sir, you just look like one *lion.*' 'Why Pompey, where have you ever seen a lion?' The Man ask, and Pompey answer back, 'Down yonder in the field the other day, massa.' 'Pompey, you foolish fellow, that was a *jackass.*' 'Was it, massa?' Pompey ask, 'Well like I said, you look just like him.' 'Why thank you, Pompey,' old Master say, and he go off to fight his duel."

We couldn't stop laughing, even Addie, who'd likely heard that story well over a hundred times. She loosened up, left off acting so trembly, and took charge of settling folks, passing blankets around, arranging us so we all got a little leg-room in that small place. She even managed to find a ledge for the lamp which I'd missed before, and then she neatened the empty food basket.

Bernette and Joe sat with me for a while, and I listened to their talk.

"Well, goodbye to Old Pig-Ass. I swear our Marse Will appeared more like to a sow than anyone I ever seen, the way he wiggled when he walked. You go on and laugh, Joe, that's a fact. Know how mean he was, Moses? The old folks made the nigger preacher promise that they wouldn't be buried near him if they died first. You know how they do with the pet house servants or the driver, drop em into the white boneyard? Well, folks wanted to make sure they wasn't laid to rest next to Marse Will, just in case the Devil got messed up in his mind and carried off the wrong body."

"Lord, go on with you, Bernette."

"Myself, I ain't superstitioned, but that man was evil. Before I got sold to him I had two good masters, got to say so, first Old Sir, and when Old Sir die, his son. That white boy and me was near in age, played together when we was small sometimes . . . and when he growed up to be Master . . . but anyways. Horse stomped him dead, estate broke up, and once I become Hughlett's Bernette it all turn bad. Evil man, Marse Will. He never done nothin to Tazwell and Addie I heard on — Taz he just figured to get free when that new baby come — but I got my reasons to hate Will Hughlett and so do Joe."

"Yeah, for one thing he wouldn't leave Bernette and me marry. See, I was only hired out to him for a while, but I done like a overseer's job for him, done him good work. That's where I gone wrong. Hughlett concluded to buy me."

"You won't believe what Joe costed, Moses. One thousand down, one thousand on time."

"Sweet Heaven, man. Hughlett's out plenty now I run you off."

"Reasoned to go with you soon's I passed to him. First day, first thing, he licked me real bad. Never touched me before, wasn't no call to then neither, ceptin he do all his new hands that way to show em they *his* niggers thereon in. And I say to myself, Next time Moses come, next time . . . Still, I trouble over one thing. You figure I put everyone here to risk on account I priced so high? The reward likely be . . ."

"Joe, don't you even think on it. That why you raised up your hands over your face when Miz Jenkins come in?"

Mrs. J. came later on with another basket of food and a clean chamber pot. When she collected the full slop buckets from the corner, everyone stared again; that was a task only for slaves. I followed her partways into the tunnel and we whispered together. Time for us to commence journeying again, I told her. She said she'd knock on the trapdoor above when it got dark, when it was safe for us to leave the shelter through the hatch. We'd done it like that before, and she mostly handed extra cloaks out as we went off through the barn. Then I went back, closed the door, and heard her shoot the bolt on the other side.

"She be back, Moses?"

"One more time."

"She leave us out then?"

"Maybe, honey. Got to see when she come back."

But she didn't come. Not that evening when the faint light from the air-slits dimmed, and we turned up the lamp. And then I turned the wick down fast, hushing everyone. There were footsteps above, several, some heavy, and voices muted by the cow's lowing. Maybe Mrs. J.'s man had returned and they were doing the chores, maybe she'd got neighbors in to help. Maybe she had unwelcome guests again and the time wasn't right.

She didn't come, not then, not that night. Folks dozed on and off, but I kept hearing things, real or imagined I wasn't sure, so I just paced about with the candle, fixing a blanket here and there, trying not to tread on anyone.

When I reached the covers up over Bernette, she commenced to thrash in her sleep.

"Get offa me . . . leave go no . . . sugar nothin get away . . . no white man's whore . . . pain me don't . . ."

Joe moved close and held her while she tossed through the

nightmare. At length she quieted, leaned against his shoulder, and after a time Joe's head drooped down till he and Bernette were resting together.

A whimper came from Shadrack. He too seemed locked in evil dreamings as he twisted about, spun over onto his belly and buried his head in the blankets. I knew he wouldn't want my comfort, knew I didn't want to give him any either, but he appeared like to smother. I lifted the blanket, loosed his shirt, and pulled it up his sweating skin. His back was all over covered with scars; lash marks on this man who'd been boasting to Martha he'd always played it so smart he never got licked, not once. I pulled his shirt down and moved off before he could wake.

"Ain't you able to rest, child?"

"Rebecca? Didn't figure you was still awake."

"Don't sleep much at my age, but you got to, you young yet. *Unless the Lord build the house, they labor in vain who build it.* Know this from the same psalm too, *He give to His beloved in sleep.*"

"You able to read?"

"Uh-huh, my first mistress showed me how. For years and years I was mostly allowed to keep a Bible. Was a comfort. They took it away after Nat Turner. Even so, I hold in my head parts I learned, a comfort still. Sometimes in the night I say what I can recollect, lull myself like . . . Come sit by me, Moses, ain't no room anywheres else for you to settle. Go on, lean back. Maybe if I tell you a psalm you feel some peace, nod off . . ."

Folks were just stirring out of their own slumberings when I awoke. It wasn't dawn yet, but my passengers had been geared up for early rising, geared to the driver's horn. Daylight commenced to filter through the air-slits after what seemed a long time, and still there was no sign from Leah Jenkins.

"Where you figure the lady's at?"

"Up and about her chores most likely. She got this farm to work all on her own what with her man away."

"Hungry, Mama . . . she gone to fetch us the basket again, Moses?"

"She get to us when she able, honey."

As the day wore on I got edgy. My head throbbed all the while I paced circles in a corner, waiting, listening, alert to the smallest sounds from the barn. Everyone else was getting restless too, cramped in the muscles, stiff in the joints, stepping on each other's hands when they tried to move about. We were all hungry. The air was sour. The slop buckets overflowed. Time and time again folks asked to go above for a breath or a stretch. Time after time I told them no. Something was wrong, had to be, but I didn't tell them that.

After a while they began nodding off again, and Addie commenced a tune to soothe the whining children. After she'd sung it through four or five times it started to grate on me.

. . . when you wake you will have
all the pretty bitty horses . . .

A noise above, I thought. Hard to tell over that droning song going on and on.

. . . all the pretty bitty horses . . .

Another faint noise overhead. Closer to where we were? I couldn't be certain with Addie's toneless voice filling my ears.

. . . when you wake you will have . . .

I would have snapped at her to stop, but just then I heard a definite, spaced knock at the trapdoor and I darted forward. Heads jerked up. Addie's singing ceased. Longing eyes followed me as I gripped the ladder and started to climb. When I opened the hatch fresher air breathed into the secret room for a moment.

Up in the lamplit barn Mrs. J. was milking the cow. She didn't turn even after I'd shut the trapdoor back down, but spoke low, as if to the animal.

"There still may be watchers on the house, stay back."

"Bad trouble?"

"Providential thee arrived early, it began last night. One search party, then another today. I dared not visit below or even risk a word till now . . . nice girl, easy, I didn't forget to milk thee this time . . . They asked after thy people. And thee of course. Searched the house; the barn."

"Heard em. Rewards posted so soon?"

"Not yet printed. Word of mouth."

"High money?"

"Indeed. Especially for thee, and the one called Josiah Bailey . . . easy girl, almost done . . . They appear to be gone now, but see that no one comes up for air all the same. One never knows."

"Sorry to make you trouble. We can clear out come nightfall."

"No matter. It would be best to stay, they might be up ahead . . . good girl, Katie, I've done with thee, a full pail . . . I must get back. I'll come down shortly if it seems safe."

She rose, patted the cow, and went off, never glancing at me. I stayed in the barn's shadows some moments, then peered out through a crack in the wall. Dusk would be falling soon. The late afternoon sun slanted in my eyes, and I stood there squinting, trying to figure a way out in case I concluded to move. Suddenly I heard the trapdoor open, and wheeled around to see Shadrack standing behind me. I sprang toward him.

"Get back down direct."

"Just after a breath."

"Just heave your ass back down, hear me?"

"Oh I *see*. You fit to see the light of day cause you Moses, and we ain't, that how you figure it?"

"*Sssht.*"

"Don't you yank on me, you got no . . ."

"Said *hush*. No ructions on this journey, now move it."

"Don't you order me around like I count for shit, won't have it. Leave go, don't you grab at me neither, ow, aha, done give Missy Moses the slip. Believe I might take me a walk, can't do no harm, this place appears just as still as . . ."

He was barely out the door, and I was almost on top of him when his back stiffened and one raised foot hung frozen in midair. Shouts came from the woods nearby, a rifle cracked. As I stuffed that blasted nigger down into the hatch I heard feet trampling toward the barn.

I dropped down onto the ladder, eased the trapdoor almost closed, then reached a hand up through the crack to grab some hay over its top. It was shut and fastened just as boots stomped in above, so many of them the noise seemed to hit with the force of a twister.

My passengers were pressed together up against the far wall. Rebecca clapped her hand over Martha's mouth, I dosed the baby, and then we all ducked. The roof had commenced to tremble. Overhead was a frenzy of bangings, boot heels, yells, slammings; it sounded like they were ripping the barn to pieces. Another shot was fired up there, jolting us clear through, and bits of straw rained through the air-slits. The crashes and shouts went on and on, while the secret room appeared to rock under that cyclone of patrollers.

Suddenly all was still.

The runaways breathed again, but I motioned for silence. No footsteps had yet quit the barn. They were still up there, figuring what to do next. If anyone spoke, if Martha cried, they'd find us.

Some hollering came from above.

"Goddamn! That nigger couldnta got away, not so quick."

"Doubt it, only the one door."

Please Lord, don't let them see the trapdoor.

"Hid here somewheres, likely with them others."

You been with me in many trials, Lord.

"We just smoke em out right now."

Don't desert me now, my Lord.

"Don't give a shit about no Quaker barn anyways."

A crackling noise started up, growing louder as the boots clumped out. The cow banged against its stall, bellowing. And then there came a great roar like wind, as the fire rushed through the barn and caught its timbers with a snap. The secret room slowly filled with smoke. Flecks of burning hay fell through the air-slits. I pushed past coughing, choking shadows to reach the tunnel door.

It was bolted fast. I slammed my shoulder against the door. It shuddered but would not give. Pulling my kerchief over my nose, I hollered for help.

"Joe, Taz, Shadrack get over here. We got to break the door down."

One more time. I threw myself at the door but couldn't budge it. Behind me, folks whinnied and knocked into each other, gasping, gagging, panicked. The smoke was thickening, the room appeared to be closing in. Looking up, I saw flames forming a square in the roof, and yelled for everyone to duck back against the walls.

The trapdoor crashed in a blazing chunk onto the floor.

Someone was next to me, I think it was Joe. We leaned on the door together just as the bolt shot clear on the other side, and then it flew open. Leah Jenkins was calling to us.

Thrashing arms, legs, heads, bodies hurtled toward the door. Folks were throwing themselves into the tunnel, climbing over each other's backs to get out, and then somehow there were seven figures crawling ahead of me in the smoky passageway. Directly after I slammed the door on the hidden room I heard a great crash. The roof must have fallen.

The tunnel came out in the cellar of the house, and we collapsed there as Mrs. J. shut another sturdy door on the passageway. We were covered with clinging soot, we coughed, choked, our bloodshot eyes flooded over, lungs and noses stung. It seemed we couldn't take enough air into our chests, but by some miracle no one was hurt, excepting for some small burns.

I beat at folks' clothes to stifle hidden smolderings, while our friend snatched a cloak off a peg and gave a quick look out a high cellar window.

"They are still watching the barn, but they may believe thee escaped in the confusion somehow. Thee had best get away before they begin a search, I'll talk to them. Godspeed, Moses."

She was gone.

◆ ◆ ◆

WE WENT OUT through a parlor window that faced away from the barn, shot across a clearing into the bushes, and ran at a crouch for the woods beyond. I kept glancing over my shoulder. No one after us. Just that Godamighty blaze and smoke against the sky back there. I could see it even as we reached the woods, it sickened me. Oh Leah. And oh my people, almost lost them; that was too close, never been that close before. No more backward glances. My whole being centered on the fugitives, rushing them toward some cover, hustling them out of that dwindling afternoon light. They didn't need much goading, fright did that. I mostly needed to steady them, to quiet them, to keep them from stampeding every whichway.

They were stumbling into holes, falling over roots, scrambling up, plunging forward, hurling themselves into the woods. The sun streaked after us, long and low, reaching between the trees, flashing patterns over backs, faces, hands. Hands thrust branches back, branches snapped back in faces, faces were clouded with steamy breath, and each breath came rough and ragged.

Martha whimpered till I grabbed hold of her, her and Rebecca both, and we crashed on, our lungs still burning from the smoke, burning afresh as we gasped the cold air. Farther along, panting, my passengers rasped a few words at me.

". . . seen us . . . followed . . .?"

"No, keep movin."

"Oh my Lord my Lord my . . ."

"Hush."

"Mamaaaa."

"Pick her up Tazwell, move."

Dashing, sprawling, up again. Deeper into the woods. No sign of a chase behind us. Getting dark. Getting colder. The weather had snapped since we'd last been out and the ground was starting to freeze. Doubted if they'd noticed yet, what with the fright pumping through them. Just as well. Darker still, hard to see. Someone cussed, flying headlong into a trunk.

"Hold it, stop. *Stop.* We cleared em for now."

They flopped where they were and I went around counting heads mostly by feel. Everyone was there, each of them smelling sour and scorched. Then I squatted down too, pressing a hand to my paining temple. Silence for a time. Just the sound of rasping breath, coughing, and Martha weeping so hard she commenced to retch. A breeze stirred the branches. Folks rustled closer together, and I knew the cold had got to them at last. The night came down full upon us. It was a clear one, thank the Lord, with stars and a quarter moon; not much light, but something. I rose and walked around the group, wondering if they'd hear my words through their weariness.

"Hope they figured we burned up in there. Like that cow. Anyways they won't be able to tell for sure till the fire dies out. Daylight tomorrow's bout when that'd be. We can go slower hereon, if they seen us, they'd been down on us long before now."

"Bless God. We real far off the mark?"

"No, and we got to keep on, in a tight line again like when we commenced. Catch hold each other's clothes, and don't nobody leave go, not to wipe noses or scratch or nothin, hear me? If we lose anyone now, I can't go back and search — you get lost, you stay lost, comprehend that?"

"Child best ride shoulders."

"You carry her first, Taz. When you feel her get too heavy on you, pass her to Joe, spell youself. We all got to take turns. Addie, best give me the baby for now, you need both hands to hold on with. Anyone feel hurted too bad to walk without help? All right, up, do as best we able. Be fine, we still on the way to freedom, still on the way north."

That last was something of a lie. I was backtracking them, looping around through these woods to the marsh again, just in case. Not all the way back, but at least a half-day's traveling would be undone, and that was about the last thing they needed to hear right then. Anyhow we were still going north, not directly was all, and thank Heaven I knew this place. I'd cut through it twice before, both times in daylight, in summer, with massy leaves clouding my path. This time it would be easier to get through the thinned trees . . . well, maybe easier . . . so much colder though, so dark . . . not supposed to happen like this . . . For an instant the woods seemed dense, almost solid. Foolishness. Only the confusion of this night made them appear so. I steadied myself. Never mind, been thrown off course before, knew the dark, and there was a clear southerly star to key on.

I turned to help my passengers form the line.

"Can't hardly see. Moses, you certain we right on?"

"Certain. Get in the middle, Taz, hold it together."

"Well, I just hope you got eyes like to a bat."

"Ain't you heard? Grab onto Addie. Addie, keep afront your man."

"The baby . . . ?"

"Fast asleep. Bernette, go back with Joe. Rebecca?"

"Right here. This where I'm to be?"

"Uh-huh, you all right?"

"Can't complain. Grateful to the Lord we ain't but cinders."

"Well, Shadrack?"

"Well what?"

"You squeeze between Taz and Bernette."

"There all ready."

"Joe?"

"To the back like before, Moses."

I passed along the row of dark figures, checking them, touching them. Then I strapped the baby between my tits, covered him up to his nose with my coat, and went up front. With the infant's fuzzy head grazing my chin, the pistol in my hand, and Rebecca clinging to the back of my coat, I moved forward. The line lurched along behind me.

For a while the fugitives followed easy enough, still partly driven by fear, but there was something else to power them on too. They'd got a taste of freedom, and for the first time in their lives they had something of their own to work for, to protect. For the first time they truly had something to lose.

As the night deepened the woods grew thicker. The trees loomed up like dim skeletons, rattling in the breeze, and when the moon disappeared behind them, we were mostly feeling our way. Warmth was draining from our bodies, folks were starting to drag, to limp. After hours of groping and straining and struggling to keep a foothold, they were losing drive. At that point fear and freedom must have seemed distant. The only thing that felt sure was the blank chilly woods.

Behind me: silence.

Then a steady wail from the baby, great gulping sobs from Martha. We stopped while Tazwell passed the girlchild over to Joe, and I handed the infant to Addie. Everyone begged to sit down and rest, but I couldn't allow it; I was afraid they'd never get up. We had to keep moving. We went on. Brambles snatched at our clothes, branches swung down against our heads. Folks jumped at noises amidst the trees, getting nerved-up, notional. Getting careless, treading on each other, cussing. Slower. Faltering.

Just as we started to go down a slope I felt the center of the line give way. Somebody tripped, lost balance, and then each passenger was pitching backwards into the one behind till Joe and Bernette had tumbled into a gully. Martha was thrown from Joe's shoulders and that child began screaming her head off.

I ran down, picked her up, felt to see if she was hurt. Not hurt, bless God, just scared out of her mind, even as Addie rocked her. Joe and Bernette scrambled out of the gully, I moved to line the group up again, but suddenly Joe's temper flared; a temper I never thought to see on so gentle a man. He turned on Shadrack.

"You mother, this all on accounta you, was you got us drove into here."

"Leave me be, didn't do nothin."

"You got that barn burnt, nigger."

"Patrollers burnt it, you the one can't stay on your feet, you the one near lost that child . . ."

The smaller figure lunged at the big one, flailing out with both fists, and then they were whirling around on the ground, locked together.

"Lord's sake, quit that, you crazy? Joe, Shadrack! Hear me!"

No use. I grabbed up a stick and cracked whoever was on top across the back. It happened to be Shadrack, and for a second he was stunned. In that second I yanked him to his feet, and prodded both men apart with the stick.

I don't recollect what I said to them. I think I swore up and down. Then I counted my passengers, formed the line again, and after that we went on in silence.

It was still dark when we finally left the woods and threaded our way back into the swamp, making directly for the Marshyhope once more. Nobody spoke even after we'd reached the creek, folks just dropped down to drink and rest while Addie suckled the baby. Holding my head, I plotted the next move. North again, have to go in the water, but there was that station. Ridley's station. They'd like him, he was one of us. Maybe everybody would smooth down once we got there too. Please God.

Joe squatted alongside me, wanting to talk. Further off, Shadrack was mouthing off at someone I couldn't see. The two voices cut across each other, their words mingling as I listened.

"Real sorry I commenced that ruction back there, Moses. It just come over me, figured Bernette been hurted and . . ."

"Get jumped on every time I turn round, get blamed every time too, always been like that with me, it ain't right . . ."

"Maybe that barn got burnt on my account after all, on account I costed so high. Godamighty, the reward . . ."

"Why don't nobody blame Hat Tubman? Maybe she the one give us away in the barn, don't nobody think on that?"

"Make me freeze up inside to think what risk I put everybody in . . ."

"She was up there too but nobody think on her, always Shadrack . . ."

"My fault if we get caught, bait's all I ever be."

I stood up. This had to stop, too early for this sort of goings-on. I told Joe if anyone was bait it was me, my reward was likely many times higher than his, and told him I'd be needing his help too. Then, gritting my teeth, I tried to make peace with Shadrack, saying we'd all best forget the barn, maybe the patrollers were getting ready to burn it anyways. Somehow it's easier to lie in the dark.

I gathered everyone else around me before we started again.

"Hereon in we walk in the creek, just ankle deep, just for a short while. Come day we be to another station, safe place, good friend. We can rest there till the trouble's past. Only a little longer now. Let's go."

And into the water, slogging along, queasy from hunger, feet numb. My passengers were silent, I couldn't guess what they were thinking. Maybe nothing. All I heard was their splashings behind me, and my mind commenced to ramble off on its own to other times, other places.

. . . *Graperoot, dandelion root, sarsaparilla. Juniper berries and stinging nettle. Catnip, tansy, elderberry blooms. Sumach and yarrow, squawvine, skullcap. Enough? No? Know you meant to go, always seen you headed for other things, child . . . Thee will see a stone marker where the roads meet on the Pennsylvania border, and beyond it thee are no longer bond. Godspeed . . . The city leaping up, welcoming with a thousand flames, and me above it all. A breeze stirring the bell's clapper, announcing me to myself and God and everyone . . . A man sitting on the bank a ways down from me. In his net the fish, silver-bodied and gleaming in the moonlight, multitudes of them flopping wet and living and beautiful. The moonlight catching the tattered hat-brim crowning his head. Him rising, gathering in his shining fish, smiling on me, nodding to show the way. My body warm as new-baked bread . . .*

Daybreak's faint beginnings. My mind returned to where we were as the marsh lifted itself out of the dark. We were close enough.

I led my passengers out of the water and settled them by the bank, a few rods from a towering, dead oak. Thereabouts the grasses reached above my eyes when I stood straight. Good. No one would spot them unless somebody moved, and the oak made a fine marker for me.

Crouching by the group, I spoke low.

"Station's nearby now, ain't much above a mile off. I be gone a short while to see all's to rights. Stay fixed here, catch some sleep."

Rustlings, whispers, a soft stir of relief. I could hear leather creaking; they were taking off their wet shoes and rubbing their feet as I mounded more reeds over them.

"Tazwell, you on lookout now. Stick by that oak so's I can find you again. No fires. Keep everybody quiet, stay hid, and leave your eye peeled to the marsh. Don't shoot outa here when you see me come back, just wait till you hear me signal, then answer same way like you done before. We straight? Good. Won't be long."

Once I'd got out of the marsh I followed the treeline bordering some fields, keeping low, sticking to the trees, watching. No one was about. Nothing moved, only the vague, swooping shape of a bird now and then. After a short time I saw the house rising up at the edge of a pasture, a small house off by itself. One light had been kindled within, though Ridley wasn't expecting us. Even so, he'd grown used to sudden visits over the years and welcomed them, living alone like he did. If anyone saw strange Negroes around his place, he'd always say he had a passle of cousins visiting; that was one clear advantage in being a colored stationkeeper.

I had just crept into the brush behind the house when I came all over queer. Cold sweat. Throbbing temple. Tight chest. Good Lord, please not a sleeping fit, not now. The house blurred, sharpened, blurred again. I pressed my fingers to my temple, and as my sight cleared I glimpsed a white man coming out back to the woodpile. He had a coat on over long underwear, and stumbled over his feet like he was scarcely awake. Within the house a baby cried, a lamp flickered, a woman's voice called.

White people dwelling there. Ridley must have moved on, else something had happened . . . white people. Maybe friendly, maybe not, couldn't risk finding out. Dared not even risk whispering a question from the shadows. Enough trouble about as it was.

Oh Lord.

Back into the marsh.

Back to my people, with nothing.

◆◆◆

"WE CAN'T GO in there."

My passengers appeared to wilt, but they didn't question me as I explained. Most heads lifted a bit when I said about the swamp island.

"Hereabouts?"

"Upstream a ways."

They sagged again.

"Just a little ways, not that far."

Lord, they appeared bad off. Daylight showed the damage done them the night before, the bruises and gashes and slivered clothing, the weariness. I'd never seen an escape party look so poorly so early on. Mostly if runaways got to looking like that at all it was way farther along the route, and we were only in Maryland. Four days gone and still in Maryland, not even clear of one slave state.

For a moment I felt weak, dizzy. It was from hunger, partly, also from a sense of having failed them. It passed, I willed it to. Then I pulled myself up and moved amongst the group, firming my voice as I spoke.

"First thing's to get safe for today, and that island's safe. Don't trouble over food, I mean to get us some once we settle in. Best get a move on now, look at that sun, we show up real plain here. Warm enough, anyways . . . no, Addie, you ain't ready to pass out . . . Come on folks, you can rest all day once we get there. Up now, try, lean on each other. We sure to make it."

*

It was less than an hour's time reaching the place, wading upstream in the Marshyhope. The creek kept growing shallower, much narrower too, as we moved toward the hideout Ridley had called a back-up waiting station. Fancy name for a small island in the middle of a reed-choked rivulet, but the ground there was solid enough, tall grasses screened it in, and a scraggly old pine on its southerly edge marked its position for me. I'd stayed there one night on my way down to make an earlier raid, and knew we could wade out to it. We'd be up to our waists in water though, and that water was steely cold.

"Take the baby and the child up on shoulders now. Blankets and bundles, whatever you don't want to get soaked, hoist. Take off all them woolens you got atop your summer-issue goods, so's you can change into dry things once we cross. Lift skirts high as you able — I got you Rebecca — all right, follow me, watch out for holes, don't want nobody to splash down. Move it, make it fast."

Everyone gasped as that water hit and climbed above knees to groins to waists, but no one fell, and the children remained clear of the creek as we crossed. One by one I pulled them up onto the island, and everyone sank down, chilled and shivering. They rose almost directly, just long enough to change into the dry woolens, and I stuffed layers of grasses up inside their clothes for warmth. Then they lay back, crowding together, pulling what blankets we had over the top of them. But for the sun, it seemed like our first night in the marsh all over again. As I hunched down nearby, Rebecca's thin voice floated out of the pile.

"Recollect when I was small the chimney burnt up, our shack too. It was so cold out, we crawled to the barn and crept right in amidst the cows . . . wasn't bad . . . didn't freeze . . ."

After that, no one spoke. We were all too beat out and miserable.

I tried to keep watch as long as I was able, fighting back the ache to sleep, fighting the pain in my head, and then someone touched my shoulder. It was Bernette, whispering she'd spell me for a time. Bless her. I crawled into the pile with the others.

When I awoke it was getting on for noon. The sun had climbed higher, warming the grasses and the air, and I felt strengthened again. Everyone else was still asleep excepting for Bernette, still on lookout, struggling to keep her eyes open. I motioned for her to rest, then crept to the edge of the island and peered out. Nothing. No stirrings beyond. No sounds at all save for the cries of wild geese and the water's rippling. It was still risky to move off the place in daylight, but I had to find us something to eat; my empty belly was churning, and my passengers surely felt the same hunger cramps.

I roused them, said I was going to find food, and put Joe on watch. Once again I repeated the signal, the warnings, the need to stay fixed and hid. Then I circled around once more, eyeing the creek, figuring my course.

We'd been following the Marshyhope along its west bank, but I concluded to wade over to the easterly side. Safer that way. If they were stilll looking for us there was a chance that the alarm hadn't spread over there yet.

Hoisting my skirts, I lifted the sack and pistol over my head, and sloshed out into that Godamighty numbing water. When I reached the bank I crouched down for a time and scanned the island. No sign of my passengers, no grasses thrashing, no voices. No ructions either, I hoped, while I was gone. Their weariness was something to be grateful about just then; it was likely enough they'd sink back into sleep for most of the afternoon.

Still watching, I tucked the pistol back into my waist, and reached a wide-brimmed felt hat out of my sack, also a shawl. These, along with my long shabby skirt, made up my nigger-granny guise. If anyone saw me from a distance it might come in useful.

Another glance at the island. All calm. I moved off, slunk away from the marsh, cut through some woods, and came out on the edge of a stubbly, picked-over cornfield.

Directly in front of me was an old gnarly-barked walnut tree surrounded by windfalls. Some of the shells were rotten from having lain too long, but I gathered up all the good ones I could find. Next, that stretch of bleached stalks; might be some cobs in there, left behind by the harvesters. Rock-hard, that corn would be, but we could mash it up, it was something, no time to be finicky.

Before moving into the field I gazed beyond.

A hill, a slow easy grade leading to faded, dun-colored earth tufted with short grass. The flat gleam of a slate roof, a peeling gable, and one side of a run-down frame house. A barn, its worn red paint making a faint spot of color against the dull land and the dark, bare trees on the far horizon. Near to the barn, an old rusting hayrake, and a small shed with a thin gray cloud rising above it. The sharp scent of curing meat blew over on the breeze, and I swallowed hard, eyeing the smokehouse. If only I could get in closer, if only I could make off with a ham. But down amidst the clumps of weeds I glimpsed two splashes of yellow and blue darting about, the blue streak chasing the yellow one, and the distant laughter of children reached me. *sally go seek clap hands sally go.* Fragile chanting, tinkling laughter, *go seek clap hands.* White, smudged faces above brightly dyed clothing, *oooh-hoo-oops go seek.* A branch from the walnut tree swung down, halving the picture, and I turned away.

The smokehouse was out, so too the barn. It would only be safe to pilfer what I could from the cornfield. Crouching and crunching around there amidst the tumbled stalks, I did find a good number of forgotten, dried ears, and these I stuffed in my sack along with the walnuts. A bit deeper into the field there looked to be more, though a few cobs had been gnawed clean by animals. I snaked down a row, shifting my eyes from the cornshocks to the house below, but just then the field commenced fading. I tried to hold on to it. Couldn't. I was falling through a vast whiteness, my voices were there, voices and pale air and a growing chill.

Then nothing.

When the sleeping fit left off, I was sprawled face-down in the dirt. My hat was tented over my head, shutting everything out, but I heard stalks creaking above me in the breeze, and remembered where I was. Something squirmed beneath me, against my chest. Only my hands, I must have landed on them somehow when I'd pitched forward . . . These sleeping fits, harder and harder to snap right out of them. Still fuzzy, weak. Got to clear my head, got to get up. Got to get out of here. In a minute. Just a minute. Be all right.

Suddenly another sound reached my ears. Laughter. Blue and yellow children. Laughter, but this time it wasn't distant. It was in the field with me. The cornshocks swished. *Can't catch me can't catch me,* the giggling came closer still, broke off suddenly.

"Oh Jeremy come quick a dead woman!" Quavery white girlchild's voice.

Another set of footsteps, light ones. Small ones, thank the Lord. A hiccupy gasp overhead.

"Maybe she been shot. Pa say they is runaway niggers hereabouts." The boy rattled the words out.

Something strange there, it came to me all of a sudden. What with the hat covering my head and my hands under me, they couldn't tell what color I was. Bless God. Best hold breath in. Best . . . oh sweet *Heaven.*

A stick was poking at my hat, once, twice, three times. I thought of the pistol strapped against my waist. But these were children . . .

"*Uckk* Jeremy, that's awful, *don't.* We best get Pa."

An instant later I heard them running off, calling for their daddy.

As soon as they were well out of sight I was running too, running before I was even upright, scrambling out of that field and into the woods, legs pumping, eyes darting, zigzagging this way, that way, in case I'd been seen or followed. When I'd got far enough away I stopped, bending over at the waist, panting, listening. Nothing. Maybe that white daddy had only thought his children were making up a tale, and if he did go look in the cornfield, he'd find no signs that I'd been there; it was doubtful anyone would count fallen walnuts or dead ears of corn. I paused a few moments longer, getting my wind back, getting my bearings, and noticed the sun had grown hazy, moving through a mesh of clouds. A larger cloudbank was moving in from the west, and there was a damp smell to the air, a smell of snow. From the way the weak light was falling I could tell it was late afternoon; been gone a long while. Quickening my pace again, I made for the swamp island. At least this time I had something to bring my passengers.

"Shadrack, what you on lookout for?"

"Joe he got tired, put Taz on, Taz got tired, he put me on. Somethin wrong with that?"

Nothing. Nothing I could point at. I just didn't trust him was all.

I turned to the others. They stirred out of their blankets, rumpled and dull-eyed from sleep, while I passed the cobs and walnuts around. Amidst the shelling and cracking we made over that meal, Joe commenced to answer my question.

"You see anyone? Hear any noise atall?"

"Horses yonder. Couldn't see em. Was a good while back."

"When's a good while back?"

"Not so long after you gone off. Bit past noon sun."

"Heard em too, Moses."

"What else, Bernette? You hear dogs?"

"Nothin but shouts. Whooped by like trash do. Sounded like plenty."

"Shadrack? You hear any more later on?"

"Horses again. Soon's I gone on watch."

"Dogs?"

"Can't say for sure."

"Well think, dogs or not?"

"They was farther off. Mighta been, might not."

"You fall asleep on lookout?"

"Shit, course not, never done. Told you, they was farther off."

"And didn't nobody see you? . . . Sure? . . . All right."

It could have been any number of things, no way of telling for certain. I had to reason my mind out fast.

We could stay where we were till the following night, till we'd gained more strength back, and move then. As for the horsemen, there were always riders about everywheres, especially during the holiday season. Even so, the neighboring farmers were already on the alert for runaway slaves, and if a search party had gone out it would find nothing up ahead. The men might very well come back, commence a search closer to home, and there'd be a risk of getting caught on the island. Then too, there was a dangerous spot along the route, not so very far away. It was Federalsburg, a town we'd have to skirt by night, and if word was spreading we'd best get past it soon.

Looking around at my passengers I saw bruised, run-down folks still in need of rest . . . Lord, if only I hadn't taken that fit, if only I hadn't been spotted I'd have felt a lot easier. But maybe that sleeping spell had been visited upon me for a reason; I'd gleaned a precious piece of news while those children were sniffing about.

"We best move at dusk. If that was search parties you heard, they be far ahead by now, and they likely be to the road what with horses and all. And even if they got dogs, they won't be able to scent us in the creek."

At dusk we were soaked to the waist again as we waded out toward the bank, then edged along in the shallows. The Marshyhope narrowed, the swampland soon sank away. Thick trees rose up on either side of us just before the weak light faded entirely. And then we couldn't see the trees, or each other, or even what was underfoot.

The darkness walled us in. For the first time on that journey there wasn't even the faint gleam of stars, and somewheres behind me Bernette swore she felt like she'd gone blind.

We inched forward, grabbing for each other, slipping and stumbling over stones, till a group of bright dots winked up ahead of us, still a good ways off. Federalsburg. I moved the fugitives out of the water, drugged the baby, and we made a wide loop around the town, clearing it safely. Then it was back into the invisible, rocky wetness of the Marshyhope once more.

Almost as soon as we set foot in the creek someone fell with a splash. A few more steps, another splash. Then silence. Just spattering footsteps, a sneeze now and then. Vague, troubled twitters from the child somewheres behind me, a gasp as someone else whisked over slippery rocks.

I skidded back and forth, feeling for my passengers, counting them, trying to help them keep their footing. Trying to keep my own. Smelling soaked wool, gripping gashed palms, touching cold hands, hands slippery as fish. Telling them they were all right. Telling myself they were all right. Telling myself that over and over.

Maybe I was pushing them too hard . . . *Pa say they is runaway niggers hereabouts* . . . tired so tired they say they just can't keep going much longer . . . *We best get Pa* . . . that town still so close, Federalsburg hidden only by a rise of land, only felt far away . . . *Horses a while back* . . . they weren't all right, I knew it, they knew it, what if they caught their death out here . . . *Whooped by like trash do* . . . what if I lost one of them this way instead of the other? . . . *Dogs? You hear dogs?* . . . dear Jesus my head . . . *Mighta been* . . . this on top of the fire and the woods and Ridley . . . *shouts yonder* . . . Lord, steady me, help me do them right . . . *sounded like plenty* . . . You gave them into my keeping . . . *runaway niggers hereabouts oooh-hoo go seek catch me tell Pa horses shouts mighta been dogs couldn't tell* . . . Lord, I'm going to hold to You, see us through . . .

Wet flakes were touching down on my cheeks. The snow had caught up with us at last, and if no one else welcomed it I did, for the moment. It meant we could get out of that Godamighty slippery creek bed and go along the edge of the woods. The storm would make some cover for us, muffle sound, and likely send nigger-hunters back to their hearths. We climbed out of the water and walked through a fringe of trees, still following the creek, which was my only guide in this blankness. I could hear it even though I couldn't see it, and the Marshyhope cut directly north, its source a good ways into Delaware.

At first things seemed just a little easier. It was some comfort to be on firm ground again, and the flurries couldn't make us any wetter than we were to begin with. But as the clinging snow came down heavier my passengers began to stray from the line. Once more I went through the endless task of counting heads by feel, touching shoulders, linking them up. The hands I reached for fell away. Up front with Rebecca again, I called their names out from time to time, just to make sure they were all there. They barely answered. Maybe they didn't hear me. Maybe they didn't care anymore. Maybe freedom didn't seem worth this struggle.

We had to keep going, had to make up for that backtracking, had to move while the snow kept coming to cover our tracks . . . Even if they hated me, as they likely did right then . . . Even so. That didn't matter . . . But Lord, why was this journey coming so hard?

My thoughts were cut short by a call, then a scream. It sounded like Addie.

"Martha? *Martha!* The child, Taz, where?"

"Up with you, ain't she?"

"Dear God, you just had her."

"Did, but she gone on to walk up with you . . . my Lord."

"Mar-*tha!*"

There was a scrambling behind me, a frenzy building. I could sense how they must have looked, even though we were only voices and footsteps to each other. Reaching, grabbing, snatching around in the dark, I finally halted them.

"Stop. Right here. Just stay still, anybody able to feel for Martha?"

"No OmyGod she gone lost Martha please Jesus no."

"Addie, Addie, easy now. I be off to find her direct, find her for certain, she couldnta wandered far . . . Taz? Who just bolted? Taz!"

"Mean to find her myself."

"Get over here. You stay put, Tazwell. Don't nobody move from this spot. Nobody. I mean that, else we all get lost all at one time. Keep rooted while I search, and when you hear me call, call back soft so's I be able to place you. *Don't stir.*"

I put my hands out before me and moved off through the woods like a blindwoman, stumbling, bumping into trees, raising my voice as loud as I dared.

"Marthaaa . . . where you at, Martha? . . . Honey?"

Please God. Never happened, never before, my fault? Should have been able to notice sooner someways or other.

"Martha . . . baby . . . me . . ."

That poor child was likely scared out of her mind, straggling around. Why couldn't I hear her crying then?

"Don't you hear me? . . . Marthaaa . . . Martha Robinson . . ."

Lord, maybe she'd hurt herself, hurt so bad she wasn't able to answer. Sweat streaked my sides, snow or not, my breathing came faster. *Martha, Lord God.*

I went deeper into the woods, calling, till I knew if I got any farther away I wouldn't be able to find the group again. Best get back to my passengers just for a moment to see if they'd noticed anything, then I'd go off in the other direction. Maybe the child had wandered up ahead somehow.

I commenced to search out the group with my voice. Thank Heaven for the storm, else I'd never be able to make soundings like that and be safe.

"Folks? Me. Talk out."

"... this way . . . her . . . right . . ."

"Again?"

"over here . . . Moses . . . all right . . ."

"Once more."

"You closer. Moses, we got Martha! Shadrack fetched her. He heard somethin, went off hisself to search, come back with her straightaway. She ain't hurt atall, just scared . . . That you?"

"Me. Right here."

Reaching around, touching them all, I felt a cluster of heads lower down. The parents kneeling over the child, it was the family together there. Weeping, one of them. Then I felt a fourth head under my hand, who?

"Bless you Shadrack, won't never forget. Honey, you sure you ain't hurted?"

"Mama, he come and pick me up like this right outa nowheres."

"Don't you never do that again Martha, hear? Thank Shadrack now."

"Wasn't nothin, them whimpers led me right on."

"Owe you man. Owe you for my girl."

It seemed a long while before they heard the rest of us, me and the others, murmuring relief. And it seemed a long while before I could get them up again, moving, pushing against the snow, this time holding on tight.

◆ ◆ ◆

BY FIRST LIGHT we'd struggled into a pine grove and stopped there. Large wet flakes were still falling, the snow had piled up fast, and the grove was one vast whiteness; it was almost a shock after that blind night. The woods were hushed, heavied, thickened. Nothing moved. No sounds reached us. It seemed we'd walked out of the dark into a different world, one that sealed us in. Another time it might have looked beautiful.

I moved toward a massive tree nearby. Its spreading branches were weighted with chunky snow, and the lower limbs had bent clear down to the earth, forming a kind of tent. Beneath those screening fronds the ground was almost untouched by the weather, and the evergreen's many sheddings had left a bed of dry needles around its trunk. It made the best shelter we'd be able to find. I settled my passengers under the pine, nudging them close together, with Martha in the middle and the baby snuggled into Addie's coat. Joe and I gathered up more needles from under other trees, mounded them up over folks, and spread out the damp blankets again.

Storm or not, I still couldn't risk a fire; a small one wouldn't have been enough to dry us out, and there was always the chance that a big blaze might be spotted. So we nested together, trying to warm one another with our bodies, pressing chilled feet against bellies, backs against backs, faces into shoulders, rag-bound hands crammed into armpits. Under the dimness of the tree, we were islanded in with each other as surely as we'd been on that hillock in the Marshyhope.

A quietness came down over the group. Even Martha was

too worn out to make the smallest whimper. The baby took suck, then nuzzled down between Addie's tits. Everyone slept uneasily at first, quivering with cold, twisting around inside wet clothing, but after a time weariness took over and folks settled down. Now and then I heard a grunt, a soft brief bleating from the baby, the snow shifting, nothing more. As the morning lengthened and folks grew a bit warmer, wisps of steam began to rise from their damp garments, and across their figures lay vague patches of light, coming through the branches from the whiteness beyond. They appeared peaceful and miserable and comforted all at once. This was at least some ease set against what had gone before.

I watched and drowsed till roundabouts midday when the snow tapered to a stop. The runaways stirred awake, sat up, and for a moment seemed confused over their whereabouts. Then they leaned back against each other again, bleary-eyed but sleepless, speaking off and on. I listened, shifting my gaze from them to the woods and back.

"Wonder what they up to in the Quarter now . . ."

". . . Hired hands come home, everybody decked out, Christmas jubilee . . ."

Frosty breath wavering at their mouths. Crusty cracked lips, raw at the corners.

"Pine's smell always put me in minda Christmas . . ."

Rags wound about their heads, covering ears, knotted under chins, rags circling their faces like bandages. A hat tied down with a muffler.

"Christmas up to the Big House, that yule log all ablaze. One master I had when I was small he give all us children pull-taffy. My mama said our eyes was round as peaches. Pull-taffy and the tree . . ."

The women's bandanas, faded colors in the shadows. Greenish-yellow. Cherry. Coppery-red. The dye washed out in places, rips in the cloth.

"Thank Heaven this tree was here for us. They say a pine point straight to God."

Gnarly hands, old ones, clasping and unclasping, chapped knuckles showing through shredded gloves.

"The tree with all them candles and ribbons. Pull-taffy."

Smooth long-fingered hands, only one of them mittened, cupping the baby's chin. A gash down toward the wrist, a thumbnail near torn off.

"Wonder what Christmas be like in Canada. Feel different, maybe?"

"They say Canada's like this all the time. Winter year round ceptin for August. Marse Will say that, but shoot. Marse Will."

Damp bluish air, the smell of wet wool and close-pressed bodies.

"Heard so many different things on freedom, all sound so fine. Seem like just tales now."

Cool light filtering in from outside, catching on the men's stubbly new-grown whiskers.

"When we get free I mean to get me some new boots, first thing. Not nigger boots with paper in the soles, good ones. When we get free. First thing. Whenever."

Salt on their boots from dried sweat, boots broken, bound up with burlap strips.

"Can't feel my feet. Was like this one winter when we raised the new barn. But no. Only flurries then. Not like this."

"Mama. Hungry. Hungry so it pains."

"Easy honey, sshhh."

"Mama-mama-maaaaa . . ."

I left the tree to find food, moving off into the grove a good ways till I found a likely looking spot to set a trap. There were a couple of walnuts in my sack which I'd kept back for such a time, and some wires I mostly carried with me on raids. I took the wires from the bag, made a loop-snare, and baited it with the nuts, hoping that would be enough to tempt some small creature out.

A while past noon the snow was still holding off, and when I went back to check the trap, I saw a squirrel dangling from the snare. It would be just barely enough to go around, it wasn't much, but it was food nonetheless. Bless God for that. I killed, gutted and skinned it out there, and carried the slippery carcass back to the group just as new flurries commenced again.

There was weak jubilation amongst my passengers when they saw my catch, and although it was a risk, we made a fire to cook the game. Joe reached up the trunk for some dry dead branches tucked amidst the live ones, and I used most of my damp sulphur matches to start a small blaze near the pine's outer boughs. Everyone gathered around to warm their hands, but I couldn't allow that fire to burn very long, and the gummy meat came out mostly raw. Nobody cared. Folks grabbed for the scraps, gnawed on the tiny bones, then scooped up snow to wash those few mouthfuls down.

As they settled back under the tree, I tried to tell them some comfort. We'd be to another station soon, we'd head for it tonight, and in the meanwhiles they could just sleep the day away. This snow was a tribulation, but it covered our tracks, so everybody could rest easy. Delaware wasn't far, I figured out loud, and likely we'd cross the state on wheels, since we had friends farther up. That was something to hope on, and I promised over and over that this misery would end soon.

It didn't.

We started moving at nightfall, went maybe an hour, and then the snow quit. I worried on the tracks we'd leave, but concluded to keep going anyways; if we waited for the right weather we'd never get out of there, and besides, this snow was the off-and-on kind. From what I'd read in the skies, more would fall next day, and, Lord willing, our trail would be covered.

With the whiteness from the ground showing up faint against the dark, it was a bit easier to see our way and no one was falling down or bashing into trees this time. Even so, we were trudging through deep snow that got an icy crust on it as the air snapped down colder, and we crunched through the surface, sinking up to our boot tops with each step. Each step became a thing in itself, a mighty effort, and that effort grew harder as the wind rose, knifing along behind us. Our strength waned, and by the middle of the night my passengers gave out, unable to stir much at all after a short rest.

I found another tree where we could take cover, but it didn't shelter us as well as that first pine. This one was smaller, thinner, and there was some snow around its trunk. We flopped beneath it nonetheless, amidst a bed of frozen needles.

For the rest of that night, and most of the next day that was where we stayed.

A bad day, that one was.

At first we were all gripped with the runs, dashing off to squat time after time, spewing out little more than water, doubled over paining bellies.

That trouble passed, but the clouded morning light brought no warmth.

The wind didn't lift.

Everyone was chilled worse than the day before.

Everyone was getting snappish and ornery.

Everyone was growing queasy from hunger again.

They had to eat, we all had to get something into us to bind up our guts, so I risked leaving my own tracks to search out some more game. One set of footsteps could very well appear like they belonged to a hunter, one set of prints wasn't really so much of a risk after all. But I didn't have any more bait for a trap, couldn't chance using my pistol for fear of the noise it would make, and figured the only hope I had was running some creature down in deep snow, then clubbing it to death. Nothing crossed my path however, and after a while I figured I'd been gone too long from my passengers.

I trudged back to their tree, signaling.

There was no answering whistle.

I signaled again.

Still no reply.

I crept up close.

My passengers were gone.

As I gazed about I saw fresh tracks, and smelled smoke a short ways off. The trail and the smoky scent led me directly to a larger tree where the whole group was huddled around a blazing big fire.

Before I said one word I dumped snow on the flames, then wheeled on them.

"Told you to stay fixed, you crazy? Who concluded to move? Who lit that Godamighty bonfire? Hear me? *Who?*"

"Well . . ."

"Shadrack?"

"Well, Taz and me we figured we'd best . . ."

"Shut up. Don't even want to hear what you figured. I got to keep a gun on you, that it?"

"We knowed you'd find us, daylight and the tracks and . . ."

"And who else mighta found you, between the tracks and the smoke? Holy God!"

"Ain't no one else around."

"You ain't able to see the whole woods."

"We was bout froze under that little measly tree. What's the difference if we sicken to death out here or get caught? Either way we . . ."

"Hush your face. Clout you both side the head if there's any more trouble. Do like I say, everybody, no questions hereon in."

They eyed me, but no one said anything as we huddled together in a cold silence. No one even mentioned I'd come back empty-handed. There was a lot of shifting around, someone kicked someone else by mistake, and a short squabble commenced. Then more silence. Then it started again.

"The mens couldnta done wrong to start that fire, Moses, my babies needed it. I begged Taz."

"And I said before bout fires, can't send up no signals. So far we ain't even been chased, got to keep it like that. Only safe way to get warm's bunched up together like you was."

"You one hard woman. Maybe my milk dry up, maybe Martha take chill, maybe both younguns even . . ."

"They won't. We be to a good shelter soon."

"You said that yesterday. Lord, when's soon going to be?"

"Maybe by tomorrow, that's what I got us aimed for."

The sky was colorless, the wind held steady. My head pained. Folks slept on and off.

"Moses?"

"Yeah, Bernette."

"Feel bad, we shouldnta moved. Joe and me stayed back to wait on you, Rebecca too, but then we was afraid you'd go direct to where the smoke was and we'd lose you."

"Well, never mind now."

"Other passengers ever do like that on you?"

"No."

Martha messed her pants and was dragged from the tree by her daddy. She howled all the while he tried to wipe her clean with snow, and after that there was a near continuous whimpering from her and the baby both.

"What gone wrong, Moses? I figured it'd be hard, but not like this."

"We be to a station tomorrow, Taz."

"But what gone wrong? Why ain't we been able to find shelter before now? Appears like every time we turn around . . ."

"Be over soon . . . Rebecca, you feel hot. You poorly?"

"Can't complain, Moses."

"Complain anyways."

"Truly, I don't feel bad atall. I just mean to wait till the Lord send me a more comfortable place before I conclude to take poorly."

Bernette said she'd go on watch around midafternoon. Joe was awake too, so I crawled under a blanket and slept, but only fitfully. Thoughts tossed about inside my head as I twisted deeper into the blanket: the lost child, those white children, the decision to leave the swamp island, the changed route, the stirrings of rebellion . . . Doubting myself again, first escape I'd ever done so; my people beginning to doubt me too, first time with passengers who didn't fully trust . . . Lord? Lord, I'm going to hold to You . . .

When I awoke the overcast sky had just begun to turn the color of pewter. The white ground was starting to dim. I went out to study the weather, saw big-bellied clouds regrouping above, and knew it was just about to storm again.

I turned around, facing the runaways under the tree. Maybe

they figured I was about to go hunt up more food, for they gazed out at me with hopeful eyes. I tried to shake my head at them, tried to speak, wasn't able. My passengers' eyes had become pinpricks of light, piercing through me, spinning, and I stepped backwards into empty space. Only these bright pinpricks remained as my voices belled in my head.

The fit loosed its grip on me. Fresh snow was pelting my face. Someone's hand pressed against my forehead. My eyes were still shut. Folks were talking above me.

"She speak with the Lord's angels when she gone off that way, best leave her be."

"Yeah, well she could still take chill, angels or not, Rebecca. Hand me a blanket. Moses? You hear me? It's Bernette."

"What if she don't come round, what happens then . . . The children? All us? . . . What?"

"Heaven's sake, she only been out a instant or two. Shadrack what you up to?"

"Well, if she don't come round soon, Taz or me best take the pistol. Somebody got to lead."

I sat bolt upright. Shadrack sprang back, and I gave him a long hard look. He lowered his eyes, and there was some twittering around me, people asking if I was all right. I didn't answer. Something hot jolted through me. I shushed them. Listened. Oh Lord yes, just barely, coming on, snow or not. My ears had long been keyed for that sound; it was dim as yet, but it was coming.

On my feet, clear-headed and moving fast, I grabbed at them.

"Get your gear, don't talk. Hurry."

They just stared at me.

"Everythin out from under the tree. Move!"

They gazed around, saw nothing, then shifted their eyes from me to the pine's small shelter. I commenced pitching sacks and blankets out from under the tree, throwing the stuff at them. There wasn't time to explain. They must have thought I'd gone mad.

"Goddammit, I said move!"

Rebecca stared at me, surprised, and picked up her walking

stick. Joe cocked his head, spun around suddenly, and squinted behind him. The others followed his gaze, shrugged, stamped their feet and blew on their hands, then stiffened a moment later as we all saw it at once.

A small cluster of lights had just appeared in the distance. Through the dusk and the thickening snow, they looked like candlewicks wavering behind cloth, wavering toward us.

We charged off, running like we had weights on our feet, plowing through the deep snow, wrenching legs free, running. I pulled on my passengers' hands, came away with empty mittens in my fingers. I grabbed for them again, touched flesh, lunged on. Heads bent against the wind, our arms flung out, we pushed harder. The snow slanted back at us, blowing in our faces.

The lights kept coming.

Stinging flakes were in our eyes, our open mouths, our noses. Folks fell, rose all whitened, dove forward once more.

The lights were still behind us.

Gasping, wheezing, kicking up spray, we ran. A voice cried out *wait up don't leave me wait,* and I groped around for Rebecca till I had her by the waist. As we struggled along together, I felt my icy collar slapping against my chin and the blood pounding in my ears.

The lights seemed to have dropped back a ways, just a little.

I fell, half-rose, got myself up by pulling on a branch. A slide of snow shushed off it and down over me, over the rest. More folks fell, hit branches, more wet chunks hilled down from the trees onto us.

The lights appeared to be dwindling, but they were still there.

We broke from the woods into an open field as the night came down full upon us. People were dropping blankets, sacks, anything that heavied them. We waded through the field, pitching ahead, looking back.

And then the lights were gone.

They'd vanished somewheres amongst the trees, but we kept moving anyways, crossing that field, another, and yet another. The lights didn't reappear, and at last we collapsed on the far edge of the third field near a fence. We herded together there for a short time, chests paining, trying to get our breath, and all the while I kept gazing back.

Those lights could have been anything; a stray farmer with lanterns on his wagon, a party of lost travelers, or slavecatchers who'd picked up our tracks. Whoever it was, they hadn't been able to see us, and had dismounted, maybe to search through the woods on foot a ways. Bless God for that, else their horses might have run us down. And bless God we'd had those two days of rest in the grove, miserable though they were, else we wouldn't have been able to make that dash.

But with that dash behind us we were weaker than ever before, beat out, burnt out, sore, and it was mercilessly cold. Martha whimpered through chattering teeth, and the baby kept up a steady wail, muffled a bit against someone's shoulder. As I counted my passengers yet again I could feel them trembling, going slack, sinking down against each other. I kept shaking them, fearing they'd fall asleep and freeze to death, fearing they wouldn't find the strength to rise. My own eyes felt suddenly heavy, but I jerked my head up and spoke low.

"Appears like they lost us. Thank the Lord that snow made cover."

"Patrollers? Nigger-hunters?"

"Don't know for sure. Can't stop here anyways. Children to rights? Everybody?"

"More or less . . ."

"We can manage. Up, easy there. Hold together like before. Take it real slow."

Slow it was, trudging, turning to look behind us every few steps, especially when the snow thinned to a weak flurry and quit a short time later. The sky began to clear till I could sight on the stars again, and a flinty moon hung above us, making more light than we'd had since we'd commenced the journey. At that point it didn't seem to matter. We dropped down to rest every few steps it seemed, and Lord knows I needed those times as much as my passengers. There was one ratty blanket left, and we tore it to shreds, wrapping the wool around our heads and hands and feet. Each time we tried to get up it took more will, more effort. Up. Down. Then up again, trying to shake the snow off us. And after a while we didn't bother to try anymore.

We dragged along like that till the middle of the night, in the middle of nowheres, we saw it. Another light. We stopped short.

At first I thought it might be one person with a lantern up ahead of us, but the light didn't move. And there was something wrong about the shape of it. No, not a lantern.

We crept closer and the light became a square.

Closer still. It had a frame around it, that light, it was a bright window surrounded by the blurred bulk of a small house.

We halted a good ways off, and I squinted at the place. Odd for a house to be so lit up at that hour. Those weren't candles in there either, that glow was coming from at least two lamps with the wicks turned up full. And the curtains had been pulled back from the window.

"That the station?"

"No. Sshh."

"You certain?"

"Shadrack, hush. I don't know that house."

"Don't you even mean to sniff around?"

"*Ssshht.* Don't like it. Too risky. Get a move on."

We'd gone only a few steps before they crunched to a stop behind me. That gleaming house had tempted them. Addie begged in a whisper for me to just see if maybe it was a friendly place after all. Martha wept softly, Tazwell began questioning me, and then Shadrack grabbed my arm.

"Can't you see we ain't able to keep on? Leastways we could steal some feed out the barn."

"Shut your mouth. Said I don't like it. The Railroad don't signal that way. Anyone could be in there, friend or not. It ain't a sure thing, and if it ain't sure it ain't safe. Now haul ass."

"Don't you shove at me. We oughta look that place over close, pilfer what we can, need to. If you gone scared, I just . . ."

I jabbed the pistol into his spine and Shadrack jumped, making a click in his throat. He kept silent while I motioned the others to go on, but suddenly we jolted to a stop. Once again there was a muffled, rhythmic beat in the distance. If it hadn't been for the snow, if it hadn't been for the quarreling, we'd have heard it sooner; maybe two riders, no more than that, coming from above us, from a northerly direction. The sound was growing larger, nearing the house, but before the horsemen reached it we'd moved off far enough. Looking back once, I could just make out a vague spill of light from the open door. The clunking of boots and a blur of voices reached us faintly. Then just a tap; the door must have shut again. We were safe, there was no need for another scramble, and a short while later I heard some weary murmurations amidst my passengers.

"Lord, you figure they was after us?"

"If they was, they wouldnta stopped."

"Mighta done, just to rest."

"Aw, likely just some young tomcats out late, and old mama waited up."

"Maybe not. Don't smell right."

I was cutting east, then southeast, then finally backtracking directly south once more, not saying anything about it. Even though I didn't know who those riders were I had a feeling about them, and I knew this much: we'd been heading in the same direction they'd come from, and I couldn't afford to gamble. There might be an alert up ahead, and we weren't fit to run away from pursuers anymore.

The wind had died down, but the cold was still sapping us. Everyone was hobbling, barely moving, leaning heavily on each other. Everyone was dizzy and sick from hunger too. More and more often folks doubled over their bellies, or wavered on their feet like they were getting ready to pass out. The spells of rest didn't help, they only made the walking times feel harder, and after a while that glowing house must have seemed but a conjuration to those folks.

As morning came upon us, the snow sparkled and the trees

dripped in the new sun. Nobody appeared to notice. Nobody appeared to notice we were backtracking either. It frightened me that they didn't speak, didn't move their fingers against mine when I reached for them. Now and then someone jumped as a pile of snow skidded off a tree, and the woods grew noisier in the thaw, but that was the only sign I had from my people, those jolts they made. Their raw faces were blank, eyes glassy and bloodshot. Swollen hands were raised to cup stinging ears, here and there a mouth twisted in pain, and I worried on frostbite. I worried on the children, especially the baby, and I worried on sickness most of all. Most folks had been coughing on and off through the night, and Rebecca was burning with fever. Joe and I were half-carrying her, and Joe himself looked like he was coming apart. His eyelids twitched, his mouth quivered, and he kept glancing around for Bernette as if he wanted to make certain she was still there.

I began stumbling as I went around touching folks, trying to get them to lean on me. No one looked up, no one looked ahead, they just kept their eyes on the ground. I moved to the front of the line again, trying to talk to them at least. If only I could talk us through it, if only I could sound firm. But my voice came out in a croak, and only a few wispy replies floated toward me.

"We be to a friend soon."

"... can't."

"Safe trial here."

"The children ..."

"Able to go slow."

"... where?"

"To a friend."

"That station?"

"Different one."

"... Lord."

"Ain't so far."

"When?"

"Soon."

"Got to eat."

"Be to the friend soon . . . sure to make it . . . almost to the friend."

They didn't believe it anymore. They didn't believe in any more promises of making it or getting there or reaching a station. They didn't believe in freedom just then. And they didn't believe in me.

I couldn't blame them. We'd been journeying almost a week, and seemed to have gotten noplace. The only shelter I'd been able to find had been so early on, it was likely forgotten. There'd been too much misery in between, misery I somehow hadn't been able to ward off, and once again we were heading back down away from freedom. I was failing them. All the doubtings I'd felt on this run pulled me down at last, and in that moment I no longer believed in myself, no longer believed in a Moses any more than they did. I stopped moving amongst them, stopped talking. Tried to pray; couldn't. Listened for my voices, and heard only Shadrack's, hollering from the end of the line.

"Holy shit, even the dumbest cornfield nigger's able to figure it, look where the sun's at, look at our shadows, they all behind us too. We ain't headed north, we been headed south all this while and you didn't even know it, Hat Tubman."

Folks stopped. They lifted their eyes, glanced from the sun to me to Shadrack, but before I could speak Addie screamed. She was staring past me up ahead, jerking her hand at something beyond us, and we all rushed forward.

Several yards away lay a man. A black man sprawled on his side, partly covered with snow along his back, one arm flung wide. Buckshot must have ripped into him at close range; half his guts had spilled out onto the ground, and frost was melting on the bluish mass. His eyes stared off at nothing. There was a stick and a sack he'd dropped nearby.

I felt the group draw back behind me, heard Martha retching, and then Tazwell led her off.

Joe dropped down by the corpse, and though he shook his head when I asked if he'd known the man, he still knelt there, shoulders heaving.

I reached down to him, trying to coax him away from the dead runaway when suddenly I felt the shock of another body slamming into me from behind. Shadrack nearly knocked me off my feet, locking one arm around my neck, while his other hand made to snatch at the gun in my belt. He spat his words out loud enough for everyone to hear.

"You said this was a safe path and it ain't, you said we was headed north and we ain't, you ain't fit to lead no more. I mean to take em north myself."

◆◆◆

I MOVED QUICK, not thinking even. My boot heel stomped back on Shadrack's foot while I aimed a bite at the arm around my neck, and grabbed his fingers before they could close over the pistol. Swinging sideways, I got him off balance just enough to loosen his grip, twist free, and spin around, shoving him hard in the face. He sprawled on the ground for a moment, started to come at me again, but by then I was sighting him over the gun.

Neither of us moved. We just glared at each other.

Dimly, I sensed that everyone else had frozen a ways off.

I kept the revolver on Shadrack and spoke at him low, through my teeth, through my anger.

"All right nigger, get up. Put a hole through your head if you ever try that again, I swear it. Risked everybody here's what you done just cause you figure you somethin big. I said get up. Look at me. That ruction coulda got us caught if anyone else was around, we was all off guard while you gone after your glory time. Just thank the Lord no one was nearby, thank the Lord no one got shot on your account. Get on your feet. You heard me. Get over there where I can see you plain, and stay put. Don't you take it into your head to run off alone neither, best believe I mean to keep my eye peeled to you every step. Haul your no-account ass over here, I said now."

Shadrack rose without glancing at me, stalked toward the edge of the group, and crouched there.

I turned to my passengers.

They were standing close together, sharply outlined against the snow, and I saw them again, clearly; saw something in them beyond their bruises and blankness and miseries, something I hadn't seen in a long while.

That challenge, that threat had jolted me back into myself. It had threatened more than my place as conductor, it had threatened this journey, these fugitives, their freedom. If I'd grown weaker, if I'd felt too low to fight, this escape might have been lost. This escape might have fallen to Shadrack. Odd that my old enemy was the one who'd brought me back, slamming into me when I'd lost faith for the first time on the Railroad and lost sight of who I had to be.

I had to be Moses even when I felt less than Harriet. I had to radiate strength and belief even when there was none left for any of us. The more my passengers faltered, the firmer I had to be. The more they doubted, the more my own faith had to grow. The Lord had asked that of me, and that was what I owed these, my people.

As I began speaking, I stuck the pistol into my waist again.

"I got us backtracked on purpose, not far, only to a sure place. Didn't say for fear I'd break your spirits, but listen now. We likely brushed slavecatchers near to that swamp island, and I feel certain two times last night. Maybe it was just horses. Maybe just lights, just nobody. That's what I pray, but I won't risk you on maybes. We ain't able to run from much now, so I got us headed below the trouble on the safest path hereabouts. That poor man laid out over there don't make it different, look on him closer. He ain't newly dead, the snow's what's kept him. Whatever happened here's a few days past, and up ahead's a friend, a farmer, he helped me before. We be to his place come noon, and this time I just ask you to believe."

They shifted around, squatting on the earth.

"Children, I know you feel like to die right here. I know you don't see no farmer or friend or freedom or the end. Everybody's bad off. But I ask you to believe. I ask just that far. You concluded for me to carry you, and I concluded to run you off, and at that time we put our faith in each other, and we all put our faith in the Lord. That covenant's what you got to hold onto. You been through a mighty tribulation on this journey, but you been through a mightier one before it. You been slaves. You lived through bondage and you was meant to live past it and you will. Believe in that freedom you can't see just a little longer. Walk a little ways with each other, help each other, and walk a little ways with me now."

I reached out for them. They slowly rose to their feet.

And so we did go on.

The walking didn't get any easier and I never ceased watching Shadrack, but a calmness had folded down around me even so, and the others seemed to feel it. That grace was still upon my soul when the noon sunlight arrowed through the woods, and we were edging along a spread of fields, neatly marked off with rail fences. Beyond was a double-chimneyed house and a barn, both of them set on high stone foundations, both standing out plain against the bright sky and the whitened ground. From a distance I could see snow glistening on the roofs and the sharp blue shadows cast by the buildings.

We drew closer, hidden within a fringe of trees that bordered a stretch of fences. Squinting through the sun, we were able to make out dark tracks circling the house and a man moving around near the well. He was shoveling it clear, stopping once or twice to brush his coat off before he lifted the lid and dropped a bucket down.

I made a whistling birdcall of a sound, the first part of the signal known to me and the farmer.

He paused, winched the bucket up after a moment, but stayed by the well.

I whistled again.

His body shifted toward the trees as if he was trying to place the sound.

One more whistle, the final call that completed the signal.

The man's head came up. He moved a few paces toward the house, set the bucket down on the porch, and ambled off. It appeared like he was just checking his fences, halting every few steps as he moved closer to where we were.

He began to grow sharper in my sight. Pie-shaped bearded face under a broad-brimmed hat, nose and cheeks reddened by the cold, clouds of breath at his mouth; green lapels on an old gray woolen coat, that coat layered over another one so that the outer buttons strained across his belly; a flash of white at throat and wrists where his long underwear was sneaking out. He kept coming, and my passengers dropped down behind me.

I stepped out from behind an elm just far enough so that he could see half of my face and my right side. The farmer's eyes passed over me, he nodded briefly but didn't cease his walking. When he reached a bend in the fence a ways past us, he turned and went back across the field.

My passengers were still crouched down on the ground. They stared up at me, silent and scared, all excepting Joe who'd covered his face like he'd done when Leah Jenkins had greeted us. I whispered that it was all right, this was the friend, and motioned for them to stay still. The farmer was being careful for some reason, and I'd just have to wait till he let me know what he wanted us to do.

For a short while the man crisscrossed the space between the barn and the house, and my eyes continuously shifted from him to my people. Shadrack especially, Rebecca too. She was shaking with fever, not fright. And then I saw our friend come out of the barn.

Never looking in our direction, he made like he was checking his fences just as he'd done earlier, but as he tramped past us he commenced to mutter partly in his own tongue, like he was talking to himself.

"*Kommen Sie, ja* safe . . . *mein* cart *ist im* barn . . . *es gibt* food. . . . *kommen Sie* . . . barn, safe . . . *schnell,* hurry . . . *mein Karre ist im Stall . . . machen Sie schnell . . .*"

He trudged off, running his fingers across the fence.

My passengers must have made out enough words to comprehend that message; they were moving as soon as I was. We skirted the field, left the trees, and crouched along the fence till we'd almost reached the barn. There was a bare expanse of ground between us and that shelter, but the railing ran up near to the door. I glanced around at the dark woods on the far side of the field, glanced behind us, saw nothing to cause alarm. Nodding, I whispered to the runaways.

"One by one. Flat down as you able. Stick to the fence. Safe inside. Go on, now. Fast."

Still keeping the tail of my eye on the woods beyond, I watched my passengers crawl out, waiting till one had vanished through the barn door before I nudged the next one off.

Tazwell first, with the infant.

Martha, not far behind.

Addie next.

Bernette.

Joe.

Shadrack.

I crabbed out last with Rebecca.

When we were all in the barn, the German shut the doors and smiled at us.

"*Haben Sie keine Angst* . . . not to fear . . . *Willkommen* Moses."

At that point my people were in no state to question our friend's strange speech, or where they were, or anything at all about the place. They were indoors for the first time in four days, and the barn looked ordinary, familiar. Everyday things surrounded us: the sounds and smells of stock and fodder, stalls and harnesses and ropes, a glint of light coming through the hayloft door and catching on the beamed ceiling, on the straw. If anyone recollected that other blazing barn, it didn't show as we slumped down on the dirt floor, snuggling under the blankets we were given almost directly. A kettle of soup was passed to us next, and we handed it around, taking turns with the ladle, breathing in the warm cabbagy vapors which rose from the thick broth; there was dark bread with the soup, milk, and slices of cold ham. I was only afraid we were eating so fast we wouldn't be able to keep the food on our bellies after having gone empty so long.

Karl Müller shook his head as he looked us over and said something I mostly didn't comprehend, excepting for the word *Sklaven*. He'd spoken it before, shaking his head over other passengers, and I figured it had to do with slavery. *Sündvoll! Sündvoll!* he spat. Sinful, I thought, and asked him if slave-catchers had been about. He nodded. Swept his hands wide. Spat again.

"Verdammte Menschen!"
"They still anywheres hereabouts, you figure?"
"Nein, nicht mehr da . . . gone, *nein."*
"Bless God."
"Gott sei Dank, ja."

While we ate, Müller hitched his team up to the broad-bedded wagon standing ready in the middle of the barn. He looked us over again, seemed to count us, then commenced lugging sacks of grain toward the cart. Tazwell and I helped him pack them around the edges of the wagon bed, lining the bottom with empty bags and blankets. We piled my passengers into the cart, spread more empty sacks over them till they were well hidden, and Müller stowed a basket of food under the seat. I scrunched down directly behind the buckboard so I'd be able to have a word with him from time to time.

With the sacks pulled over us, we could only hear the barn door sliding open, the wagon groaning as our driver climbed on, and his throaty calls to the team. Then nothing but the creak of leather and wood, the muted thudding of hoofs. Müller had to go slow on account of the snowy ground and the weighted cart, but we were moving, we were on wheels at last.

Another wagon rumbled past us and away. No one had bothered over the farmer lumbering along with his load of grain, and after that no one else seemed to be on the road at all.

Warmed by the soup, nestled amidst the sacks and blankets and each other, folks began to go limp around me. My own eyes closed, and I slept longer than I'd meant to. It couldn't have been more than an hour, but I woke with a start, wondering if there'd been any signs of danger, anything amiss. I listened. The same sounds. The same motion. Nearly the same kind of strong light filtering through the burlap over us. Everyone still asleep. Everything quiet on the road. Even so, I whispered to Müller, taking care not to show myself.

"Hsst. Me. You able to hear? Still safe?"
"Safe, *ja.* More up. Delavare."
"Slavecatchers? Patrollers?"
"Die Patrouillen sind . . . now behind."

"Thank Heaven. Where we headed?"

"Odessa, *heute Nacht* in Odessa."

The light was draining off our scratchy coverings when I sank into another shallow sleep. Next time I stirred the light was gone, and the noises of a town quickened just beyond. Likely Odessa. Likely we'd head for the Quaker Meeting House on Main Street, that was a good station.

I hushed the newly awakened runaways before the wagon rolled to a stop, swaying a little as Müller jumped down. His boots crunched away from us, voices mumbled somewheres up ahead. The boots returned at a faster clip, and we started up again.

Maybe we'd hit trouble, maybe we'd only been sent on to another place, but I didn't dare ask questions while we were trundling through town. As soon as the noises fell behind us, Müller said a few words, and although I couldn't catch them, his voice didn't sound alarmed.

Moments later when we were just beyond Odessa's outskirts, the team slowed up. A door squealed open directly ahead of us, the cart jolted over a small rise, drew to a halt, and the horses snuffled out their breath. There was some whispering near the wagon seat. Not a one of us stirred.

The cart shifted slightly. Two sets of footfalls reached my ears, one pair going away from us, the farmer's tread coming around to the back of the wagon. He spoke in easy tones as he peeled the sacks off us, and I climbed down into a dusky, deserted livery stable. A low-burning lantern stood nearby, and in the faint yellowish light Müller smiled at me, motioning past a row of empty stalls.

"Safe. *Schnell, komm.*"

He helped the rest of the folks down and nudged them toward another wagon, a large one, already hitched up to a fresh team. It too held feed bags, but when the German pushed some of them away I saw a hatch in the wagon's broad bed and knew the bottom was false. A slave runner must have left it for us — no one but Underground workers owned such rigs. I supposed our route had been changed on account of this.

My passengers held back. The thing did look like a rolling trap, but I told them we'd hit upon one of the Railroad's best cars, and Müller said something about Wilmington. Wilmington. Wilmington and Thomas Garrett. All the way to Wilmington without having to walk. The runaways must have seen the relief and gratefulness on my face; in another instant they began to squeeze themselves down through the hatch.

The German stowed the food basket under the new wagon's seat, touched my fingers, and murmured to me once more.

"*Geh mit Gott,* Moses."

That was what he always said in parting. That was when I comprehended he wasn't taking us himself.

I looked around for our driver and finally glimpsed a man standing just within a shadowed stall, facing the bolted doors like he was guarding them. But not like he was guarding them fiercely; there was that gentle air about him I remembered, the weary slump of his shoulders, the hat-brim. I wedged myself down into the wagon bed with the others.

Karl Müller's face hung above me for a moment, and then it was shut off from my sight as he closed the trapdoor. Up above, I could hear him locking the hatch and shuffling sacks over the top. More footsteps, voices. Then the door screeched and wheels creaked under us as the wagon trundled out of the stable.

We rode all night in that tight space, pressed together like lovers, breathing through the air-holes in the bottom, stopping only to rest the horses. Although it was like traveling in a cupboard, everyone lay still, hushed, sleeping mostly. Rebecca's fever seemed to have lessened. There wasn't so much as a whimper from the baby or the child. The wagon's swaying motion felt soothing. A deep peacefulness settled over us for the first time in many days.

As we rocked along, I dimly heard a church bell ring twelve and realized with a start that we had driven straight into New Year's Day.

◆ ◆ ◆

Bless Thomas Garrett.

We lay sheltered in his secret room for three days, swathed in flannel, muffled in blankets, recovering, resting. Thomas dosed us, fed us, gave out fresh clothing, and arranged for our transport through Pennsylvania. He also passed along some much-needed funds which had been sent me through him, from a Scottish society that had taken an interest in our cause.

And then we were on our way again.

I figured to have Shadrack upfront in my sights the rest of the way north, but after we'd passed through New York City the passenger foremost in my mind wasn't Shadrack after all. It was Joe.

The trouble started in the office of *The National Anti-Slavery Banner* almost as soon as my friend Oliver Johnson took us in there. I tried to stop it; wasn't able to. Johnson meant well, he couldn't have known. I hadn't expected that trouble myself.

Oliver Johnson had recognized Joe rightoff. Congratulated him. Said he was glad to see the man who was worth fifteen hundred dollars to his master, and had gotten so far away. Joe put his hand up to his face, then lowered it. Too late. He stammered. Asked Johnson how he'd been able to pick him out so quick, asked him twice. Oliver waved a reward poster, and like for a lark, began to read it aloud. I motioned for him to stop. Johnson didn't see me, and went on as Joe's face commenced to twitch.

"HEAVY REWARD FIFTEEN HUNDRED DOLLARS REWARD: Ran away from subscriber on Saturday night, Christmas Eve, Jo-

siah Bailey. Joe is about 6 feet 2 inches in height, of a chestnut color, bald head, with a remarkable scar on one of his cheeks, not positive which it is, but think it is on the left, under the eye, has intelligent countenance, active and well-made. A reward of fifteen hundred dollars will be given to any person who will apprehend the said Joe Bailey, and lodge him safely in jail. . . . W. R. Hughlett."

Joe asked only one more question, how far it was to Canada. Johnson showed him on a map. And from that time on Joe went silent.

"Just started to feel so good, but look at Joe. Must be he got it figured anyone be able to spot him like that now. Lord, Moses, he won't even speak to *me*."

"He will Bernette, he will. Bound to get over it soon."

Out of New York City, up the Hudson River, on a steamboat, on a ferry, then switching to a stagecoach for a while. Mostly the easiest part of a journey thereabouts, since the Valley was safe enough, clear of big cities, and I knew the river captains, they knew me. Back on the water again. Martha was seasick, sick all over the place, other folks too. But still, moving north, getting there. And still Joe did not speak.

"Can't do nothin with him, he just don't seem able to shake it."

"He will, maybe next time you turn round, surely when we cross the line."

Off the boat again, going overland along the Hudson, nearing its source.

"If they spot us, can they send us back from here?"

"Won't nobody spot us, Taz."

"Appears like everything turned so smooth so sudden, almost don't believe it."

"Believe it. We be all right, be to Albany soon."

West from Albany, past Schenectady, Fonda to Little Falls, west on the surface lines. Always dangerous, those public steam-cars, but we had our forged free-papers and our tickets. No one looked our way more than twice. No bounty hunters seemed to be about either, and I was surely on the lookout for such. My people tried not to stare around at this, the first train they'd ever ridden. They sat still and rigid, hands folded, ankles crossed, their eyes on me. I watched them, watched the car, mostly watched Joe. His knees had given way when we'd boarded, and I'd half-dragged him to a seat, hissing at Shadrack to help me.

"He gone off his wood is all, broke right down to a fool."

"Hush up, Shadrack."

"He don't hear nothin."

"He don't *say* nothin. Best you do likewise."

"Big buck like him, figured to beat the shit outa me more'n once, well."

"*Sshht.* Can't even feel bad for him, can you? Born evil you was, now look out the window and keep your face shut."

Fields were jumping by, cows, splotches of trees, patches of old snow. Martha's nose was flattened against the window. Cows, towns, more fields, people getting on and off; it really felt like we were moving then. The fugitives loosened up, sensing that. Signs flashed by in the stations we passed, there were signs up front in the car too. Martha fixed her eyes on one of them, then tugged on her mother's sleeve, pointing. Addie shook her head and turned to me.

"Always did have a notion to learn my letters, tried to learn myself one time. Stole a book offa. . . ."

". . . sssh . . . don't say his name . . ."

". . . offa the Man. I'd look at it, then put it back quick, take it out the shelf again, put it back — in the end I got so scared he'd catch me, I quit."

"You learn up to Canada, right alongside Martha."

"In a children's schoolhouse? Be ashamed . . . once we get free maybe Rebecca can show me."

Off from Oneida by foot, snow on the ground, but we were so rested it didn't seem bad, and the weather held clear. From

Oneida to Peterboro and my friend Gerrit Smith. Richest white man I ever knew, and he kept his estate open to fugitives all hours. That time we stayed hidden in his kitchen, clustered around the stove, keeping warm, whispering about the mansion; concluding it was grander than the Big Houses we'd known. Next day Mr. Smith sent us off in his carriage, and like always I found money tucked in my coat as we clattered away. West, northwest, north. Closer.

"We come so far, got so much, I just pray nothin don't happen so's we lose it all sudden."

"Rebecca! That don't sound like you atall."

"Appears easier for me to keep ahold my faith in hard times, ain't that somethin?"

Syracuse, Jarm Loguen's station. Edging up on the line, nearer still. Jarm Loguen, the colored preacher, my friend. Everyone took to him rightoff. Everyone excepting Joe. Joe still hadn't changed, hadn't spoken.

On across to Auburn, to my own folks' place. Homecoming in a way, though I didn't really think of that house on South Street as home. Daddy and Mama looked to rights, and we squatted by their hearth, listening to them tell of their own escape. Mama pressed a big bundle of food on us when we left in the morning, even as she pleaded with me to stay on longer. We couldn't, had to get along for Williamson, riding again, riding out of that abolitionist town in Senator Seward's carriage.

"Man, we gone in style today. Wish old Pig-Ass could see us in this rig."

"Bug his eyes out, that's for sure, Taz. You, me, everybody, like this . . . mercy, he'd drop a load's what he'd do."

"Both you mens just thank Heaven he can't see us, not him, not a single nigger-chaser."

"Yeah . . . must be way up now . . . never really comprehended how it would be, never got it pictured in my mind what was out here. Course they didn't tell us nothin on it, ceptin for scare stories."

"Well, it ain't likely old Master been this far from home hisself, or got the North pictured right besides. Most white folks stick in one place too, don't see much beyond the next nearest town."

"Wish Joe could see it all."

"Shame, yeah. Talk him up again Bernette, maybe this town."

Williamson, Milham House was where we stayed. Joe was off his food, didn't touch the supper my mama had packed for us. He lay awake nearly all night, eyes open, silent. The rest barely slept either, but that was from excitement; I'd told them we were almost onto the last lap. Bernette passed some of the hours kneeling by Joe, murmuring to him, then came and sat by me, sat down hard. After she'd dozed off I crept forward, hoping to get a word out of him, trying again like I'd been all along.

"Joe? . . . Me again. Won't you just say somethin? It's all right, told you, won't nobody get caught on your account, not Bernette, not nobody, believe me. Told you my reward's the big one . . . Joe? . . . Canada ain't far now, not like on that map, not anymore. Almost to the Falls, the Falls is the line and then you know you safe. Cross that line soon . . . Joe?"

I didn't know what to do. I'd never carried a fugitive who'd broken like that, and all the while it was getting easier and we were getting closer and the joy was getting bigger, Joe didn't comprehend. It broke my heart to see him so, such a big man with a child's eyes. Other times, in other trials, I'd known what moves to make, even when I'd been at my worst. You seek shelter from snow. You look for food when the food runs out. You hide or run from danger, else you fight it. But this was different, this was one kind of tribulation I didn't know how to lift. I didn't know how to heal this man's spirit.

"Won't be much longer now."

"The Lord been good to us, Moses. Never ceased to pray

for this, and once we cross, don't guess I be able to cease my thank-prayers."

"Keep Joe in your prayers for now, Rebecca, we all got to."

"I been, always."

Over to Rochester, almost the last stop. We didn't stay with Frederick Douglass that time, we slept in the A.M.E. Zion Church at Spring and Favor streets, bedded down on the pews, warmed by the coal stove in the corner. Off early the next morning, folks moving quick and jerky, folks worked up, knowing what lay ahead.

"How many niggers in St. Catharines?"

"No niggers atall."

"C'mon, Moses."

"That's the truth, no niggers. Free colored people."

"The white Canada folks don't bother us none?"

"Lord no, Queen Victoria got different ideas from Uncle Sam. Ready folks? . . . Good. Walk easy, just to the depot. Let's go."

The final run, on the steam-cars again, out of Rochester. Rochester to the Falls, Canada, St. Catharines.

"Mama, when's the Falls?"

"Moses say a good while yet, honey. Sit still, keep your eyes on the window. You tell us all when."

On past Parma. A danger point there, they often watched the trains at Parma. I'd seen bounty hunters get on at that stop before. By the grace of God, not this time. Nothing seemed amiss. Only I was growing desperate about Joe. He no longer appeared strapping; shrunken into himself, slump-shouldered and blank in the face, he just stared at his knees. When he moved at all, he'd only rub his fingers across his mouth over and over, that was all he did.

The train was nearing the Suspension Bridge, I knew that, though we couldn't see it yet. Gently, I commenced to shake Joe. He was limp between my hands. It seemed cruel to shake a man who appeared so beaten. I patted his knee. He didn't notice.

"Think on Canada, Joe, you heard us talk on it. Maybe you get your own place there, you and Bernette. Maybe you get some land. Bernette and you. Your own place, land. With . . . with cows. Cows, maybe you get milk cows, dairy farm. You both work it together. Be a barn and a house, fields with rail fences . . . fences on accounta the cows, fields and . . ."

"That's right, Joe. We be together and . . . Joe? . . . Oh Moses, we all be across that line soon but for him. If he don't comprehend he got free, then he still ain't free after all. It won't make no difference."

"He bound to comprehend . . . Bernette, honey, don't cry. Don't leave up on him, talk him through."

"The Falls, Joe, almost there, the bridge, the line . . ."

The Suspension Bridge.

We weren't truly safe till we'd reached its center, the center was the actual line. My passengers knew that, I'd told them. Everyone was silent, gripping hands, pressing against the windows. Mist began rising below us as the earth dropped away. A thundering came from outside, we could hear it over the noise of the train. And then the Falls appeared upriver. The Falls and the rise at the middle of the bridge and the downgrade right after.

Someone let out a whoop. My folks bolted from their seats; shouting, stomping, telling everyone and each other and whoever *made it we made it,* clasping one another over and over *God thank God* clasping, laughing *OmyLord clear,* in the aisle, weeping, reaching for more hands, reaching for me *bless you Moses bless.* The dusty train was swimming before my eyes.

Almost blindly, I embraced my people, one by one.

And suddenly remembered Joe.

He was still sitting hunched over like he wasn't able to hear the joyfulness around him, still staring at his knees, while Bernette jerked on his hand.

I took him by the shoulders.

"*Joe!* You crossed the line."

He didn't look up.

"The Falls, the line, we all crossed safe."

He shifted his eyes to me, but they were still blank.

"Oh my Lord, Joe *please.*"

I took his face in my hands and wrenched it around so he could look out the window.

"You gone free, Joe. Free. You done it, Lord God, it's over."

Slowly Joe stood.

He looked at me and Bernette, reached for us both at once, and held us close for a moment. And then he strode to the middle of the aisle. Raised up to his full height, raised up his arms. Touched the ceiling with spread fingers. Wept openly, unashamed. Tried to speak. Kept on standing there, legs wide apart, fists against the roof, filling the car with his dignity, his manhood.

His face was still streaming when the train jerked to a stop, and Josiah Bailey was the first one to leap off, shouting, as he planted his feet in the new earth.

◆◆ ◆◆ ◆◆

Auburn rests in the dark.

The house is quiet, resting too.

The porch below the window is just a porch, mine.

It's chilly, but I feel a growing warmth within me now. Best get some wood for morning all the same. I pull on my shoes, wrap up in a cloak, and go outside, out into the moonlit September night. The air feels cool against my skin, cleansing, and as I stride across the yard strength seems to flow through me, more with each step. Passing along the fence, I skim the top of the railing with my hand, moving on toward the gate.

I push the gate open, shut, open, and hold it that way, standing there with my arm stretched forward. Yes. They did go through. It wasn't wiped out. Not that journey, none of them. They passed through, and whatever happened afterwards, they crossed over into their time, they had that. And what I gave them, their freedom, they held dear. Dear enough so that they chose to try and share it with their brothers and sisters. Just as I did. They followed me in that way too. I could have stayed set, they could have stayed set. We didn't. They fought for those others in the war same as me, even Shadrack, even him. And so those lives weren't really lost. They were given.

Lives given, still gone; and yet they are with me even so, and all the passengers that followed, that stood behind me, stand here now in the dark. It was worth it, the work, the mission. Yes. They went through, I brought them through according to Him who called me.

I move past the gate to the woodpile, and gather up kindling till my arms are full. As I turn to go back in I see a man's form wavering in the dimness, coming toward me.

"Hat? Baby, what you up for?"

My daddy's white nightshirt catches the moonlight, and when he comes closer I see he's pulled his trousers up over it. His boots flap open and unlaced.

"Thought I heard you, honey. What you about?"

I hold out my laden arms in answer.

"*This* time a night?"

"It's a good time, Daddy."

We walk back together. As we reach the porch I nearly tread on a figure huddled against the bottom step; someone sleeping wound up in a ball, knees against chest, head tucked under a coat sleeve.

"Another one, Hat. Seen him when I come out."

We go on inside, but after Daddy's climbed the stairs, and I've laid the wood by, I open the door again and try to rouse the man hunkered down by the porch. He's too deep in his slumberings, too weary to wake, so I hunt up a blanket, fetch it out, and cover him where he lies. Another one. Another pilgrim seeking shelter here.

My train stands still now, it has become a station, but yet the passengers come, and the vocation has only changed shape, not vanished. And I must warm these passengers, warm this house, this station I keep for them. Morning's coming soon.

I fill the kitchen stove with wood, add kindling, and touch a match to crumpled paper. The fire grows under my tending, and as I crouch before the stove's open belly the flames lick up, the wood snaps. I am held within the fire's rippling light-circle, and it spills color over me. I kneel there, dressed in its red.

certainly I shall be with thee

Stirrings over my head.

and this shall be a token to thee

Bedsprings squeak, feet touch the floor.

that I have sent thee

A clink, a cough, feet on the stair.

My passengers await me.

◀▶

Historical Afterword
Author's Note
Acknowledgments

Historical Afterword

HARRIET TUBMAN spent the second half of her long life in Auburn, New York. Her parents lived in her home there, and were believed to be centenarians when they died in the 1870s. In October, 1867, John Tubman was murdered during a quarrel with a white man near Airey, Maryland. Harriet Tubman subsequently married Nelson Davis, a young veteran of the Civil War. It is thought that she married Davis at least partially to "take care of him," as he was afflicted with tuberculosis, and died in 1888 at the age of forty-four.

Tubman continued to help and house the poor, the aged, and the infirm, despite increasing ailments of her own. She was eventually crippled by rheumatism, and her sleeping seizures became more severe. Nonetheless she contributed to the support of black schools in the South, and became more actively involved with the Women's Suffrage movement, addressing meetings with Susan B. Anthony and Elizabeth Cady Stanton.

She was honored by Queen Victoria who sent her a Diamond Jubilee medal, a silk shawl, and an invitation to the British court, but Tubman received no remuneration for services to her own country until thirty-five years after the Civil War had ended. During those years she earned a meager living by selling garden produce, but had to borrow funds and accept donations as her financial situation grew more precarious. Her friends continued to petition Congress on her behalf, and in 1890 she was awarded a widow's pension of eight dollars a month. In 1899 the sum was increased to twenty dollars. This was not compensation for her own work in the war, however; the pension was awarded only because she was the widow of a Union soldier.

In 1896 she came into possession of twenty-five acres of land near her house, where she had wanted to found a home for aged, indigent blacks, and to name it for John Brown. She deeded the land to the A.M.E. Zion Church, and in 1908 the John Brown Home was opened.

Harriet Tubman died on March 10, 1913, and was buried with military honors in Auburn's Fort Hill cemetery. The following year the town honored her again with a special ceremony. After tributes from Dr. Booker T. Washington and Mayor Charles W. Brister, the citizens of Auburn dedicated a bronze tablet in her memory.

Author's Note

THIS IS of course a fictional work, but it is grounded in historical fact and follows the general outline of Harriet Tubman's life. There are many gaps in what we know about that life owing to the lack of primary sources, the scarcity of written records pertaining to her slavery, and the peripatetic nature of her vocation. Tubman's dictated letters, interviews, and transcribed speeches were often shaped by the perceptions of those who put them into print. Many of the secondary and tertiary sources conflict with each other as well, but the gaps and conflicting accounts have provided me with room for reasonable invention and interpretation.

Several nineteenth-century sources were particularly important to this novel. Foremost of these are Sarah H. Bradford's two biographies, *Scenes in the Life of Harriet Tubman* (1869), and *Harriet Tubman: The Moses of Her People* (1886), both of which contain personal interviews with Tubman herself. Other helpful sources were Harriet Tubman's dictated letters and speeches; the journal kept by William Still at the Vigilance Committee of the Pennsylvania Anti-Slavery Society which is bound in a book titled *The Underground Railroad;* the letters of Harkless Bowley, John Brown, Frederick Douglass, Thomas Garrett, Thomas Wentworth Higginson, Wendell Phillips, William H. Seward, Gerrit Smith, and others of the period; newspaper articles, especially those appearing in the *Troy Whig* (1859), the *Auburn Citizen* (1914), and Franklin Sanborn's article in the *Boston Commonwealth* (1863), and Wilbur Seibert's *The Underground Railroad* (1898). Other important modern sources are acknowledged elsewhere.

Harriet Tubman was born into slavery about 1820 in the Bucktown District of Dorchester County on Maryland's Eastern Shore. As the daughter of Benjamin Ross and Rit Green, Harriet belonged to a large family. Information on the ages of the Ross children is sketchy, but there are certain indications that Harriet was the youngest which I have followed. I focused on the family members who have the most bearing on this particular story, omitting mention of those who do not, to avoid unnecessary loose ends and confusion.

Although there is some disagreement as to the exact name of Harriet's first master, Edward Brodas remains consistent with the majority of the sources. His wife's name has never been accurately determined, so I have telescoped her with the Miss Susan who appears in several sources, sometimes as Harriet's mistress, sometimes as a woman to whom she was hired out. In any event, Miss Susan's treatment of the child Harriet remains unchanged. Throughout the novel, major events are drawn from available source material, and this is true of Harriet's childhood as well. Some of the early events may have occurred on other plantations, but because I find discrepancies among certain sources, interviews, and the census tracts, I felt it was reasonable to place most of these events on the Brodas plantation. This was done for the sake of clarity, and in no way affects what actually happened.

It should be noted that Harriet's sleeping spells are not my invention, nor were they psychological in nature. Evidently, they were a form of chronic narcolepsy, a result of the injury to her head from the overseer's blow.

There is uniform agreement that Harriet's physical strength returned and increased substantially, well before her attempt to buy her freedom, although no clear dates are given for the incidents with John Stewart and Dr. Anthony Thompson.

The marriage of Harriet and John Tubman probably took place about 1845. Some time during the marriage, Harriet Tubman discovered the will of her mother's first master. The precise date of this discovery is not definite either, when one closely examines the sources, and so I felt free to place it where it best serves the story.

Some accounts indicate that Harriet Tubman began her escape in the company of her brothers who turned back almost immediately, leaving her to run off by herself. Other accounts suggest that she started out alone, after signaling with a song near the slave quarters or the kitchen building. I have chosen the interpretation which seems the most plausible to me, and included a portion of the song she is believed to have used. Her escape occurred about 1849.

The amount of time Tubman initially spent in the North is disputed.

I have rounded it out to a year. Though she occasionally worked on Cape May during this period, her most important activity was in Philadelphia, so I centered her there. The sources disagree over the number of trips she made to northern Maryland before her return home. I have touched on the one that is best documented. In any event, her rescue journey to Dorchester County did signal the start of her own vocation, which extended beyond the rescue of her family.

It is appropriate to include a note about Tubman's mysticism here. Again, this is not fictive invention. She was deeply religious and often spoke of Divine warnings which, she felt, guided her. She also experienced visionary states, and told Sarah Bradford that she spoke with the Lord every day as she would with a friend. According to Bradford, she felt prompted by mystical voices to escape bondage, and had a presentiment of danger to her father before she rescued him, and a graphic precognitive dream about John Brown. Her earliest precognitive dream was the one about flying over fields and rivers until she was helped across a final barrier. The most important aspect of her mysticism is her conviction that God had called her to lead her people out of bondage.

The techniques used by Tubman on the Underground Railroad are faithful to the sources, as is the legend of Moses which grew up around her, firmly establishing her code-name. It is impossible to relate all her adventures on the Underground Railroad and maintain the coherency of the novel, but I have included many of the important ones, combining some of them in the final section of the book. She apparently directed her raids at the Eastern Shore of Maryland, though one source suggests she may have ventured farther south. The letters from the stationkeepers which are reproduced in the Underground Railroad section were drawn from writings which did not directly pertain to Tubman, although they might have, and in some cases I abridged them slightly.

Tubman did receive some kind of warning that her remaining brothers were about to be sold before she rescued them. There is disagreement as to whether this warning was a letter from William Still or a premonition. I have chosen the former approach.

The incident with the bounty hunters on the train, involving the ruse with the tract or book, is derived from several reports. The only change I have made here was to place the incident on a train rather than in a train station or a park.

Harriet Tubman rescued her parents from slavery in June, 1857, at which time her father finally abandoned the idiosyncrasy of blindfolding his eyes in the presence of his runaway daughter. One source says her parents were rescued from Caroline County on the Eastern Shore, but the majority state that Ben and Rit were still living in their original home on the Brodas-Thompson plantation.

My depiction of Tubman's relationship with John Brown is as close to historical veracity as possible. This episode was pieced together from a wide variety of sources, owing to the dearth of records concerning Brown's private meetings with Tubman. These meetings are partially based on the letters of Brown and certain abolitionists, and on accounts of Frederick Douglass's meetings with John Brown.

Several incidents in the final escape were derived from existing reports of Tubman's journeys. Josiah Bailey did follow her north in the company of others, but their names were different from the ones I used, as was the size and composition of the group. However, I wanted to use this particular journey as a paradigm for many of Tubman's raids, and therefore I wove several strands into one escape here. The episode about the missing black stationkeeper conforms with other accounts of it in the main, with the exception of a small piece of dialogue. The encounter with the German farmer has been changed slightly. This story sometimes involves a Quaker or, in other accounts, simply "a man." I gave "the man" a German origin in order to show the variety of people who composed the Underground Railroad. Tubman led many Christmas escapes, and often had to deal with difficult weather conditions.

It is factual that Harriet Tubman served in the Civil War, reaching the front at a time when neither blacks nor women were permitted induction into the Union Army. (Blacks were inducted after the Emancipation Proclamation). She was based with the Union Army's headquarters of the Department of the South in Beaufort, South Carolina, and acted as a scout, spy, raider, and nurse. She received no rank and no pay. The fragments of letters which appear in the novel's prologue are derived from actual letters written by friends and colleagues in an effort to secure payment for her duty after the war.

One final note is necessary, pertaining to word usage. Certain expressions, such as "the Man" and "Uncle Sam" sound quite modern, but were actually part of the colloquial speech of the period. I have tried to keep idiomatic terms or phrases consistent with nineteenth-century usage.

Acknowledgments

I WISH to thank my editor, Anne N. Barrett; Linda M. Arnold, Ph.D., for her assistance with the final phase of research; Margaret Bacon of the American Friends Service Committee in Philadelphia; Richard W. Badger, Secretary of the Wilmington Monthly Meeting of Friends; Carol Golab and the Philadelphia Social History Project; Dr. James Johnson, President of the Dorchester County Historical Society; Nerissa L. Milton of the Association for the Study of Afro-American Life and History, Inc., in Washington, D.C.; and Nana Rinehart, who translated the German dialogue.

A special note of thanks to my friends Sheila Freeman and Carole LaMarca Steininger. Ms. Freeman offered many creative insights and feedback; Ms. Steininger typed the final draft and did much to help me polish it.

Grateful acknowledgments to Eugene Genovese's *Roll, Jordan, Roll: The World the Slaves Made,* and to Gilbert Osofsky's *Puttin' On Ole Massa: The Slave Narratives of Henry Bibb, William Wells Brown, and Solomon Northup;* and to Anne Parrish's *A Clouded Star,* from which I derived the code-phrase "Journey from midnight through hope to God be praised."

Rather than include a lengthy bibliography, I would like to express my appreciation to these other authors and sources in particular: W.E.B. Du Bois's numerous works; Ira Berlin's *Slaves Without Masters: The Free Negro in the Antelbellum South;* Benjamin A. Botkin, who edited *Lay My Burden Down: A Folk History of Slavery;* James B. Cade's article "Out of the Mouths of Ex-Slaves" in *The Journal of Negro History;* Earl Conrad's *Harriet Tubman;* "The Charles P. Wood Manuscripts of Harriet Tubman," edited by Earl Conrad for *The Negro History Bulletin;* Benjamin Quarles's many works, especially *The Negro American,* which he edited with Leslie H. Fishel,

Jr.; several biographers of John Brown, particularly Jules Abels, Truman Nelson, and Stephen Oates; the "Garrison Family Papers" of the Sophia Smith Collection, Smith College; and the works of Kenneth Stampp.

I am also grateful for the help I received from the staffs of Founders Library at Howard University, the Library of Congress, the Central Branch of the Arlington County Public Library, and the Schomberg Collection of the New York Public Library.

My affectionate thanks to the following friends for their supportiveness: Mary Fay Bourgoin, Jean A. Conaty, Judith Caswell, Hanna Emrich, the Rev. Thomas P. Gavigan, S.J., Sherry E. Joslin, Sandra Kalenik, Richard C. Squires, and Melanne Verveer.

Most of all I wish to thank my husband, Jim, for his concern with this project and the contributions he made to it.